LETTERS
FROM
BRAZIL

A Cultural-Historical Narrative Made Fiction

MARK J. CURRAN

 www.trafford.com
North America & international
toll-free: 1 888 232 4444 (USA & Canada)
fax: 812 355 4082

It started with Sputnik - "A silver bowling ball with antennae" rotating around the earth - and ended with a case of the clap.

"Living is very dangerous" ["Viver é muito perigoso"] João Guimarães Rosa in "The Devil to Pay in the Backlands"

PREFACE

In 1957 the Soviet Union sent the first satellite into space; it looked like a round, silver "bowling ball" with antennae. It was no more than a radio orbiting the earth from near space, but it scared the crap out of the United States. After all, it might not only catch the generals' planning in the Pentagon, but might overhear your private conversation in the living room, or worse, in the bed room. The Russians had the drop on us.

The space race was on and of course would culminate in a neck to neck finish in 1969. The Soviets would fail to get their rocket to the moon and just a few days later the United States, fulfilling John F. Kennedy's campaign promise, would land men on the moon. "That's one small step for man, one giant leap for mankind."

What became NASA figured you better have some good scientists who knew what they were doing, folks who were geniuses in science and math. And it would not hurt to have liberated, bribed and made an offer he could not refuse to Wernher von Braun. The Russians grabbed some of the topnotch German V-1 and V-2 scientists, but the U.S. landed their share as well. Von Braun would be the brains behind the development of the rockets and the whole moon-shot program, and in an amazing aside, in our truly free press Democracy previewed it all on Walt Disney's "Wonderful World of Color" on NBC for anyone interested. The movie "The Right Stuff" would be Hollywood's telling of the story.

There was much more than dominion in space or landing a man on the moon at play; that was just the symbolic part. What really was at stake was world domination, either the free world's Capitalistic system with its free market or Russia's Marxist Communism with its planned economy and state. The U.S. needed a strategy.

One of the pieces in the puzzle was the National Defense Education Act (NDEA), a congressional brainstorm to train red-blooded, patriotic, healthy, and yes, brainy U.S. young men and women to speak the languages and understand the cultures of countries deemed essential and critical in this race for knowledge. There were two essential ingredients: language study and area studies, the latter a hodgepodge of disciplines to understand a given area of the world, i.e. geography, history, politics, economics, religion, society and even a smattering of culture. It would be a better plan than the old U.S. foreign aid program so heatedly debated in the 1950s with the barbs lanced at giving iceboxes to Eskimos and camels to Bedouin nomads (the national foreign aid policy even became the topic for all the debate teams in U.S. high schools in the 1950s, so you know it had become important, this along with a stodgy debate about "ability grouping" and the British system of education as far superior to the U.S. "education for all" idea).

Russian, Arabic, Chinese, Japanese, Urdu and others became "essential" and "critical" languages, but surprisingly enough Spanish was high on the list and Portuguese, the latter aimed at figuring out what was happening in Brazil, South America's largest country. The program would train young college professors who in turn would train their students in language and area study. Russia was already sending hundreds of "volunteers" and "cultural friends" to the far corners of Asia, Africa and South America, not the least, Cuba. We had to catch up, and the theory was that the "products" of this plan would help in the fray.

On New Year's Day of 1959 Fidel Castro had liberated Cuba from the tin-horn dictator Fulgencio Batista who was frolicking with the boys and girls of the Mafia in Havana while ignoring the well-being of the populace at large. Fidel was the product of an arrangement between his Spanish-Cuban father who ran a sugar cane plantation in eastern Cuba and the housekeeper. Fidel, a precocious Jesuit trained scholar and athlete in high school (he wanted to become a major - league ball player and if the Dodgers' Walter O'Malley had signed him, history would have been rewritten), was an idealistic thinker who changed the region and the Americas. Castro, lauded and cheered in a tickertape parade in New York City and a guest on Jack Paar's "Tonight" show in 1960 was deemed a new "savior" for Cuba. We will never know how that might have turned out. After Cuban dissidents, exiles in Miami, garnered the lukewarm support of the State Department and trained for an invasion to "liberate" Cuba from the "Marxist Castro," (training in the U.S. Everglades with full logistic support of the U.S. Military), the ill-fated "Bay of Pigs" invasion was welcomed by a fully prepared Fidel Castro and his soldiers and was soundly defeated within hours of the landing, this with the help of Soviet fighter jets. Grumbling anti-Castro folks blamed then President John F. Kennedy for not sending in the full force of the U.S. military to secure success.

Years would pass, Fidel was now completely in the pro-Marxist, pro-Russian camp, now unashamedly pronouncing his belief in Marxist Revolutionary Principles, announcing his strong allegiance to Russia and his vows to defend Cuba against United States Imperialism. The assassination attempts by the CIA began, but never succeeded. The economic Embargo was put into place and Cuba was really forced to remain in the Russian camp. It would all culminate with Russia's placing of intercontinental ballistic missiles in Cuba in 1962, the discovery of the same via U.S. high altitude spy planes, and the tense confrontation between Kennedy and Khrushchev which brought the planet to the brink of nuclear war in 1962. Fortunately, wise and cool heads prevailed; Kennedy coerced Khrushchev to withdraw his missiles in exchange for the U.S. doing the same in Turkey. So, it was a draw.

Another card in the deck in Spanish speaking South America was fiery Marxist revolutionary Ché Guevara (from where else with this moniker, but Argentina). Ché was trained in traditional medicine but was converted to the Revolution, a conversion reinforced on a strange motorcycle trip from Argentina through the entire west coast of South America; Ché was particularly impressed by the poverty, misery and downtrodden peoples of the Andes, especially the laborers in the mines. He joined Fidel's cause when the two met in Mexico after Castro's release from prison for inciting revolution against Batista in 1956 and his exile to Mexico. In hindsight, it may have been Ché who was more brutal and non-compromising in his fervor for the cause for he was named the head of the kangaroo court tribunals of all the Batista folks who did not get away and any dissidents to the cause. He gave the orders and at times fired the gun in the firing squads. After the early years of the Revolution, the evolution of the same in Cuba, it was Ché who would lead the Cuba "Liberating" force in Angola in the 1960s. But the final move was his disappearance and then arriving in Bolivia to lead the peoples' revolution in that country.

All the above was a big fly in the ointment that bothered United States' politicians, military leaders and others all the way up to the President. Just one small facet of the plan to combat Fidel, Ché, and international Communism was that National Defense Education Act and the Fulbright Grants that would finance the young scholars who would perhaps help save the day.

Cuba, Fidel and Ché were not the only headaches. Another was the massive, rich country of Brazil with its almost 200 million population, the Amazon Basin in its back yard and one very disturbing factor: the impoverished Northeast where millions of peasants worked the land in the early 1960s, living in a state of semi-servitude under their all - powerful, rich masters: the landowners of the "coronel" (colonel's system). Brazil, long a developing democracy, friend of the United States, rapidly growing industrial and agriculture power in the southern hemisphere, had a problem. There was a political leader in the Northeast, one Francisco Julião, who was spearheading a peasants' movement ["A Liga Camponesa"] patterned on Cuba with the main issue of land reform. As well, there was a leftist governor in Pernambuco State, Miguel Arraes, who was making noise about doing something about the unjust land tenure system in the same area. A leftist movement, the MEB, the Base Educational Movement ("Movimento Educacional de Base") was in full swing to alphabetize the illiterate peasant class so they could get the right to vote and change things. And the MEB received the staunch support of the leftist leaning, Fidel - sympathizing UNE (National Union of Students).

All this brought a major change to this old democracy in Latin America in 1964. Espousing an anti-communist rhetoric along with saving the country for God and family, the right-wing generals fomented and carried out an almost bloodless revolution, its name alone a sign of the times: "The Redemptor" ["A Redentora"]. It was April,1964, when tanks rumbled down Avenida Atlântica along Copacabana Beach to attack the military fort located between Copacabana and Ipanema. Eye witnesses recall the tanks, but more revealing to any understanding of Brazil was the reality of thousands of "cariocas" tanning and playing on the beach, body surfing in the waves, and checking out all the skin, this in the middle of a startling and profound military coup. The regime would last for twenty-one years until 1985 and would be in cahoots with similar causes in Argentina ("The Dirty War") and Chile (Augusto Pinochet's battle against the left).

Soon, peaceful, fun-loving, prosperous Brazil would be at the epicenter of the same global Capitalist-Marxist conflict and how it would turn out would affect the bigger picture.

The generals' answer was a crackdown on the left, innocuous at first (taking away political rights of suspected leftists, thus their right to vote and hold office) but later evolving into a full blown fierce dictatorship with no holds barred: the capture and imprisonment of dissidents, torture and even death. The Brazilian Left, without resources and really fighting alone, did its best: there were street protests culminating in the beating of marching students by the military police, the reaction of some leftist leaders who kidnapped important foreign diplomats for ransom, robbed banks for funds and opposed the military any way they could. Many fled the country into voluntary or otherwise exile, and some were "disappeared" by the military.

This is the background for my story.

LETTER I

THE BEGINNINGS

1

My name is Mike Gaherty and I was born on a small farm in southeast Nebraska, but the family moved later to a larger place just west of Lincoln. My people had immigrated from Ireland in the early 19th century to southeast Ohio and work in the coal mines, but had saved to get another chance at farming, the tradition in the Ireland days. The farm was of average size in those days of the 1940s and 1950s, a half-section dedicated to raising wheat, alfalfa and corn. The upbringing was middle class and traditional Catholic. The work on the farm was hard and I enjoyed the experience but soon discovered I had no mechanical aptitude and in fact, to coin a term of the times, was "mechanically declined." This meant I would not be a candidate to run the farm after school.

I was good in debate (the Lincoln High School won the state debate championship my senior year with myself a veteran debater on the squad), history, and had a knack for languages, first two formal years of study of Latin by the dedicated school marm in the public school, but more so in Spanish. What was lousy was any effort in math other than arithmetic, or sciences, barely passing Geometry and Chemistry in high school.

The Gahertys although with a modest farm income had education as a high priority. My dad only had an 8th grade education because in those days the boys had to leave to run the farms. My mother was bit more fortunate attaining two years of college at a Catholic girls' school, studying to be a school teacher, and living some amazing years as a schoolmarm in one-room country schools in western Nebraska and neighboring Colorado, even living in a sod house and getting to school walking or on horseback. It was she who wanted the kids to have a good education and a chance at life. The choice was the Jesuits, probably because they would come to the small towns on the west frontier to give fiery Lenten missions with sermons of fire and brimstone. She said, "They are good teachers."

My older brother went to Creighton University on a GI Bill scholarship, middle brother Sean to Marquette on a Naval ROTC scholarship with a subsequent career on a ship in the Pacific, and I to the small Jesuit school in Kansas City. I went for all the wrong reasons – Kansas City was an exciting place for a farm boy from central Nebraska; the city had a major league ball team, the Kansas City A's, migrants themselves from Philadelphia and lousy. I had seen the likes of Ted

Williams and Mickey Mantle in forays to the city while in high school. Omaha just had a minor - league team.

So, I enrolled at Rockhurst College in the late 1950s, became a business management major to avoid the math and science but thrived in Spanish under a terrific teacher and mentor from Tulane University in New Orleans. It was what went on outside the classroom that marked the future: friendships with the Latinos at school and dating some very upper-class Latin American young ladies being "finished" at the local nuns' school. A lot of Spanish was learned amidst some good times that included a traditional "serenata" at the girls' school when I and my Latino buddies got juiced up at a local tavern and then hopped over the fence at the Catholic school and planted ourselves in front of the girls' dorm. I played guitar so the group sang the traditional "Mañanitas" below the dorm window, but failed in the following numbers due to the disturbing barking of the Dobermans guarding the place. The cops came, red lights blinking, and the boys were told to "go home" and sleep it off.

The final note that would determine the future was the decision to attend summer school at the UNAM (National University of Mexico in Mexico City), the moment and the choice upon the advice of my Spanish teacher and mentor at college: "If you are going to compete in the business world in Latin America or even teach Spanish, you better get some in-country experience and develop the necessary skills." I borrowed $500 from the local Lincoln National Bank, co-signed with my father's signature, packed a trunk with clothes and my trusty Sears-Roebuck classic guitar, and hopped a bus from Lincoln to Omaha, on to Kansas City, Tulsa, Austin, San Antonio and across the border to Mexico. On the other side, the bus passed by Monterrey, Querétaro and on to D.F., a grand total of 55 hours on the Greyhound. The summer went well with no muggings or assaults on the small town naïve boy from Nebraska; I learned some Spanish and saw a lot of central Mexico.

The next chapter was icing on the cake, a 35-hour bus ride through large and small towns of southern Mexico, through Maya country, to the border at Guatemala, a harrowing bus ride over the top of the mountains (Guatemalans told the joke "Did you hear about the Indian who got drunk and fell out of his corn field?") in Guatemala to meet friend Jaime from Rockhurst days. I experienced for the first-time life with upper class Latin Americans and needless to say enjoyed the experience. I was offered a job with the friend's family's business, a pharmaceutical manufacturing firm, after graduation the following year.

Wisely knowing my propensity for being a true blooded "gringo" and realizing I would never be able to adapt to living permanently in a foreign country, I choose instead to graduate from Rockhurst, and study for that Ph.D. in Spanish and Latin American Studies at Georgetown in D.C., this on the NDEA Scholarship. After three years of intense study, academic success and more learning of Spanish and especially Portuguese, I arrived at the crucial moment of the comprehensive exams, and if successful, the dissertation to follow.

This is where all the threads of the story come together. I won a Fulbright-Hays Research Grant to Brazil to study its folk-popular literature ("a literatura de cordel") and its relation to Brazilian erudite literature and history. I would leave in June of 1966 for Brazil, spend a year, and hopefully write that damned dissertation and fulfill the wishes of the NDEA program.

But then the phone call came.

2

I'm back on the farm in Nebraska with my folks and getting all my stuff ready for the extended stay in Brazil for the Fulbright-Hays and dissertation research beginning in June 1966. I've never traveled anywhere for that long a period so packing clothes and other necessities, documents, notes on research contacts in Brazil graciously given me by graduate school professors, and a research plan is no small deal. For sure I will not be lugging a trunk of clothes and a classic guitar on this trip as I had in Mexico and Guatemala for that summer of 1962, my first introduction to Latin America.

The phone rings and it is James Hansen from the International Section of the <u>New York Times</u>. When you are twenty-five years old, getting ready to do a commercial airline flight for the first time to a place you've never been, you've got enough to worry about. I was suspicious of the caller, after all, was this a joke? What did I know?

"Hello Mike. This is James Hansen from the <u>Times</u> (I was supposed to know it was the big paper in New York). Mike, we had someone on the Fulbright-Hays selection committee for your interview for the grant. Sometimes those old stodgy professors have more than one iron in the fire. Not only were you deserving of the grant, but he passed on to us a couple of ideas that coincided with a notion we've had for some time about coverage in Latin America, in this case Brazil."

"At the <u>Times</u>, of course I'm talking about the International Section; we need to understand the reality of these Third World nations and pass that understanding on to our millions of readers, a pretty sophisticated crowd. We want them to know what is cooking in those countries – the big view – economically, politically, militarily and otherwise. We do not require a CIA mission report or a news report from a stringer; we already have access to all that. What we have in mind is a little different and you fill the bill to do it, that is, if what you hear from me appeals to you. We think a person in your situation may bring something fresh, interesting and important to our readers (we've checked out your background, your observation skills and your writing and oral communications skills from your graduate professors). And we think you have the curiosity and adventurous spirit to fit our plan. What we have in mind is a genuine account of what you see in Brazil from all angles sent to us in the form of an occasional long LETTER from the USIS, USAID or consular offices (this guarantees safety and confidentiality with government mail). We think a young, red-blooded, virile man may have a chance to write of a couple of angles that will catch the attention of the readers. We will publish the letter periodically for twelve months and if it "clicks" do a final NYT travel book with the segments. You will do your "normal" Fulbright research, living in Brazil and seeing whatever comes up. If it all works out, at the end you will be compensated in cash payment and will have a fine book to add to your Curriculum Vitae in academia."

"Remember it's the full account of what you see and experience in Brazil – the whole kit and caboodle. Most of our readers know about Copacabana beach, Brazilian soccer, Pelé and the World Cup victories, the music from old Carmen Miranda to the Bossa Nova, and that there is a lot of jungle in the Amazon. A helluva lot more is happening down there and it is a big place important not only to the International Section reader, but for our country's interests. So, think it over, give me a call at the Times (you've got a week before you leave, so ponder the matter) and we will formalize the agreement."

I thought "holy shit" and stammered an answer that yes, thank you, yes, I'm flattered, and yes, I'll certainly give it due consideration (not telling the man I had already made up my mind; I'd be crazy to not do this and get this chance). Two days later, to not let James think I was too anxious, I made the call, ironed out a few more details of exactly what he wanted, and agreed to the offer. James indicated that there would be no formal contract but not to worry; all that would come later.

Done deal.

3

Mom and Dad drove me to Omaha where I would catch the TWA flight to New York and then the international flight on Pan Am to Rio de Janeiro. We arrived at the airport, lugged my two big suitcases to the TWA check in counter and there was the first surprise - the ticket that was supposed to be waiting for me from the Fulbright commission was not there. An on the ball agent looked at my Fulbright papers (kind of an "insurance policy" I had in my packet), made a quick call to the Fulbright Commission in Washington, D.C., nodded his head a few times, saying "yes, yes, okay" and in a few minutes a one-half inch packet of those old cardboard thin tickets was spit out by the machine at the counter. Saying, "You're all set, good travels and the best of luck," he handed me the tickets which were stuffed in my carry-on briefcase. And TWA checked the bags.

After a hurried goodbye to Mom and Dad (there was no time for a proper teary good-bye due to the circumstances), I literally ran down the concourse, out the departure door, down the steps to the tarmac and rushed to a 707 already warming up the engines. I ran up the steps to the plane, was greeted by the stewardess, directed to a seat and collapsed in a heap. "Fasten your seatbelt for departure," she said. Breathing a bit harder than usual the country boy obeyed.

After the flight from Omaha, Kennedy airport was crowded and I don't recall a thing except boarding the Pan Am flight, being ushered to the front row in tourist class and seated between two young Peace Corps Volunteers headed for a two-year stint in Brazil. We took turns saying what we were going to do in Brazil and the eight-hour flight to Rio took off. Contact with the Volunteers in Brazil would ensue in the coming months and would be frequent and important with some memorable times drinking beer with Volunteers on R and R in Recife and Bahia, swapping stories and sharing what we thought about Brazil and the Brazilians. As to what we would do in Brazil, the matter stopped there; we were in two different worlds in that big hunk of the world.

After what was decent service in those days – a hot towel to do something with (did they think the farm boy needed to get the hayseed out of his ears?), large colorful maps of Brazil as souvenirs, paper slippers for those swollen feet during the flight, a drink and fine meal, I probably only slept an hour or two until the plane gradually descended into the Galeão, the international airport in Rio de Janeiro.

ARRIVAL IN BRAZIL AND ON TO RECIFE

We arrived at the Galeão amidst fog and smog, stood in line at customs for the passport stamp at the tiny booths populated by bored, surly bureaucrats in dark suits, thin black ties and constantly smoking. I was introduced to that nifty piece of paper that said: "DO NOT LOSE. THIS PAPER IS NECESSARY FOR YOUR DEPARTURE FROM BRAZIL." So, I was presented this flimsy slip of paper which seemingly guaranteed getting out of Brazil in one year's time. I stuffed it into the packet with the other documents – the passport and that thick cardboard wad of airline tickets.

The customs check in 1966 meant standing in long lines with all international passengers from the dozens of flights arriving in Rio, all groggy from the overnight flights, all in a hurry to navigate another of the introductions to Brazil's famous bureaucracy. You put the bags on the revolving caravel and waited for the green (hopefully) or red light. I drew red so this meant undoing both large suitcases and carry-ons and a meticulous check of everything; the customs people acted like they had never opened a bag before – it was a big novelty. They got a kick out of my J.C Penney gringo white briefs. Finally, they finished, no questions, the green light flashed and I got to repack the bags.

Out the door and I had truly arrived at the chaos and color of Brazil. Using the free baggage cart (a good Brazilian custom), I rolled it all outside the terminal door and was greeted by the crammed taxi row in front and the deafening noise coming from the bus lanes on the other side of the curb and the immense pollution. Grabbing the first cab I could, taxi meter soon running, a cultural experience awaited me. First, I got about 70 per cent of his Portuguese and stammered my first words in that language in Brazil. It soon was apparent that three years of graduate study of Portuguese and Brazilian Literature from near-native professors plus the beery practice with buddy Joe Hayes worked only up to a certain point. There is no way that could prepare for real life in Brazil; it's one thing to study it all, another thing to be there.

Ah, being there! After passing through the terrifically smoggy and ugly north zone of Rio from the "Ilha do Governador" where Galeão was located, along a coal black sludge canal which appeared you could cut with a knife, along the two lanes of traffic heading into the city, we headed into Avenida Getúlio Vargas with its sixteen lanes of traffic and turned on Avenida Rio Branco for the ride down the main street of commerce in downtown Rio. Then I saw it: the hazy Bay of Guanabara and the Sugar Loaf Mountain in the distance. For a graduate student of things

Brazilian in the mid-1960s, <u>this</u> was finally what I was waiting for: it was a scene right out of the classic film "Black Orpheus" ["Orféu Negro"].

We were all weaned on that film and it charged our batteries to get to Brazil. It's worth a note in this first LETTER. It was directed by a Frenchman, Marcel Camus, and was intended to provide France and the world a beautiful view of an exotic Brazil. It dealt with the theme of the Greek singer Orpheus and his lost love Eurídice, but in the setting of a totally romanticized Rio "favela" or slum. The cast was almost totally black and set at Carnival time in Rio with a handsome leading man (who really was a Brazilian soccer star and first-time actor), a beautiful leading woman (who turned out to be from the U.S., Marpessa Dawn, who had to have her dialogue dubbed) and the "cast" of hundreds of real people from the old Babylonia "favela" on the granite rock above the Sugar Loaf cable car station. Aside from terrific recreations of carnival scenes, there were many scenes of the old electric street car (Orféu was a conductor) in downtown Rio going over the Lapa aqueduct, beautiful scenes of the Bay, of "Pão de Açúcar" and the "Cristo Redentor" on top of Corcovado mountain. There was also an eye-opening scene with a real Afro-Brazilian cult of "Umbanda" with drums, chants, trances and the rest, all a bit scary but certainly exotic to the non-Brazilian viewer. Most impressive and very smart and creative was the background music by the best of the new, then, "Bossa Nova" music and screenplay by one of Brazil's favorite and best poets, Vinícius de Morais. All this was on my mind during that taxi ride and first view of Rio.

Also interesting was the taxi driver's "introduction" to Rio. After learning I was a bachelor and open to come what may in Rio, he said (and I translate from the vernacular), "All the women in Rio like to fuck, but some like to fuck more than others. You're a "gringo," have lots of cash and are not bad looking, so have a good time." I intended to check it out. An aside: being from a conservative Roman Catholic background, real sex was pretty limited up to this point for the Nebraska farm boy. The <u>Times</u> wanted the "big picture" and I would supply some chapters on sexual satisfaction. Besides, the "easy" women in Brazil had all kinds of customers, including big shots and politicos, so something else might be learned aside from experiencing the "sensation" as the folk poets would say, of the oral sex or the "whole works," depending on your pocketbook.

After reaching the end of Avenida Rio Branco the taxi driver in effect gave me "the tour" in the normal drive to my hotel – through the Glória Section, the 18th century baroque Glória church up on the hill to the right, along the beach of Flamengo, around the curve to the spectacular but totally polluted Botafogo Bay and beach with the Sugar Loaf high up to the left, through several tunnels (Rio is a city of mountains and beaches) and then to yet another of the dreamed of sites: famous Copacabana Beach. Once again from the movie, my eyes were filled with one of the most iconic and spectacular sights of Rio (called the "marvelous city" by its residents the "Cariocas") – the six-kilometer-long crescent of beautiful beach, the surf and waves to one side, and the unending row of twenty-story apartment house buildings, hotels, and restaurants and nightclubs to the right. I thought, "If this is heaven, I have arrived." This is where I would see the "Carioca" beauties in their bikinis, called "tangas" and even "fio dental" [dental floss] bikinis.

We arrived at a modest hotel at the end of Copacabana in Posto 6 and the view from the sidewalk out front was the entire six - kilometer crescent with the Sugar Loaf at its end and the Christ figure far up in the sky to the left. It was gorgeous and I was in culture shock.

5

That night I got up my courage and made my first phone call in Brazil, and in Portuguese to boot! This is a test for all language majors for the first time in the foreign country, and surprisingly it went well. The objective was to talk with Colonel Manuel Cavalcanti Proença (Brazilian Army, forced retirement) in Flamengo, one of a handful of contacts arranged for me by the Portuguese-Brazilian Literature professor at Georgetown.

Colonel Proença was a professor of Brazilian Literature at the Army's War College ["Escola Superior Militar"]; I guessed even the big brass in Brazil were interested in culture! Major books on the romantic novelist José de Alencar, on the major Modernist Poet Mário de Andrade, forwards and introductions to the novels of José Lins do Rego, one of the Novelists of the Northeast, and an important guide to the greatest of all Brazil's novelists' masterpiece "The Devil to Pay in the Backlands" ["Grande Sertáo: Veredas"] were among his credentials.

There is more. The colonel's military "curriculum" comes into play. In 1924 as a young officer he participated in the now famous "Prestes Column" ["A Coluna Prestes"], a mad, crazy, largely ineffectual man-hunt by the military to chase down, arrest or kill Luís Carlos Prestes, a Marxist fomenter of revolution in São Paulo in 1924 who had slipped out of the noose to the huge Brazilian Interior. Prestes' aim was to contact the poor, rural masses and educate, convince and convert them to the revolutionary cause. To do so he made a wide swing through western São Paulo State, up through Goiás, Minas Gerais, Bahia and the states of the Brazilian Bulge – the Northeast. He failed, the current theory for the failure being the absolute unwillingness (probably out of fear) of the poor workers to be made politically conscious ["concientizados"] and their choice to remain under the power of the politics and land system characterized by the rule of large landholders called "colonels" ["coronéis"]. Prestes was caught, imprisoned and would only appear on the national scene after his amnesty in 1945, immediately giving a fiery political speech in Paecambu Soccer Stadium in São Paulo to the delirious fans, but being war time, surprisingly enough espousing the cause of then Brazilian hero and dictator, Getúlio Vargas. He would enter my story again come the 1960s.

It was that wild goose chase then that only coincidentally awakened Colonel Proença's eyes to the flora and fauna of that great Brazil and made him originally a specialist in Botany. It was only later after massive amounts of reading that he was converted to be a writer, critic and professor of Brazilian Literature. Then came a glitch: with the 1964 Military Revolution (and its ramifications for me in Recife in 1966), Proença was on the wrong side; he was with the progressive, socially conscious officers and not the fiery new "redeemers" of the Constitution waging a war against Communism, the Left, and the new, evil morality in Brazil. So Proença was "reformed" ["cassado"], his political rights taken away but in the amazing, surprisingly at times, tolerant Brazil stuck into a corner of the War College to teach literature. In effect, "Keep your mouth shut about politics and stick to the novels and poetry." Hard-liner General Castelo Branco, by chance a northeasterner from Ceará, would shepherd the first years of the revolution, begin the first efforts at "tightening down" Brazil for the coming years, gradually introducing Brazilians and their recent healthy democratic tradition to a new way of looking at things. He would be followed by the generals' choice for a "democratic succession in command" by General Costa e Silva and events to come – a terrorist bomb attempt on his life in Recife and the fierce military response – the hardline repression during my stay in Brazil.

So why would Colonel Proença enter this story? There was yet another facet of the Colonel's intellectual life. On that wild and wooly "tour" of the interior of Brazil in 1924 he also became aware of Brazil's folk-popular poetry, both the oral, improvised verse of the poet-singers ["cantadores"] and the broadsides of the poets of the popular literature in verse ["literatura popular em verso"] called by its popular name of "cordel" in subsequent years. He was instrumental in the rescue and collection of old "cordel" for the Ruy Barbosa Foundation in Rio in the late 1950s, along with scholars Manuel Diégues Júnior, a cultural anthropologist, and Orígenes Lessa, a journalist, fan and collector of old "cordel" (there will be a lot more about this in December of 1966 and my time in Rio). Thus, Proença was "my man in Rio" for the Fulbright research.

I took a bus that first night from Copacabana, trusting the driver to let me know where to get off, passed through what seemed a myriad of tunnels through Copa and Botafogo and into the district of Flamengo where Proença lived. After arriving, they ushered me immediately into his office-library and we had the talk that would mark the next six months of research in Brazil. Due to the letter of introduction from Professor Parry of Georgetown I was welcomed, we chatted of Proença's military days and interest in "cordel" and he agreed to be my first research mentor in Brazil. It was short and sweet: "Mike, go up to Recife, to the fair at Caruaru with the blind folk singers, read the basic books on "cordel," start a collection, and come back here in six months in December and we'll set to work." I left his amazing library (having been introduced to "bibliophiles" in Brazil), took a bus home to the hotel and got ready for Recife, Pernambuco.

There was one lesser but no less important item: I called my old friend from undergraduate days at Rockhurst, Caetano Forti, went over to the luxury apartment of his family overlooking Botafogo Bay and Sugar Loaf, was introduced to his mom and brother, and arranged to stay with the family upon my return to Rio just before Christmas of 1966. Things were looking up. So far so good; there were no muggings from the Rio thieves, things were relatively quiet in the Rio streets and the military was in charge. That would soon become evident in Recife.

6

The flight to Recife was on the Varig Electra direct from Rio where I was introduced to the incredible "Varig Service" modeled after Air France. The seats were large and comfortable, there was lots of leg space and tourists were treated like first class: drinks before dinner, appetizers ["aperitivos e tira-gostos"], a steak dinner with wine, all with crystal glasses, silver and china. And I was introduced to that great Brazilian institution of the fiery hot, sweet demitasse coffee ["cafezinho"]. It made the international flight on Pan Am look shabby!

The passenger to my side offered a current view of Brazil. He was a businessman from Fortaleza, Ceará, who traveled the entire east coast selling northeastern goods to the rest of Brazil. He spoke directly and sincerely to me, the novice in Brazil: "We've got a new government with the generals. Even though he is from my home state, I really don't much like General Castelo Branco and the signs of change in the present regime. I'm a Juscelino Kubitschek fan, our terrific president from the 1950s who brought major economic development to Brazil, made us a strong Third World nation with the continuation of the Getúlio Vargas era – steel mills and production, the new Brazilian automobile industry with the VWs ["fusca"] made available to even the middle class, and prosperity. The generals are promising a great "March to the West," colonizing and developing the Amazon and a big economic cake they promise to divide and make a few slices available to the middle class and to the poor. We'll see."

I would run into the businessman totally by accident in future months, first in Recife on the beach and once again on Copacabana Beach near its center at Santa Clara. They say Brazil is a big place, so go figure! I would remember his words and caution for the future.

7

The Electra zoomed into Guararapes Airport (an introduction to those macho, adventurous Brazilian airline pilots and their far more adventurous flying and demeanor than U.S. pilots with its regulation); we had seen the brilliant blue of the Atlantic and then the straight as an arrow reef along shore, the reason for the name Recife ["arrecife"].

Recife would be my "home base" of research and introduction to Brazilian ways and life for the next six months. It was euphemistically called the "Venice of Brazil" due to the three rivers entering the ocean in and around the city. There was another name: "The Calcutta of Brazil," darkly referring to the immense poverty in the city, that is, in parts of Recife, "the wrong side of the tracks" as we would say in Nebraska. The prosperity of Recife, on the other hand, was due to incipient industrialization of the Northeast bulge, the regional development entity SUDENE (Superintendency for the Development of the Northeast, its largest bureaucracy) and in no small way to the massive number of potential laborers migrating from the poverty-stricken interior. Recife's economic foundation however was still mainly the old economic mainstay dating back to the 16th century and early Portuguese discovery and colonization: the sugar cane industry. These potential laborers who made the city run (they built the sidewalks and the streets) were descendants of slaves but also poor white sharecroppers and farmers who made up a good portion of the population. I would soon learn that Recife and the Northeast was also the center of a major, regional cultural and literary movement with nationally famous novelists, playwrights, poets, and musicians – my "bread and butter" for future research. Ariano Suassuna and João Cabral de Melo Neto of "Severe Life and Death" ["Morte e Vida Severina"] fame were just a couple of examples.

It was the poor rural migrants along with some amazingly talented individuals that explained my choice in residence for the next six months: a good many of the major poets of "cordel" lived in Recife, its suburbs, and small towns of the interior of Pernambuco state and its neighbors in Paraíba State. The São José Market, the hub of commerce for food and other necessities for Recife, was in the old downtown, the hangout for the maids sent to do the weekly market or "fair" for their middle and upper-class patrons. It also was the epicenter for "cordel" poets and salesmen and their market stands, where they sold the thousands of "cordel" broadsides to an avid public. It would be important in my story.

My first night in Recife was spent at the 4th of October Hotel in the downtown along the Capibaribe River; the "tariff" was expensive, USD $32, and my modest Fulbright budget would soon be eaten up at that rate. It was located near to the infamous "Restaurante Leite" where presidential candidate João Pessoa was assassinated by a member of the Pernambuco Dantas clan, setting off the spark for the 1930 Revolution which eventually would bring Getúlio Vargas to power. My future mentor, Ariano Suassuna, a small child in Paraíba at the time, was shaken when his father, an ally of Dantas, was assassinated in Rio days later.

Along the Capibaribe river running through that part of Recife, there was heavy traffic on the footbridges linking Boa Vista District to the downtown on the other side. There were always beggars, some afflicted with swollen, bandage wrapped legs, often with blood oozing from the bandages. "Recifenses" either ignored them or dropped a couple of coins in their laps. The river itself was swollen when I arrived in late June of 1966, the result of intense rains in the interior and the floods that ensued when the three main rivers emptied into Recife proper. This was "winter" for the "Pernambucanos," only slightly changed hot tropical temperatures but downpours of rain, often lasting the night through from June to perhaps October. The floods would be repeated in 1967.

8

⁓⁓

Since the hotel tariff was biting into my budget, I contacted yet another person indicated by the graduate professor at Georgetown, Fábio de Holanda, an intellectual, short story writer and collector of folklore. Fábio was a colleague of Ariano Suassuna, the playwright and major writer of plays using the "cordel;" he had participated in the Northeastern intellectual movement of the 1940s and 1950s using folklore as a basis for literature (not unlike Federico García Lorca in his time in Spain). He invited me to the house in a calm, distant suburb from downtown (I would soon learn that suburb or "subúrbio" had an altogether different meaning in Recife: "subúrbio" was a poor slum; other districts were called "bairros"). I took a taxi to his house, met him and his large family of wife and ten children, and basically asked for help. There were no college dormitories in Recife; students lived in apartments call "republics" ["repúblicas"]; all the modest hotels and boarding houses were full due to a national volleyball tournament. What to do? Fábio made a phone call and said I could bunk at an art studio located in an old colonial mansion in Olinda, a district some ten kilometers from city center via a beat up two lane asphalt road. Major northeastern painters and artisans lived there and would find a place for me. Olinda was the first capital of Pernambuco in the days of the original "captaincies" ["capitanias"] of the 1500s.

There was a cultural aside at Fábio's house: his ample collection of northeastern clay dolls ["bonecos de barro"] on the shelves in his office. In a way, this was my introduction to northeast Brazil's folklore, prior to any contact with "cordel" poets or their verse. Three to four inches in height, unpainted with the original color of the clay, they depicted all manner of folk life: northeastern trio musicians with triangle, drum and guitar, depictions of the famous bandits Antônio Silvino and Lampião and Maria Bonita, Padre Cícero a famous miracle working priest from the interior of Ceará State, wild bulls and horses, northeastern cowboys and images of St. Francis, a favorite. The dolls came originally from Caruaru (the reader may recall Colonel Proença's advice to get to that city and its market) and became known for one artisan – Master Vitalino ["Mestre Vitalino"] and his family. The master became famous, the dolls were sold soon at airports and folk-art shops in Rio and São Paulo, and Vitalino made nothing. He was cheated by big city art dealers. I would buy some of the clay dolls later, none I think signed by Vitalino, and would wrap them in dirty clothes in my luggage with the idea of getting them home to Lincoln.

So, I loaded my suitcases, thankfully, and took a taxi to the colonial three-story mansion ["sobrado"] in Olinda, knocked on the door and was given a cot in a corner of the art studio itself. The young artists welcomed me, invited me to smoke some weed, and showed me how to sleep in a hammock (would this be my "bunk" for the next two weeks?). I thought hammocks were for Indians and with a gringo's lack of "getting it" [o "jeito"] fell out a couple of times until they showed me you must get in sideways. The hammock was a big deal; most were made from fine weaving from the State of Ceará and they even had a "married hammock" ["rede de casal"] for two.

The painters were upcoming stars of the artistic scene in Olinda, Recife, and Pernambuco; some would become famous and make a good living. The paintings seemed to me to be a "marriage" between avant-garde, surrealism and folk art. These guys were curious what a naturally wealthy North-American was doing in Brazil in 1966 and when I told them I was on a Fulbright research grant to study northeastern folklore and the booklets of verse of the "cordel," they nodded their heads, smirked and even laughed. Why would a "gringo" be interested in that shit? There had to be more to the story. It was just the first time my motives were questioned and would lead to some interesting circumstances later.

During those two weeks in colonial Olinda there were several introductions to life in the Northeast, all surprises but essential to getting used to Brazil. You could hear, see and feel the rain dripping from the high tile roof (the building was probably 400 years old) and see bits of sunshine or grey through the holes. The bathroom and shower was folkloric enough – the water dripping from a single faucet, the stool with no lid and in need of a good cleaning. (You can take the kid out of Nebraska ...). It was hot and humid day and night (hey, we were in the tropics). I slept little those first few nights, not incidentally from an introduction to Brazilian music, but not the samba or Bossa Nova one might have expected.

During a few nights of the week from about ten p.m. to about 4 a.m. there was loud drumming reverberating through the tiles; it was the pounding of drums from the Xangô ceremonies a few blocks away. The "TA da da, TA da da, TA da da" sound I would learn later was from "Pai Edu's" Xangô rite, one of many "houses" ["terreiros"] of this Afro-Brazilian religious rite all over Olinda and Recife.

So, bleary enough from that we awoke to a different sound coming from the plaza right outside the mansion: the trumpets and drums of a military band doing its daily drill about 6 a.m. They played marches and they marched every day. It was part of the military presence all over the Recife area, a reminder of who was in charge but not really an unpleasant side of the ubiquitous army presence. A more sinister side of all that would come later.

During those days, I finally did get a taste of the Brazil I expected – the sound of samba, northeastern music and the most indicative of music in all of Brazil at that time – the MPB, Brazilian Popular Music, and even more the "yeah-yeah-yeah" "iê-iê-iê" of the ersatz Rock and Roll storming the country at that time. A handsome young rock singer from Espírito Santo State, Roberto Carlos and his buddy Erasmo Carlos were taking Brazil by storm with the local version of the Beatles. It was a storm that inundated all the teenagers, college kids and even adults of the time: boys with long hair to their shoulder, girls and boys with tight pants, all sprinkling their Portuguese with the new slang Roberto Carlos used in his songs. Brazilians said it was the "Golden Age" of the national music. There were political ramifications: Rock was immoral for the Brazilian hardline generals, the degradation of the national morality, but at least it was <u>not</u> subversive or Communist.

One more northeastern custom became evident in those first days, to my mind a great Brazilian institution: the "serenade" ["serenata"] on the sidewalks outside the old mansions, small groups of Brazilians with guitar in hand playing samba or its northeastern version, the "baião." It was quiet, it was acoustic, and even the farm boy learned two or three ditties on the guitar and the guitar accompaniment – the best a "baião" supposedly written by no less than the infamous bandit Lampião: "Mulher Rendeira." It was on one of those sidewalks one evening I was introduced to another North American researcher (the Brazilians said there was a "plethora" of them hanging out in the Northeast, more spies from the CIA?) It was Mark Lisboa on a Ford Foundation Grant from Princeton who was studying the history of the sugar cane economy and industry in the Northeast. Mark was Jewish, probably no accident since the Jewish colony in Pernambuco was instrumental in establishing that thriving economy for colonial Brazil; the Jews were encouraged to leave when Brazil retook the Northeast from the Dutch (and their Jewish connection) who ruled for about forty years when the Spanish King Felipe II ruled Portugal as a descendant through marriage to the Portuguese crown, this from 1578 to 1640 until the Battle of Guararapes threw out the Dutch. 1578 incidentally was a watershed moment for Portuguese and Brazilian history: the young, religiously inspired king Sebastião, overly ambitious it turns out, took the "reconquest" of Portugal a step farther, leading an invading army into North Africa in Morocco and being totally vanquished by the Moslems, losing his life in the process. There was no legitimate Portuguese successor to the throne available, hence the Spanish takeover. All this became known as Sebastianism and would produce astounding moments in northeastern Brazil's history in the years to come, one of the many chapters told in "cordel."

Mark, unlike me, adapted well to the local scene. He bought a "Lambreta" small motor scooter and whizzed through the traffic from Olinda to Recife proper to the research institutes to do his work. I would have been terrified and with reason. Driving in Brazil was often more akin to Formula One and Indianapolis than a Third World country; maybe it was Emerson Fittipaldi and friends from São Paulo who would dominate at Indianapolis in those years. Brazilians told the story that all these guys trained as taxi drivers in Rio and São Paulo. And Emerson added a chapter to Indianapolis: in the winner's circle, instead of quaffing the traditional bottle of milk, he insisted on orange juice – he owned groves in Brazil and Florida. There was a compromise: the authorities allowed him to drink the OJ before the Brazilian TV cameras, but only after the bottle of milk. The "lambreta" would become the title of a hilarious Brazilian chronicle by the immensely talented Luís Fernando Veríssimo. Incidentally, Mark met, courted and later married one of those cute young ladies from Olinda. We would meet months later in Ouro Preto, Minas Gerais under different circumstances.

Not only did I not marry a Brazilian, although romance in Brazil will enter my story, but I also did not buy a motor scooter, first because I was saving money for something else, and secondly for one better reason: fear! On the other hand, in those weeks in Olinda I would become "sort of" Brazilian, catching the "local," the "drip-drip" ["pinga-pinga"] bus that took about an hour or more each way into Recife where the work was to get done. The fare was right, just a few cents, and you got to know Brazil. The buses were jammed, mostly with poor black Brazilians but also the mixed blood northeasterners of Indian-White roots, and a few "brancos." They were incredibly hot with no air conditioning and like a sauna in the sun and heat of Recife; a keen sense of smell on my part would reveal those who did and did not use deodorant (or who could even afford it). I put up with this routine during those two weeks going to Recife to the Law School Library to read books on "cordel" and the renowned Joaquim Nabuco Research Institute for more of the same, but wasting lots of day time hours in the process.

There is a famous nineteenth century novel in Brazil which tells of an ambitious Portuguese immigrant who arrives in Brazil ready to conquer all obstacles and basically, like all the Portuguese, to get rich. Something happens: the tropical heat, the life style of Brazil gets to him, he loses all ambition and becomes indolent in the tropics. In other words, he loses his momentum. I was beginning to feel like the "Portuga" (the Brazilians used this nickname for anyone associated with the mother country) and that heat, rain, and suffocating bus rides were indeed causing me to lose my momentum. Something had to be done.

9

I had the good fortune of finding a young men's boarding house in a terrific location for work – the "Rose House" ["Chácara das Rosas"] – a euphemistic name at best, very near the Pernambuco Law School ["Faculdade de Direito de Pernambuco"] where I would do the first important background readings on "cordel." It was centrally located in the Boa Vista district and merits a few pages in this early phase of work in Pernambuco. It was a two-story affair, with a "garden" out front facing the street with just a few roses. The "Chácara" itself was in the shape of a U with rooms on the three sides and a small dining room and kitchen in the center; the "bath house" was in a small building to the side. The latter would be a learning experience for the "gringo" from Nebraska: there was a narrow pipe from the ceiling where water either dripped or barely came out, cold water only – this was the shower. The stool was enough to take your breath away and I soon learned the reason for the smelly waste basket to the side: you don't flush paper down the fragile drain and you bring your own toilet paper (the thin pages of the international edition of "Time" magazine served in an emergency). The Rose House did not all smell like roses. There was a sink, once again with cold water only, where you could shave, carefully hoarding those few stainless-steel Gillette blades from home. Outside the outhouse there was another spigot and many of the guys brushed their teeth there.

The owner Antônio would show up once a week in his shiny new VW Bug (the Brazilian name was "fusca," and if you got the larger version it was the "fuscão" or "big fusca"), the result of an ingenious national finance plan for the middle class to get a new car in Brazil – a lottery! You paid a small fee for the ticket and if your number was called you got your car right away; what was left was the hefty down payment and monthly payments to follow. In slow moving Brazil, it was a "hurry up and wait" system. VWs were the most common cars in that new auto industry in Brazil, but the locally manufactured "Rural" (a bi-product of Willys Jeeps of Brazil) was around too. Unlike Mexico from my earlier days there were no black Mercedes, but the contraband U.S. Mustang took their places. Antônio would have the gay black "maid" wash the car while he whiled away a couple of hour's bullshitting with the tenants. All the guys liked to trade stories of their latest sexual escapades, tell dirty jokes and hang out until he collected the rents and was on his way until next time.

Life in the Chácara tells volumes of what really was going on in Recife at the time, stuff you didn't read in the newspaper or see on TV but was the "essence" of much of the male mentality and the task of living at the time. (The <u>Times</u> readers would get their money's worth just with this.) If you kept your ears open, and I did, it was a new world.

The boarders were young men mainly from the interior of Pernambuco State, but with a smattering from neighboring states like Paraíba, Ceará, and a couple of guys were from Piauí to the NW of the bulge, so big and small of the Northeast were there. <u>Realidade</u> magazine, a truly excellent publication maybe combining "Life" and "Look" in Brazil did an article on Piauí probably the poorest state in Brazil with a title catching the locals' attention: "Piauí Exists." Most Brazilians were happy to get that news but had no plans to visit. Some of the fellows were studying at various schools, a couple at the ubiquitous English Language Institutes, but just as many were working and trying to make it in that northeastern economy. A snapshot of them told and taught me a primer on life in the Northeast. First, the Chácara was cheap rent even for Brazil – the equivalent of USD $35 per month, room and board – the latter folkloric.

Mário was smart, full of humor, studying at the Yazigi English Institute, and trying to get a foothold in that economy. He told me that if you knew just a smattering of English it would double your salary, and the example he liked to give was to get a job as a steward on the old "Tariff 3" DC - 3s plying the skies of northeast and northern Brazil at the time. Tariff 1 was the modern jet, Tariff 2 the jet-props like the Electra, but Tariff 3 was what most modest income people used, if they flew at all. I noted on several trips on them later that Varig, Paraense and other airlines insisted on giving the passenger instructions in three languages: Portuguese, French and English. I can't vouch for the French, but the English was unintelligible. It all seemed classy to the passengers and delayed takeoff times. This was the Brazil I came to know well in that year.

"Peba" ("armadillo" in English) was a chunky guy from the interior, representative of probably thousands of migrants to Recife. He made a living at the big central São José Market trading in cereals, a couple sacks of beans or rice always stacked in his room. He was illiterate but working diligently to learn written Portuguese using the old ABC books; more than once I saw and read his painstaking efforts at writing his first letters and words in the language. Off work he had an interesting hobby: screwing all the maids in the neighborhood. The colorful language he used to describe this endeavor was to "levar para o mato e derrubá-las" (take them out to the boonies and "lay" them).

Paraibano (of course from Paraíba State) never did do much that I could see but he was one of the champion dirty joke tellers.

"Matuto" or hillbilly was my roommate in our room on the ground floor; I never did figure out what he did and could only catch a fraction of his Portuguese from the interior.

"Marujo" was a main character in this cast of characters. "Swabbie" was a veteran of the the Brazilian Navy and had training as a para-medic. He brought a couple of skills to the boarding house, most important, giving shots of Vitamin B-12 to cure the nasty colds that came with a change of season. As a newcomer, late that rainy June I sure enough caught a whale of a cold and decided to take him up on his offer to get rid of it. I got the shot in the forearm and it immediately swelled up to the size of a Mickey Mantle baseball bat and scared the crap out of me. Soon enough the swelling went down and the cold disappeared. Like Don Quixote who fabricated his helmet and visor out of cardboard, tested it with his trusty sword and smashed it to pieces, made it again and this time wisely did not test it, I never repeated the shot. There was an alternative in treatment at the time in Recife: you went to the pharmacy, bought a small vial of Vitamin B-12 and then waited in the back of the store where a person in a white smock administered the shot. Just an aside: "Swabbie" was also available to give shots or anti-biotics to the misfortunate guys who had visited the red-light zones in Recife in those days. I never did need or get that shot, at least not then. "Swabbie," by the way, regaled us all with stories of conquests of beauties in far off lands, thus combining his medical training with on – site experiments.

Guerra Souza was the son of a rich insurance man in Piauí State. We got along well and one day he said, "You want to take a ride?" He was talking about me joining him in his two-place Paulista airplane for a high-level tour of Recife and said it would be great for photos. Why not? We took a city bus to the north end of Boa Viagem Beach, the main local and tourist hangout for the Recife beach scene which is coming up in my narrative. There was a clay, narrow landing strip with just room enough for the takeoffs. The Paulista turned out to be my idea of the old Piper Cub in the U.S.; the motor looked like the ones in the VW Bugs, almost the same size. So, we strapped in, Guerra revved the engine (no headphones as I recall; he never used the radio and I don't know if he had one) and we were soon zooming out over the Atlantic Ocean, the long reef directly below us and the beach to the right. Guerra, perhaps an amateur version of those hot-shot Brazilian airlines pilots already encountered, began to maneuver the plane in big circles and then up and down, diving close to water level, "So you can see the waves." It was like a ride in "cordel's" most famous airplane – the "Magic Peacock" - from one its most famous stories, a light weight contraption which was both peacock and airplane, made of aluminum with both an electric and gas engine and lots of lights, made by the way on "Industrial Street" in old Egypt! We saw the ocean freighters, the small fishing boats, a few people on the beach, soccer games on the sand and the whole view of greater Recife – land, island and peninsula. I noticed from that height how the muddy water from the floods of Recife's three rivers created a large brown band for a mile or two from shore but beyond that there was beautiful blue-green water. The wind was whipping in our faces with no side windows on the plane but I did get those promised pictures in Kodak Kodachrome and managed to develop them into slides at an exorbitant cost in Recife.

It was only when we landed that Guerra, all smiles and very proud, told me, "Congratuations! ["Felicidades"] You are my first passenger! I soloed just last Friday." I noted the plane had neither parachute nor life vests. "Living is very dangerous," novelist Guimarães Rosa's saying in his masterpiece novel, came to mind.

There was only one elderly gentleman in the Chácara: Míster Raimundo. He was pleasant enough but was always taking pills, lots of them. The "word" was he had a mysterious liver disease (a sign of the times in Recife in 1966 was that most of the young guys took liver pills as well, but the reasons and the symptoms were never explained to my satisfaction; was this like "Carter's Little Liver Pills" of U.S. fame in the 1940s and 1950s?). He was from somewhere in the South, had been given a fatal diagnosis and out of desperation had traveled to the interior of Minas Gerais State to the tiny town of Congonhas do Campo where Brazil's most famous Spiritist healer resided. Arigó was most known for his "surgeries" for cataracts but using primitive tools like pen knives or table knives and no anesthesia; gossip had it that Princeton University Medical School sent a team of doctors and a film maker to record these surgeries. They did so, saw the incredible procedures with surgical "instruments" coming out of an old rusty coffee can with water in it, and medical science could not disprove the cures. In Recife, we had our own Spiritist healer who received the spirit of a German physician from the 19th century and was a regular operator on breast cancers. Raimundo had the consult with Arigó in Minas Gerais and later moved to Recife and took his pills.

There was one other young guy in the Chácara who opened an entire slice of Brazilian life to me, something that would relate to the "cordel" and my research. Jefferson was a bright engineering student in one of the local colleges (Brazil in those days had a penchant for using U.S. presidents' names as first names: Washington, Wilson, Jefferson, Lincoln and the like but with Portuguese pronunciation – a hoot!) One afternoon after that less than "hearty" Brazilian mid-day meal at the Chácara we got into an unlikely conversation. I was saying how great classical music was while Jefferson said there was nothing as good, as creative, as Brazilian samba. "How about J.S. Bach?" I asked. He said, "Who's that? Never heard of him." I retorted, "Holy Mother, you've never heard of Bach and here you are in college, studying Engineering." Jefferson was quiet for a minute, then said, "And you, you gringo son of a bitch, have you ever heard of Chico Heráclio?"

It was an amazing exchange. Chico Heráclio was a big landholder and a local political boss in the interior of the state, famous and a household world to any northeasterner. He was one of the last of the true "colonels" ["coronéis" in Portuguese] and represented an essential part of economic and social life in that part of Brazil. Once again "Realidade" magazine did a feature article on the "colonels," their historic importance in old Brazil and how Chico was not only an iconic figure in the Northeast but a dying breed. He reflects an entire chapter explaining life in northeast Brazil: most of the land in huge plantations or ranches, no middle class, and a huge rural workers' class living on the edges of the ranches, sharecroppers or lowly paid laborers, and totally subservient to the commands and wishes of the "coronel." It was a major slice of northeastern economic reality yet in the 1960s, a vital component of literature in the novels, plays and poems of the region, but even more important as a major character and topic of "cordel."

Bach on the other hand was this German from 400 years ago who composed some pretty uninteresting stuff for snooty, upper class Germans who wore wigs, frilly clothes and minced about a great deal. Jefferson indeed "schooled me" on "coronelismo." I'd say it was a tie.

Talk, shooting the bull and more serious matters for me in those first months in the Chácara were interesting enough and would set the scene for the coming months in Brazil. The guys were delighted but totally surprised to have a "gringo" amongst them; we were supposed to be in the expensive high-rise apartments in the beach district of Boa Viagem along with the American "colony" of USIS, USAID, consulate workers and business people. No one spoke conversational English, so it was great training for me and fulfilled the Fulbright goal of "learning a critical language." At least in one sense. We had a nice cultural exchange: I taught them all the swear words I knew in English (at their request) and they plied me with every foul word they knew in their ample vocabulary ("Portuguese is the most difficult and richest language on earth; English pales by comparison.") It was an education and probably I learned more about Brazilian social "mores" there than I could have in any textbook. Over those months there were some great friendships, and the "goodbye" party six months later included a "cordel poem" dedicated to the "gringo" and written with every swear word they had taught me those last few months, all inspired by many hours of drinking those liter bottles of Brahma beer.

However, politics, rumor, curiosity and maybe some fear or anger raised its ugly head (food for fodder for the <u>Times</u>). It boiled down to: "Mike, what in the hell are you doing in Brazil and why the Northeast and, in particular, Recife? And why do you go to USIS (United States Information Service) or USAID (United States Agency of International Development) to get your mail?" I recited the mantra I would repeat time and again in Brazil: "I'm on a Fulbright Hays research grant for Ph.D. dissertation research. The topic is folk-popular literature in verse in those chapbooks you see for sale in the markets and its relation to Brazilian Literature and History. You people call it "a literatura de cordel" ["string literature" the literal but bad translation in English]. Recife is one of the centers for the chapbooks and the poets; they are right next door to us in the São José Market in old Recife. And I'll be going to the markets and famous fairs in the interior of Pernambuco and Paraíba and Ceará States to build a collection. And since I don't have a permanent address, USIS is the most reliable place to get my mail which includes money to live on while I'm here."

The Northeast and much of Brazil was replete with probably a couple dozen such researchers, all on grants, all getting ready to do the Ph.D., and from the top schools in the U.S. I would meet many of them over the next six months. The Brazilians were used to having these geeky folks poking their noses into all sorts of things from politics, to economic development to African religion, all understandable, but only one "wierdo" doing the "cordel."

The response was immediate and did not go away: "Gringo, this is bull shit. Why would a rich north - American come to Brazil and not be involved in international business or the Alliance for Progress or some such thing? You've got to be CIA. We know the "gringos" are in cahoots with the military, are scared shitless of communists, subversives, anything "smelling" of Fidel, Ché and Cuba, and even Francisco Julião and the Peasant Movements here a while back. Your cover is pretty piss poor."

We all laughed (not really) and I said, "Hell no" to the accusation. Over the next few months I would compile a small but fine collection of the "cordel" booklets, all stashed in the two suitcases in my room at the Chácara. I would take the long folkloric walk to the São José Market two or three times a week and always come home with a handful of twenty or thirty booklets of verse, and that was just the beginning, hundreds more would pile up on my bus trips to the interior. A funny thing happened: gradually, slowly, the guys would come home to the Chácara from visits to their home towns in the northeast interior and bring me one, five or ten "folhetos" of verse. And even more curious, I would educate them a time or two on their own folklore, long "scorned" or ignored by anyone professing upward mobility.

I forgot to mention, my first name was unfortunate in Brazil: "Vou falar com Miguel" ["I'm going to talk to Mike"] in local parlance was "I have to take a piss." Oh well. Some more of those US researchers published a book on Brazilian popular Portuguese, and they told me most of the research was in the "pé-sujos" ["sticky feet"] bars everywhere in Brazil and involved a lot of bathroom humor as well.

This brings me to Brazilian hyperbole or ultra-nationalism. The conversations at the Chácara were sprinkled with braggadocio: "Brazil is first in everything; Portuguese is the world's most difficult language (Brazilian statesman Ruy Barbosa was a polyglot and could have taught English to the Queen of England); Brazil has the world's most beautiful girls, and one day will overtake the USA in economics and power!" Such statements and beliefs were common and not only in the Northeast. The sociologists attributed it to Third World dreaming and an inferiority complex. There was a sense of humor to it as well; a popular song in 1966 and everyone had the words memorized was "We are underdeveloped" ["Somos subdesenvolvidos"]. It went something like this: "We are underdeveloped; we are underdeveloped. We drink Coca-Cola, we shave with Gillette, and we smoke Marlboros. We are underdeveloped."

Finally, I need to talk about the food at the Chácara. Breakfast was a roll or two with butter and a large "café com leite." Lunch (supposedly the largest meal of the day in Brazil) was a piece of fried meat, a small portion of white rice, more bread, and guava jam and a slice of cheese for dessert. Supper was like lunch, but smaller portions. I'm not a big guy, but that went a long way to explain the cheap monthly rent and why we all had to supplement our diet at that great Brazilian institution of the "corner bar" or "pé sujo" [sticky foot]. Ours was just across the street and aptly called the "Bar Acadêmico" due to the proximity to the Pernambuco Law School. We could get fried eggs with bread and a soft drink, (the Northeasterners loved big drinking water glasses filled with buttermilk, watery at the bottom, curdling at the top and best slugged down after two, three or even four spoonsful of sugar) and bananas for breakfast and meat and cheese sandwiches to supplement the meager evening fare of the Chácara.

The corner bar was far more than for eating. It was a major part of our social life; hours were spent drinking large bottles of Brahma Choppe beer, smoking cigarettes ("Hollywood" was the most popular brand), and shooting the bull. It was there I heard more of those Brazilian jokes, was continually kidded about the CIA (or not) and in a muted way was filled in on Brazilian politics, student protests and the military. 1966 was still early in the dictatorship and the violence was just beginning. When you went to the movies before the main feature there was always ten minutes of clips of the military's latest projects, generally a new statue honoring some one. (Damn, this reminds me of another Brazilian saying: "Pee behind the statue," ["Vá atrás da estátua"] thus explaining the smelly statues in all the towns of the interior, the men letting it go after swigging beer in the bars by the plazas.) Yet in 1966 you might hear hissing or whistling when these scenes appeared; that all changed later.

10

The reason for the move to the boarding house in Recife was work; it started and continued the next six months both in and out of the city. All began with taking a big breath and telephoning the writer in Recife who knew most about "cordel:" Ariano Suassuna. He lived in a beautiful colonial style house in the district of Casa Forte, some distance from the Recife center, the entire façade with blue Portuguese colonial tiles, the interior furniture of caned rosewood. Ariano wrote poetry and plays and later novels at home but made a living doing weekly columns for the local newspapers and teaching aesthetics at the Federal University of Pernambuco in Recife. His original claim to fame was simple and modest: a three-act play taken largely from the stories of "cordel" but adapted in great part: "The Rogues' Trial" ["Auto da Compadecida"]. The play was first performed in Recife, then São Paulo, later in all Brazil and eventually made into a movie. Ariano told me to come by, set a time, and welcomed me into his tropical living room where I introduced myself, shared my reasons for coming to Brazil (Suassuna was not worried about the CIA) and he gave me some simple directions. "Go to the Law School Library and check out the known books on "cordel," give them a reading, get to the São José Market to see the poets in action and then get to the interior towns and markets to meet even more of them."

The Law School Library of Pernambuco State was located about two blocks from the Chácara; it was an imposing early 19th century edifice and its most imposing room being the huge open-air reading room. I found that if you wanted the atmosphere of high school and college kids in those days, the "jovem guarda" of those heady days of Brazilian rock and roll and MPB [Brazilian Popular Music] with Chico Buarque and Caetano Veloso, it was all in that one huge room.

You could get a library card showing your i.d. card (in this case my passport) and check books out, but you could not take them out of the library (a wise thing I learned later when entire collections of "cordel" vanished). So, I checked out two or three of the most important books, probably by folklorist Câmara Cascudo, and grabbed a chair at one of the long wooden tables. That was when things got interesting. The library was jammed with high school and college age kids including lots of very pretty Pernambuco girls with those dark eyes and hair and very ample figures. They were all talking at once, gossiping and flirting with the boys, including the blue-eyed "gringo." It was a mutual admiration society. If that were not enough to keep me from concentrating on the reading (and taking hand written notes in some spiral grade school lined notebooks from a nearby bookstore), there was the infernal street noise from the wide open tall windows on all three sides of the reading room. Traffic noise from busy streets, including the many buses and trucks on the main traffic artery, and the blaring noise of the soccer games (it was World Cup Time) came through those windows.

There was one more surprise and I was told it was in integral part of old Pernambuco culture, soon to vanish into history. While reading yet another chapter and taking more notes with my handy, cheap BIC ball point pen, suddenly there was a loud shouting in the room, "Oh peanuts, who wants peanuts? Fresh, tasty and at the right price." ["Ó amendoim, amendoim! Quem quer? Fresco, gostoso e o melhor preço!"] This was one of the "pregões" or "street cryers – vendors" of old Recife, evidently with free reign to sell in this, the oldest and most prestigious library of colonial Pernambuco! Guess what? You get used to it. This scene like Hansen said, was not in CIA reports and the stringer articles for the <u>Times</u>.

I probably spent at least a month reading for several hours each day in that library, but it was not where the real field work took place. That began at the old central market located in a labyrinth of tiny streets with little or no sidewalks, many dead ends and five days a week a beehive of humanity – the São José Market.

In that "winter" of 1966 I walked from Boa Vista District along Guararapes Avenue across the bridge at the Capibaribe River, through the modern shopping area and then gradually getting into the "real" old Recife: narrow streets in a labyrinth winding, turning, often ending in dead ends ["becos"], all heading to the market. The streets were jammed with mainly dark-skinned people, in poor, mended clothing with rubber thongs or sandals on their feet, and carrying a shopping bag – these were the maids or doormen of the middle and upper class "Recifenses" who sent the hired help to "do the market" ["fazer feira"], an institution still of those times – in other words, to get the groceries for the week and anything else the household needed. There was one more item – a sturdy black umbrella – for the immense downpours.

I never wore "good clothes," knowing what I was facing – the tropical rains, mud in the streets, getting splashed by passing cars and trucks on the way to the market. And I never carried much cash, just enough to buy a few folk poems in the market and a soft drink or beer on the way home. More than once I would be trying to negotiate the crowds and suddenly people were running in the streets and shouting, "Catch the thief, catch the thief" ["Pega o ladrão, pega o ladrão"]. I was a bit frightened the first time it happened, but later figured out what was going on – normal life on the streets near the market. Police or military police would soon show up and by then the pickpocket had vanished. The moral: take no official documents or much money; I had Xerox copies of passport and visa on me and never had their validity tested.

There's a well-known piece of Brazilian literature from those times: the "Gaúcho" novelist from the southernmost state of Brazil – Rio Grande do Sul – Érico Veríssimo wrote a novella when he was a diplomat in Washington D.C. "A Black Cat in a Field of Snow" ["Gato Preto em Campo de Neve"] referring of course to his complexion (and he was not black or mulatto, just "Brazilian") in the U.S.A. Many times in this story I will paraphrase it - "White Cat in a Field of Black" – such was my presence on those streets heading to the market – white, blue eyes, a "gringo" spotted from a mile away. And best of all, never robbed or mugged!

So, with muddy shoes, white socks stained with mud, I arrived at that "New World" of the market, the real reason I was in Recife. People have written books about it, so I've just got to hit the highlights: a huge indoor market in a pavilion with vegetables, fish, meat with flies on it, household gadgets or tools, cheap clothing, sandals, shoes, and then what interested me: artisan shops with real rosewood carvings of the bandit Lampião and his consort Maria Bonita, Father Cícero of Juazeiro fame, and the "cedro" carvings of the local folkloric fishing boats, the "jangadas," a raft of four or five balsa logs, a six foot wooden mast, a tiller, and a mended sail that poor local fisherman would take to the high seas! Early on I spent some of my very limited budget on a few of these items.

What mattered to the Fulbright scholar was what was going on outside the market. In the shaded plaza of the São José Church was an extension of the market: the outdoors market. This became my destination two or three times a week. In 1966, the poets of "cordel" or their "agents" would come to the atrium – plaza to sell Brazilian folk-popular poetry. It was a scene that might have taken place 300 years earlier in Lisbon, Salamanca or Madrid. The poets would arrive early in the morning, spread out a sheet of plastic or perhaps open a beat up wooden suitcase upon a stand and display the story-poems [chapbooks or "folhetos de cordel"] and when a crowd gathered proceed to "sing" or "recite" the wonderful story-poems. My first incursions into northeastern folk life happened here in 1966. The door to another world and reality was opened. The whole kaleidoscope of Brazilian life was opened to me in these story-poems: daily life, customs of the Northeast, Brazilian folk-popular religion, the poor peoples' "National Enquirer," national politics, everything making this folk-popular, narrative poetry the poor people's "History of Brazil." The military dictatorship and the students' opposition was part of it all. I only came to realize this months later. Field work was two or three days at the market, and incidentally a visit to the major source of the folk poems in a simple, wooden market stand by Edson Pinto who bought and sold all the chapbooks the poets would bring each week from the interior. I would listen to the poets "sing" or recite their poems to avid audiences, all male by the way, over those initial months of fieldwork.

Funny enough, there was a cheap movie theater on the street across from the plaza. This was where the "hillbillies" in town would see the movies, and many of its titles ended up as stories of "cordel," like "Joan of Arc" or "Samson and Delilah" or a John Wayne Western.

I did not hang out at the market or plaza at night upon the advice of those in the know: it became the old time, downtown red-light zone and with some unsavory characters. I would check out that scene at a better part of town – Boa Viagem Beach.

11

Boa Viagem Beach was the only beach where I and my buddies from the Chácara would spend time, but once again it offered an entirely new chapter of northeastern Brazil customs and social mores. It was located about five miles south of downtown Recife and like the reef off shore was straight as an arrow for several miles. The north end was the district of Pina, one of the poorer slums in Recife, called "mocambos." The main feature aside from the abject poverty was that most of the shacks were on stilts due to incoming tides; when these went out you had a mud plain and the boys' main job was to dig clams out of the mud. An irony was you had to drive through Pina out on the peninsula to get to the Recife "yate" club; I knew this just from hearsay, the former not being a hangout for me or the Chácara buddies. The renowned sociologist Gilberto Freyre, an iconic figure in Recife and the Northeast at that time for his book "The Masters and the Slaves" and the founder of the Joaquim Nabuco Socal Science Research Center wrote a treatise on the "mocambos," calling them colorful and picturesque with blowing palms in the ocean breezes. He obviously never spent that much time in them; a much more accurate picture was João Cabral de Melo Neto's beautiful "Morte e Vida Severina" and the TV version which showed the slum accurately yet with a saving grace.

So, my good friend Pedro Oliveira and others from the boarding house would walk from Boa Vista to Guararapes Avenue in the city center and catch a bus from the bus stop by the Capibaribe River which headed south to the beach (none of our crowd had a car). The bus on a good day would take twenty minutes, but in traffic or if there was an accident it could be an hour. There was no air conditioning, all windows were open to the view of the old run-down area of south Recife, then the airport road and finally to the beach. The return trip was along the old warehouse district of the docks.

Boa Viagem was the district for the upper middle class Recifenses and the foreign "colony," the latter a mixture of various consular personnel, employees of USIS and USAID and SUDENE, all living in 10 to 15 story apartment buildings facing the beach. Even one or two blocks back there were no paved streets and some pretty basic houses of the poor. The main street facing the ocean with the tall buildings, dozens of palm trees and beautiful white sand made it all worthwhile.

The first thing I learned in this most Catholic country of the planet was that you went to the beach, mainly, on Sunday morning. It was jammed by ten or eleven o'clock with girls (and often their mothers or aunts) in the one-piece swimsuits of the day ["mailloux" in the local parlance]; the bikini would only come later and in 1966 when I got there was associated with Rio and Copacabana and the "balzaquianas" or women of little repute with whom the "cordel" poets would populate their many story-poems to titillate the northeastern hillbillies looking for vicarious thrills. I discovered that the guys, despite all their "macho" stories back home and escapades with I concluded only the "easy" women, did little more than ogle the local chicks, not really making any "scores," but then neither did I. I would be considered a transient, albeit a rich "gringo" from the US. The girls first question when we would meet would be, "How long are you going to be in Brazil?" We sat on the sand, smoked those Hollywoods and checked out all the chicks who paraded by. I loved the swimming, a somewhat unique experience after those big waves and ocean at Acapulco when I was a student in Mexico in 1962: tide pools protected by the large razor - straight reef about a mile off shore. The pools were full of cool and sometimes warmer yet refreshing water and at times were only four or five feet in depth closer to shore. I was a good swimmer so I ventured farther out in deeper water where it was possible to just float on your back or do back strokes. It was here that I discovered that many of these people who lived by the sea could not swim and just waded near the shore. I thought this amazing; it would not be the case in deeper waters in Salvador or Rio de Janeiro.

The guys introduced me to coconut water ["água de coco"] from a fresh coconut with the top sliced off by a local vendor and a long straw. These guys were artists, taking the large coconut in one hand, bouncing it into the air, and - "whack" - knocking off the top with one of those machete like "fishing knives" ["pesqueira"] used in the Northeast. There was a hazard of the trade: many had less than the full complement of fingers.

And the guys "pulled my leg" telling me not to confuse "coco" with "cocó," another of the nuances of spoken Brazilian Portuguese; the first is indeed "cococut," the second "baby poop."

I never did get "into" Brazilian soccer; there were dozens of games each Sunday along the beach. My take on "futebol" would be a story to be told months later when I was introduced to it in no less than the Maracanã Stadium in Rio. I did spend many days at that beach, mainly swimming or just lying in the sun (many a fierce sunburn resulted but fortunately with no major consequences). One minor entertainment was to watch the tiny, white, sand crabs ["Maria Farinhas,]" white like their manioc flour name, come out of their holes, "stare" for a while from the little black eyes at the end of their antennae and then skitter down the beach — a lesson for how to deal with the local and national politics – walk sideways with your antennae up - it was best to keep an eye out and with a quick get a way in mind.

Since Hansen from the <u>Times</u> said he wanted the whole story, I'll have to tell it like it was but maybe not in all the lurid detail. I'm Irish-American, from a small town in Nebraska, a church goer (maybe not by choice) all my life at home on the farm and sporadically during college. That means traditional Roman Catholic morality – confession followed sin or else it was the fires of hell. I already said my sexual experience was limited before Brazil and there was a conscious decision to remedy all that during this one year. So, when in Brazil, do like the Brazilians do, at least the Brazilians I knew – check out the red-light zones. Recife's was on the back streets of Boa Viagem and the guys from the Chácara helped the beach economy on more than one occasion. It wasn't only the US or British "swabbies" from the aircraft carriers that flooded the zone (a sea of white uniforms) but us locals as well. And with some interesting consequences but mainly good times.

These were not the luxurious brothels of Mexico City, and not those raucous full of fun party houses ["castelos"] from Jorge Amado's novels in Salvador da Bahia, but a simple house with a "living room" where you could drink a cold beer, look over the girls, pick one to your liking and head to her room for what generally amounted to a "quicky." The girls were pretty and they were good, offering quick, efficient oral sex or for a few more "cruzeiros" the full works. Even then they had a job to do and could get you out the door in a hurry, knowing how to expertly move things along. What they did for hygiene and protection I never discovered, but there were no condoms used or suggested. (One of the "cordel" poets told me at the time, "It is not our custom.") Good fortune was with me until round two when I would come back to Recife to tie up loose strings at the end of the year in 1967, but that comes later. Like Mick Jagger would sing in those days, "Are you satisfied, really satisfied?" Who knows, but we all would either catch the bus home or repair to a local bar in the zone for more beers and to swap stories.

It was in one of those bars that I would spend one of the best nights ever in all Brazil with plenty of cold liter bottles of "Brahma Choppe" beer, lots of cigarettes, and some of the most memorable music I had heard up to that time in Brazil. A trio of musicians, "off work" from one of the red-light bars, was taking it easy in this bar, accepting beers from the customers and in return playing an incredible repertoire of northeastern folk songs until the wee hours of the morning, "Asa Branca" and "Mulher Rendeira" among them. They played the traditional instruments of the backlands or "sertão," – the triangle, drum and sound box (like a small accordion) – the same the nationally known "fancy" "baião" singer Luís Gonzaga was making famous in "forró" music. I've forgotten many of the tunes, but never came across music like it the next few months in Brazil.

12

The balance of work those months in Recife was at the renowned Joaquim Nabuco Social Science Research Center in Casa Forte, a distant district in far west Recife and at the State Library downtown, but it was the former that became important to this story. For a couple of reasons.

The CJNPS was founded by no less than Gilberto Freyre, the intellectual "kingpin" and "shaker and mover" ["manda-chuva" - "he who makes it rain" or "bamba do bairro" – "the big man in the neighborhood"] in northeastern culture. Freyre had done his masters at Columbia University in New York and his thesis, modified and translated into Portuguese in Recife became the famous "Masters and the Slaves," a treatise on colonial Brazil, the Northeast and sugar cane development, but mainly the ethic and sociological makeup of the people – white slaveholders and the black slave cast, their respective living quarters "casa grande e senzala" ["big house and slave quarters"]. "The man" was a descendant of sugar cane aristocracy in Pernambuco and converted part of one of the family sugar cane plantation on the outskirts of Recife into the park where the CJNPS was built.

The main building was a modified and modernized "big house" on the old plantation; the entire front and side walls were covered with beautiful blue Portuguese tiles ["azulejos"] and the entrance "salon" was all with polished, tropical hardwood floors and a gorgeous rosewood stairway to the upper level and the offices. A large auditorium for lectures was on the first floor. Outside the main building was an incredible tropical garden with palm trees, all manner of ferns and flowers, including orchids. To the side and the back was the "Sugar Cane Museum" depicting the history and workings of the old plantations. It indeed was a "small kingdom" and on the western boundary was another "big house," Gilberto's home and office.

My purpose for spending so much time at the Institute's library was that it had a good collection of the story-poems of "cordel," in fact the first one I consulted in the Northeast. There also were three or four important lectures each week by the real experts ["peritos"] of Northeastern culture, some on staff at the Institute but others with special invitations to speak. I fell asleep in one of Freyre's lectures as he droned on one of those incredibly hot tropical afternoons. This was a "mortal" sin in those parts. Either the monotony of his voice or perhaps the tiredness due to a big night at the "pé sujo" with buddies the night before brought on the intermittent snoozing. Another case was not the same – the vibrant and important lectures of Luís da Câmara Cascudo,

Brazil's most important folklorist – he would entertain and inform us in wonderful talks with a vibrant voice, many gestures and snappy presentation. Luís would become one of my mentors on the "cordel" in coming months, but this in Natal in Rio Grande do Norte State.

It was here I met two important characters in this narration. First was a Fulbrighter, Steve Baldini with a fine academic pedigree – a B.A. in Economics and Politics from Harvard – researching "economic development" in the Brazil of the 1960s. It would only be months later that Steve would reveal to me (by accident) a second reason to be in Brazil, but that is jumping ahead in the story. Steve lived in an apartment with some college students from Brazil in the Boa Vista District and our paths would cross in those bull sessions in the "Academic Bar" across the street from the Chácara.

The second would become my most important Brazilian "informant" on the "cordel" in Recife – José Atayde, one of the twenty-three children of the scion of modern "cordel" in Recife and the entire Northeast – João Martins de Atayde. Zé worked in the Sugar Cane Museum and was in fact preparing to study "museum administration" or something of the sort, but his modest background, and so far, lack of a university degree, kept him pigeonholed in that old class structure in the Northeast. He would guide me at times at the São José Market and invite me to the modest Atayde house in that old district of Recife, tell me stories of the "empire" in "cordel" founded by his father – an iconic but very close mouthed and somewhat mysterious "entrepreneur" ["empresário"] of "cordel" at its height in Brazil from the 1920s to the end of the 1950s when he grew ill and sold his entire stock to another poet-publisher in far off Ceará State. I'll get back to this.

Zé inherited the close-mouthed demeanor of his famous father, perhaps just another example of why southern Brazilians called the Pernambucans "fechados" or close-mouthed, hard to get to know. As the weeks and months went by and Zé would accompany me on forays to the interior to meet poets and buy the story-poems, the friendship grew as well as the trust level. Only then would he "open up" on a few matters that almost brought me to a foul, evil end in Brazil.

This brought me to the end of the first phase of research and life in Brazil and I sent the first LETTER, the entire missive, to Hansen in New York in a large 81/2 by 11 sealed envelope mailed at the USIS office on the peninsula in downtown Recife. This is the same place I would walk to once a week from the Chácara, across the big bridge of the Capibaribe River into Guararapes in downtown Recife and on to the tall USIS building. I collected the letters from home, walked back along Guararapes, bought a <u>Time</u> magazine in English, the international edition on that thin paper, stopped at a bar, bought an icy Brahma Choppe beer, smoked a cigarette and read those long letters from home. Oh yeah, once a month they contained the expense check from Fulbright, not to be missed.

13

It was Hansen's response to that first LETTER that would change life in Brazil. By the time I got it I was ready to begin short trips to the northeast interior, to the towns and cities and their markets, to buy story-poems, meet and interview poets and study the folklore of the region. Coincidentally this was the part of northeastern Brazil that was central to the peasant movement of leftist, land-reform (Cuban style) local politician Francisco Julião prior to the Revolution in 1964 and under threat by the military now in 1966. The travel was part of the plan to get material for the dissertation; Hansen's letter would not change that, in fact it might intensify the effort, but all with a different slant, all this after his getting LETTER I.

"Mike, our hunch was right – your journal is exactly what we wanted and thought you were capable of doing. There is no other document we know of that puts the reader into a "real living experience" in Brazil right now; I mean the total experience – living, people and customs, politics, food and drink, fun and games. Keep it up; we are looking forward to the next batch. It's a little rough and we'll have to edit it, but that's understandable. However, I have a communication I'm passing along since it puts a new light on what you are doing and may change our plans. It is from Stanley Iverson from the Bureau of Intelligence Research (INR), Western Hemisphere Affairs Section (WHA) – the main research gathering entity for the U.S. Department of State, established in 1947 around the time of the Marshall Plan and crucial intelligence needs in West-East Germany. Stanley wants to sound you out on a couple of ideas for your research and the rest of the time in Brazil. I want you to know that whatever you decide it will not affect our prior agreement of the LETTERS, in effect chapters for the book we will publish when you get home. Stanley came to know of you via your Fulbright grant proposal, knew of our joint project with you and called me the other day. I took the the step of showing him your LETTER I. Give his letter some consideration. Thanks, James Hansen."

Iverson's letter was as follows:

"Dear Mr. Gaherty, hopefully I can just call you Mike. I'm in close contact with James Hansen and I've read your first LETTER from Brazil. I find it a very interesting and direct narrative of a young man your age; mainly it's honest and accurate. As requested you have reported "all" and in so doing given the <u>Times</u> readers a broad look at what is going on in Brazil. What the INR – WHA finds interesting is the actual research – the study and collecting of your primary sources, the booklets of the "literatura de cordel" which seem to describe very accurately the vision of the peasant class of the Northeast. You have not really gotten into much detail in the first LETTER to Hansen, but it is clear you may be heading in a direction that not only is interesting, but perhaps vital to our knowledge of what is happening to a large, significant part of the Brazilian population and their tendencies to act in the future. I think you are familiar with Francisco Julião's "peasant movement" of the early 1960s, just a few years ago. It boils down to a call for social action and even revolution of the landless peasants following the Cuban model. Even though Julião is now "persona non-grata" to the military and has disappeared from the Northeast and his main ally former governor Miguel Arraes is under house arrest and at the Brazilian penal colony on Fernando de Noronha out in the Atlantic, there are many former officials of the Arraes government and their sympathizers who would love to see the success of the movement – mainly land reform in some fashion and the removal of the old ruling class in the Northeast.

We realize it is early in your research, but we would like to be apprised of any of the story-poems which clearly mark the attitudes of the rural-urban poor class – how they view the current government, both from the left and right, and how they view social issues. And of course, if they report on any specific event of local, regional or even national significance, we would want your "take" on it. There is no need of a separate letter to us, but if we see something that really gets our attention we would like to contact you directly. There is always an INR man in every major city, oftentimes with a consular title but sometimes a direct employee of U.S. government projects like food distribution for the Alliance for Progress, road building for the Alliance, and a select few Peace Corps volunteers working on special projects. If you need to contact us or are ever in any danger, call the following number (linked to all consulates and to the DOPS of the Brazilian government – their information and police agency) – 437-0094-5588. This number must not be revealed to anyone else; it is for your private use only. If you do have to use it, eventually I will be contacted and can explain the situation. I realize you may not want anything to do with the Brazilian Department of Political Security [DOPS], but I assure you a link to them is necessary in case of dire emergency."

I weighed the "offer," and wondered what if I refuse? Would these characters be keeping an eye on me anyway? Probably. Better to be on the right side, so I mailed an affirmative response to Hansen, the "go between" as it were. Shortly afterwards and in the coming months there would be significant matters to report.

14

The Roman Catholic Church in Brazil was not immune to the far - reaching tentacles of the military regime, but you had to be aware of broad developments taking place across Latin America. Coinciding with but not linked to the "Aggorniamento" or "Opening" of the Roman Church by rotund Pope John XXIII in the 1960s, a new social theology was being developed by the progressive clergy of the church in Latin America. Started by a Peruvian, Father Gustavo Gutiérrez, Liberation Theology became a prime mover for much of the clergy in many countries, and it was adopted by the Council of Latin American Bishops. Complex and with variations in each country, the theology first and foremost was an official siding with the poor, what came to be known as the "preference for the poor," with broad ramifications for the Church from Mexico to Argentina. It was the idea that salvation in an ethereal heaven sometime after death was not the only important idea – but freedom from poverty, misery and perhaps starvation would be equally important for the Bishops' flock. The "Base Communities" involving tens of thousands of Catholics came into being to promote the cause. The Jesuits came to be leaders in the movement (Gutiérrez was a Jesuit) but were far from the only ones – Archbishop Romero in Salvador was assassinated for his support of the poor. Brazilian theologian Leonardo Boff was later "silenced" by Rome for his writings.

Closer to home, that July in Recife a Jesuit priest known for links to the Base Communities was murdered outside his parish home. The story made all the papers, and all lamented the violence but it was never clear who exactly was responsible, the most likely theory - "para-military" in cahoots with the dictatorship. The Northeast was supposedly a hotbed of subversive, leftist activity, not only a carryover from the Julião days but growing opposition to the fairly "benign" dictatorship, up to that point! More important was the attack on the home of Recife's "Red Bishop" Dom Hélder Câmara, a major leader in the National Council of Brazilian Bishops and representative in the Latin American conclave. His house was machine gunned, the bullets tearing into the outside walls of the compound. Fortunately, no one was hurt but the message was sent. Dom Hélder's message-mantra was simple: "The worst violence is hunger."

All this was going on in Recife during my second month. Studying folklore and folk poetry seemed to be a safe way to go, but maybe not. The local press reported the murder of the Jesuit priest, the attack on Dom Hélder's home, lamenting the violence but placing no blame. One of my research techniques during those months which turned out to be amazingly successful was a simple questionnaire to the main poets in the region via a letter through the mail. I asked the poets if they believed they were "the representatives of the masses" and the "voice of the people" and if they were ever stopped from writing, printing and selling their story poems. One of the major poets at this very time wrote, "I don't write anything about all this. Politics is a very dangerous plate" (analogy with "prato" a plate of food). Maybe his opinion was shared at the moment around Recife because I encountered no story-poems on the anti-church violence. Significant for Hansen and Iverson was this attitude; the poets were in no position to make waves. I'm sure this was the main attitude of the poor of all the interior of the Northeast forty years earlier when Marxist Carlos Prestes tried to stir the masses into revolution and got no response. This did not mean however that things could not change in 1966, after all, Fidel and Ché <u>did</u> make waves.

It was July when the significant event happened. Someone – leftists, "terrorists," "subversives," opposition to the military – planted a bomb at the main Recife Airport – "O Aeroporto dos Guararapes". This would be one of the first violent attacks on the military in Brazil and would have devastating consequences in the following months. "President Elect" General Costa e Silva was doing a "campaign" tour throughout Brazil and was coming south from Ceará, Rio Grande do Norte and Paraíba States to Recife for a major "address." Everyone knew he was the man selected by the junta led by current general, Castelo Branco, to be the successor, so the whole thing was a charade of sorts. The entire event was reported in a very hastily written "cordel" poem which actually "scooped the newspapers;" it was hot off the press the same day as the attack and was penned by an iconoclastic poet reporting "A Bomba no Aeroporto dos Guararapes" ["Bomb at Guararapes Airport"]. The poet detailed the events: the plane carrying the "president-elect" was delayed in João Pessoa, Paraíba, for minor engine problems. The bomb in Recife set with a timer to go off with the original arrival went off as planned, minus the arrival of the plane. Multiple deaths took place, crew at the airport and some bystanders. The plane with Costa e Silva landed later, he gave a speech lamenting the incident and promised that the government would look into, find and punish the terrorists.

More important for my LETTER was what the "cordel" poem and poet said. The iconoclast "cordel" poet Lucena de Mossoró wrote, paraphrasing, "This act was done by evil people, terrorists trying to disrupt the election and future of Brazil. The military will know how to deal with such an act." An understatement to be sure! Truer words were never spoken! In a few months, General Costa e Silva would take command in Brazil and together with the other generals would institute and publish the famous IA - 5, "Institutional Act – 5." This promulgation would in effect "cement" the dictatorship, establishing total military control in Brazil and severe consequences for any opposition to it.

The <u>Times</u> and the INR would be very interested in this single, modest, "cordel" poem for it expressed the view from the people and from the Right that the Military Solution was the best for Brazil, not expressing any leftist opposition as might be expected. For the moment, my research would not reveal any other tendencies.

15

Later that July my time in Recife was spent with the already mentioned research work at the IJNPS, the State Library and the Law Library. Social life was busy enough with the trips to Boa Viagem Beach and the "serenades" on the beach with Chácara and local friends – these revealed much of the Brazil of the 1960s. There was a big bonfire, girls and guys gathered round, and there was much conversation and much singing of the "iê-iê-iê" music and samba and "baião" but all in a very innocent, "chaperoned" situation. It was the closest thing to a Brazilian "hootenanny" atmosphere.

At the same time, I experienced much more of the northeastern folk experience of the times: the great festival of São João (St. John's day) on June 24th, almost like July 4th in the USA: "caipira" or northeastern Brazil country music, the "quadrilhas" or what amounted to northeastern Brazil "square dancing," the fireworks, the "invasion" of 1960s rock and "ie-ie-ie," beer drinking and some "cachaça" rum drinking, but with no major or minor consequences for me. In my case it was all innocent fun.

There was still a certain amount of "static" from the guys from the Chácara to the suspected "gringo:" "What in the hell was going on with the United States Peace Corps volunteers in Brazil?" There were rumors that they were distributing birth control information and pills in the "favelas" in Rio, all with the "imperialistic" idea of limiting Brazil's population growth. And there were the rumors that the U.S. had plans to flood the entire Amazon Basin, move in the U.S. Navy and control all of Brazil's North. "Míster Gaherty, what do you know about this?" I told the guys it was all bullshit, that I knew nothing, besides I was studying "cordel."

That was not the only problem I encountered in that hot July and August of 1966. Maybe because I was away from home in Nebraska and truly on my own once again, I decided to grow a beard for the first time in my life. It grew for a month, my face itched in the heat and humidity of Recife and it was probably scraggly to look at. That was just one consequence; there were others. These were the days of Fidel Castro, Cuba and the Revolution, and Ché Guevara. They all had beards. My Brazilian friends at the Chácara called me a "barbudo" ["bearded one"], "leftist," "fidelista," and "comunista," this in strange contrast to the suspicions of CIA and a very weak alibi according to them of me being just a "folklorist" in the Northeast. Probably because of the former, heat, humidity and itching, I shaved the beard with one of those Imperialist Gillette Stainless Steel Razor Blades and continued on my way.

LETTER II

THE NORTHEAST INTERIOR

1

It was in late July that my first trips to the northeastern interior took place, first to Caruaru in Pernambuco State, then to Campina Grande in Paraíba State and then in August to Juazeiro do Norte in Ceará State. In all these places, the first objective would be to collect the story-poems of "cordel" in the markets and fairs, meet the major poets of the region and interview them, but also absorb the atmosphere of the Northeast interior. That meant travel.

For a person on a limited budget there was only one option: bus travel. This opened my eyes (and those of the <u>Times</u> readers) to an important aspect of the 1960s: economic reality, lower and middle class social mores and in a few instances politics and violence. I should say, however, that the most immediate violence was a bus crash resulting from macho bus driver behavior and that of the drivers ["motoristas"] of the cargo trucks on the same roads. It did not happen to me but there were some close calls. The bus drivers would amble along in the countryside, perhaps to avoid all the potholes in the horrible roads, or just as likely to flirt with the country girls walking along the sides of the roads. But once they got to the city, be it Recife, João Pessoa or Campina Grande with the paved streets (maybe concrete or asphalt but more likely the rectangular cobblestones ["paralelepípedos"] in most cities, it was "Katie, bar the door" ["Deus nos acuda!"] when they raced through the streets on the way to the central bus station. It should be noted that in most of the Northeast there were at best just very narrow sidewalks to the side of the streets, and many times not that. And you could still see carts hauled by oxen or even human beings.

Most of the bus rides were on the "drip-drip" ["pinga-pinga"] routes from the coast at Recife, João Pessoa, Natal or Maceió on to the deep backlands, the clever Brazilian name because the buses stopped at every large and small town and crossroads in the middle of nowhere. I soon learned that a "direto" was the best option although it never was "direct." Passengers were largely from the poor class with a sprinkling of middle class riders; most were hillbillies in from the outback to visit relatives in the coastal cities or maybe just to visit the major markets in the latter.

The first trip was a real eye opener. José Atayde my contact from the "empresário" of "cordel" in Recife, his father João Martins de Atayde, and the Joaquim Nabuco Social Science Research Sugar Cane Museum was my guide ["cicerone"] - informant - and occasional translator for the trip. Caruaru, Pernambuco, was only two hours by a rough concrete paved road from Recife and the coast, but seemed light years away from the hustle and bustle of Recife. We passed through that first climatic zone of the Northeast, the "zona da mata" ["sugar cane zone"] with total greenness, sugar cane, banana trees, citrus, a land of incessant rains in season, to the second zone, the "zona do agreste" ["the pastoral zone"]. The latter was a land of rolling hills, still verdant with sugar cane but now with small farms and ranches with the ubiquitous northeastern cattle, "zebu" or Brahma stock (I had seen the latter as the main feature of the rodeos in Nebraska with the cowboys riding those fierce Brahma bulls). Our destination was Caruaru, "The Princess of the Agreste" a bit of a euphemism depending on your point of view.

The main attraction was the huge fair and for me the blind girls singing ballads in the fair (this was what Colonel Proença in Rio had encouraged me to see first on these trips). There were supposed to be "cordel" poets in the fair as well, singing or reciting the story-poems. It turned out to not be the case this trip, but the experience with the blind singers was a highlight of folklore research in the entire trip. The girls sang in what to me seemed to be a monotone with minor variation, accompanying themselves by tapping on gourds to keep the rhythm of the verse. It was a shock to hear their interior Portuguese and truthfully, I only got a portion of the lyrics (José translated some for me), but this was one of the historical ties to the origins of "cordel" in Portugal in the 18th century when the booklets of verse were sold by blind men in the fairs who recited the story-poems. The girls were not singing story-poems but genuine ballads ["romances"], some centuries old, some new reflecting life in the "agreste" with its cowboys, roundups, fierce chases after bulls and ferocious cougars ["onças"] in the mix.

There was one well-known "cordel" poet in Caruaru, "Dila" by name, and he was a "corker." A terrific introduction to all the "cordel" in the region, Dila was also a printer and had a primitive hand press in the back of his modest house in a proletarian part of Caruaru. He was just as well known for his woodcuts decorating the covers of the story-poems he printed, but with a unique variation in the "cordel:" his woodcuts were actually cuts made on pieces of rubber tire, the end product serving the same purpose as the traditional wood block or "taco" (no pun on Mexican food). That day he was gone but later would provide me with one of the most colorful if not exactly "normal" interviews which would become a chapter in the dissertation months later. Dila claimed to have an unusual knowledge of the stars, astrology and astronomy and that his poetic talent was a result of the "influence of the Sun and Mercury!" Or as he said in another way: "common verse – mixed ideas!" and "terrain explored in the fields of dreams." Hmmm.

There was yet another idiosyncrasy in his story poems: the most popular topic was northeastern banditry and the most famous and infamous bandit "Lampião." That was common enough to all the "cordel" poets but Dila at times claimed to "be" the incarnation of the deceased Lampião. Hmmm again.

Caruaru was also the place of the famous maker of clay dolls – Vitalino – already mentioned in LETTER I. For whatever stupid reason (my own ignorance of Vitalino at the time or maybe José's understanding that I was interested only in "cordel"), we did not go to his place of residence, the "Alto do Moura" some seven kilometers from Caruaru. This was a pity in one way because his workshop was still in business in 1966, run by his son Vitalino Júnior and eventually by other children and his grandchildren. The story is long and complicated, and I was certainly not "clued in" at the time; Vitalino at the age of six or seven years began making his own toys or dolls out of the left-over clay his mother used to make bowls and pottery to sell in the market. If you dropped one, you just made another. He chose themes of wild bulls, cougars, country folks going to the market and much more. The dolls became famous and an artist in Rio invited him to an exposition on northeastern folklore in Rio in 1960 and paid for the trip, including his first airplane ride. With the coming notoriety, it was only after that that he began signing his dolls which would appear in museums throughout Brazil and even in Europe. But according to the "cordel" poet Azulão in his story-poem "The Voice of the Artist Treated Unjustly," Vitalino was cheated out of any real profits, another of the victims of "commercial, capitalistic galleries."

And finally, the fair of Caruaru is related to one of the great works of Northeastern Literature I had come to study: a book by one of the Novelists of the Northeast. There are four of them and their novels began in the 1930s and continued through the 1960s, and in two cases, much later. All this was related to my work on northeastern folklore and the "cordel" because these major national writers borrowed from both to write masterpieces. I'll talk of José Lins do Rego and the sugar cane zone novels later, of Raquel de Queiróz and the backlands novels of Ceará and the São Francisco River and mainly Jorge Amado of Bahia, but the fair of Caruaru suggests the scene from one of Graciliano Ramos' novels "Barren Lives," ["Vidas Secas"] when the main characters the cowboy Fabiano, his wife and children go into town for the market and fair and what happens to them. The novel takes place in Alagoas, but the scene is identical to Caruaru. Between the lines the social injustice of the Northeast prevails, as is the case in most of the novels of the 1930s when Communism, Marxism, land reform and social justice offered an alternative to four hundred years of social domination by the upper class. It was this alternative that interested Iverson and the INR and got me into trouble.

A small and significantly minor moment occurred during that first visit to Caruaru. José de Atayde introduced me to a minor novelist living in Caruaru who knew the former Communist and Leftist Jorge Amado well (Amado will enter the story later in Salvador da Bahia) and as well a currently famous figure from the slums of São Paulo – Carolina de Jesus. Carolina became famous in the 1960s because of a small book "Quarto de Despejo" which told of her life in the huge slums of São Paulo where she was one of hundreds who managed to survive by picking remnants of trash in the huge garbage dumps. Carolina supposedly kept a diary and when a local journalist discovered it and her story and edited her "slum" Portuguese, it became a best seller, a "must" read for the sociology people, an example of how the poorest of the poor might climb out of poverty. I think the writer was Lycio de Neves; I scarcely knew him, but I found out later the DOPS knew of the encounter.

After this all too brief first encounter with the interior of the Northeast, I returned alone to Recife on the "pinga-pinga" bus, an experience that would be repeated several times in the next few months. The bus was filled with country people who had been to the market in Caruaru, women with small babies wrapped in shawls, and men dressed in the local cowboy hats, all returning to their shacks in the countryside between Caruaru and Recife. There were no regular bus stops; the people just talked to the driver and asked to be let off along the road. Many of the men were drunk on "cachaça" or sugar cane rum from the city fair and argued about the fare. And the bus broke down after an hour and we were all towed into Recife. This was the introduction to the "other Brazil" of the interior.

2

Shortly after the return to Recife my research continued but with a different twist or at least a minor detour. The chapbooks of "cordel" which were my main item of interest were written by the poets of "cordel," but they had a "country cousin," the poet-singers who improvised oral verse in a sort of oral poetic duel called the "peleja" or "cantoria." It is a long and involved story essential to understanding northeastern folklore but secondary to my research on the "cordel," the reason honestly because of a personal problem in hearing by me (a weakness in catching certain sounds and tones) and a more basic reason. The oral, poetic duel of two poet-singers was done in local parlance, mainly the Portuguese of the small farmers and others of the Northeastern interior, in effect, "a country Portuguese" difficult to understand even by middle or upper-class city dwellers. These duels once written down in the "cordel" were perfectly understandable, that is, with a good dictionary, but damned near impossible to get in performance. Suffice to say, I did not specialize on the oral poets. But the themes they used, the metrical forms they employed were all an antecedent to "cordel" and an important part of it. No self-respecting "cordel" poet would be without a "peleja" in his repertoire.

After Caruaru, once again due to my forays in the São José Market in Recife, I met some of the singer-poets and not wanting to ignore this important aspect of northeastern folklore, arranged to record one of their performances – a poetic "duel" called "cantoria" or "peleja." The "rub" was that it was to be held in the Santa Rita Market in Recife, an old area along the docks known for derelicts, drugs, prostitution, thieves and I don't know what else. I arrived with a friend from the Chácara and with my tiny portable tape recorder to the side and recorded only one of two such performances in the research. We were seated on rough wooden stools with a dirt floor when the "cantadores" arrived, very poor in appearance but with the requisite "violas" or 10 - string "guitars" used for accompaniment to the rhythms. They performed for about two hours, me recording with those tiny cassette tapes: all manner of traditional songs like "você cai," and other modalities. I ponied up all the extra "cruzeiros" I had for the performance and the many beers imbibed by the singers and somehow safely made it back to the Chácara with recorder and tapes in hand.

3

Days passed and it was time for a second foray to the interior, this time to Campina Grande in neighboring Paraiba State where new adventures and challenges would await. Hansen and Iverson both encouraged me to "proceed." It was the "pinga-pinga" bus again, this time first for two hours north from Recife to João Pessoa, the capital of Paraiba State, all in the "wet zone" ["zona da mata"] with sugar cane all the way. Then a second bus headed west from the big coastal city to the "interior" city of Campina Grande, an extremely important spot for my research. The road once again was paved with concrete for the two hours stretch to "Campina" as they called it, a city of about 200,000 people with another large market and fair, my main reason for the trip. There were however some other aspects of Brazilian culture that showed up on this trip, all important for Hansen and Iverson's interests.

I lodged at the home of a good friend from the Chácara times in Recife, Pedro Oliveira; he would be instrumental several times in research and travels in these months in the Northeast. The family was upper middle class, his father Otacílio an important personage in the entire area. The elder Oliveira made his living with gas stations in Campina; his family was large with four boys and three girls, all early teens and older when I visited. Pedro would be my guide around town to the huge market and fair, but his family introduced lessons for the "gringo" to the reality of that old Northeast. It was a reality matched in the story poems of "cordel."

One story was that of one of Pedro's sisters. She was engaged to a young, handsome fellow from Campina; they were madly in love and a marriage was planned. But Uiara the beautiful daughter had a previous boyfriend and a relationship that did not work out. The guy was the scion of a wealthy backlands family, his father one of the old "coroneis" or political bosses of the region. When the relationship fell through and Uiara began to date her current boyfriend, he met up with the former "noivo" on a downtown street and the spoiled brat of a kid pulled a gun and shot him. To make a long story short, the killer was never arrested, much less brought to trial, and despite efforts by the Oliveira family, no local sheriff, or judge was interested in further investigation of the case. All the Oliveira efforts came to naught. Northeast politics ruled the day. My lesson from Jefferson and "Coronel Heráclio" from the Chácara days was becoming more meaningful.

All this had not one but many precedents in the Northeast, the most famous coming from the real-life history of bandits in the region. The story is complicated and long, but you can boil it down to two cases: the famous real - life bandit ["cangaceiro"] Antônio Silvino and the even more famous case of Lampião and his consort Maria Bonita. Their story and the historic reality are one of the largest chapters of the "cordel" told in literally hundreds of story poems. Both bandits have much in common: they became bandits ["cangaceiros"] because of a basic lack of justice in the backlands. Both had fathers who were murdered in cold blood during local political strife, both victims of powerful backlands "coronéis" or political bosses, both whose complaints to local law officials were never heard, and the killers ran free. (The INR and Iverson were interested in all this because of the possibility of unrest and possible social upheaval. Would the bandits be the "seed" for massive social upheaval in the Northeast?)

Silvino was a generation earlier than Lampião but the stories are much the same; both saw that the only justice would be by the "rifle de ouro" as the Winchester 73 was called, so they took up arms and took justice into their own hands. Silvino survived by robbing trains, stores and banks in small towns and became known as a local "Robin Hood" who more than once emptied coffers of coins into the streets for the poor people. He became legend in Paraíba and neighboring states, evaded the law for years but was finally captured and put in the penitentiary in Recife to serve out his long sentence. There was a happy ending when after years as a model prisoner, he made enough money in the jail to educate his children and left as a free man.

Lampião was the same yet different. He became notorious for his cruelty, a "no holds barred" attitude, many blood curdling murders, stories of cutting off victims' fingers for their gold rings or worse. He evaded the law for more than twenty years before he and his consort were riddled with bullets in an ambush by the police in Sergipe State in 1938. By this time there was such a loyal allegiance to him by the back landers that the authorities and police decided to do a "macabre" funeral march through the backlands of the Northeast with the bandit, his consort and fellow bandits heads severed, soaked in large cans of queresene to show the people he really was dead. Otherwise they feared a new "messianic" legend could arise. I would see the heads in large vials of formaldehyde in the museum at the side of the School of Medicine in Salvador in the coming months.

All this is just to show the state, yet in 1966 of backlands justice. The "cordel" is full of such stories and in fact they are a mainstay in the whole body of story poems: the hero unjustly treated who takes the law into his own hands, wreaks vengeance and becomes a local folk hero.

When I heard Uiara's story in Campina Grande in those innocent first days in Brazil in 1966 I was amazed, "Living is very dangerous" says the writer.

A second but no less important slice of Brazilian life was revealed in those days in Campina Grande: Brazilian Kardec Spiritism. Pedro's father Otacílio was a successful businessman with the gas stations and he as well was a founding president of the Campina Grande "Campo Campestre" or Country Club. But there was more to the story – Otacílio was a famous "médium" in Kardec Spiritism in the city. Allan Kardec from France founded this variant of religion in the mid - 1850s explaining it all in his "Book of the Spirits." We had never heard of it in Nebraska, but it was sporadically successful in parts of the U.S. and more so in England, but especially successful in that broad spectrum of religion in Brazil that I would come to appreciate in the coming months.

It was a bit "down the totem pole" from the major religions, but was nevertheless important. Kardec founded his beliefs on both the Old and New Testament, "cherry-picking" from each for the foundation of Brazilian Spiritism: a belief in the Golden Rule, in Reincarnation (as you live so will you be rewarded or vice-versa), thus each person's "heaven" or "hell" is his own creation by how he lives (God is not involved). If you live and act well, in the next life you will be lifted to a life of a "higher elevation;" if you do the opposite, the next life will be at a lesser level. More important than all this for Mr. Oliveira was the belief in the communications with the spirits of the deceased – family, friends and an entire pantheon of beings of the past – thus the power of the medium, but also a corollary: the power to heal.

In a long session in the back patio of the Oliveira compound Otacílio explained all this to me, and if it is fuzzy as I write this LETTER, it's my fault, not his. Basically, the medium gifted with the healing power possesses the same gift as Jesus Christ but of course to a lesser degree: Otacílio could discern the "sickness" of the hundreds of people who came to his compound, lined up in the street outside and patiently waiting for a consult. They were from all social classes, the rich to the poor, but shared the desperation to be healed. If the ailment were mental, he would refer them to psychiatric help, if it were physical he would apply a remedy from the huge "pharmacy" in two rooms in his house, all the medicines donated by pharmaceutical salesmen in the region. And most importantly if it were spiritual, he would pray over the person. He stated in a modest way that his "practice" had a far better successful cure record than the local M.D.s or psychiatric hospital. In this he was akin to the famous Arigó of Congonhas do Campo, Minas Gerais, Brazil's most famous Spiritist healer. And there was yet another aspect of Spiritism he explained to me: that of the "seer" or spiritist medium who could in effect predict the future, Chico Xavier of Minas Gerais the most famous of that group.

So I'm twenty-five, a cradle Catholic although not an everyday practitioner, and now I'm knocked over the head with yet another Brazilian religious phenomenon, not the first nor the last. If I was learning anything in Brazil in these early months it was religious tolerance, that no one religion had all the answers and more importantly, you should respect them all. My mentors in folklore would pound this home time and time again. This was just one more of the religious encounters I would have the next few months.

All this was just the unexpected on my first foray to Paraíba State. The main reason to go to Campina Grande was to meet one of the most famous of all "cordel" poet-publishers of the times – Manoel Camilo dos Santos. There was a large weekly fair, comparable in size to that of Caruaru in Pernambuco, with all the accoutrements of the Northeast including "cordel" poet-singers and poets. My friend Pedro guided me to the fair first and after we determined that Manoel no longer actively sold his verse in the fair but rather from his house-printing shop, there was a long, convoluted search to find his neighborhood, then his house and finally the poet. We walked on muddy streets and sidewalks from the rain that day to a poor, proletarian section of Campina and relying on the street address on the back of one of Manoel's story-poems I had purchased in Recife finally came to his house. Up to this point in Brazil this was the highlight of my research.

After knocking on the door of the row house and shouting the northeastern "ó de casa" ["Is anybody home?"] a woman cracked the door and suspiciously asked who we were and what we wanted (a white Brazilian in sport shirt and slacks and a foreigner were not the usual visitors). After Pedro helped me explain (my Portuguese was still not that of the poor interior folks), Manoel came to the door, his short-sleeved shirt and pants stained by printers' ink and wearing the sun glasses many poets sported in those days. I would learn only later after collecting and reading many of his story-poems that he specialized in the 32 - page "romance" – a story of love, and adventure in the "cordel." He was a former singer-poet so his was a complete mastery of the metrics and traditions of the poetry and he had many titles of the poetic duels. A final and important facet to his personality was that he was <u>a master</u> of the back cover "editorial" page of the story poems, an important aspect of "cordel" at that time. Aside from giving biographical information, place of residence and printing, the poet truly did "editorialize" – in this case putting up a "front" of having a stable of lawyers at his service ready to immediately sue the crooked, vile, immoral, "parasites" who were stealing his poems.

I don't think I garnered any crucial information from our meeting even though I did come away with a large handful of his poems to take back to the Chácara in Recife, but Manoel would provide me with one of the best written interviews via the mail for later research. Most important was I met "the man."

It was coming back from Campina Grande by bus to João Pessoa on the coast that another lesson in Brazilian folklore and life took place. The driver was zooming along at a good pace on a country road when suddenly, he slammed on the brakes and we all fell forward in our seats. Someone shouted "PEBA, PEBA, PEGA A PEBA" ["Armadillo, armadillo, catch the armadillo"] and the bus emptied, that is, except for the gringo in the back of the bus. Driver and passengers were running helter-skelter in the countryside beside the bus after the object of their obsession: an armadillo ("peba" in Portuguese). This gringo not yet knowing the word "peba" as a result of my academic Portuguese (no reference to the same in the classics of Portuguese or Brazilian Literature) remained in his place watching the wild scramble. Soon all returned to the bus, no "peba" in hand, but evidently satisfied with the effort. A passenger clued me in: "They have aphrodisiacal powers." Graduate school had not prepared me for "pebas," much less their vital bodily fluids. The driver started the engine and ambled on into João Pessoa.

And so ended the second foray to the interior in that rainy, hot "winter" of 1966. So far things were going much as planned; I was experiencing and writing of major aspects of northeastern life, folklore and the "cordel" and just occasional bits and pieces for Iverson.

4

It was August 1966, and adventure beckoned again with an important motive: a trip to the distant interior of the Northeast to Ceará State and to the stomping grounds of one of the most important figures of Northeastern religion, folklore and life – Father Cícero ["Padre Cícero Romão] of Juazeiro do Norte, Ceará. My motives were purely those of research, but more lay in store. Some background is necessary for anyone who might see this LETTER. Father Cícero is arguably among the top two or three main characters of the entire cast of the "Literatura de Cordel;" he is in the company of Carlos Magno, Lampião and Getúlio Vargas. If one is to understand Brazil and Brazil in the 20th century, his is a necessary chapter.

Father Cícero is an icon of the Northeast, perhaps its most important. Born in the interior of Ceará State in 1834, the part of Brazil most ravaged by the droughts (the area of the most famous drought of all, the 1877 "seca dos dois 77" when an estimated one million northeasterners died), the poverty, misery and outright starvation due to an unjust land distribution system and colonial class structure, Cícero would be ordained a priest of the Catholic Church, assigned to an "end of the world" poverty stricken parish in the middle of nowhere and evolve to become the region's religious leader, revered for near "messianic" powers. I would discover that the entire story was best told in the "cordel" and thus a "command" performance in my visits to the markets of the Northeast. Just as introduction, one needs to know that in the late 1800s while saying mass in Juazeiro, the host purportedly turned to blood in the mouth of the recipient, a "holy lady' ["beata"] in Father Cícero's parish, and the legend began. It evolved to make Juazeiro the main religious pilgrimage site of the entire Northeast, a legend in its time. And it produced hundreds of titles of "cordel" story-poems.

So, I made the trip in August of 1966. We traveled by the usual "pinga-pinga" bus leaving Recife about 4:00 a.m. and no seats were empty. The "easy" part of the trip was the first two hours by concrete paved road to Caruaru the "Princess of the Agreste," [The green pastoral region west of the sugar cane coastal zone] but then reality set in: the end of the paved road and a muddy, pot hole filled two lanes and then a rutty "path" for the next twenty hours to our destination in Ceará State. The bus bogged down in mud after Caruaru and then continued the described road. The bus reminded me some of the old school buses in the 1950s in Nebraska – straight backed seats, little padding, and windows you could slide down to get some air. We needed this since the rough road with all the pot holes caused the many children aboard to get sick and vomit; the driver tried to keep a semblance of order by wiping it up with newspapers but soon gave up. Even adults vomited later in the stifling heat. From Caruaru in the "agreste" or cattle zone we soon passed into the dry, cacti filled interior, the famous "sertão" or backlands of the Northeast.

This was the land I had read about back at Georgetown in the literature classes on Northeastern Brazil – the Novel of the 1930s with all the tales of the dry backlands filled with brave cowboys dressed in leather from head to foot who brought down ferocious brahma bulls in the maze of cacti and thick underbrush in the dry desert, religious fanatics, messianic leaders, cruel political bosses and landholders and bloodthirsty bandits, the cast of characters of those novels but also the mainstay of the "cordel." The first time I saw one of those cowboys dressed in leather hat, vest, chaps and boots was a vision come true from that old literary and folk literature reality. For the Brazilians, it was no less romantic and admirable than our stories of the western cowboys, cattle drives from Texas to Abilene, Kansas, and killers like Billy the Kid and others. The crossing of the backlands had a name in Brazilian lore – the "travessia" or heroic crossing – told in myriad stories of "cordel" but also in the Brazilian novel: "Grande Sertão: Veredas" ["The Devil to Pay in the Backlands"] by João Guimarães Rosa in 1956, considered the best of all Brazil's modern novels, and linked closely to the "cordel." The novel told in heroic fashion the battle between Good and Evil, the Devil and the "saints," the bandits, political bosses, and most of all love in the backlands.

After Caruaru, well into the trip, we stopped for the first meal, an eye-opener for me and not a bit like Nebraska. The place was called an "arraial" or sort of a cross-roads spot in the road with an open air thatched "restaurant." We sat at open tables with straight backed wooden chairs and ate "family style," with large bowls of rice, pinto beans, manioc, and the main dish of salted meat or "charque," the mainstay of backlands protein. I had bought some sweet rolls and crackers at the bus station in Recife, hoping to sustain myself for the entire trip, but hunger got the best of me and I dug in with the rest of the folks. Saying all those Catholic prayers from early years on the farm, I prayed for sustenance but mainly for a calm stomach. The prayer must have been heard because I made it to Juazeiro with no revolutions.

There was a long haul across the large state of Pernambuco before we entered Ceará and eventually into Juazeiro well into the latter state. I can't remember all the towns but there were many, and they all looked the same: a single, main street through town with cobblestones ["paralelepípedos"], row houses with no sidewalk, and maybe a single plaza with a few flowers. One of my acquaintances on the bus was a young fellow who worked at a branch of the Bank of Brazil ["O Banco do Brasil"] in Recife who was going home for a few days to visit the family. We eventually arrived at the town of Serra Talhada in the high backlands of Pernambuco, dry, dusty but with a low mountain range of perhaps 300 meters in height. This was the birthplace of the most famous bandit-outlaw of the entire Northeast – the infamous "Lampião" ["Flash of Light"]. I've already talked of him and his famous lover-consort Maria Bonita and the curious but similar ending to their lives as Bonnie and Clyde in the late 1930s in the U.S. What was of interest on the bus trip was that some of my Bank of Brazil friend's relatives had been killed in cold blood by the bandit. Lampião would become along with Padre Cícero of Juazeiro and Getúlio Vargas of Brazilian political fame the most famous of the cast of "cordel." Just one of the "cordel" story-poems, "The Arrival of Lampião in Hell" by José Pacheco would be a classic in the genre.

After several more bone-crushing hours on the road in that little school bus we finally arrived at our destination – Juazeiro do Norte do Ceará. It was well after midnight and we arrived in the darkened streets to a modest hotel – no lights – so the driver performed the northeastern greeting: he clapped his hands and yelled "Ó de casa!" [Is anybody there?] and after a while a short northeastern night watchman showed up and said, "No rooms here." Pardon the crude comparison, but my thought was "no rooms at the inn." The bus driver knew his way around and basically dropped me off at 2:00 a.m. in the main town plaza and said, "There's a religious pilgrim house over there." I don't recall all the details, but I roused someone who directed me to a "rancho do romeiro" ["pilgrim's hostel"] and that night I not only was introduced to Juazeiro do Norte and Father Cícero's land but to a true "pilgrim's" experience. My lodging was in a mud wattle shack with no lights, no floor other than the bare clay, no furniture other than two hooks that had a hammock attached. The "bathroom" was the yard out back. I dropped my light satchel on the floor, climbed into the hammock, pulled my jacket over my head to ward off the mosquitoes and slept fitfully until awakened by a real chill in the air in that dry, high, backlands town. I awakened, "Was I delirious?" to the sound of angels, or so it seemed. It was the high - pitched singing of the ladies in the dawn services in the church Father Cícero himself had founded in the plaza of the town, Nossa Senhora das Dores [Our Lady of the Sufferings].

You learn about Brazil taking baby steps and this was one of them. The poor, miserable outlanders flock to Juazeiro to "pay promises" for the favors bestowed upon them by Father Cícero's intercession with those on high, or more likely, to ask for favors, both spiritual and material, to survive. If granted, they say they received "a grace." Not then, but later I came to understand that my experience that night and coming days was no less, even though I came as a folklorist and "gringo" tourist. What better way to experience Juazeiro than the "rancho dos romeiros," the hammock, the mosquitoes, the near freezing air that a.m. and the singing of the holy women ["beatas"] in the nearby church?

The temporary religious fervor was soon replaced by practicality: I contacted a local pharmacist, a friend of José Atayde in Recife and was soon greeted by him and his son who would be my personal "guide' or "cicerone" as they say in the Northeast, and I also welcomed their hospitality and lodging in a quite comfortable middle-class home in Juazeiro. Orestes the son would take me to the "sister" city of Juazeiro – Crato – and there getting to know the prosperous city of the area, he would show me the nightlife, such as it was, typical of the Brazilian interior in 1966, a dance at a local club. The dance merits special attention for a folklorist, first its great title: a "foot dragger" ["arrasta-pé"]. It was the epitome of social life for the teenagers and younger crowd of Juazeiro in those days and featured both northeastern music of the "forró" and the ubiquitous "iê-iê-iê" of early Brazilian rock of Roberto Carlos. The guys stood on one side, the girls on the other and soon a lively mixture took place, but it was quintessential "country."

It was in that hot August of 1966 in Juazeiro that I also experienced a scene long gone in later years: in the hot evening (this was just at the time of the beginning of television in the Northeast) folks would drag chairs out on the narrow sidewalks in front of the row houses and talk and laugh far into the night until the air cooled and you would go back inside to sleep. And there were guitars and much singing of ballads and folk music. To my mind, it was one of the most beautiful of the old customs of the Northeast, and it was related to "cordel" – folks would talk of people gathering on the sidewalk to hear someone read or recite one of the latest "cordel" romantic stories.

I would be on my own, my choice for the wanderings in town the next two or three days, this because I wanted to experience the phenomenon of Father Cícero as a researcher and not a tourist. It was best to wander about alone. Father Cícero was and still is one of a half dozen of the main characters of <u>all</u> "cordel," and even though I was not inclined to the old, conservative religious vision of the story-poems (I preferred the stories about bandits or politics) I could not ignore this. After all this is why I made that trip to Juazeiro.

The next day, now settled in comfortable lodging with the pharmacist's family, I took off on my own to see the Juazeiro of Father Cícero. The first was the huge plaza in front of the main church; in its center was a small glass enclosed shrine marking the place, unobtrusive in nature, but to its side was the main church where the tomb is located. The church was not huge in size, was white washed on the plain exterior with open windows on the second floor and a bell tower on top. That day the plaza was practically empty but when I returned the next day for the commemorative mass (each month on the anniversary of his death) the huge plaza was jammed with religious pilgrims, mostly very humble people, the men dressed in loose white trousers, shirt, straw pilgrim's hat and leather sandals ("alpargatas"), the women in simple country dresses. I entered the church during the celebration of the mass and could not understand a thing due to the poor p.a. system with a priest giving a sermon in northeastern, country vernacular. What was impressive was that the church was also jammed with the same poor pilgrims and even the open - air windows high above had people standing in them. I recall little but that the church was very clean, white washed on walls and ceilings and with large blue stars on the latter with the names of donors to the church.

Outside the plaza just down the street was a far more striking place for me – the "Casa dos Milagres" [The Miracle House] also called the "Casa das Promessas" [The Promise House]. In effect, it was a series of almost darkened rooms lit only by hundreds of candles, the walls and ceiling sooty from the years of candle smoke, the floor of beaten down clay. This was the <u>essence</u> of Juazeiro and the Padre, a place I would see later, but in better surroundings, at the Igreja do Bonfim in Salvador, Bahia, and more importantly along the banks of the São Francisco River in the interior of Minas Gerais-Bahia States. There is a basic Brazilian religious phenomenon, really of Brazilian Popular Catholicism or Brazilian Folk Catholicism that takes place here – the "paying of promises" ["pagar promessas"] I would run into later in the aforementioned places. It boils down to a couple of simple concepts: if you believe in all this, are a Catholic of the traditional Northeast, and have a great difficulty in your life – a serious sickness like cancer, a broken marital relationship – your wife or husband has left you for another - you've lost your job and are destitute, or myriad other circumstances, you pray for a cure or solution. The prayer is directed to a powerful person known with special abilities to intercede with God himself, or Jesus Christ, or the Virgin Mary, or a powerful saint. If your prayer is answered you have the most serious religious and moral obligation to go to a shrine where the "Saint" is known and leave proof of your healing, generally called an "ex - voto" in the Northeast. It may be a simple photograph but can just as likely be a plaster of paris hand, leg, head or other body part symbolizing the cure.

The "miracle house" was jammed with such objects and photographs, evidence of almost 80 years of religious pilgrimage to Juazeiro since the first miracle attributed to the Padre in 1879; as mentioned, the host turned to blood in the mouth of a communicant, the "holy lady" Maria de Araújo in a mass by Father Cicero.

When I walked in I was practically accosted by the "holy women" [beatas] in charge of the place, all wanting a few coins from the obvious foreigner to tell the story of "Meu Padim Cícero." They grabbed the sleeves of my shirt and in high pitched, almost whining voices, insisted on the "ritual," the most important part the payment expected in local currency. I managed to get a few "cruzeiro" bills out of my pockets to satisfy them but stood transfixed by the atmosphere of the place. This was not like any Catholic Church in Nebraska and did not seem "civilized" to me, but was just the first in another lesson of the Brazilian backlands, the "other" Brazil of ignorance, poverty and folklore. I could not help thinking of a scene from an art movie I had seen recently in D.C. at Georgetown, "Zorba the Greek" with the wailing harpies at a funeral in rural Greece.

A truly folkloric experience followed, not as intense but important just the same. As I was walking down the long street back to the downtown of Juazeiro, there was a blind singer performing for a few coins' donation at the side of the street. He was poor, and I really caught little of the ballads, but mainly they were songs telling of the life and miracles of Father Cícero, but what was most important for me was that he was accompanying himself on a backlands version of the old Arabia Viol – the "rabeca," in Juazeiro a crude instrument in the form of a violin but with perhaps only two strings, played by a bow across the strings. This was the same instrument used by the original singer-poets of the old Northeast of the 19th century in their poetic duels that later were handed down to the "cordel" and became an important chapter in it.

Important though they might be, of much lesser emotional impact on me were the remaining highlights of researching Father Cícero in Juazeiro – the original home of the priest and the modern, huge complex of religious buildings inspired by him and built on a hill on the outskirts of the city. It took me another full day to see them. Father Cícero's house, a small place, was converted into a museum. There was the tiny bed where he slept – a short "nordestino" he was - the daguerreotypes on the walls with photos of his parents, the old vestments in a glass case, and many gifts from the penitents. The main thing I remember was that Father Cícero each evening would give a small sermon and lead the rosary from the window of the place to the crowds outside the house waiting for a glimpse of him and words of inspiration. The religious complex on a hill outside of town called the "Horto" seemed like just "another" religious compound with buildings and church. I was young, naïve and just beginning to study this phenomenon so that was about all I had to report.

The rest of this amazing experience was only indirectly related to Father Cícero but was just as important. This chapter in the Brazilian "odyssey" was to understand the importance of the backland's priest and miracle worker, but more importantly for me, his role in the "cordel."

The most important publisher of "cordel" in the mid-1960s in Northeastern Brazil was the "Typografia São Francisco" run by an elderly black man named José Bernardo da Silva. This was a second major reason I went to Juazeiro. It's a long story and better told in the annals of "cordel," but suffice to say, José Bernardo had been an employee in the printing shop of João Martins de Atayde in Recife in the 1930s, 1940s and 1950s. He must have learned the ins and outs of the trade of printing and publishing the booklets of verse of the story-poems because he was not really a poet. What did happen is that he somehow purchased the entire operation when Atayde fell ill in the late 1950s and moved the whole thing kit and caboodle to Juazeiro do Norte. He inherited or rather "purchased" the entire stock of "cordel" poems of Atayde in Recife, but in addition the remaining stock of poems of the great pioneer of "cordel" Leandro Gomes de Barros that Atayde had purchased from Leandro's widow in 1921.

José Bernardo in the mid -1960s had three or four mechanical presses putting out new printings of all those old classics of "cordel," most often putting his own name on them as author or at least "author-publisher." The old standing rule in "cordel" was at that time: if you bought the rights you could put your name on the cover and claim authorship! My host the pharmacist was an old acquaintance if not close friend of Zé Bernardo's and garnered me an interview. The printer was stand offish, probably with good reason because he was "twisting the rules" on "cordel" publication, and was probably a bit suspicious of white "gringos" asking a lot of questions. The interview was gracious, in his living room, a house a step or two up from that of the normal "cordel" poet. He talked of his arrival in Juazeiro, his skepticism about Father Cícero and the gradual acceptance of his "miracles," but he spoke little of the "business." He allowed no photos, but did have an interesting trait – he spit occasionally into a spittoon at his feet, probably that old "fumo de rolo" tobacco from the Northeast. He was gracious, but guarded. I always said later that it was not the information he provided which was little, but just the chance to meet him and be in his "mere presence." His is an important chapter in the history of "cordel."

There was one more "cordel" person to meet and this encounter was much more "productive" regarding research. My young guide Orestes got me to the house of Manoel Caboclo e Silva who was a known publisher of "cordel" in another part of Juazeiro. Manoel received me in the sparse living room of his house but was very congenial and chatted a good while. The main thing I learned was that poetry was not exactly his "cup of tea," but rather he was an astrologer and printed at that time the major almanac in all the Northeast. His model was the most famous almanac in the years preceding him; he took over the task and his annual almanac appeared at the side of the "cordel" booklets in all the fairs of the Northeast. Being from Nebraska I had memories of my father's "The Farmer's Almanac" and how it really did help in annual planning. Manoel years later would purchase the "cordel" stock of Joaquim Batista de Sena of Fortaleza and would sell both his and Manoel's own poems in the markets.

The last moments in Juazeiro were also related to my growing up on that wheat, alfalfa and corn farm in Nebraska. Orestes' father, the pharmacist, had what the northeasterners called a "sítio" or small farm out of town, and it was there I learned all about agriculture in this small oasis in the dry backlands of the Northeast. Oriosvaldo, the father, explained how he planted, nursed and harvested myriad products on that irrigated farm: corn, sugar cane, manioc, all manner of garden vegetables and even palm fronds and palm oil from the tall "carnauba" palm trees, the latter used in the original production of the wax for vinyl records.

5

It was at the end of those pleasant and fruitful days in Juazeiro that the unexpected happened. It's a long story but here's the condensed version: my friend José Atayde back in Recife who had been so good to me and instrumental in the early research both in Recife and later Caruaru, knowing I was planning on the trip to Juazeiro, had said, "Can you do me a small favor?" How could I refuse? He said that my host in Juazeiro, a friend José had given to me as a contact and his son, a good buddy of José back in school days in Recife, could help us out. Oriosvaldo's pharmacy also was a sort of "country store" which provided all kinds of goods to the locals in Juazeiro, among other things, small arms and ammunition for hunting. José said he was in the market for a small pistol, probably just a .22 caliber for "bird hunting" or the like. Could I get it from Oriosvaldo, just put it in my pack and bring it to him in Recife? He assured me, "Hey you are a 'gringo,' no one will ever suspect you are carrying a firearm, far from it." There has not been any reason up to this point to explain that in those early days of the military dictatorship, even then no one of the public could carry arms, and if they already had them, they kept it a secret from the police or the military. So, the "ingenuous, naïve" but faithful friend, the gringo, me, picked up the gun and a box of bullets, rolled them up in some dirty clothes and put them in my pack for the return trip to Recife. No big deal. No harm done. One of my graduate literature professors from Georgetown, the Jesuit Father Cunningham, had a habit of teasing the kids in his classes, kind of a comedy "shtick" but with some truth to it. In my case, he would growl, "Yeah, that Gaherty, he's so damned naïve and such a goody-goody he'll probably help an old lady across the street and she'll stab him with her umbrella."

I had decided I could not manage that 20 - hour bus trip over those so-called "roads" in the backlands all the way back to Recife and had used the rest of my few remaining cruzeiros to buy a ticket on a third-class "puddle jumper" back to the city – in this case an old DC - 3 that Varig Airlines still used in the interior cities of the Northeast. All I had was a very small suitcase with my "necessaries" as we used to say on the farm in Nebraska, and that small pack. The trip was a hoot with the old DC - 3 sitting like a tired old sheep dog on its tail, the pilot revving the two propeller engines and zoom down the runway and we were air born. The best thing was it flew so low you really could appreciate the countryside as we passed through a good deal of the state of Ceará and the length of Pernambuco back to the coast. And there was even a Varig Steward in a starched, white, long-sleeved dress shirt with black tie and trousers serving soft drinks, coffee and sandwiches.

I still am a bit fuzzy about what happened but after we bumped to a landing at Guararapes Airport alongside the jet-props and the big international jets, the few passengers climbed down the metal staircase they rolled up to the door behind the pilot's cabin and began walking across the tarmac to the terminal. At that point at the entrance gate and fence this guy in military attire with the whole works, cap, white shirt and tie, pistol strapped to his waist, blue slacks and military boots, drew me aside and in a polite but stern Portuguese said,

"Mr. Gaherty, we'd like to have a word with you. Would you step this way?"

"Oh, shit!" was my only thought. I had that goddamed gun in the pack with a small box of shells, and to make matters worse only had a Xeroxed copy of my passport that contained the special one-year student visa stamped in it. I had been advised to never carry the passport with visa for fear of pickpockets or thieves in the markets and fairs so just carried a Xeroxed copy of the front page of the passport and the visa. Recife is in the tropics, but I was sweating more that moment than all those hot moments on the cramped city buses the last two months. I was so rattled that I really wasn't thinking too clearly about anything. I just remembered wondering, "What in the hell would they want with this blue-eyed gringo who only stood out on the streets of Pernambuco like a hot dog with mustard at a black bean Brazilian stew dinner?"

They escorted me into a small office in one wing of the terminal with glass windows all around and, you notice such things, an air conditioner that could freeze water. In minutes, the sweat was dry and I was shivering from the cold. It all started out innocently enough, what I imagine was standard procedure. "Let us see your documents, please." After my stammering explanation about Brazilian pickpockets and street thieves (true but possibly misconstrued as an insult to Brazilian law and order since I was in the presence of these protectors of the same) and the Xeroxed papers, they wanted to know what I was doing in Brazil, how long had I been in Recife and the Northeast and why had I been to Juazeiro ("No 'gringo' goes there much less knows anything about it."). It was only as I was trying to explain I was on a Fulbright Study grant to do Ph.D. research on Brazilian folklore and the story-poems of the "literatura de cordel" (none of the officers had heard of it or knew what the hell it was) and the role of Father Cícero in Juazeiro, that they produced the gun and ammo box and theatrically slid both across the table in front of me.

"Think fast asshole," I said to myself. Oh crap. What do I do? What do I say? Do I spill the beans about José Atayde and the "simple" favor, not knowing if he would get a knock on the door a few minutes later and even worse, what that conversation might reveal and what the DOPS would do to him, or me now invent some cockamamy as yet unthought of explanation for the pistol? Gahertys were not brought up lying, even "fibbing" was confessed to that old priest in the tiny torture box in the church on Saturday afternoons, and I was not any good at anything but the truth (maybe that's why "cordel" agreed so much with me; its heroes never lie ["falsedade"] or are arrogant ["querendo ser maior do que Deus"]). I told the now three officers in the room about José Atayde, his innocent request to pick up a small pistol for shooting birds, and my returning the "favor" for his work as guide and informant for me in the Northeast. And that's all there was to it.

"Senhor Gaherty, either you are a very clever person or exceedingly stupid. I think you have been here long enough to know that Brazil is going through a very difficult time, a tense time, and that there are serious enemies of the government and the Revolution led by the glorious generals who have saved our country from Fidel's Communists, and even a revolt here in the Northeast under ex-governor Arraes' and Francisco Julião's leadership. We are surrounded by those who want to disrupt the public order and even overthrow the established democratic government and its principles, witness the bomb detonated in this very airport just a few weeks ago. It could have, except for an accident of fate, killed our future president! It is for that reason that firearms are not allowed by the public under <u>any</u> circumstances at present without due permission or reason and of course proper documents. You have none of the above and even beyond that are supposedly a researcher, a serious scholar, and a guest in our country. Why in Jesus's name did you not think of that before you agreed to transport this illegal weapon? You're supposed to be smart, you gringo son of a bitch researcher. Christ Jesus. I'm not sure at present of the penalty but at the least you will be expelled immediately from the country. If you were Brazilian, your ass would be grass and your momma would not recognize you after we were done with you."

It was at that point that I remembered the phone number of the INR given to me by Iverson that I carried on a folded note card in my billfold. I gave it to the Pernambuco Police, they called the number, it went through a series of delays and eventually there was a voice on the line. It was Ron Wellseley from the U.S. Embassy in Brasília (an agent of the INR) and he wanted to know what was going on. I explained the whole situation, my link to Hansen, then Iverson and now to him. After putting me on hold for an interminable time he got back on and said, "Mike, we are handling all this and there is a contingency plan for such matters. Put me back on the line with the officer in charge of the State of Pernambuco Intelligence Office (these were the officers behind my being detained), I'll explain a few things and then you follow <u>explicitly</u> their instructions. I won't be back on, but know you can call me at the same number later if there are complications."

I handed the telephone to Geroaldo of the OIEP (Estado de Pernambuco, Oficina de Inteligencia, what turned out to be a regional offshoot of the Brazilian DOPS), he talked for another twenty minutes, hung up, went around the table and gave me some straight talk:

"Senhor Gaherty, you indeed have friends in high places. The matter is resolved but you must follow my explicit directions when you get out of here, and here they are: Deliver the pistol to your friend José Atayde, say nothing of this meeting with us and go on about your "business" of "cordel" research. I assure you we will be keeping an eye on Atayde; it may be as he says, nothing serious, but I want you to know it's damned serious from our perspective and from now on in Brazil, we will know where you travel, what you do, who you see and how things evolve. After my conversation with Mr. Wellseley, I think you are on the right side and may even be doing a service to your country and ours, but there are those on the other side who are just as interested in what you are doing. If they contact you, you contact us. You can use the same number. You are free to go."

A day or two later I saw José out at the Sugar Cane Museum, delivered the pistol and the ammo, thanked him profusely for the contact with Oriosvaldo and Orestes in Juazeiro, told of my "cordel" and Father Cícero research and the matter was closed. I would see José off and on the next two months in Recife and then again, the following June. Only later would I hear the end of this story.

6

After that return to Recife in August of 1966 and before my next foray to the interior in September a vivid chapter of northeastern Brazilian culture was opened to me – an introduction to the Afro-Brazilian ritual of Xangô. It was August 24th, night of St. Bartholomew and the "devil" or "Exú," and I went to my first Xangô ceremony with Mark Lisboa from the old neighborhood in Olinda; Mark had a good camera and took some fine photos in black and white. My description of it all has a disclaimer: I was not studying Afro-Brazilian religion per se, and at that time had an impressionistic knowledge of it, so what I would send Hansen and the Times would reflect that place and time.

Xangô is one of the major Afro-Brazilian religious rites in Brazil and one of the most "pure," that is, not mixed with Eastern Religion like "Umbanda" in Rio or even "Quimbanda" in the Southeast. It is most closely related to the purest of Afro rites in Brazil, the "Candomblé" of Salvador, Bahia, that will enter this story later when I am doing research in that city. A thumb nail sketch, imperfect as is my knowledge, goes something like this. The religion came from Africa and has its roots in a polytheistic view of life with much in common with "Candomblé" and less with "Santería" in Cuba and other Afro rituals in countries in northern South America and the Caribbean. It arrived in Brazil with the slaves and developed and evolved over 400 years of Portuguese colonization and domination. There are many facets to the religion and countless books, magazine articles, Ph.D. dissertations, documentary films and TV and movies have dealt with it. I can only hit the high points here.

There are multiple gods or spirits, called by various names in Portuguese like "santos," "encantados" and the like. The gods are "called down" in the Xangô ritual by the "Mother" or "Father" of the saints in a ceremony characterized by dances and chants, this figure akin to the Catholic Priest and the mass in Western Culture. The basic concept is that each member of the ritual has her or his own saint or god, much like the saint of traditional Catholics according to their first name, but that is the only similarity; it is much more complex in Xangô. When a person is initiated into Xangô, whether purposefully by a mother who takes her young daughter to a ritual, or "accidentally" when a person just "knows" they are to have a personal saint, and the choice is not of the member but of the saint, generally the person while dancing and participating in the ritual becomes "possessed" by the spirt. The members have a term for it: "Cair no santo"

["Fall into the saint"] or "O santo cavalgou no cavalo," ["The saint came down and "rode" its horse or mount"]. Once this happens, if all goes as per customary ritual and plan, the "initiate" goes through a long "training" and finally a formal initiation into the ritual.

What I needed to know, and any foreigner for that matter, is that when you are "possessed" by the saint, you take on the saint's appearance, personality and other traits: the clothing the saint is known for, the dance steps of that saint, the symbolic accoutrements of the saint like a sword, a bow and arrow, and the foods of the saint. In effect, you begin to dance, sing and dress like the saint. Psychologists and other non-believers say the member "goes into trance," but don't tell any true believer that, and especially not me. I'm writing this just as an introduction to that night of August 24th, a scary experience indeed for the Catholic from a small town and local parish in Nebraska. Needless to say, or maybe not, I knew generally about all this before arriving in Brazil (we graduate students in Portuguese and Brazilian Studies were all mesmerized by the possession of the saint in the "Umbanda" scene in the movie "Black Orpheus") and one of my research goals, albeit not the main one, was as a "folklorist" to experience the ritual. And besides, one of the two most important Brazilian writers I would need to deal with for the dissertation was the Bahian Jorge Amado whose novels were "soaked" in Afro-Brazilian religion.

A second basic fact is that all the Afro-Brazilian religions in Brazil, some closer to Africa than others, survived only to the extent their members, black slaves, could convince the white Portuguese masters that they were really practicing a version of the Catholicism forced upon them by the slave owners. Thus, each African "saint" corresponded closely or loosely to a Catholic saint or deity, from God the Father, to Jesus Christ, to the Blessed Virgin Mary and the phalanx of Catholic saints – each African saint was tied to Catholicism.

Mark and I arrived at the ritual site called "terreiro" in Portuguese in the hills of Olinda at about ten p.m. The ritual was to start around 10:30 but no one seemed to be in a hurry or watching the clock. The building was one – story, whitewashed and totally simple both on the outside and inside. It was a "compound" run by the Father of the Sant – "Pai Edu" - famous in those parts. His success was a well - known item of discussion in the Recife area, and his new VW Bug ["fusca"] was just one sign of his success. There was a large rectangular main room where the ritual took place, but many "back rooms" where food was prepared, where participants dressed for the night's ritual and where the "possessed" were taken to rest until the possession or trance wore off. In that main room, there were three or four rows of "bleachers" as it were where guests (and tourists could come if they did not interfere with the ritual) would sit on long wooden benches.

We filed in along with a few others and took a seat in a still uncrowded scene. That soon changed: by the time the ritual began with the circle dances, chanting and loud accompanied drumming by a group of young men all dressed in white, the place was jammed. And the heat was stifling; participants and guests were all sweating. This evening, at that time, was near the top of my list in emersion into Brazilian culture and I can't overstate the impact it had upon me. There would be other moments like it, New Years' Eve in Rio and Carnival in Rio, but nothing that "visceral."

The night of the "Devil" or "Exu" – just one of the major "saints" of Afro-Brazilian Religion – did not disappoint. I learned that Exu, among his many traits, was an essential part in all the rituals, no matter the specific saint being celebrated that night, this because he was "mischievous" and had the habit of perturbing the cult. You had to initiate any service with a prayer and offering to Exu or he would disrupt and perhaps even ruin the evening. Thus, the first chant of the night led by a spectacularly robed Father of the Saint Edu dressed in a long red velvet cape with a purple collar was: "Sem Exu Nada se Faz" sung and repeated by all the participants dancing slowly in circles in the room. "Without Exu, nothing is done." Beyond this initial chant dozens of others followed, many dedicated directly to him, but many others to the myriad other "saints" of Xangô.

I grew up in Nebraska in a nearly all -white community; we had a smattering of black folks (called "Negroes" then) and a few Mexicans (they were all "legal" and worked construction on the railroads like the Santa Fe, the Rock Island and the Union Pacific). I had been exposed to the "mestizo" population of Mexico in the early 1960s and of course to large black populations both in Kansas City and Washington D.C. in college, and was getting used to the predominately black population of the Northeast and the mixed blood "caboclos" of the interior. But this night was a real Baptism into the black race and culture of Brazil.

The participants in the ritual, both men and women, were dressed predominately in white, the men in white shirt, trousers and shoes. The only other men were the young boys with their drums for accompanying the chants. The women known as the "daughters of the saint" were also largely in white but in splendid woven dresses with a preponderance of the decorative weaving of the northeast on the sleeves and collar. They all had a lot of jewelry, many bracelets on both wrists, earrings and many necklaces. I have no experience in all this and I'm told that most practitioners of xangô are of the poor class, but the jewelry looked expensive, much of it the color of silver or gold. Most also wore a sort of cloth turban on their heads, but their feet were bare, this I found out later was due to the rituals of the dancing.

After that introductory chant or prayer to ask for Exu's good graces to continue the ceremony, the ritual really began: it was a series of songs or chants, all in response to the leading voice of Pai Edu. I could not understand the Portuguese at all and there was also a mixture of the African Nagó language, but the melodies were beautiful especially with many voices chiming in. They all danced in a large circle around the room, and each new chant was led by Pai Edu with the others answering, and the dances gradually speeded up until the movements of the dancers were exceedingly fast. It was then that the "saints" began to take possession of the dancers, some but not all, and the demeanor of the possessed "daughters of the saint" seemed to vary. Some now in "trance" were quiet, almost somnolent, but others began to dance faster and faster, whirling in circles outside the main dance circle, and these ladies (there were a few men, "Filhos do santo") moved rapidly up and down the room, their hair now outside the turbans, straightened up in some cases, sweating profusely, and making groaning and whimpering sounds. They came close to our bleacher seats and frankly scared the hell out of me. Some would slap the shoulders or face of other dancers and one immense woman came close to doing the same to me. The room was by then extremely overheated and I was feeling a bit queasy. I whispered to Mark, "Let's get the hell out of here," but he was busy taking photos and said, "Just be patient." At this point, some of the "filhas" would seem to collapse or almost faint, eyes closed, and some other women would guide them to chairs to sit down and rest or even take them from the room. All of a sudden, the room turned dark and all I remember was falling to the floor, head spinning. I don't know how long I was "out," but woke up with two of the "daughters of the saints" beside me with wet towels wiping my face and with huge smiles on their face. One said, "You have "mediunidade!" Exu visited you. You are definitely a "son of the saint." Welcome to Pai Edu's celebration!" Still shaken, I thanked them, sat still to collect my wits, and with Mark by my side just basically sat for a while waiting for developments. It turns out I was not the only one. Several of the "daughters" previously in "trance," now serene, returned to the ceremony.

At about this time a different chant and rhythm started, led by the drums and Pai Edu, the large circle started again, and soon all came to a stop. People entered with huge silver trays and bowls of food - a sort of fried chicken with manioc flour and I don't know what else, and bottles of beer. It was an offering to the Saint, to the "Pai de Santo" and to all present – all were expected to partake, including the tourist guests. Mark and I just sat watching.

One other moment later that night freaked me out. After the food offering, the chants and dancing started again and once again grew faster and men and women fell into trance, but one "son of the saint" suddenly seemed to take over the room. He began to dance, almost at a run, from one end of the room to the other and at one point, I swear, seemed to climb-walk-run up the wall on either end and then come down, running ever faster up and down the room.

It was at this point that I told Mark, "It's late, I've seen enough, let's split." He reluctantly agreed, and we quietly walked behind the dancers and edged out the door into the fresh breeze from the nearby sea and outside that hot and stifling, crowded building. As I said before, in 1966 I knew little about "Xangô" or "Candomblé" and really did not understand most of what was going on, but quite honestly, I found the experience terrifying when that huge black women with wild hair, bugged out eyes, and frantic behavior was dancing, moaning and groaning and heaving her chest in front of me, and making the slapping motions to all those around her. I was ready for a "rain check" on it all and would not attend again until a few months later, this after an introduction to Afro-Brazilian culture via the novels of Jorge Amado in Salvador and more experience at the "Candomblé" cult in Bahia. This was Afro-Brazilian culture at its best, the vestiges of a religion and cult originating in Africa, brought to the tropical coast of Brazil, adapted to survive the strict Catholicism of its masters, and thriving to the present. It was not a show, a play, a dramatic representation or the like, but a legitimate, sincere, genuine moment where people connected with their gods.

I can only say and write in this LETTER that it was quite like that scene from "Black Orpheus" when Orpheus goes to the "Umbanda" (another African cult in Rio) to search for his lost lover. I always wondered if the scene from the movie was staged for the camera; after this night of Exu there were no longer any doubts in my mind. I sent this LETTER, minus the dealings with the police in Pernambuco, to Hansen of the Times, number II.

7

The next phase of the research in the old Northeast and its close relationship to "cordel" was a foray once again into the interior, this time to the birthplace, "o berço" as the "cordel" poets like to say, not only of "cordel" but of its antecedent, the homeland of the "singer-poets" ["os cantadores"] – the interior of the State of Paraíba and the sugar cane plantations of one of the renowned "Novelists of the Northeast," José Lins do Rego. Throughout this entire first phase of research in Brazil the goal was first to study and learn of the "cordel" and collect the story-poems, but also to relate it to the larger view of Brazilian culture: erudite literature and history. In the end, none of the three could be separated. A short "primer" on the literature may help.

Back at Georgetown I had studied the basics of Brazilian Literature in the Ph.D. graduate courses: first, a survey of highlights from colonial times to the present twentieth century including prose and poetry, then, a seminar on Brazil's greatest author (at least until the mid-twentieth century,) the cerebral prose stylist Joaquim Maria Machado de Assis, then a course on the Novelists of the Northeast, and a final seminar on Twentieth Century Modernism and its poets. Most directly related to my study of folklore and the "cordel" were the Novelists of the Northeast, four stellar writers from the 1930s to the 1950s, and in the case of Jorge Amado beyond to the 1980s. These four writers were "children" of the 1930s and the literary side of Gilberto Freyre's sociological classic "The Masters and the Slaves" and the movement of "Regionalism of the Northeast" from a seminal meeting in 1926. Some became more important for my studies than others and I had my favorites. Raquel de Queiróz was from Ceará and wrote about life along the São Francisco River, the northeastern bandits and of course her own story of growing up in the backlands of Ceará ravaged by the droughts. Graciliano Ramos was perhaps the most "esoteric" of the four in terms of literature but would be important to me with his classic "Barren Lives" ["Vidas Secas"] the story of the drought and effect on the cowboys of the interior of Alagoas State. Jorge Amado would be most important because of his novels utilizing the folklore, the popular ballads and the personages of "cordel" and its poets, although these were minor in his total works – his thesis was joining Afro-Brazilian culture to his novels.

It was the fourth, equally important if not so famous of the Novelists of the Northeast who now would come into play – José Lins do Rego of the sugar cane zone of Paraíba. He in effect would "translate" into literature (fiction) the precepts that sociologist Gilberto Freyre had made central to the intellectual movement of the times: he would portray in a series of novels the history and life and conflicts of the sugar cane zone in what became known as the "Sugar Cane Cycle" in Northeastern Literature. His style was a bit more modern – he used the interior monologue extensively – but in his dozen or so novels the Northeast came to life. Some Brazilian critics likened him to our own William Faulkner, although he never reached the literary heights of the latter, that is, true "stream of consciousness" narrative technique, probably a good thing for me, a much more "down to earth" direct narration type of reader. Always much more attuned to history, journalism and "real life", I always saw him as a literary chronicler of the role of sugar cane for several centuries in the Northeast.

Lins do Rego never used the story-poems of "cordel" as a direct source as Ariano Suassuna and Jorge Amado and others would, but the "atmosphere" of much of what "cordel" told was central to his novels: the "Masters and Slaves" of the sugar cane zone, the rich landholders ("coronéis") and the slaves and then poor dirt farmers of later days. The themes of the rich and poor in "cordel," the evil landholders and the struggle of the poor to survive an unjust social situation, and especially the saga of the real northeastern bandits appeared in his stories. And of course, there was much more. Lins do Rego loved to use the verse of the singer-poets ["os cantadores"] and the folk songs and ballads as a "mortar" to the foundation of his novels. I had an idea of this prior to the trip (thus fueling my interest) due to mentor Manuel Cavalcanti Proença's explanation of the same in his introduction to one of Lins do Rego's novels which I had read in the U.S.)

Being just barely aware of all this, still a neophyte in Brazilian culture and literature, I knew of Lins do Rego's importance, and once again that graduate school professor of Brazilian Literature at Georgetown opened the door to this important, not to be missed, slice of the cultural reality of the Northeast. I used one more letter of introduction, this time to a professor of Brazilian Literature at the University of Paraíba in João Pessoa, Dr. Juárez Batista, to see if he could help me arrange travel to the sugar zone. Not only did he do this, one more example of the incredible hospitality of the Brazilian intellectuals to those who truly were interested in their culture, but he went "above and beyond" in the arrangement: a private car with chauffeur ("motorista") from the Federal University of Paraíba and a guide who was the major collector and publisher of the prose folk stories of the Northeast, a young Altimar Pimentel! This trip would be perfect for Hansen and the Times and would paint a cultural picture of an important part of Brazil and its social, literary reality.

The university car picked us up at Professor Batista's house and we headed just a few kilometers west to the rolling hills of sugar cane not far from the Atlantic coast. The Lins do Rego family was one of the major sugar cane "dynasty" families in that region of Paraíba. José, grandson of José Paulino, grew up on one of the plantations, a microcosm of the entire region, and as an adult wrote the "literary history" in a series of novels that became known as the "Sugar Cane Cycle." The most famous of the books was "Menino de Engenho" ["Plantation Boy"] and in it Zé Lins recreated his youth in fiction. This trip was to see the plantations of the Lins do Rego family. I personally was astounded as the long day progressed and we drove through several of the local plantations depicted through the years in José Lins' books. The cliché came true: Life imitated

Literature and Literature imitated Life. Having read three or four of the major novels back at Georgetown before coming to Brazil in 1966, I was amazed as we drove through the plantations — it all was as I had imagined in the readings, thus confirming one of the major aspect of Lins' style: an amazing gift of description.

The most famous of the plantations in the novels, "Itapuá," the one José Lins do Rego grew up on, was now the residence of a grand-daughter of the "pater-familias" "Coronel José Paulino," José's grandfather who was not only the richest landholder in the area, but the political boss as well; it had originally been a wedding gift from Coronel José Paulino to his daughter. The original mill was built in 1819 and was still in use, but the "big house," built in two stories with a highly-decorated façade, many interior rooms and with the traditional chapel to its side, was in a state of decadent grandeur in 1966 (not an oxymoron in this case) but still "oozed" history of the region. An irony at the Itapuá plantation was that the only restored building was the former slaves' quarters, the "senzala," a long rectangular building in a single story, now white washed and with a television antenna on its roof. In Lins' novels, slavery had passed (it was finally outlawed in 1888 in Brazil, the last country in the Western Hemisphere to do so). What replaced slave labor was the land-tenant system that still was operative in 1966: large plantations where the descendants of slaves worked as indentured servants, or in some cases perhaps a little better off, as poorly paid day laborers or sharecroppers on the edges of the vast sugar cane fields of the plantations. Theoretically they were free men and to be paid a wage ["alugados" or rented labor] but during this visit in 1966 the entire sugar cane industry was in crisis, the international markets were at a dismal low, and in fact the workers had not been paid wages in two months. I was shocked to see these workers in the fields, dressed in rags and bare foot, only with machetes to chop the tall cane, strip off the leaves and stack the stalks of cane on the ground, and not surprised when my guide Altimar told of "invasions" of the small local towns where warehouses were ransacked by starving peasants in search of basic foodstuffs (another scene in Lins' novels).

There were poor whites as well who might perform semi-skilled work like blacksmithing or making harnesses, or other jobs, but with little advantage over the blacks. All these people were among the masses that Carlos Prestes, "The Knight of Hope" as then Marxist Jorge Amado called him in the 1920s, tried to bring into the Communist revolution of 1924 and failed, and that Francisco Julião wanted to unite in the Peasants' Leagues of the 1960s in the Fidel inspired revolution put to a temporary stop by the Brazilian Generals in their "Redemptive Revolution" of 1964. "Cordel" would tell their story, lamenting the poverty, misery and downright starvation and the mass exodus of northeasterners to Rio de Janeiro and São Paulo in the twentieth century and happening right in front of my eyes in the 1960s. These were the stories that Iverson of the INR-WHA was most interested in, yet to come.

What was most evident from the low hill of the next plantation we visited, the "Oiteiro," was the view: as far as the eye could see there was an ocean of green fields, "cana caiana," sugar cane, tall and blowing in the wind. (Gaherty the Nebraskan could not help but remember the waving fields of wheat back home). As we drove down the hill from that first plantation we came to another scene, almost "photographic" to me from my reading of the novels: the Paraíba River valley with the wide stream dividing fields of sugar cane. In Zé Lins' novels during the dry season poor tenants would plant vegetable gardens in the rich soil, and famous bandits like Antônio Silvino and his gang would camp at night at the edge of the fields, bathe in the river and drink the water, all the while on the lookout for the state and local militia and police with orders to shoot the bandits on sight! Lins populated the scene with local superstition including the strange white man Zé Amaro who was rumored to be a werewolf and haunt the area at night! ("Cordel" would depict this entire society and scene.) Lins' masterpiece (in my opinion) "Fogo Morto" ["Dead Fire"] had many scenes near the river.

All the area we had just seen was the real - life scenario for a major Brazilian art movie of the 1960s, in black and white and with primitive equipment and scenes – "Menino de Engenho" or "Plantation Boy" by a cinematographer I would meet later in Rio – Nelson Pereira dos Santos. I forgot to mention that a young, pretty, black girl accompanied us on the trip; in the movie, she played Zefa Cateta, one of the "women of easy virtue" on the plantation, one who had initiated the "Plantation Boy" in his early adventures with the opposite sex, by the way, a custom of the times. An unreal aside: In those days after the trip Juárez Batista offered me a job as an actor in a coming art flick: I would play a British capitalist and plantation owner in the region. He said it would be easy: dress in the white linen suit of the English of those times and tall, black leather boots, carry a whip and sport a wide brimmed straw hat and I would be perfect for the part. I never did hear any details beyond that first casual offer. A good thing.

After the Paraíba River we moved on to other plantations central to the novels and two stick to my mind: the one in ruins which was that of the Quixotic poor plantation owner "Coronel Lula," the "Santa Fe" plantation, and then the most important one, still in good shape and operating in 1966, the "Corredor" operated by José Lins do Rego's cousin in real life, now owned outside the family, but in the fiction, operated by José Paulino, the feared and almost mythic "Coronel" of the entire region. It was quite different from the old ruin of Itapuã, but was no less impressive. It was a rectangular, long, one-story structure with a tile roof and a large veranda in front with columns. Inside, much of the old house had been preserved for tourists. What I remember were the polished wooden floors throughout, I can't say what kind of wood but perhaps "jacaranda" or Brazilian rosewood, the old black and white photos of family members on the walls throughout (daguerreotypes) and the caned furniture, probably jacaranda as well – straight backed chairs, rocking chairs and divans. The current owners and caretakers pointed out José Lins do Rego's childhood bed in one room.

Before they escorted us outside to see other parts of the sugar cane mill ("engenho" in Portuguese) they had a treat for the "gringo" researcher: a huge bowl of black molasses, a sugar cane derivative, covered with manioc flour, a delicacy of those parts! I tasted a spoonful or two and then had to apologize and say I could not handle the rest ("a delicate gringo stomach"). They smiled and I am sure laughed after we had left.

The rest of the tour was amazing, a one-time experience for me and harkening back to the most famous of the pre-1930s Novels of the Northeast by one José Américo de Almeida in the late 1920s, "Sugar Cane Trash" ["A Bagaceira"], which told of life on these very plantations giving emphasis to the annual cycle of wet and dry seasons and the harvest of the cane using manual labor of the poor migrants ["retirantes"] from the northeast interior. I've mentioned its author before – the famous politician and governor of Paraíba, José Américo de Almeida – and how I missed meeting him in João Pessoa, a real goof up on my part.

We left the "big house" and went a few yards to the real "nuts and bolts" of the old mill – the "casa da purga." It was a large single-story building with a thatch roof emanating an almost sickening, sweet smell through the open windows. This was where in days' past they brought in the cut stalks of sugar cane, placing them on a stone floor where a huge stone grinding wheel drawn by oxen rolled over them and crushed the sugar cane liquid from the stalks. The liquid sugar flowed down a canal and was poured into wooden molds where it would dry. The molds would then be turned upside down and become solid "loaves" of sugar; these were the "sugar loaves" or "pão de açucar" (I finally got the connection to Rios' Sugar Loaf Mountain, the iconic tourist site in Guanabara bay.)

The final building was the working "casa de moagem," or grinding house. A large round grinding stone once again crushed the stalks of cane; the result was a "caldo," green in color, that flowed down a canal into a heating vat and there became the dark "melaço" or molasses; this in turn was scooped with big large ladles into a large form made up of squares. When the "melaço" dried, it became that northeastern staple of sweet, hard "sugar candy" or "rapadura," a food used to sweeten coffee or eaten alone for dessert in the interior. The squares looked like gold bricks to me because of the color. What I remember most was the intense heat in the building, the workers' shirts soaked to the skin in sweat, and the drying blocks of "rapadura." On the outside of the building were tall stacks of the remaining sugar cane trash, the leaves from the stalks of cane; they would be used as fodder for the local cattle. These piles were what gave José Américo the title for his book, already mentioned, "Sugar Cane Trash," that and the metaphor of the poor migrant workers, "sugar cane trash" as well.

I learned and it's important to know: all that I have described to you from the trip and Lins do Rego's novels evolved into modern days and the huge sugar cane refineries. The old Lins plantations and many like them because sugar cane suppliers to the refineries; José Lins do Rego's last novel dated from that change from the colonial to modern times: "Usina" or "Refinery" and marked the last phase in the gradual evolution and decadence of the whole history and era. That explained why the mill we saw did not produce actual sugar or alcohol, but just the "rapadura" so described, but sold its cane to the big "usina" for the more famous products.

The last part of the trip that day was no less important. We left the Lins do Rego plantations and passed through the town of Itaibiana where I had hoped to meet a well - known "cordel" poet but he was gone, on the road to other markets to sell his verse, and the town of Pilar. This last stop was significant for me and the "journey" through Brazilian Literature and José Lins do Rego's novels and their link to history, folklore and the "cordel." I can't really leave it out. In the real-life times of the early twentieth century there was a phase of banditry in a "wild and wooly" Northeast; it corresponds in Brazil to the days of cowboys, ranchers and outlaws in the American west and even to the twentieth century story of the real - life Bonnie and Clyde in both real life and the cinema.

In the teens and twenties of the Twentieth Century the region was affected by these real-life bandits. Among them was Antônio Silvino and his gang who lived, loved, robbed and marauded the northeastern interior of the sugar cane zone. They hid from the law at times on the very plantations we saw, protected by locals who kept an eye out for the police or military troops coming in on horseback to try to catch them. It's all a long story told in detail in the "cordel" (the bandits were the major heroes of "cordel" in the early twentieth century) and central to our last stop on the tour. Antônio Silvino and his gang in real life "invaded" the town of Pilar, rode down the lone central street and ransacked the local stores and warehouses and here's where it got interesting. They supposedly emptied the coffers of the stores into the streets for the poor sugar cane locals to pick up the coins. This really did happen more than once in the tiny burgs of the interior and thus Silvino became known as a local "Robin Hood" hero. So, when our car drove into Pilar all this was on my mind. Once again, life and literature, literature and life. But the town was indeed humble, a small plaza in front of the whitewashed church with a single bell tower, the plaza to be sure with flowers, and rudimentary electric power lines along the only paved street, and that with the famous northeastern cobblestones called "paralelpípedos." This was the image for all such places in the "cordel" and even the main street in hell as depicted in one of the great story-poems when the bandit Lampião and his gang take over hell from the devil.

One last cultural note on the trip: the driver or "motorista" addressed me the entire time as "capitão" or "coronel," the same titles used for the great plantation owners one hundred years prior. Sorry to say it has not happened since. So, that marked the end of this amazing trip where I did not collect a single poem of "cordel" but reaped an unforgettable chapter of Brazilian literature, life and folklore. Even the last term has a northeastern story: most people mispronounced the term "folklorist" in Portuguese, saying "folquelore" – four syllables - instead of "folklore" – three syllables. I was known as one of this group, better than an agent of the CIA!

8

The final part of first research in the Northeast would be a last trip to the interior, this time by bus from Recife to João Pessoa, then the interior of Paraíba State through Guarabira and Sapé to the dry cotton fields of Rio Grande do Norte State where I would pick up more story-poems in Natal and meet and experience mentoring from the most famous of all Brazilian folklorists – Luís da Câmara Cascudo, a pioneering scholar on the "cordel" as well. Along the way, I would run into the most threatening leftist story-poem I would ever see in the "cordel" – prime material for Iverson and the INR-WHA. The trip would end with an unexpected encounter with John F. Kennedy's "Alliance for Progress" and another move from the Left in Brazil.

The bus trip turned out to match and even go beyond the "travessia" or "crossing" from Recife to Juazeiro do Norte the previous month. I started early with a comfortable bus (not the straight backed "school bus" to Juazeiro) so there were high hopes. By now the two hours to João Pessoa paralleling the Atlantic were "old hat" on good pavement with nothing but sugar cane on the horizon. Then it turned "folkloric." We switched buses to a "pinga-pinga" school bus type heading west from the Paraíba capital; the pavement vanished and once again was a rut filled, potholed muddy road to Guarabira about three hours' northwest of João Pessoa. Guarabira that September was incredibly hot and dry, dust permeating the air as our bus plodded along that country "highway." Just as dusty was the main plaza in town with a two - hour lunch stop, time enough for me to rush via taxi to the important "cordel" printing shop known as the "Folhetaria Pontes" still doing high quality story-poems by local authors as well as important "cordel" poets in the markets of Rio and São Paulo.

In that dusty market, I saw what Iverson had been getting at and why he wanted me to be involved at the INR. Amongst dozens of story-poems displayed on a suitcase by a "cordel" poet, there was one called "Letter to Mr. Kennedy" ["Carta a Míster Kennedy"]. The "folheto" jumped out at me because of the title but also the cover: it was a line sketch – a caricature – of President John F. Kennedy, impossible to mistake in that year of 1966 since his image was world renowned. He was dressed in a tall ten-gallon cowboy hat, chaps, a big six-gun strapped to his waist and tall cowboy boots, the image many Brazilians had of a "western cowboy in charge in Washington, D.C." In front of him was a short, poorly dressed northeastern country bumpkin with the long hoe of a sharecropper in one hand and a letter in another.

Anyone familiar with real "cordel" knew right away this was something different, not really "legitimate" because there was no precedent for any of it in traditional "cordel." Once I opened the story-poem and read just a few verses the whole thing became evident: it was a virulent attack on capitalism and the international imperialism of the United States, the role of the Kennedy regime and its failure in Cuba (the Bay of Pigs fiasco leading to Fidel's ultimate turn to the USSR, Krushchev and Marxism as a solution in Cuba), and U.S. involvement in Viet Nam. The poem sang the praises of Castro and spoke of the capitalist-socialist battle going on at the current time in several countries in Latin America. In ended with the verses in capital letters (a stylistic technique never used in "cordel"): LIBERTY? PROGRESS? ONLY AFTER WE EXPULSE YOU! This was a poem written by a "pseudo-popular poet," that is, a poet writing story-poems in the "cordel" format but as paid, political propaganda. The "folheto" was indeed propaganda from the Left, but the format was intended to give the appearance of a "legitimate" "cordel" poem in the markets. As I would come to realize later after more experience with all this, the paid political poem was a normal thing in "cordel," both from the Left and the Right. In 1966, it was a daring story-poem — a "dangerous plate" in the words of one of the legitimate poets of "cordel," a theme in his mind not to be touched upon without danger to the traditional, non-political "cordel" poet. This one was done evidently by "politicians" and intended to be sold in the fair and the markets and heard and read by the peasants. It was just one of the many tactics of Francisco Julião's Leftist Peasant Revolt. I would only run into similar stuff a few times, but along with the Left's "Movimento Educacional de Base" [The Educational Base Movement] to make literate the poor peasants so they could vote (supporting the Left and Julião), these were the items the Brazilian Military, the DOPS, and Right-Wing Brazil were searching out to squelch any opposition to them. I would write of it in detail to Iverson on the return to Recife; it proved that all this was no "fairy tale" I was living in Brazil. There would be more cases to come, and many from the Right, but this was my "baptism" to the reality of the battle for the minds of the peasants of the Northeast.

It recalled other things going on in Recife during those months that I have not thought of saying: a general commentary on the political and economic times. In the 1960s, it was general knowledge in the Northeast that all North Americans were rich simply due to the fact they were from the land of Uncle Sam ["Tio Sam"]. Although my research grant paid for normal expenses, and this with much care, I had no other funds. In those days of the mid - 1960s there were large second-hand book stores in Recife but also in the South; they enabled me to buy many of the "classics" on "cordel" and Brazilian Literature I would mail back to the U.S. and form the basis of a future professor's library. These bookstores however had bigger fish to fry: they had contracts with several large universities and libraries in the U.S. receiving what amounted to a "blank check" for the books they would amass to satisfy the voracious appetite of the "gringos." The practice would eventually be outlawed nationally, those in the know protesting the fact that entire libraries of Brazilian bibliophiles were sold off and transported to the U.S., a true example of cultural imperialism. Unwittingly I got caught in the web of this phenomenon and reality and could have come to a bad end indeed if circumstances had turned out differently.

A few days before this trip, knowing of rich Americans and my presence in Recife, and that I was American, I was invited to go to João Pessoa to see the formidable collection of "cordel" of a local journalist, the invitation coming from the journalist's widow. So, with the quantity of $50 USD in my pocket, all I had available at the time, I caught the bus and went to see the collection which turned out to be of high quality. Like the Lins do Rego black molasses with manioc flour that would come later, the good lady offered me one of the "delicacies" of the region – a huge bowl of "gerimum" (like pumpkin) in warm milk. I've already commented on the delicate stomach of this "gringo," but in this case if I wanted to see the collection and not offend my hostess, it was "down the hatch" with it all. I could only think of the famous short story by Monteiro Lobato, "The Indiscrete Liver ["O Fígado Indiscreto"], the story of a tongue-tied, innocent young man who could not stand even the sight of liver but had to eat and eat a lot of it when he had been invited to dinner at his fiancée's house. It is a hilarious story I recommend. I finished the bowl of "gerimum" and looked at the collection. I ended up choosing some thirty titles for all the dollars I had (the lady wanted "One million cruzeiros" or 500 dollars for the complete collection). Keep in mind an 8-page story-poem in the market in Recife cost about 5 cents U.S. I heard years later that "An American" had taken the best of the collection, "robbing" the widow. I can only say in my defense that the story-poems were few, and in my mind, I was not taking advantage of the kind lady. I spent every cent I had! It did not end there. Back in the Chácara boarding house in Recife days later I got a letter, no sender address, special delivery, that in effect said, "You thieving gringo son of a bitch, if you ever set foot near Mrs. Gomes' house again there won't be enough left of you for the buzzards." That precluded any idea I had of returning, returning the few "folhetos" to her and getting the hell out of Dodge. I've thought of it all many times since, but my conscience is clear and it's just one more case of the "naïve" gringo. "Living is very dangerous," said the master Guimarães Rosa in "The Devil to Pay in the Backlands."

The road from Guarabira, Paraíba, to my destination, the city of Natal, turned out to be a trip of four hours on the worst road I had experienced up to that time in Brazil, including the trip to Juazeiro do Norte, already described, a trip as the locals say of "pure folklore." We forded initially several small streams, and the driver would stop along the road, interrupting the trip, to converse with, I suppose, old and new friends and flirt with the girls walking along the road. Upon entering Rio Grande do Norte State the terrain became extremely dry with many poor plantations of cotton; this was in direct contrast to the green of the coastal areas of Pernambuco and Paraíba, the lands of sugar cane. We finally rolled into Natal at breakneck speed over the old cobblestones once you got inside the city limits, and on my limited budget I settled into a local "hotel" near the bus station.

The hotel merits a telling. It was like a hundred others in the Northeast, the most modest of lodgings for the poor able to travel by bus in the region, thus its proximity to the bus station. "Cordel" poets might pick such a place when in town for the market. The place had a painted sign in front, scarcely a sidewalk between it and the busy city street, a tiny ground floor room serving as registration with a surly clerk who looked at my Xeroxed passport (notwithstanding the warning from the police in Recife), took my 10,000 cruzeiro bank note ($5 USD), gave me a huge skeleton key and said, "You're up on the second floor, number 202." The "lobby" had a plastic covered divan and there were two straight back wooden chairs across from it on a bare concrete floor. The room was about the same: tiny, a narrow bed, one short threadbare bedsheet and pillow, a wooden chair and a couple of hooks on the wall for your clothes. The "community" bathroom with a single stool, one sink with a single cold-water faucet, and a 2X2 shower with a single spigot (no hot water, we were in the tropics) topped off the place. The main attraction was yet to come that night after I piled into bed exhausted from the bus trip.

After a couple of those large Brahma Beers in the corner bar outside the hotel, I collapsed into bed, exhausted from the bus trip, but soon enough got the urge to go down the hallway to the community bathroom. I awoke to a slight buzzing sound and wondered what in the hell that was (there was deafening noise from the outside main street and the buses). The room had a small corner lamp and that was all, so I depended upon one of those small boxes of wooden matches used for lighting cigarettes for light in the room. Soon enough the matches gave me a huge lesson in Brazilian entomology (My Mom back in Nebraska always told me: there are only two real professions for a farm boy like you Mike – learning to be an auctioneer at the local cattle auctions or study bugs and how to get rid of them.) The floor and walls were covered with an array or you might say an entomologist's delight of every kind of bug and cockroach I had ever seen. I managed to put on my tennis shoes, after shaking them out, go take the piss and crunch my way back to the bed. Strangely enough, I still managed to get a few hours' sleep despite all manner of disruption – the lights coming in from the street through the gauze curtain, the infernal noise of the buses arriving and yeah, wondering if this was going to be a Brazilian reenactment of one of my old nightmares from U.S. horror movies – the "Thing" or "The Fly."

After a "cafezinho" and sweet roll in a tiny hole-in-the-wall café near the hotel the next morning, the first order of business was to get directions to the poetry-printing shop of one Mr. Mário Brito in the district of Alecrim in the city. The basic way you did "cordel" fieldwork in those days was to check the back cover of one of the story-poems from the region you were headed to (most purchased at the market in Recife), and oftentimes it would offer the name and address and a small list of publications of that poet or printer. Not knowing for sure if the guy was still alive, I caught a local bus to Alecrim, a proletarian district in town. I was now getting used to wild goose chases to such places; the poets did not quite use the classified sections of the local papers!

I found the place and the man who had an enormous stock of poems from authors of Rio Grande do Norte and many from Ceará, the latter I had mostly purchased in Juazeiro do Norte. The problem was he kept the entire stock in a damp, dark basement. It was truly hard to believe, but the basement floor seemed literally "paved" with story-poems of "cordel," all severely damaged by mold. Mr. Brito, an "agent" of "cordel" for years, dating back to the Golden Age of João Martins de Atayde in Recife from the 1920s to the 1950s, was now in his 80s and was nearly blind with cataracts in his eyes. I estimate I purchased some 70 titles and emphasize again that most were nearly beyond use, moldy from that storage area.

The highlight of Natal, and perhaps of the entire first research stage in Brazil's Northeast was my encounter with Luís da Câmara Cascudo, the master of Northeastern Folklore. This is yet another "chapter" of Brazilian culture interesting to the <u>Times'</u> readers for no other reason than it highlights an important part of the country that you don't get in the newspapers in Rio or São Paulo or national TV, but is essential to a broad cultural view of the country – this is what Hansen wanted!

Luís da Câmara Cascudo was a major figure in Brazilian culture in the 1960s; he exemplified a very Brazilian concept: "The intellectual from the provinces." Just as Spain still claimed to be a large country of "patrias chicas," so Brazil was (and is) a huge country of several large geographic and cultural regions. Cascudo, formed in History in the "insignificant" northeastern state of Rio Grande do Norte, came to be the best folklorist in a country with a lot of folklore; he wrote more than 100 treatises on the subject and among them seminal works on the "literatura de cordel." My introduction to him were the lectures at the Joaquim Nabuco Institute of Socal Sciences in Recife early in those Brazilian "winter" months of 1966, and my trip to Natal had as its major purpose to spend time with him. The encounter went far beyond my expectations!

On the afternoon of the second day in Natal I grabbed a city bus outside the hotel and took it up the long, steep avenue to Cascudo's home (I had written him from Recife asking for an appointment). It marked a great moment in my young life as a researcher in Brazil. I arrived at the house, knocked on the door, explained who I was and received entry directly into his airy office-library. Professor Cascudo was in his 70s; he was extremely hard of hearing with a full shock of grey hair and thick eyebrows, but a person full of energy and enthusiasm. I noticed the large plaque on the door to his incredible office-library: "In Honor of Service to the Historical Society of Rio Grande do Norte, to the State and to the Nation!" He was dressed in a short-sleeved shirt and had the famous unlit cigar in his hand. With light colored eyes with a penetrating look, a pursing of his lips before accenting a word or an idea, his pronunciation marked the clearest and sharpest Portuguese that I had heard in Brazil! Perhaps from the custom of being a professor and lecturing so much over the years, he had the habit of conversing while standing on his feet, taking small steps to the right, back to the left, raising a hand in the air, the forefinger pointing upward, this to emphasize a point, and touching me occasionally on the shoulder to make a point! He gave me great lessons in a short space of time!

Luís da Câmara Cascudo spoke of the great and absolute necessity of fieldwork for the folklorist and his scorn for the "office researcher" who consults a book or two before writing his theses. He praised the fieldwork I had done thus far in Brazil. Discussing the topic of the dissertation, the poets of "cordel" and the singer-poets ["cantadores"] of the fairs, he spoke of personal experience with famous "cantadores" of the Northeast, of the old-timers who still improvised in four-line strophes ["quadras" or "versos de quarto pés"]. He spoke of Fábio das Queixadas, a slave who won his freedom through the "cantoria," and of other poets he had met while growing up and maturing in Rio Grande do Norte State. He spoke of the old Arabic viol ["a rabeca"] the singer-poet used for accompaniment, this before the singer-poets began to use the five course-ten stringed "viola" in the 1960s. The "rabeca," according to Cascudo, comes from the true troubadour tradition, from Provence of old France. He told of his contact and personal friendship with the great Leandro Gomes de Barros, the most famous of the poets of the old "literatura de cordel" at the beginning of the twentieth century. I was planning that a chapter of my future dissertation would treat the poet. For Cascudo, Leandro from the era of 1914 was the greatest of the troubadours of the Northeast!

He spoke of the changes in popular poetry, from the "cantoria" or "peleja" of the old poets to the "cantadores" of the mid-1960s, dividing them chronologically into two categories: before 1910-1915 and after. He criticized the studies that do not make such a division, noting an enormous difference between the modern "cantador" who does his "performance" on television or the radio in Rio and the original "cantador" who never left the region. He cited as an example the case of Inácio da Catingueira, an illiterate slave but a great improviser of verse.

Cascudo spoke of his books, old and new, and about the Northeastern "vaqueijada" ["rodeo"]. We talked of my origin in Nebraska, of the ranches, cowboys and rodeos, and even of the cattle drives of the Longhorns from Texas to Abilene, Kansas, and then on to Nebraska. We compared, at his request, the "vaqueijada" with the Mexican or the North American rodeo. He was trying to understand "bull dogging," the event in the North American rodeo when two cowboys, each with a strong horse, place themselves respectively on either side of the steer in the wooden chute. Steer, horses and cowboys flash outside the chute to start the event. The cowboy on the left leaps from the back of his horse onto the back of the running steer, grabbing the horns, and tries to turn its head and wrestle the steer to the ground. Note this involves a steer, not the full - grown bull. In exchange for my help on this matter the master promised to mail me the "vaqueijada" study as soon as it came out, this plus an honorary diploma of the Society of Northeastern Folklore. He was as good as his word!

I'm going on, but I've got to put all this in perspective; it's not small potatoes. Cascudo's library left me astonished and with a bit of envy. The book shelves were surrounded by art and ceramics of the region, and especially work from Africa where the master had been doing research for years. Also worth mentioning was the huge, life-size wood carving of a northeastern bandit on his door, an important theme in the "cordel."

He was in the gradual process of aging: his deafness, his poor eyesight and never traveling from Natal. Cascudo for me was not only a true master, but a great hero, a man who had nothing to gain from spending so much time with a young student he had never met before. A model of a professor!

After this, I was indeed ready to leave Natal, but with a little time on my hands the next morning before the time for the bus to head back to Recife, a seemingly small event jolted my mind back to political reality. I took a walk down by the docks of Natal and was astonished by the number of large Caterpillar Tractors and heavy road working machines I saw on the docks. There were large cranes to load and unload the large transatlantic cargo ships that came to the port. The cranes were huge, on tracks like railroad cars, thus ready for the great ships docked alongside. And there were many dock workers reminding me of the description of Jorge Amado of the black stevedores in Bahia in "Jubiabá." There were warehouses full of sacks of manioc meal and huge bags of salt, all ready to leave port. The salt industry was in fact "infamous" in Rio Grande do

Norte due to the horrible working conditions of the salt gatherers who "slaved" on the salt flats near the port.

I ran into a red faced, pardon me, red neck tractor operator of heavy equipment on the dock, a U.S. construction guy, he seemingly hanging around, me just a tourist, and we had quite a conversation. He had spent the entire previous year in Natal as an operator of the huge Caterpillar tractors. He was a specialist in road construction and was working on a project funded by the famous Alliance for Progress of the Kennedy regime of the U.S., but he told a sad story.

He said there were in port many huge tractors meant for road construction on roads in the entire Northeast. Each tractor in those days cost approximately U.S. 35,000 dollars. One could add to this initial cost the phenomenal expense of transporting the vehicles from the U.S. to Brazil. Due to bureaucracy and its paperwork, at that time it took seven months between ordering, shipping and the arrival of the tractor in Brazil. Worse yet, the due "permission" to unload the tractors from the ships had not been issued. In Brazilian bureaucratic parlance, "They had not been liberated." The operator had not been able to figure out the conundrum of "the permission slip." From whom? By whom? He could give me no answers; it was all a mystery to him. He surmised the problem have might have been the actual payment of transportation costs. So, these beautiful tractors remained exposed to the tropical sun, the salt, and the sea air and were in effect rusting in the port. One huge tractor was in effect ready to go, but was awaiting the windscreen. Each state in the Northeast should have received a total of nine tractors. One can only imagine the frustration of the operator waiting each new day for the permission to go through, thus "liberating" the tractors but also himself! It all remained as an anecdote of the Alliance for Progress and the efforts of economic development for Brazil in the era.

Except for one thing. As I was leaving the dock area, headed back up to the bus and that dismal bus station and return to Recife, once again an officer from the military police stopped me. He said, "You are Gaherty, right? Come this way with me."

"Oh crap, not again, I was just doing some tourism in Natal before heading "home" to Recife."

The police wanted to know what was I doing wandering around down by the docks. "Hey," I said, "I'm a folklorist, I want to see the stuff the tourists don't see. I'm a fan of Jorge Amado, I've read "Jubiabá" and scenes of the stevedores loading the international cargo ships. This stuff is interesting to people like me. And I'm sending LETTERS to the New York Times at their request for the topics."

He said, "That very well may be, Mr. Gringo and Folklorist, but this is serious shit! There's a good reason the Alliance for Progress equipment has not been landed, approved to unload and on to its projects. It's the Left! Those bastards still have a hand in the bureaucracy and paper work of the ports and operations here in Rio Grande do Norte. Who in the hell do you think might want to stop all road construction in the Northeast, stop any positive help from the U.S. and hinder the Revolution's moves against the Communists? I suggest you move it right along, get on your bus to Recife and forget any conversations you had with that redneck comrade of yours! Stick to those folk poets who you say are so important, but sure as hell not to us."

9

What do do? You can't fight city hall and this crowd was the rough side of that. No sense going against the grain on this deal. I walked back to the bus station and got on the "pinga-pinga" back to Recife. After a few days, I would do one last jaunt to the interior, this time the long road south to Alagoas State and Maceió its capital, the purpose to talk to a well- known "cordel" poet. He was out of town but through a connection from the Georgetown Portuguese professor once again, I received lodging in the modest hotel Varig Airline used and a tour of the town. I saw the fresh water lake, had some tasty local shrimp and was on my way "home" to Recife. Once again there was an abundance of fertile soil and the great plantations of sugar cane almost from one capital city to the other. We woke up at 4:00 a.m. for the long bus ride back to Recife, arriving that night, and not being able to sleep, it indeed was a lesson by bus. It seemed the richest land that I had seen in the Northeast, right or wrong (there is serious competition in such matters by the respective neighboring states). There were fields of cane on the entire route from the northern part of Alagoas to Recife. The cane was in its final stage, the season of cutting and grinding. It was three or four meters tall and field workers were cutting it by hand, leaving the leaves on the ground and stacking the stalks of cane together. They were piled in stacks in the field which were later picked up by hand, put on the backs of burros and taken to the roadside where they were tossed into big trucks to be taken to the refinery for processing. I saw in the distance the tiny "Maria Fumaças" ["Smokey Marias"], the small steam trains working in the area, incredibly picturesque for the gringo, recalling compositions of the same name by the great Brazilian classical composer, Heitor Villa Lobos.

The land seemed to me to be incredibly fertile, rich and well-watered, but also covered with small hills, something I did not expect in the coastal zone. I saw all the phases of harvest, and from the bus to boot! Harvesting and preparing the soil for the new planting. It seemed the greater part of the work was being done by hand, men and women in the fields.

So, it was that at this point, the end of October 1966, I finished the initial phase of research, having done all that I could in the collection of primary material, buying a good and in part impressive stock of "romances" and "folhetos de cordel," reading the basic academic works for the study of the same, meeting, interviewing and documenting visits with important poets and publishers, and immersing myself in northeastern life.

Finally, important for this last large LETTER to Hansen and the <u>Times</u> would be the social scene of those last weeks in Recife. In those final days of June to the end of October there was much day-to-day reading but a lot of partying (Americans wanted to know about Brazil and the beach scene in Carnival, that was to come, but this was indicative of the times). The northeastern college kids had "basement parties" ["festa de porão"] and "serenatas" on the beach in the evening at Boa Viagem, and I got my share of flirting and dating northeastern girls. In particular there was one very pretty, quiet girl from the interior just outside of Recife and we "sparked" some. It was my fault the friendship went no farther, partly out of laziness one Sunday when I failed to meet her and her family for Sunday dinner, instead taking the easy way out and just going to the beach. It turned out the family had really put on the dog and the bastard gringo never showed up. She confronted me with it later and yours truly felt like and got what he deserved – feeling like a real shithead. I apologized but words are cheap. We Gahertys were not raised to act like assholes and I just did.

On a happier note, on two occasions in those days I managed to sing and play electric guitar, songs principally from the pioneer Rock in the U.S.: songs of Bill Haley and the Comets, from Elvis Presley, "That'll Be the Day" and "Peggy Sue" from Buddy Holly, stuff all prior to the Beatles. I played first at a night club in Campina Grande, Paraíba and then at the "Veleiro" nightclub in Boa Viagem. It was interesting to see the role of gossip, the spreading of the news of the nightclub in an interior city in the 1960s, of the comments ("Did you hear about the 'gringo' who put on a show in the nightclub last night in town?") Not to speak disparagingly of Campina Grande, but it was no big deal. The fact one guy pulled a gun on all of us outside the nightclub could have turned out worse; he made his point as a tough guy and put it away. My singing was not the main show – the records played featured the predominant singer in Brazil at the time - the great Roberto Carlos and the "iê-iê-iê," particularly his song "I Want Everyone To Go To Hell" ["Quero que todo mundo vá p'ra o inferno"], a song the poets of "cordel" went crazy over, creating letters to the devil, letters from the devil and many discussions about Roberto Carlos and the devil, an important protagonist of "cordel."

In the end I think I became "a little bit Brazilian" during the months spent at the Chácara das Rosas and with the good buddies who were also had a bit of "northeastern rogue" ["malandro"] in them. The friendships made with them, with adults, parents of close friends, with the one girl friend I already mentioned and with the people involved in folklore and "cordel" would become an important part of this narrative and the LETTERS to Hansen. Friend and Fulbright buddy Steve Baldini who was also a part of the Bar Acadêmico crowd would enter my story in a more significant way later.

There were really two goodbye parties: Part I was with the buddies at the "Chácara," a night of icy cold Brahma and Antarctica beers in the liter bottles, smoking Hollywood Cigarettes and lots of jokes. There was a part II the next morning when the same buddies from the Chácara gave me a goodbye party at the Bar Acadêmico including two glasses (those buttermilk glasses) of conhac they insisted I get down ("Hey, can the American drink like us?"). A bleary ride to the airport capped it all off.

The next plan for research was to travel to and become familiar with the great and old city of Bahia de Todos os Santos, to get to know the world of the writer Jorge Amado and finally to get to see what was going on in "cordel" in the region. In the latter sense I ran into a bit of prejudice in those days: the Pernambucans and Paraíbans would not admit to any "good" "cordel" coming out of Bahia. I was not so sure; research up to that point led me to believe the notion was incorrect. Bahia was one of the "hottest" markets for 'literatura de cordel" in the 1940s, 1950s and 1960s with several poets living in Salvador, among them two of the most important of modern "cordel;" the conservative Rodolfo Coelho Cavalcante of whom I shall speak later, and his competitor, the folk-popular "hell's mouth" [my term] Cuíca de Santo Amaro, a bad poet but a fantastic "reporter" in "cordel." There were other poets of renown in the period of the famous transportation strike in the 1930s (I would cross paths with both Right and Left in the coming weeks and have to explain a few things to the DOPS), among them Permínio Válter Lírio. The strike was a major theme in Amado's "Jubiabá" which dealt with poor stevedores, the labor unions and Communist unrest in the 1930s. The Bahian "cordel" seemed to have a more political tone than other areas of the Northeast. And of course, there were stories about Bom Jesus da Lapa, to come in these LETTERS. After Bahia, the research plan would be to acquire and read the "cordel" of the migrants to the south-southeast of the country, the famous "parrot cagers" ["pau de arara"] of Rio de Janeiro and São Paulo.

I sent this LETTER, minus the dealings with the police in Pernambuco, to Hansen just a day or two after arriving at my next stop, Salvador, Bahia de Todos os Santos.

LETTER III

SALVADOR DA BAHIA
AND JORGE AMADO

1

November and December 1966. The plan was to spend two months in Salvador and surroundings checking out the situation of the "literatura de cordel" with its half-dozen poets and printers, but as it turned out, in truth, "cordel" would have to wait. There were other priorities, among them, principally, that of getting to know this, the most "African" part of Brazil. The city of Salvador da Bahia de Todos os Santos was the scene of the novels of Jorge Amado, the Brazilian writer best known at that time outside of Brazil, and one of my favorites. I say this despite the controversy in academia dealing with erudite literature and Jorge Amado with his "populist" and "commercialized" novels (This attitude was "bull shit" to those in the know. Just try to write "Gabriela!" or "Dona Flor" or "The Miracle Shop"!). There was a "war" between Amado and the literary critics who gave him hell throughout his incredibly successful run as a novelist. The first thing I did was purchase the book-guide to the city of Salvador by the same Jorge Amado, "Bahia de Todos os Santos," read it from cover to cover and tried to see and familiarize myself with all that Amado told in the book, with an original printing of 1944. What I wanted to capture, once again as a reader with a romantic sensibility, was "the magical night of Bahia, city of mysteries." I did find the mystery or what it could be for me. I walked day and night investigating in my forays about the city, including having good times including taking in "candomblé" and "capoeira." I also found the mystery in the great baroque churches like São Francisco and the Third Order Church, Santa Bárbara of the famous "Payer of Promises" play and movie and African Syncretism at the Igreja do Bomfim; an Irish-American Catholic could do no less.

The city impressed me right away as possessing the most beautiful natural scenery I had seen to that point in Brazil, even in comparison to Rio de Janeiro and the Bay of Guanabara. The road from the airport to the city center followed the beaches - the beach of Itapuã, the district of Amaralina, Ondina and then Barra Beach. Then the road climbed up the hill on Avenue 7th of September, passing through Vitória, Campo Grande and Piedade, finally arriving at the "old upper city" with the main plaza [A Praça Municipal]. Beyond, one saw the Church of São Francisco, the Church of the Third Order and then the old slave block, O Pelourinho. The view looking out on the bay from the upper city from the Lacerda Elevator, the old fort with its arm to the sea, the passenger boats of the old Bahiana Line, the lower city with its famous Modelo Market to the side of the Praça Cayrú and the dock of the small sailing boats ["os saveiros"] was a chapter directly from the novels of Amado. Once again, as in the case of José Lins do Rego and the sugar plantations of Paraíba, it all seemed familiar from my readings in the United States. And in the distance, across the Bay of Bahia of All the Saints, was the Island of Itaparica, as the Rotarians say, "a post card" of Brazil.

Fittingly, seeing the sun set on Barra Beach completed my first impression of what Jorge Amado had described so many times in his novels, this, in his words, the most mysterious, poetic and African of all Brazilian cities. The upper city with the Lacerda Elevator and the old government buildings in the upper city main plaza were all impressive, but more so were the people themselves. In the 1960s, you could still see men in white, linen suits (the British capitalists – railway builders' contribution to the Northeast from the 19th century on), beautiful and elegant ladies dressed in white, huge bellowing skirts, blouses and "turbans," and necklaces and bracelets, the same clothing to be seen in the rituals of Candomblé or even Xangô in Recife. The same ladies sold regional foods on the street corners, in front of the Lacerda Elevator and in the lower city in front of the Modelo Market. What did shock the gringo from Nebraska was the fact that the population was black in the majority, something I soon grew accustomed to. There was one occasion late at night when I rode a crowded bus to my destination, and I was the only white person on board.

I had arrived in the city of folk festivals in the "festival season," beginning with that of Conceição da Praia. I crisscrossed the city, seeing all through the lens and perspective that Jorge Amado placed in his guide-book in the 1940s. I saw the "rampa do mercado" [the dock] with the fishing-cargo boats ["os saveiros"], the cast of characters populating Amado's "Dead Sea" [Mar Morto], and the fair at the dock, the fish market, and the great Modelo Market. I also saw the fair of "Água dos Meninos," recalling Corporal Martim in "The Death and the Death of Quincas Water Yell" [A Morte e a Morte de Quincas Berro D'Água"], always searching for that "Bahia de Jorge."

The first days in Bahia were spent in a modest hotel on the hill of Avenida 7, the Hotel Caramuru, lodging in those days for North Americans with a modest budget. Peace Corps Volunteers from the city or the interior would do their R and R here near the sea. On one of such nights over "caipirinhas" in the hotel bar one volunteer told me one of the best stories of the entire time in Brazil and one I could relate to from Pernambuco days, a great vignette of northeastern Brazilian culture. Here's the "aside:"

If you spent any length of time in Brazil's Northeast in those days you soon came to know and feel the difference in the concept of space between the U.S. and the locals. Basically, when the northeasterners talk to each other, and this includes all classes, they get close; I can't speak so much for the women, but one then gets into the business of the "air kisses" on one or both cheeks and how many and when. I do know that men greeted close female friends in the same way. This is where the "naïve" north American did not adapt so well. I got into the "formal" embraces but not the kisses and never did figure out the "proper" routine. Conversation with buddies did reveal other customs: the Brazilians got right in front of you, continued perhaps a casual conversation, perhaps touching your arm or shoulder to make a point or even touching the collar of your shirt.

As far as I could tell there was no gender ramification and certainly nothing homosexual in nature. My peace corps buddy told me of all this in extreme.

He swore that in the interior of Bahia State while in a lengthy conversation with a close friend that the Brazilian unbuttoned his shirt from top to the belt and, geez, back up again by the end of the conversation!

I had no such experience but do recall that many times the Brazilians would touch my arm or shoulder and a time or two when they fiddled with my shirt collar. I leave any speculation to the experts or the reader. But it won't happen in New York or Lincoln! We tend to keep our distance.

From the modest second floor of the Caramuru Hotel there was a view of the sea, especially exotic and mysterious for me at night. I would stay there a few days until finding "permanent" lodging in another boarding house, a business run by Portuguese owners and immigrants themselves to Brazil; they would importantly add to the Brazilian experience a strong flavor from the "Metrópoli," the home country, something I'll describe in a bit.

I did a lot of partying in Bahia (man does not live by research alone), going to the Brazilian nightclubs with Brazilian and North American friends. One spot was famous, the "Tabaris," in the upper city near Avenida 7. This was one of the clubs Jorge Amado liked to talk about in his novels on Salvador (I surmise from many nights spent there as a student in his younger days, "on the lam" from the Jesuit Prep school his cacao rich parents sent him to in order to "straighten him out" from reckless days and a bad crowd in his home town of Ilhéus) the Tabaris was a combination of tavern, dance hall and place where the girls of ill repute could be found; a fun time was always had by all. There was a beery night there with friends and only later did Brazilians tell me, "Gaherty, YOU a gringo were at the Tabaris? That's Bahian history! You're lucky you got out of there alive." That was the night about 3:00 a.m. we were all shooting the breeze, sitting on the low wall of the street that winds down from the upper city to the lower, everybody pretty - well sloshed. I recall someone almost falling over the side to what would have been at least a fractured skull. In my case, Catholic beliefs and prayers to the Guardian Angel of my Irish youth weren't all a waste of time. Years later and as so often mentioned in this text I would always recall the macho bandit leader and his love in João Guimarães Rosa's "The Devil to Pay in the Backlands" and how Riobaldo called Diadorim his "anjo de guarda" ["guardian angel"].

Yet at the Caramurú Hotel, I went to my first session of Candomblé (I think it was the "terreiro" of the famous Mãe Menininha), with its chants and dances. Candomblé was considered to be the "most pure" of African rites in Brazil, a beautiful introduction to Salvador. And there was some dating of an American girl; we were both influenced by the "magical nights" of the "mysterious city" of the novels of Jorge Amado. In the beginning, there were "caipirinhas" (those powerful drinks one American called "rubber hammers") and days and evenings with no "obligation." As for Brazilian romance, there had been a wonderful Pernambuco young lady and then a beautiful friendship in Rio to come.

In the coming days, I would meet Hildegardes Vianna, director of the Department of Tourism in Salvador. Professor and writer on themes of folklore in Bahia, she would enter this story later speaking of her knowledge of "cordel" poetry in Bahia. She spoke to me of "candomblé," saying it was totally commercialized in Brazil, but with a few "secret" meeting places where one could yet see it "in its purest form." She declared that Jorge Amado was not really "a friend of the people" and that his link to "candomblé" as an "ogun" [male leader] existed mainly for publicity. Hildegardes told me that the pure "old steps" of candomblé were now mixed in with completely new dance steps, these created by influence from the cinema, and in particular American tap dancing of the 1930s! I think the lady knew some things most people did not, but it was a stretch to believe it for Gaherty the neophyte.

Save for two or three moments there were no major political encounters to report to either Hansen or Iverson, but "cordel" did reveal important data for the latter.

2

I had much more contact with North Americans in Salvador than in Recife, meeting officials from USIS (United States Information Service) the agency linked to contracts with the Alliance for Progress, and with Peace Corps Volunteers. Among the latter was a good friend who taught English at the IBEU [Instituto Brazil-Estados Unidos] in Vitória, a job that did not seem to me at first to be in the spirit of the "economic development" model or difficult living of the Peace Corps volunteers working in the northeastern interior, but as I learned later, there was more to the Peace Corps Mission. Don did provide an important service - teaching English to the middle and upper - class students at IBEU. Such people-to-people contacts would prove invaluable in fulfilling a "diplomatic" part of Peace Corps; such students with English and favorably disposed to the U.S. would become future leaders in Brazil. I learned this was part of the modus-operandi of the Peace Corps worldwide.

I also met Fulbright Scholar-Researchers (I was one of them). Some became well-known "Brazilianists" of my generation of the 1960s, still a "Golden Age" of U.S. research in Brazil. It was through one of the volunteers, Don, that I found out about the Portuguese in Brazil (and the jokes about them which I had heard in Pernambuco, and in the texts of "cordel"). My friend took me to the "Portuguesa," a boarding house where I would live the next two months in Bahia. The Portuguese owners were good folks, ambitious to a fault, fitting the stereotyped notion of the Portuguese in Brazil. The boarding house, "A Portuguesa," was divided in two parts: the "dormitory" on Avenida 7 near Piedade Praça with small but always scrupulously clean sleeping rooms, bathroom with shower and a small central room for breakfast, with a TV set to the side. (Contrast my Bahia experience to the Chácara das Rosas in Recife.)

The main noon time meal and dinner in the evening were served at the second part, the Portuguese restaurant on Barra Beach; you would go down the hill on the "Ladeira da Barra" to the plaza of the same name to a restaurant at the side of the beach. For me it was an incredible place: Barra Beach, alongside the famous Barra Light House, in those years was one of the most popular places of the city, still in vogue with many middle - class people in the neighborhood, whites and blacks, fishing boats and the most beautiful sunset in Brazil! Beautiful young girls, tourists in the nearby hotels, and best of all, the green-blue, cool but not cold, waters of the Bay of Bahia, made this a paradise for the "gringo" from Nebraska. We caught super crowded buses two times a day, sweating in the Bahian tropics, and made our way down to the Barra and the restaurant, many times swimming in the bay before the big mid-day meal. The food was excellent, a combination of Portuguese and Brazilian, always abundant and tasty (in comparison to the "cuisine" already described in the Chácara das Rosas in Recife, and of course for a very different price.) A big mid-day meal might be codfish-Portuguese style [bacalhau] with a lot of garlic, rice and beans, the beans flavored with pieces of ham. On other days, there was even filet mignon with fried potatoes, always preceded by the soup of the day, excellent French bread, fruit salad for dessert, and a wonderful demitasse coffee [cafezinho]. There was also another local custom for the Portuguese and others: a large mug [caneca] of red wine from Portugal or icy cold Brazilian beer. My mouth waters recalling this! I quickly regained the kilo or so I lost in Recife with the meager diet of the preceding months and those sometimes - difficult trips to the interior of the Northeast.

Just as in Recife, there were "characters" in the Portuguese boarding house - the Portuguese gentleman, a salesman of Barsa Encyclopedias, who also gave English classes "even to the wife of the governor." I confess that when he spoke to me in English, I understood almost nothing. Brazilian students in Recife and Bahia complained about the same thing - teachers whose English was from another planet. There were "granfinos" or "suits," politicians and administrators from the federal government in Brasília (or so I thought) on duty in Bahia, men who wore dark suits, coats and ties in that Bahian heat. One became a good friend and made a point of introducing me to his idea of "Bahian night life." The main clients of the boarding house restaurant were the Portuguese themselves; it was difficult to know the exact relationship between them and the owners. These were young men, bachelors, recently arrived from the shores of Portugal to "make a new life and living" in Brazil, businessmen dealing with textiles in the Lower City, one of them eventually marrying the marriageable daughter ["filha casadeira"], granddaughter of the owners.

The person in charge was a round, good humored lady, but with a hand of steel in the kitchen, Dona Carmina. She was always kidding with us, Don and I the gringos, happy as long as we paid our rent on time. I recall so well the dinner hour which was filled with noise, lots of laughter, and lots of conversation. Good times. These were the times to hear that Portuguese accent from the continent without having to travel a couple of thousand miles to the other side of the sea to Lisbon to hear it. The boarding house closed one month each year when the owners went on vacation to the old country, Portugal. In the "Portuguesa" I heard "barbaridades" and strong words of prejudice against the Brazilians, especially the blacks of Bahia. An aside: I recall well the conversations with a North American Peace Corps Volunteer during my stay in Bahia, a black man, and his stories of racial prejudice in Bahia. Always, always in the Brazil of those years, we, the North Americans, were accused of being racists, and with some reason due to our history. But in Bahia, I discovered a Brazil far from free of the same prejudice, not only of race but of region. The "literatura de cordel" is replete with such notions in the stories when the northeasterner migrates to the South and must confront not only a new and difficult economic life, but terrific prejudice as well.

3

The prejudice also had to do with the public perception of the "literatura de cordel;" it was deemed a literature of little value in the "Aurelião;" Aurélio Buarque de Holanda was the author of this major Brazilian dictionary of Portuguese of the times (in my opinion, unfortunate, since he was the uncle of my favorite Brazilian singer, Chico Buarque de Holanda). Within that world of "cordel" Bahia was held in even lesser esteem than the bards of Pernambuco or Paraíba. Recalling the priorities of this first stay in Bahia, as to "literatura de cordel," I found little, even then, the texts and value of the "cordel" would be of great interest to Hansen of the <u>Times</u> but even more for Iverson of the INR.

The famous personage of "cordel" in the city in the 1940s, 1950s and beginning of the 1960s, Cuíca de Santo Amaro, the "Hell's Mouth" of popular literature in the era, died in 1964 just two years before my stay in Bahia. The coincidence, and it was only that, of his death the same year as the military revolution in 1964 and the threat of the "Peasant Leagues" by Francisco Julião in Pernambuco at the same time were related. Cuíca prided himself on being the "reporter of the masses," a popular poetry-journalistic gadfly unafraid to ferret out the most scurrilous political and social scandal of the days from the 1940s to 1964. He would become aligned with the workers' party of the dictator Getúlio Vargas, the "Father of the Poor" in Brazilian politics in the early 1960s. It's a long story, but Cuíca chronicled in minute detail major daily events in the society of Salvador, crime, local politics and even national politics (he claimed to be a "personal" friend of Vargas and to be "protected" by him). In 1966, I never ran across any story-poems by Cuíca directly related to the Peasants' Leagues, but there was an abundance of accounts praising Vargas, the workers' party and ferocious attacks on the conservatives headed by Carlos Lacerda who would eventually help to create the atmosphere that led to Getúlio's unheard of suicide in 1954 and then ally themselves with the military.

Another fine poet, the "Apostolic Troubador" Minelvino Francisco Silva, lived some distance away from Salvador, in Itabuna in the southern part of the state. He was important but was never active in commentary on politics.

Such was not the case of the most important poet of "cordel" in Salvador from the 1940s to the mid – 1960s. When I arrived in the city in 1966 Rodolfo Coelho Cavalcante was not in Bahia at the time, but "exiled" in poverty in the town of Jequié in the Bahia interior where he had a modest home. I contacted Rodolfo later via the mail and it was the beginning of a long correspondence, friendship, reading and future research. Rodolfo was a person who would make an impact on my life. He was extremely important to the INR and Iverson because a significant amount of his story-poems over the years and decades were from the Right; he was a staunch defender of the current military regime and the dictatorship and a defender of Brazilian democracy dating from the 1940s by his anti-Fascist, anti-Germany, anti-Nazi poems written on the streets of the tiny backlands capital of Teresina, Piaui.

More important was Rodolfo's anti-communism. The story is worth telling for this LETTER. As I mentioned when talking of that virulent anti-Kennedy poem found in the market in Paraíba, there was and still is a tradition of the "paid political poem" in "cordel," but from an apolitical stance. The poets, poor, barely able to come up with the funds to print their story-poems in the local typography, had a tradition of writing a poem for a local political candidate, from the Left or Right, for very small amounts of money. Rodolfo was approached when he still lived in Maceió, Alagoas, by the people of the local Communist candidate for a local office to write a political story-poem in favor of the candidate. Being inclined to Democracy and aware of the history of Leninism and Stalinism in the Soviet Union, Rodolfo refused the "offer" and was later attacked by thugs in the payroll of the candidate, beaten, tied up and tossed into a canal to drown. The poet somehow got loose from his bonds and survived, so it is no surprise he became the most virulent anti-communist poet of "cordel" of all times and thus a principal supporter of the "Redeemer" Revolution of 1964 and the Generals. There was more, and more closely tied to the traditions of "cordel," a Catholic, conservative phenomenon for at least its first 60 years: Rodolfo was in lock-step with the military in the "moral cleansing" they espoused for Brazil and thus ranted and raved about the new morality of the 1960s, the long-hairs and hippies and fans of the Beatles, in short of social change. His story-poems were a sociological gold mine for such views and important, at least in a minor way, of seeing what the poor masses believed from the right. And theirs was by far the majority view. I would be questioned by the DOPS once again, now in Rio de Janeiro, for my knowledge of all these story-poems as humble as they were. All this was really discovered and came to light in later months in Rio.

In that hot November and December in Salvador I found only one printing shop dealing with "cordel," that of Waldemar Santos in the Pelourinho District, still printing "cordel" story-poems in 1966. In a subsequent trip to the interior to the great fair of Feira de Santana, I encountered another poet who made a living with humorous poems of sexual innuendo - Erotildes Miranda dos Santos. Therefore, the months in Bahia were spent, as I said, with another priority - that of really getting to know the city and absorb its culture through the reading of the novels of Jorge Amado that I had not already read, and especially his book-guide, seeing both the "good" places and the morally "doubtful" places indicated by the master.

One of the latter was one of the "castelos" or houses of ill repute on a scruffy third floor of one of the old colonial mansions on the road from the upper to lower city. I was accompanied by, or rather I went with, that Brasília bureaucrat from the Portuguese boading house who said I needed to get out more and see some "highlights" of Bahia. It was not exactly like the idealized, fun scenes I had read about in Jorge Amado's novels; in them the houses of prostitution are more like nightclubs with an international cast of girls from all over Latin America, many from exotic Buenos Aires. A gang of Amado's fictitious-gambling buddies from "Dona Flor" fiction is present; there is much singing, dancing, eating and drinking before folks repair to the bedrooms. In this case, the "living room" was a bit dark and dingy and after cold beers we were looking over the available girls when the police knocked on the door: "Elections tomorrow; this place has to close at midnight." So, my carousing ended with just a couple of beers, ogling the "merchandise" and back to the boarding house. Samuel promised to make up for it later if I came to Brasília where "It's quality 'stuff' and I'll show you a good time." He said the girls there are all "business associates" of the politicians and know more about what's going on in Brazil than the folks in congress. I would find out a bit about this months later in Brasília. The sex would have to wait. Not the politics although from a very unexpected source!

4

Using another of the addresses from my Brazilian Literature professor at Georgetown, I looked up Professor Olinto from the School of Humanities of the University of Bahia, my naïve, ostensible purpose just to learn more about Jorge Amado and the cultural and literary scene in Bahia. We met at the university and had a lengthy conversation about several things. There was a "lesson" on Brazilian literature with the professor's likes, dislikes and all, many not agreeing with my taste based just on an introduction at Georgetown, but important for the LETTER to the Times. Here are my recollections of the conversation:

"The best modern Brazilian novelist is Graciliano Ramos and his masterpiece "Barren Lives," but this does not take anything away from our local hero Jorge Amado who like José Lins do Rego in Paraíba has really chronicled our region in literature. "Barren Lives" is a literary masterpiece written in literary language; Amado's works are entertaining, informative, but heavily propagandistic from the left, at least the early novels. You know, he is a Marxist, or least he was until he reneged on the Soviet Union and Marxism when he found out about the Gulag in the late 1950s. It was only then that in my opinion he began to write fun, entertaining novels about Bahia, like "Gabriela" and "Dona Flor." But he is an "icon" in Bahia, really "untouchable" locally."

"In theater that scoundrel in Rio, Nelson Rodrigues with plays like "Beijo no Asfalto" is really our best dramatist. (Olinto did not mention my favorite in Salvador, Dias Gomes and his "Payer of Promises," and even more importantly, Ariano Suassuna in Recife with the "Rogues' Trial)." He certainly was not clued in nor interested in Pernambuco, Paraíba, Ceará or the "cordel."

It was Professor Olinto's talk about politics that caught my attention. "Mike, you have to know we are really in a tight situation today in Brazil. The Revolution is two years old and the military is really tightening its grips on the country. So far it is ostensibly crackdowns on student demonstrations (the National Students' Union – "União Nacional dos Estudantes") and a witch - hunt for the old leftists from the 1960s – people like Francisco Julião of the "Peasant Leagues" and Miguel Arraes, governor of Pernambuco, and of course Luís Carlos Prestes the old Marxist from São Paulo dating to the 1920s, and the MEB "Base Educational Movement" for literacy and the ballot for the poor has of course been squelched. That bomb at Guararapes Airport in August in Recife, and you were there to witness it, has upped the ante. General Costa e Silva will come in later this year, replacing our northeasterner Castelo Branco from Ceará and who knows what will follow (Olinto and none of us knew then of the infamous Institutional Act AI -5 that would come in the next months, the unofficial beginning of the true military dictatorship). Bahia has our congressional leader Antônio de Magalhães who seems to be in line with the military for its share of federal revenue, so we cannot complain about that."

Far more would come in my next few months in Brazil, but I was informed this interview, somehow, was known about by the DOPS who were keeping an eye on me. But, "What me worry?" as "Mad Magazine" would say in those days, I would move on to fun and tourism in Bahia.

5

~~~~~~

Most of my "tourism" was done with just my one good "buddy" – Jorge's "Bahia de Todos os Santos" guidebook to Salvador under my arm. From the Portuguese boarding house on Avenida 7 near the Piedade Praça which was close to the Benedictine Monastery from the 17th century, the hot, crowded, smelly city bus would take us all to the Municipal Plaza ["A Praça Municipal"] with the four - hundred – year - old government buildings including the mayor's office, the city council and the statue of Bahia's founder Tomé de Souza gathering pigeon droppings. The plaza was a huge parking lot "populated" by most of all VW Bugs ["fuscas"] the rage in all Brazil in the 1960s, written about in Recife already. There were others: the "refugees" from the U.S. auto industry, the "Willys" Jeeps and the luxury version the "Rural," a kind of station wagon of the times.

Off to one side was the Lacerda Elevator ["O Elevador Lacerda"] that amazing device that would whisk a real melting pot of "Bahianos" from upper to lower city and vice versa. Bahians bragged about it being the first outdoor passenger elevator in the world done in 1873 fittingly enough on the day of "Nossa Senhora da Conceição" holiday. It would link the Praça Cayru (the port, the Modelo Market and business section of the lower city) to the Praça Tomé de Sousa, the government section in the upper city. The cost was literally pennies dropped in the glass collection boxes; the wait in line varied, long during rush hour but often just a minute or two in off-hours. Many the time I was the only white person aboard in the cabin they would jam with perhaps thirty passengers, Bahians of all the many racial possibilities (there supposedly were 90 racial categories listed by the Federal Government at that time). Despite an attempt at air conditioning or at least air moving about, the heat was stifling and some interesting odors – the sweet perfume of the ladies and the body odor of those of us of the "proletariat." I loved that ride; it was fast and there was an actual "rush" feeling the gravity change. The thought did enter my mind that I would not want to get caught in the area and especially in the elevator cabin with the "wrong crowd."

The Municipal Plaza would fill me with those great images garnered from the readings of Jorge's novels at Georgetown: the beautiful "Bahianas" in the huge bellowing skirts, blouses, jewelry at the neck and wrists and the turbans – the clothing from the Afro-Brazilian "candomblé" rituals. There seemed to be a team of two ladies in each corner of the plaza and the neighboring "Praça da Sé" with their low table, simmering cooking pots, stools, selling the Bahian delicacies of "xinxin de galinha, caruru" or "acarajé." I never did learn about all that cooking and for sure never knew all the ingredients. The "acarajé" had a bean base, deep fried in "dendé" or peanut oil, sliced and filled with shrimp or other delicacies. My gringo's stomach from farm country in Nebraska unfortunately never did get used to it, but the Bahians loved it, that "acarajé" was like a hot dog back home.

The other item was the frequent appearance of the old iconic tradition for northeastern men: the white, linen suit. A perfect fit (not really, the linen jacket and slacks were baggy, prone to wrinkles and to getting dirty in a hurry) for the hot tropics, the outfit was always white and fit for that humid, hot northeast and especially Salvador. I was always amazed how many businessmen and government workers still wore the outfit, the inheritance I understood, from the British capitalists who swarmed through 19th and 20 century Brazil building the railway system. I do know that if you could afford one you wore it. "Cordel's" master pioneer poet Leandro Gomes de Barros would lambast the British in his satiric "cordel" poems, one of the most famous "borrowed" by Ariano Suassuna as one of three major texts for his "The Rogues' Trial."

In those wanderings in hot November and December of 1966 after traversing the Municipal Plaza I would walk on down to the just as famous "Praça da Sé" or "Cathedral Plaza." Although the building was terrifically in need of fixing up and a good paint job in those days you could still make out the Jesuit Priest high above the central portal, dressed in Alb and chasuble ready to say mass. Anyone studying Latin America, Spanish or Portuguese, would have learned that along with the Franciscans and Benedictines, the Jesuits were the primary order establishing the famous Missions in Southern Brazil and Paraguay, but also churches, hospitals and schools throughout Colonial Brazil. Father Nóbrega was one of the first, head of the Society of Jesus in Salvador and first provincial of Jesuits in Brazil in 1555 and then founding the Jesuits in São Paulo. Father Anchieta was not only a missionary but wrote some of the early works of Brazilian Literature and the first Grammar of Portuguese and the Tupi Language of the Guarani Indians. In the 17th century came Padre Antônio Vieira who did his novitiate in Salvador in 1625 and became known for his famous sermons and other discourses and a diplomat in Portugal. He was instrumental in defending the Brazilian natives against the slave and gold hunters who wanted the Jesuit lands, missions and the Indians as slaves. And you also learned that the entire order was thrown out of Latin American in 1767 by the Portuguese Crown by direction of the Marquis de Pombal; the causes were political, jealousy of other orders but mainly the Jesuits' own success with the Missions which were economically independent from the Crown and had garnered much wealth for the Order. The famous gold and slave hunters coveted not only their land and wealth but their protected flocks, the Indians of southern Brazil.

Also in that same, venerable, historic square, the "Terreiro de Jesus," was the famous or infamous building of the old School of Medicine ["Faculdade de Medicina"], the oldest medical school in Brazil, and the Nina Rodrigues Museum to the side, the medical school the most venerable, but in my circle of interests, Jorge Amado's novels and Brazilian folklore, not quite so venerable. Hansen's Jewish, Sephardic public in New York would have agreed with Amado's thesis in his "Tenda dos Milagres" ["The Miracle Shop"] – the miscegenation of race in Brazil and the contribution of Afro-Brazilian Culture. A sidebar to the main theme was the atmosphere of philosophical Positivism in the School of Medicine and the biological determinism that resulted, all led in the novel by Fascist – Leaning, Axis - Favoring professors of the times.

A final stop and one I would repeat often in those days was a visit to the most famous baroque church in all Brazil, the "Igreja de São Francisco" in its own plaza down the way from the others just mentioned. For someone steeped in the great churches of Europe, this place may have been "old hat," but for me the farm boy from Nebraska, it was truly amazing. Built by the Franciscans in the 17th and 18th centuries, it is the best example of the Baroque style in Brazil; my only basis of comparison would be the great churches I saw in Mexico City in 1962, including the national cathedral in the "Zócalo." The entire inside is sculpted gilt wood, and it is dazzling. For me the church will always have another memory: Jorge Amado's film "Dona Flor and Her Two Husbands" and the playboy male lead Vadinho who notes the lascivious looks of all those angels, this while hitting the pastor up for a loan! The other incredible feature is the vast collection of Portuguese blue tiles ["azulejos"] decorating the walls of the interior patio next door, perhaps the best collection in all Brazil.

I'm getting nervous that Hansen and the <u>Times</u> will be getting bored with all this tourism, common stuff for the hundreds of thousands of those folks who visit Bahia each year, and I have nothing unusual to add. But what can you do? They say Bahia has a different church for each day of the year. Among them is the Church of the Third Order of St. Francis next door with the stone carved baroque façade covered for years with plaster to avoid destruction by the Dutch and other foreign invaders to colonial Brazil. And there is more to come.

As I walked away from the São Francisco Plaza through a dingy narrow, cobblestoned street (and this was in the daytime), women would motion to me from dark, smelly doorways to come in and "have some fun." As a red blooded young American, I was ready to investigate fun aspects of Bahian culture, but this was not the ticket. I had read Amado's novel "Sweat" ["Suor"] back in graduate school in D.C., the unentertaining 1940s social protest-Marxist inspired fiction of the people who lived in the district – among them poor dockworkers and the bottom of the barrel whores relegated to the dingy inside rooms of old, dilapidated colonial buildings constructed 400 years earlier. Amado had lived some months in the district after fleeing the Jesuit Prep School in Salvador and wanting to investigate and live the proletarian life of a young Marxist. The book tells it all in a realism that makes the reader squirm.

Beyond these narrow alleys and worn building the tiny streets suddenly opened to one of the most amazing and famous plazas in all Brazil – the "Pelourinho" or old slave block of Bahia. The "pillory" plaza was the center of colonial Salvador where slaves were disciplined and auctioned to the wealthy sugar cane plantation owners, and much later to the cacao plantation owners as well. For around three hundred years, the business of slavery made things tick, and after 1888 and the final Abolition, the buildings and traditions remained. On my visits in 1966 it was dingy, dirty, all in need of a serious paint job, and a place you did not go at night.

From that triangular plaza, you walked ever so carefully on the 400-year-old cobblestones down the steep hill to the "Baixa dos Sapateiros" ["Shoemakers' Plaza"] and continued up a diagonal street to another of Bahia's great churches – The Church of St. Barbara ["A Igreja de

Santa Bárbara"]. For me, the student of Brazilian Literature, folklore and "cordel," (and any other North American studying Brazil in the 1960s) it had immense importance. The playwright and Brazilian soap opera ["telenovela"] writer Dias Gomes had written a short play which would become famous in those days, later made into one of the most celebrated black and white "art films" of the times: "Payer of Promises" ["Pagador de Promessas"]. It along with Amado's works, José Lins do Rego's novels, and Ariano Suassuna's plays were the mortar for the brick foundation of my studies in Brazil including the coming dissertation. Its thesis would go a long way for an accurate understanding of Brazil and its culture for the dilettante bookstore readers and readers of the <u>Times</u>' dailies – something Hansen had envisioned when we made the "deal."

The play dealt with the prejudice and discrimination of the white population of Salvador and the Roman Catholic Church vis a vis the black population and its intrinsic belief in Afro-Brazilian Spiritualism, but it was a bit more complicated than that. The "high falutin" term "religious syncretism" was common in those days; in short it meant the mixture of two or more religions. In this case it was the long-standing, ever present mixture of Roman Catholicism and Afro-Brazilian spiritualist religion ("candomblé" in Bahia) in daily life. In the play, a peasant from the interior of Bahia State, a believer in both Catholicism and "Candomblé'" (and he was far from alone) had experienced what he believed to be a miracle: his donkey recovered from illness after he, Zé the peasant, had prayed to Iansan (a goddess of the Afro-Brazilian religion). Zé, in thanks, decided to sell his land, carry his own cross like Christ, go to Salvador to the Church of St. Barbara (the Catholic correlative of "Iansan") and offer the cross to the local pastor in thanksgiving for the miracle (it would be his very large "ex-voto").

Zé's simple idea became enmeshed in the politics of the times (some saw him selling his land as the precursor of the land reform movement bandied about by Francisco Julião in Pernambuco, i.e. Cuba and Fidel and Ché), and when the local parish priest refused him because of his African religious "abomination" – the "miracle" of Iansan-Santa Barbara – all hell broke loose. There was a tragic denouement. Incidental to the story was the minor yet important role of a "cordelian" poet who discovered the story and wanted to publicize it all in a "cordel" poem sold on the streets like "hot pancakes" – the real-life poet Cuíca de Santo Amaro.

This was the great scene in front of me after leaving the "Pelourinho" and the "Baixa dos Sapateiros" in 1966.

Where I did go for many nights in those hot, tropical days of November and December was to a relatively modest venue in the tourist center near the Lacerda Elevator; it was there that the Bahia Center for Tourism (with meager funding) sponsored a nightly "capoeira" show. Little did I realize the amazing opportunity that the show was for me or for anyone fortunate enough and maybe with their eyes open to experience a long, gone cultural age in Salvador. This was good "stuff" for Hansen!

The night I went for the first time to see "capoeira" was a true revelation for me and was perhaps the best folkloric "performance" I would appreciate in all my time in Brazil. The important folklorist Hildegardes Vianna and the journalist Vasconcelos Maia were the persons behind the endeavor. The "capoeira" Master was Canjiquinha who played an important but minor role in "Payer of Promises."

Capoeira can only be described as a combination of dance and self-defense. Master Luís da Câmara Cascudo described it in his "Dictionary of Brazilian Folklore" saying it came originally from a ritual of the Masai Tribe in Africa, that of a young man reaching adulthood. The dance commemorated the act of a young man killing his first lion. The slaves in Brazil learned a version of the same and grew to be super-efficient in the "dance." The white slave masters discovered that there was more to it than "dance" and therefore opposed the ritual which the slaves had masqueraded as a dance.

I experienced in 1966 the unadulterated true art form. I learned there were twelve rhythmic patterns which accompanied the dance, the rhythms played on the berimbau, a long, curved piece of wood (like a wooden bow of bow and arrows) with an empty gourd at one end. The gourd would resonate when a metallic wire strung between the two ends of the "bow" was struck by a stick producing a "metallic" low sound. The player of the berimbau, in addition, would push a metal washer against the steel wire which would vibrate with a series of different sounds, each obeying the different requirements of each "toque." The "dance" was also accompanied by small drums. Along with the different "toques" or rhythms there were different "songs" or "chants." Some of the dances or "toques" were called "Hail Mary" ["Ave Maria], "Holy Mary" ["Santa Maria"], "Samba Style" ["Sambada"], "Angola Style" ["Angola"], and "Knight Style" ["Cavalheiro"], etc. The rhythms varied from a slow movement, almost seeming like a ballet movement, to incredibly fast steps of battle or self-defense. One of the latter was called a "half-moon" ["meia-lua"] when the capoeirista spins in rapid circles with a leg extended at waist level and then turns the spin into a rapid kick. Another begins with the capoeirista's hands on the ground and then turns into a type of high leap executed from the side ending in a kick from the opposite direction. I made these not-easy notes without tape recorder or the like; I was in the mysterious, difficult and romantic time of pre-technical 1966. In addition, there was the cadence in which the capoeirista "balanced" ["balançava"] with the entire body swinging back and forth with the rhythm ("gingando"), this before launching into another "attack." All members of the group learned the words to the various chants and the diverse rhythms and how to play all the instruments, but some were "specialists" in certain "toques."

I attended "capoeira" night after night. The "Master" explained each "toque" before the group demonstrated it. Then he would dance with four or five of the "disciples" at a time, creating a very theatrical effect. There was also a demonstration of "street capoeira" (which I would run into in a "favela" in Rio later) when the "Master" and the "Disciples" battled in a true to life street scenario. One reads in Brazilian folklore that there were famous "capoeiristas" employed as body guards by politicians in the poor districts of Rio de Janeiro, descriptions coming from the 19th century.

In the 1960s there were famous capoeira clubs in Bahia with old, well-known and even famous Masters like "Mestre Bimba" and "Mestre Pastinha' in the Pelourinho District who would practice capoeira into his 90s! For me, the Fulbright Scholar and unofficial "folklorist," this was one of the highlights of Brazil and Hansen and the <u>Times</u> when they received this LETTER and learned of it in its heyday.

6

Another of my points of interest in the stay in Bahia was the old Modelo Market, an historic market and tourist center in Salvador, famous for its commerce and handicrafts. The original market was at its peak in the 1930s and 1940s during the time of the first novels of Jorge Amado. Burned down by a "mysterious fire" in the 1950s, it would be reconstructed later in the place where one finds the "Praça Cayru." In my days in Salvador there was a restaurant on the third floor and its owner Camaféu de Oxossi, a friend and minor character in several of Jorge Amado's novels, "commanded the scene." My main purpose to spend time in that restaurant in 1966 was to absorb the atmosphere of Amado's novels like "Mar Morto" or even "Dona Flor and Her Two Husbands."

The original purpose of hanging out at the market was to contact the poets and publishers of "cordel" in Bahia. There was in the old days a certain gentleman named Nigro Silva who had a poetry stand in the "Golden Age" of "cordel" and was an "agent" of João Martins de Atayde of Recife, receiving and selling the story-poems of Atayde in Bahia, this in the 1940s and 1950s. Unhappily, the man and his stand were no more. Still, I frequented the market and its stalls, watched the loading and unloading of "saveiros" at its side: single-masted, small cargo boats loaded with jute, cotton, fish, vegetables and fruit. It was a very busy place with the atmosphere of a "fair," many people just hanging out, passing the time of day. The slides I took in 1966 portrayed that vibrant life still like the heyday of the market in the 1940s, the "Golden Age" of Rodolfo Coelho Cavalcante and Cuíca de Santo Amaro selling their poems outside the market and at the foot of the Lacerda Elevator. This was the folk-popular life described by Jorge Amado in his novels and in the guide "Bahia de Todos os Santos."

So, all seemed to be coming along, my stay in the city a success, but my past in Recife caught up with me. On one of the forays to the Market, while I was just watching the "saveiros" come in, a fellow in a white-linen suit, straw hat and sunglasses sidled up to me and surprised me with a greeting in English, "Mr. Gaherty, it appears you are enjoying yourself in Bahia, but we can't see that you are doing much poetry research. Isn't that why you are here? We know you had that conversation with that Marxist Literature professor from the University of Bahia, and we know you seem obsessed with Marxist Jorge Amado and his tales of capitalist oppression here in Salvador. You know, you were supposed to keep your nose clean (he mentioned the pistol episode from Juazeiro and José Atayde) and just study folklore."

I was first surprised, then a bit shaken. Indeed, the DOPS continued to find me a "person of interest." The good news is I was innocent as the veritable lilies of the field and tried to explain to the fellow. But first I did ask, "Who in the hell are you, show me some identification and why you are coming on with the detective shit?" So, Sérgio (that was the agent's name) politely flashed a DOPS identification card and we continued the conversation. It turned out to be like an early Ph.D. defense: I said I was not doing much "cordel" research because one of the main poets, Cuíca de Santo Amaro, had died in 1964, that the old veteran Nigro Silva was long gone from the scene and that my main research target Rodolfo Coelho Cavalcante was not even in Salvador, "exiled" in poverty to a tiny house he owned in Jequié in the interior of the State and living from hand to mouth selling tourist trinkets and just one "cordel" story in the interior of the state (I knew this from letters from him). And I explained that to "salvage" the time in Bahia I was immersing myself in the street life described by Jorge Amado in his Bahian novels.

Sérgio the agent said, "Look, I know you are training to be a scholar and that you have done some serious study of Brazil and its literature, but you may have picked the wrong writer to fall in love with. Amado is a filthy Communist, he was a member of the Brazilian Communist Party in 1947, was kicked out of Brazil, went to eastern Europe where he worked as an activist for the International in Hungary, and only came back here a few years ago."

I had done my homework: "Sérgio, did you know that Amado totally reneged on Stalin and the Soviet Union when he found out about the Gulag in the 1950s and ever since has been writing wonderful, humorous, novels on Bahia totally different from that Marxist period of the 1930s and 1940s?"

"Once a Commie, always a Commie" was Sérgio's response. He then closed the conversation saying, "Just watch it. Don't do anything stupid. We know you have friends in high places and we think you are on the right side, but reading Jorge Amado and becoming his lap dog does not help your case. We'll be in touch." And he walked away from the dock.

So, what to do? In 1966 the Market and the dock to the side were the most colorful of all the "folkloric" scenes in Bahia and I was determined to see them and absorb the atmosphere, so I continued my wanderings. To the side of the busy dock there were literally dozens of "saveiros," the ones with one or two masts on the small sailboats that carried cargo from the entire "Recôncavo" to the main market in Salvador. Nebraska was never like this; I saw strong black men, naked to the waist, sweating in that hot tropical sun, unloading bales of cotton and jute to the docks. To the side was the old fish market, a very busy place from early in the morning when the fishermen of the bay showed up with their catch. It was always busy every time I went, and hot and smelly, in other words, a good market!

I would return to the same scene a few days later under different circumstances. I got up at 5:00 a.m. to see the sunrise and the early morning activity at the dock. Walking from the Portuguese boarding house on Avenida 7 de Setembro past Piedade Plaza I would arrive at the small plaza with the statue of Bahia's most famous poet Castro Alves and take a somewhat precarious and perhaps stupid and certainly naïve walk down the dark, narrow street to the lower city where the market, dock and "saveiros" were located. What the reader should remember was that Gaherty was not only a student of folklore and folk poetry but of Brazilian literature, and once again, the most romantic tales in fiction were by Jorge Amado who spun wild tales of the Bahian nightlife, including "castelos" or whorehouses and the parties in them, in this part of the city. So it was that in those wee hours I walked by early risers headed for work but also the partiers in wrinkled white linen suits coming home (or maybe to work) after a long night on the town. One only must remember Amado's "Dona Flor and Her Two Husbands" and the carousing first husband Vadinho and his friends partying into all hours of the night with their gambling and drunken carnival escapades and good times in the "castelos" in an orgy of wild living to get an idea of the "mysterious night" of Bahia and the spirit of the place I was searching for. Maybe a bit of vicarious pleasure on my part, who knows? I was the only white person in sight, and the best of society were not on the streets at that hour and that place, so maybe that's why the epigraph of this book of LETTERS is Guimarães Rosa's saying from "The Devil to Pay in the Backlands," "Living is very dangerous." I did not get mugged and that morning was one of my best times to that point in Brazil.

Early on that walk and from up above the lower city I heard the whistle of a huge cargo ship, saw it sliding into port, and another two going in the opposite direction, out to sea. From far off one could barely make out the lights of Itaparica and Maragogipe across the bay. Rays of colored light were reflected on the clouds and back to the Lacerda Elevator.

Upon seeing the lightening of the day with the sun's rays poking through the clouds, I saw an entirely different world. You could see the sails of the "saveiros" in front of the lower city, recently arrived from Itaparica, and far off, the whiteness of a huge, transatlantic passenger ship. Little by little this ship became the center of attention of the dozens of people on the dock.

Now walking slowly and carefully (the cobblestones were slippery and there was barely a sidewalk) downward on the Avenida Contorno (the street that winds from the upper city and the Castro Alves Plaza down to the lower city), I walked in front of old colonial houses of some three or four stories, all in decadence and disrepair. There was dirty water running from under their doors into the gutter, feral cats searching out something to eat, broken and dirty narrow sidewalks to the left, and to the right a tall wall separating the avenue from the upper city.

When I arrived at the Praça Cayru and the "Rampa dos Saveiros" later that early morning their world was open to me. The sailors, crew or workers on the "saveiros" were waking up, in all manner of dress – shorts, t-shirt, or bare to the waist, most in sandals or rubber flip flops. A veteran sailor, perhaps in his 60s was seated in a "saveiro," seemingly just "hanging out," ["a toa"] watching the world go by, a Bahian pastime of the dozens of people scattered about on the streets in the lower city.

An old codger with a red-striped shirt was in a small boat that rowed men who had slept in the city, taking them from the dock to their own small boats anchored a bit farther out in the bay between the dock and the sea arm. The pungent smell of cooking fish was everywhere, and many "saveiros" were now in the process of unloading their wares on the Ramp of the Market. Some men sang while they worked, and I heard pieces of popular songs of the day.

Old and young, weak and strong near where I was seated on the wall of the dock were watching the "movement." All noted the arrival of the Transatlantic Passenger Ship, an event that quickly provoked all manner of commentary. One of the old men seated near me, looked over at this white gringo in the midst of black Bahia, after giving his opinion as to the home port of the great ship, said, "There's more luxury there than the life of a "coronel," (the political bosses of the Northeast). Another said it was "arretado" – very cool – and falling into an improvised dance step, winked at me and said it ought to be great "for whiskey and white girls." The scene came from what I imagined, and with some reason, right out of the pages of a Jorge Amado novel. In fact Jorge's famous "Mar Morto" ["Dead Sea"] of the late 1940s described a terrific storm in the bay, a transatlantic taking on water and soon to go down, and the rescue of the passengers by a passel of black men on their "saveiros."

I took great photos with my little slide camera. I had wanted to capture that "mysterious night" and life in Bahia. Mission accomplished. Maybe both the Times's readers and the DOPS would agree with me when I would send in the next LETTER.

A lesser but similar scene took place just days later when I took a rickety bus from the "Praça Cayru" to the market-fair of "Água dos Meninos" ["The Boys' Water"]. It was a horrible day weather-wise, incredibly hot in the sun, but the muddy streets a mess from recent rains. I did see little boys playing in the water where "saveiros" were unloading fruit, vegetables, bags of manioc flour and fish to be sold in the market stalls to what seemed to me to be very poor Bahians, almost all black. The stench of the place was almost overwhelming, but I succeeded in walking through the aisles between the market stalls and taking some pictures, often being glared at by the locals. As expected, there was no sign of "cordel" poets or poetry stands, but once again, in part, I made the trek because of Jorge Amado. In a short story, "Death and the Death of Quincas Water-Yell" ["A Morte e a Morte de Quincas Berro D'Agua"] a small back room in the market was the scene for the card games of some of Quincas' rowdy friends. And an aside: a few weeks later I would experience an incredible nightclub behind Leblon Beach in Rio de Janeiro, high in an unfinished skyscraper with the name "Berro DÁgua."

There were moments, and not few of them, when someone must have been watching over me, perhaps a Catholic guardian angel (the Gahertys still believed in such old-Catholic stuff), but for me, always a reflection of "The Devil to Pay in the Backlands" when the bandit hero Riobaldo continually lived remembering his own "anjo de guarda," Diadorim.

Perhaps not quite so colorful, but another point of interest, and related to my research was the old "Vila Velha" Park located near the governor's palace up the hill in Campo Grande. The park was filled with huge tropical trees and held a beautiful view of the "Bahia de Todos os Santos" far below; it also had a small theater with a café to its side. It was the theater that held my attention because a local reporter had produced a play just months before my arrival with short sketches, each based on a story-poem from "cordel." They told me it was a huge success, something to be repeated in the same years by Ariano Suassuna and friends in Recife.

Naïve as usual, I did not realize at the time that one of the young actor-singers in 1966 was a fellow named Caetano Veloso who would go on to be among the elite of popular composers and singers in all Brazil. I did meet a young actor who also went on to national fame, Othon Bastos, who at that time was picking up whatever small rolls were available locally – one of them a mini role in Dias Gomes' film "Payer of Promisses" ["Pagador de Promessas"].

In the same neighborhood, I also found an unlikely hangout given a tip by Peace Corps Volunteer friend Don Brooks – the English Club. We used to go there and drink cold Brahma beer and shoot the breeze, but one event marked the scene: the arrival of a British aircraft carrier to Salvador and the club and the streets of the city were filled with the white uniformed sailors, some of whom we met one night at the club. This scene would be matched and trumped only one time in Brazil: a North American aircraft carrier docked in that hot summer of 1967 in Rio and it seemed like the entire beachfront at Copacabana was filled with the "swabbies" looking for a good time and the famous Carioca girls of the night.

7

A "detour" from Salvador took place in those same days – a trip to the interior of Bahia State to Feira de Santana. The agricultural zone between Salvador da Bahia and Feira de Santana is once again "zona da mata," tropical with lots of rain. After that one passes through the ranching zone with rolling hills of pasture. The city of Feira lies at the division of the ranching zone and the dry backlands and is known as the city with the largest cattle fair in the entire Northeast. The city seemed to me in those days very dry, dusty and hot, reminding me of Guarabira in Paraíba State or yet Caruaru in Pernambuco. There were two large avenues, one the zone of commerce, the other the place of the huge cattle fair, thus the city was divided into two parts: that of the cattle and that of "normal" commerce; I went only to the commercial side because that is where I would possibly find poets of "cordel." I saw leather articles, vegetables, food, clothing and the like. I saw an old lady selling manioc flour and occasionally she would eat the same from a paper bag, "tossing" a bit from her hand into her mouth, like a North American might eat popcorn. There was another lady smoking a clay pipe producing huge clouds of billowing smoke in the area. As the day advanced, the heat increased as did the coming and going in the fair.

There were several vendors of "cordel." I met and photographed Erotildes Miranda dos Santos, a very dark-skinned man, bald in front, long hair at the back of his head, with sun glasses and the hat of the trade. Known for his story-poems which were a bit risqué, with sexual themes and covers of naked, young girls among them, the stories were really intended for humor ["gracejos"], with double entendre, among them one title "Modern Dating."

That was the extent of any "cordel" I found in the fair. The return to Salvador was "déjà vu" all over again, as Yogi Berra would say, like other trips to Caruaru or Campina Grande – a jammed local bus, many people standing in the aisle. Then the brakes failed and we had to wait for another bus, destined for Salvador, and wave our hands for it to stop. And then the whole mess of passengers climbed on board the passing bus and the rest of the trip was a highly uncomfortable bus ride to Salvador. The Feira-Salvador highway would be bad luck for me in the future, another scene to tell in a while. At least, the DOPS could not complain about me not doing research.

In those final days in Bahia I would go to parties with Rodolfo, a Brazilian buddy from the boarding house, where we would flirt with the young bahian beauties, drink icy Brahma Choppe Beer, and listen to and dance to the "hot" Brazilian music of the times: the "iê-iê-iê" or

"Yeah-Yeah-Yeah" Beatles' inspired music of Brazil's hottest recording artist, Roberto Carlos. And since there was extra time with no "cordel" in sight we went to the nightclubs for more of the same.

There was one truly folkloric event that took place that would mark my last foray into Bahian folklore – the huge festival of "Conceição da Praia" in the lower city on December 12th.

One of the great folk-popular festivals of Bahia, this festival opens the "season of popular festivals." I walked from the lower city to the Praça Cayru where I saw a multitude of market stands set up in front of the old colonial, famous church of Conceição da Praia. I could only think of the black and white photographs of the albums of Pierre Verger treating popular life in Bahia, collector's pieces today. One could see all manner of fruit in big mounds piled on the ground. There were many drunken people, drinking "cachaça" from the stands along the street which sported bottles of all the brands mixed with local fruits. There were "capoeiristas" practicing their craft in the streets, this the original form of "capoeira" in Salvador. There was a procession of religious statues including the "Virgen da Conceição," patron saint of Bahia. And there was a small park with a carnival and Ferris Wheel. It was credibly hot, that summer of 1966, humidity in the 90 per-cent range.

I walked from the Lower City to the Baixa dos Sapateiros where thousands of people filled the streets, many in the "Blocos de Samba," Salvador's version of a "Samba School" from the carnival parades in Rio. The participants were all dressed in the Block's costume, all dancing in the streets. One block had white-red striped shirts and tall straw hats, another with young girls with Indian headdresses and short skirts. The "Block" is traditionally tied together by a cord or rope to keep out "crashers" ["penetras"]. Almost all the participants were black and were great dancers. I saw some drunken persons, but causing no trouble. Those Nebraska 4-H Square Dances wouldn't draw a glance here!

I understand that these "Blocos" are a variation on the old "Afoxé" of the Bahia of the 1930s and the novel "Miracle Shop" ["Tenda dos Milagres"] by Jorge Amado. The rhythm comes from the pounding drums, ear-splitting to me. And wonderful for me were other participants, the "typical" Bahianas with long, full, beautiful skirts, necklances, bracelets, "turban" style hats, dressed in all their finery.

The whole scene frightened me some because of the drunks and me feeling like one of the few white folks on the streets. The terrific heat was a factor as well. Ah! Folklore!

8

In those political times of 1966 and 1967, as I will not tire of repeating, being a "folklorist," a foreigner at that, was still "safe" in the eyes of the nationalistic generals. This endeavor although not always related to "cordel" brought one or two last moments in Bahia, moments important for any "gringo" really wanting to understand Brasil. This meeting and conversation was with another university professor but this time with no link to the Left and the paranoia of the DOPS. Professor José Calasans was the expert on an historical event that marked the course of modern Brazilian History and Folklore: The War of Canudos. My link to the War and to Calasans was that one of the earlier extant story-poems of journalistic "cordel" treated the event – "A Guerra de Canudos" by Francisco das Chagas Batista, brother-in-law and colleague of Leandro Gomes de Barros. Chagas Batista was a combatant and in his story-poem written in retirement years later detailed the battle and provided a folk insight into its causes and history.

Professor Calasans spoke of his research on folklore and "cachaça" but mainly Canudos. In 1896-97 there took place one of the few violent conflicts in Brazilian History at an end of the world - forlorn, poverty stricken area in the backlands of Bahia State. A self-proclaimed "Messicanic" leader, Antônio Conselheiro, a fugitive from the law in Ceará State where he had killed several people including his own mother (!) settled in the "arraial" or "burg" of the Bahian backlands preaching a messianic message (many said he learned his craft or at least was influenced by Father Cicero of Juazeiro-Ceará fame, the priest being one of the major characters of the cast of "cordel"). He promised the overthrow of the Republic, a return to the heady days of the Empire, and material and spiritual salvation for the poor masses of the area. A strange snapshot of the days, it was believed he could accomplish miracles because of a strict celibacy, finding "sacred" stones to build his church and turn the Vassa-Barris river into milk and honey. Starting with some cattle rustling from nearby ranches, Canudos was threatened by the hired hands of ranchers with the goal of eliminating Antônio Conselheiro, however, surprisingly enough he defeated them, then the local police, then the local and state militia and finally took on the federal troops of the national army. In the end, the troops bombarded the town, killing all but a few who managed to escape to tell the story, but ironically the accounting of the event became national news in Brazil due to a reporter from Rio de Janeiro, Euclides da Cunha, who documented the war and its tragedy in newspaper reports that he turned into what would become Brazil's most famous book up to that time – "Rebellion in the Backlands" ["Os Sertões"]. More than the actual reporting of day to day combat, the book had a larger view and purpose; it revealed the "other Brazil," the impoverished, helpless, "fanatical" Northeast to the middle and upper-class public in Rio de Janeiro and São Paulo and for the first time made city dwellers aware of this "Two Brazils" reality. I had read the book at Georgetown, so I recognized its importance. Calasans graciously filled me in on the details. It is difficult to understate the importance of both the event and the book.

The second and last important moment related to both folklore and history took place on my final day in Bahia, almost an afterthought – a visit to the Nina Rodrigues Museum lodged in the Medical School of Bahia to see the museum's holdings on Afro-Brazilian culture and especially "candomblé" but with a huge and macabre surprise – the yellowed heads of the infamous northeastern bandit ["cangaceiro"] Lampião, his consort Maria Bonita, and other bandits in his gang like Corisco. The correlation to my research – the "cordel" (also a distant relative of the Sephardic Romance tradition in the 14th and 15th centuries in Spain before 1492) was to a major theme of the poetry in the "real" northeast – Brazilian banditry this time in the form of Lampião, his consort Maria Bonita and the gang. The entire group was cornered in 1938 on a ranch in tiny Sergipe State and shot to pieces (in our own cinema "Bonnie and Clyde" was an interesting parallel). To prove to the uneducated back landers that their bandit heroes were indeed dead, the heads were cut off, put in kerosene cans and taken on a macabre "tour" of the interior; otherwise the locals were apt to believe they either had not died or would come back as "messianic" figures to save the poor of the Northeast. The heads ended in the Medical school and later the museum, ostensibly to study the cranium and figure out what "caused" banditry!

9

There are things that just don't fit into box or maybe a suitcase or certainly in a cultural LETTER to the <u>Times</u>, and this is an example. A lot that followed in the final days in Salvador was not earth shaking and not controversial, but these small, cultural "vignettes" tell a lot about a Brazil that few North Americans were aware of in 1966.

A. "Candomblé" is the visible and most important of Afro-Brazilian rites in Bahia and I've mentioned it a bit in a past LETTER. On one of those final nights I attended one of the most famous of all the "terreiros" or places of worship – the "candomblé" of Mãe Menininha in Federação District, she perhaps the most famous of the "mothers-of-the-saint" ["mãe de santo"] or ritual leader. The "terreiro" was jammed with tourists and was highly commercialized but just the same beautiful. It all began about 10:30 at night and continued into the wee hours of the following morning; there were beautiful chants and dances, homage to the "mother of the saint" and to various "daughters" and "sons" who were possessed by the saints, "caindo no santo." It was very similar to the Xangô ritual in Pernambuco already described, and of course to North Americans somewhat similar with the famous "Umbanda" scene in "Black Orpheus."

B. At the end of November 1966, in front of the tourist hotel in the Barra and in the tremendous heat, we heard "White Christmas" and other Christmas carols by no less than Bing Crosby, blaring out of the sound system into the plaza in front of the beach. As the Brazilians never tire of repeating: "Only in Brazil!"

C. I had the opportunity to visit the district of Tororó, a poor district inland from the coast of Salvador, inner city as it were, and my host was a Peace Corps volunteer from New York. He was black and spoke at length of his personal experience of racial prejudice in Bahia. The slum or "favela" in later years was demolished in the name of progress – an interior freeway in the city- and I never learned of the fate of its thousands of inhabitants. I would hear a lot more about such government goings-on in Rio a few months later. And I would wonder when I would meet a beautiful black girl – Miss Chicago – who was invited to Salvador on a trip sponsored by the Brazilian airlines to get more tourists from that city to spend their money in Brazil, and how she found the racial situation.

D. Brazilian hospitality – the shoemaker Manoel and his wife Maria. In that year of study in Brazil there were many occasions of amazing hospitality shown to me, and from all social classes. The Brazilians took immense pride in their generous giving and it was part of the national "character" both spoken and written about in the treatises on the subject. In fact, they bragged about it, especially the "old guard" or adult generation, always with a note of nostalgia of better times. I cite just one example but worthy of all.

I was invited for the main noon meal at the house of Manoel and Maria, friends of my Portuguese professor from Georgetown during her stay in Bahia. Manoel was a shoemaker and repairman and he and his wife and children lived in a tiny, humble house not far from Piedade Plaza near the Portuguese boarding house. It was evident that they had spent the food budget for at least a week or more to prepare lunch ["almoço"] for this gringo they had never met. I left very impressed with their kindness, their good will, and their genuine hospitality. This is what the Brazilians mean when they talk of this characteristic of the Brazilian personality. The trait may be a product of other and better times, but it was certainly present for me during this stay in Brazil.

E. Finally, and a part of an unforgettable and quintessential Bahia was my visit to the peninsula and the Itapagipe District to the famous church of "Nosso Senhor do Bonfim" ["Our Lord of the Good End"]. Already declared a basilica by Rome, the place is famous in Bahia, a church dedicated to Jesus but famous in local folklore for its festivals when the Catholic faith is mixed with the ritual of "candomblé" when the Mothers of the Saint and many of their daughters dressed in all their religious finery come to wash the steps of the church and place flowers upon them, but thinking of their "Jesus" of the "candomblé": Oxalá. The place is the most famous in all Brazil for the mixture of Catholicism and African Religion, what the scholars call "religious syncretism." What I did not get to see was the equally impressive procession when these dozens of ladies walk the many kilometers from the oldest church in Bahia, "Conceição da Praia" from the 16th century all the way to Bonfim.

Maybe the folks interested in Brazil and readers of the Times would begin to see why Salvador was so important in the big scheme of things during the times.

Bahia was done! All these notes of the latest LETTER would be sent in a packet "air mail, registered" to Hansen in New York with the promise of more to come. Next in the big plan was to head down to Rio de Janeiro for work on the dissertation research with Professor Manuel Cavalcanti Proença, the advisor who had sent me to the Northeast for fieldwork and collection on the "cordel" six months ago. Just as important was to do in depth reading of the "cordel" collection at the Casa de Rui Barbosa in Rio, check out the famous northeastern fair and market in the São Cristóvão district in Rio's north zone and discover what else in northeastern folklore could be found, after all Rio was the main destination, along with São Paulo, for one of the nation's most important internal migrations – the poor, impoverished "nordestinos" looking for survival and a better life in the South.

Gaherty is also a young red-blooded enthusiastic "gringo" wanting to experience the famous Rio – the beaches and those gorgeous "cariocas" in the string bikinis, the sights and sounds of Rio and most importantly, Carnival. That would come in due course with just a couple of surprises, altogether unintended, from my "watchdogs" the DOPS.

The only way to get to Rio from Bahia for a Jorge Amado reader was to take the old Lloyd Brasileira Maritime ship, the "slow boat" to Rio, but after several attempts at buying passage and running into a bureaucracy at least as inefficient as the U.S. railway system of the 1960s, I ended up "flying down to Rio."

LETTER IV

RIO DE JANEIRO

1

As planned some six months ago, the beginning of the transition from my now familiar Northeast back to the jazzy city of Rio was easy: I took a taxi to Caetano Forti's very comfortable apartment where he, his brother and his mother Dona Glória were waiting for me and had arranged very comfortable lodging for a few days until I could find something more permanent. The luxury apartment with several maids, fine food and mainly exceptional hospitality fit the ticket. Caetano's father had migrated from Austria and done well in business in Brazil and his mother was descended from aristocratic northeastern literary people – specifically from Ceará and related to Brazil's most famous 19th century Romantic Novelist – José de Alencar. Maybe that explained the vast library with the leather-bound volumes that Caetano for sure had never opened, and the expensive collection of Brazilian paintings. It was through this family that I was exposed to the "other Brazil" – the sophisticated, upper class – a far cry from most of my acquaintances and certainly folk-popular poets of the "Literatura de Cordel."

The experience began right away; Caetano and a friend and their obviously chic, upper-class dates allowed me to tag along on a night on the town. We started in a decent place – the "Castelhinho" Bar facing Ipanema Beach at probably about 10:00 p.m. This "in" place later became a hangout for the people associated with the "Bossa Nova" music in Brazil (along with the "Garota de Ipanema" bar nearby, the place from which Vinicius de Morais and Tom Jobin saw "her" and were inspired over a lot of beer and scotch to write "The Girl from Ipanema"), and even later with Chico Buarque de Holanda who would become my favorite Brazilian composer and singer of all time! In short, it was the cream of the intellectual and social class in Rio; for me there was nowhere to go after that but down! As they say in Rio, "the night is young" ["a noite está começando"]; from there we went to the "in" place on Copacabana Beach in those years - "Sacha's Nightclub." It was party night: there was high volume Brazilian and rock music and the customers – the elite of Rio's youth, the young men dressed in tuxedos ["smoking" in Portuguese], the girls in long, formal dresses, this mixed in with many in the crowd in "elegant casual" attire. We blearily arrived home at 4:00 a.m.; this was my introduction to high living "carioca" style.

It was not to last. The next day I suffered the biggest shock (except for DOPS' dealings) up to that time in my tenure in Brazil while watching the evening news on "Repórter Esso" (like NBC or CBS). We had drinks and were not paying much attention to the news stories when one caught my attention: the TV was announcing the death that day and planned funeral of Professor Manuel Cavalcanti Proença, "Retired Army Colonel and Professor in the 'Escola Superior de Guerra,' the West Point of Brazil!" Then it hit me – "holy shit!" – this was the guy who was supposed to be my thesis director in Brazil! It was the same person who six months earlier had advised me to go to the Northeast, do my fieldwork, return to Rio and we would begin to work on the dissertation. I was stupefied, in shock, not knowing what would become of me and my project.

The <u>Times'</u> readers might vaguely recall what I wrote in LETTER I of our brief, but important encounter at the family home in Flamengo on my first shaky night in Rio, but it's important to repeat some of it because of what would happen later. Professor Proença had been a colonel in the Army before 1964 and the Military Revolution and was teaching at the military academy. His original field was biology and botany, and it was only later that he evolved to become a nationally known professor of Brazilian Literature with a strong interest in folklore. He was an incredible intellectual, a master of many areas. As a young soldier, he had taken part in the famous "Prestes Column" of 1924 in pursuit of the then "communist" in the backlands of the Northeast all the way north to Ceará. He parlayed the experience into writing a famous book about the fauna and flora of the backlands and its folklore: "O Termo de Cuiabá." After that he wrote major literary criticism on many of the greats of Brazilian Literature.

The next day I went to the deceased professor's apartment to express my condolences to the family and attend the wake with all the family remembering better days. He left us, but not his memory. It was only after leaving the apartment, going down the steps to the street that I had my first introduction to the on-going operations of the military government in Rio. Once again, a fellow in a dark suit and tie gave me that Brazilian wave of "come on over here" – hand with the palm facing down and waving the fingers. He said, "Mr. Gaherty, I'm Heitor Dias. I've been assigned to keep track of you here in Rio. There's no problem but you know that the deceased was on the Left and that's why he was "demoted" from active service, "retired" but allowed to teach safe stuff like literature at the Academy. You may know by now that in Brazil it's not just who you are but who you associate with. Your research and activity studying the "so-called" folklore you swear by is creating a bit of a dossier with us. Like I say, no problem yet, but watch your step."

"Nossa!" "I'm just paying my respects to a man who treated me so kindly and really was instrumental in my studies. What else do you expect me to do? I've done nothing wrong and wish you would get it through your heads that I **am** just trying to do research so I can write the damned dissertation a year from now back home. Cavalcanti Proença was one of the greatest literary critics in Brazil and a pioneer in the collection of "cordel" for the Casa de Rui Barbosa here in Rio. That's my connection. I don't suppose you people have anything against Rui Barbosa for god's sake?"

The guy put a firm hand on my shoulder and said, "I'll ignore your smart alecky ways for now, but don't do anything stupid" and walked off.

I said to myself, "Puta que pariu!" I was shaking as I got on the bus and got off at the Forti's apartment. I didn't say anything to anyone about the encounter but just recounted the time at the wake. As it turned out plenty was going to happen to take my mind off it.

2

There is a small chapter in "Cordel" but important – the reporting of soccer games both local and national – which would come later in my research and reading that hot summer in Rio, but it held second stage to this! My introduction to soccer ["futebol" in Brazil], perhaps one of the most important parts of Brazilian culture, could not have been more impressive. I went by car with Caetano Forti and his friend Chico Ramiro who directed an office for investments in Amazonia to the "Carioca" Soccer Championship in Maracaná Stadium.

An aside: there was a national campaign by the military government in the 1960s to open the Amazon area to private economic development; it was accompanied by a huge public relations campaign, i.e. propaganda, by the Military in its "March to the West" ["Marcha para o Oeste"] in the spirit of "new discovers and explorers" ["Os Novos Bandeirantes"]. It was a little like a gold rush, but this was land. It promised riches for the investors and a bright future for Brazil.

Back to the game. We arrived at the famous Maracaná traveling through the Rebouças Tunnel under Corcovado mountain, an adventure itself in the never-ending semi-darkness of the tunnel. It was downright scary for a Nebraskan used to open plains and country roads. The stadium was said to have a standing-room only capacity of 200,000! On that day, it was jammed with 143,000 enthusiastic fans. The "gringo" had never seen anything like it in his life.

The favorite team was "the team of the people" – Flamengo - versus Bangu. I cannot comment with any authority, being a total newcomer to such things, but my hosts said that it was a good game. Bangu won 3-0 but the interesting thing was that one of the players of Flamengo was badly injured but could not come out of the game due I think to a rule of stipulated number of substitutions. He played the final period limping badly from one end of the field to the other. The game was called by one of the field judges before the official time ending the game by the clock, an extremely rare event in the history of Brazilian soccer. I only know that "old-timers" recall this game and its role in the "lore" of Brazilian "futebol."

The following description of the moment and the atmosphere in the stadium by a person totally new to the phenomenon is taken directly from my notes, untouched.

"There are two levels in the gigantic stadium, the "arquibancada" above and the "plateia" below; Caetano, his friend and I were seated in the lower deck under the partial cover of the upper deck. The upper deck according to Caetano was a better seat, more exciting and with a better view of the playing field, but also dangerous. The men sat shirtless, cursing the referees, the opponents and their fans, many on both sides inebriated. The second period was never completed due to scuffles on the field and the stadium turned into bedlam, confusion and chaos that lasted some forty minutes. The result: the game was suspended and nine players were removed from the field by the judges.

"In the standing room section, a kind of moat surrounding the playing field, I saw people literally being trampled by groups of 100 to 150 youths who were running crazily around the oval. From my seat far from the playing field, it seemed like worms or maggots oozing around the moat below the playing field. Dangerous it was for those who got in their way! Nearer to us in the lower deck there were fights breaking out all over. And when the game was suspended the people in the upper deck had rolled up balls of newspaper, set them afire, and were hurling them down on us in the lower deck. I estimate I saw two or three dozen balls of fire around us. One could not help but think of a famous soccer riot of the times in Lima, Peru, when the security guards had padlocked the gates to the stadium with the result that many people were trampled and crushed by a panicked crowd trying to exit the stadium. In the Maracanã I recalled the intense heat and wondered if things would get worse."

"I forgot to comment the beginning of the game; it was incredible! When the players entered the playing field via a tunnel on one side of the field, thousands of huge flags were waved by the fans. The noise was deafening with rockets and fireworks shooting into the air and the entire stadium was filled with a thick cloud of acrimonious smoke. There was a tremendous uproar of fans shouting for their teams. I had never seen anything like it; this made the "Big Red Cornhuskers" displays of enthusiasm seem like tiddlywinks. My impression, and I was keeping it to myself, was "How could a game be taken so seriously?"

"Equally impressive was the traffic flow out of the stadium after the game: all the traffic seemed to flow so easily, and I saw no traffic jams or wrecks. This, I thought, was not the Rio I would see with the massive traffic jams in Copacabana and the insane jockeying of "cariocas" just going back and forth to work downtown. The folkloric notion bandied about in the times that the Brazilian race car drivers at Indianapolis Speedway with all their success were former taxi drivers from Rio or São Paulo came to mind."

"That night was a special night to remember at dinner at the Fortis – peals of laughter, much shouting and carrying on about the game. It was then I learned, coincidentally, that "Flamengo" was indeed the "team of the people" ["o time do povo"] and Fluminense "the team of the rich." As a folklorist and fan of "cordel" my choice of a favorite was to be obvious. Studying the story-poems of "cordel" and their relation to Brazilian Literature seemed a whole lot safer. I would have made a lousy Brazilian!"

3

Time to introduce my "new love" – the DiGorgio Classic Guitar! It was during this stay with the Forti Family that I realized a great dream in Brazil. On "Carioca Street" in the downtown there was a shop called the "Silver Guitar" ["Guitarra da Prata," the best in Rio.] I went there, saw the fine collection of classic guitars and played many of them, experimenting with the tone and fret action and of course considered the workmanship and the looks. The major guitar makers in Brazil at that time were from São Paulo and all Italian descent (like the famous violins from Italian makers). Among the best brands were DiGiorgio and Giannini, the second extremely expensive. The best of all was a "Del Vecchio" for hundreds of cruzeiros, well beyond my meager budget! Among the DiGiorgios there were some fine instruments. The room where one tried out the guitar was small but with fine acoustics – I thought I had arrived in heaven playing that fine rosewood DiGiorgio. I ended up buying it, taking advantage of the "cash sale." It was explained to me later that Brazil happened to be in one of its many economic crises of the times, thus the unusual price; I paid for what would become perhaps the best investment of my life, but still it was all the money I had, this the money saved during those spartan six months in Recife at the "Chácara das Rosas" boarding house in Recife. I would see the music festivals on TV in the coming month and suspected that Chico Buarque de Holanda or Roberto Carlos or others from the Bossa Nova and Brazilian Popular Music movements played this model!

So I took the guitar ensconced in its hard case, handling it like a new born baby, in a taxi to the Fortis where I left it until my planned departure for the USA in July of 1967.

4

In those days research began, first at the National Campaign for Folklore in downtown Rio opposite the old Ministry of Education Building, the one famous for its columns and windows done by the avant-garde architect Corbusier and then no less than Oscar Niemeyer, Brazil's most famous architect. It was there I met Renato Almeida, director of the Campaign and a top-flight folklorist of those times. Also important was the friendship with Vicente Salles, second in command, director of the "Brazililian Folklore Magazine" ["Revista Brasileira de Folclore"], by chance a native of Belém do Pará and a scholar of the "literatura de cordel" of the Guajarina Press in the same city. "Guajarina" was the primary publisher in Brazil of story-poems of WWI and WWII and Iverson of the INR would be extremely interested in such poems because they reflected the accurate Brazilian "take" on both wars and Brazil's relation to the United States. Belém, curiously enough, would be tied to another tight spot and "hot soup" moment for me in Rio in the coming months.

Vicente facilitated the use of the Campaign's small but excellent folklore library, giving me great hints ["dicas"] for research in Rio, not the least a first contact with Orígenes Lessa, one of the main journalists interested in the "cordel" with articles in "Anhembi" and "Revista Esso," seminal works on "cordel." Orígenes' life was in a bit of a state of flux in 1967, but a short and intense meeting gave me great guidance. Vicente also directed me to the Northeastern Fair at São Cristóvão Market in the north zone of Rio, the best place to meet "cordel" writers living in Rio and getting their poetry.

Finally, there was a related cultural moment to those halcyon days of the mid-1960s in Rio: Vicente's wife was a member of the Rio de Janeiro Symphonic Orchestra and my guide to the classical music scene in the city. You don't think of such a thing in the tropics, but it existed and was important, not the least because of Brazil's most famous composer, Heitor Villa - Lobos.

5

In those first days in Rio in December of 1966 I walked about the downtown getting to know Avenida Rio Branco well. It was on one of those occasions that I met Dr. Orlando Gomes of the Fulbright Commission in Brazil; he was to provide liaison between the Commission and the grantees like me, and help to iron out any problems. I considered telling him about Hansen and the <u>Times</u>, Iverson and the INR, and my moments with the DOPS, but thought better of it; no sense complicating things. I did skirt the issue a bit with some general, naïve inquiries into Brazil, the government, politics and literature. Answering one of my questions, he said none of the Fulbrighters had gotten into any "real" trouble other than perhaps some loud parties reported by neighbors (certainly not my case living in a boarding house of one of the ubiquitous widows in Rio trying to eke out a living by renting out rooms). And he advised to just keep on the straight and narrow, "like all the Brazilians in these times." I did consider that in a real emergency, a last resort kind of situation, he might be helpful.

He did however enlighten me on a major aspect of my work and research in Brazil: in his own words, he "tried to open my eyes" to the truth about northeastern culture and the culture of Modernisn in southern Brazil. He was a sociologist by trade and had a rather negative attitude toward Gilberto Freyre, that "icon" of Northeastern Culture. He maintained that Freyre's intellectual movement "The Regionalist Movement of the Northeast" was really second to the Modernist Movement of Mário de Andrade and others in the South, modeling itself on the latter. In short, Freyre's contribution was not as great as the notions bandied about in the Northeast. Was this envy or the truth? For certain the conversation demonstrated the prejudice or even enmity between intellectuals in the Northeast and the South, something that I would run into in the coming months in Brazil. And I'm speaking of the "big players" of erudite culture; don't even dare to talk of the attitude toward folklore, "cordel" and the "colorful" dances and songs of the Northeast, including those of the Afro-Brazilian Religion. As mentioned, in the 1960s one of the famous Buarques de Holanda, an uncle of my music hero Chico, had written the standard Portuguese Dictionary respected greatly across the nation; in it he would call "cordel" "a literature of little value and prestige." So am I making my point? The downright racial and cultural prejudice would only gradually become apparent to me in conversations with "Cariocas" and keeping my eyes open in the coming months – on the buses, at the Northeastern Fair, and especially on the beaches and streets of the "rich" parts of Rio's South Zone. I recalled conversations with Ariano Suassuna in Recife and Luís da Câmara Cascuo in Natal; both preferred to be "intellectuals from the provinces" and stay far away from Rio or São Paulo. I suspected even then that the prejudice was a two-sided coin.

6

In Rio I would go to the movies regularly, almost always interested in those with northeastern themes based upon its literature and folklore. I saw "Blood Stream" ["Riacho de Sangue"] filmed in Bahia and Pernambuco, in color, a film that tells in a free and liberal manner the story of "Holy Lourenço" ["O Beato Lourenço"] and Father Cícero's "sacred bull" in Juazeiro. There were battle scenes with the government soldiers, with bandits, and the traditional conflict betwee the courageous backlander and the rich landholder. It was a plot that came directly from "cordel." The movie was a totally romanticized and idealized version of the same, but it was the first time I saw movies in the South on Northeastern culture, an important topic for the dissertation. The INR people would be interested in the "cordel" version because Father Cícero was considered a rebel against the established state and national governments at the time, and any local backlander who threatened rebellion against the landholder was a red flag for DOPS and the military.

A lot more innocent was a film considered a "classic" in later days in the Brazilian cinema, Lima Barreto's "Bandit" ["O Cangaceiro"] which was done about 1954. The film was black and white with poor sound but was one of the first in Brazil to treat the phenomenon of banditry ["o cangaço"] and it did so in a romanticized way. It brought back memories to me of Saturday afternoons in the small-town cinema in Nebraska where we might see an old Gene Autry or Roy Rogers "oater." An entirely different matter was the film by Glauber Rocha – "God and the Devil in the Land of the Sun" ["Deus e o Diabo na Terra do Sol"] of Brazil's "New Cinema" from the 1950s and 1960s with its stark realism and undercurrents of social unrest. After all, this film as well depicted the northeastern bandit, but wrapped in a wildly surrealistic and artistic covering.

7

In stark contrast to that impoverished, folkloric northeast would be my next experience in Rio. I would spend Christmas Eve once again with the Fortis. I think it was Dona Glória (Caetano's mother) who made it a point for me not to be homesick, being so far away from home and family in the U.S. There was first an exchange of presents at home and then we went to Glória's sister's house for Christmas Eve dinner of ham, turkey and much more and the traditional champagne toasts. Then they took me for a drive along the beaches of Leblon and Ipanema to see the Christmas decorations. There were few that year; the Fortis said that it was a bad year for the economy; sales were down thirty-five per cent from the previous year, inflation was increasing and prices going up (I wondered: was this why I got that incredible deal on the Di Giorgio?) We were at the height of the regime of the first military president General Castelo Branco of Ceará and his secretary of commerce Roberto Campos who was famous for his austerity program "to straighten out the Brazilian economy." It would be he and his colleagues who would bring about the devaluation of the Brazilian currency and the change to the "new cruzeiro" a short time later.

The Christmas Dinner was another snapshot of upper class "carioca" life: there was much conversation, a bit of singing of Christmas carols, the dinner itself and more singing. Among the guests was a diplomat who served in Lima and Montevideo and was the set-up man for Castelo Branco's trips within Brazil. There was a relative of the family who had designed the "Museu de Arte Sacra" in Salvador and was now a professor at one of the big universities in Rio. Equally impressive for me was the end of the night: Caetano, his brother and friends once again went to the nightclub-bar "Sacha's" in Copacabana the large discoteque crowded with the "cream" of upper class Rio – some in tuxedo, the girls in long formal dresses. We dragged in at 4:00 a.m.

Mass was later that day and a Gaherty never would miss Christmas Day mass. It was a bit anti-climactic, an open-air mass at the end of Copacabana Beach, but a new experience for this gringo. Most in attendance were young folks, the "jovem guarda" as the generation was called in the mid-1960s, and there was a decidedly modern priest from the new Catholic Church, "Um padre p'ra frente."

In those days, it was raining incessantly in Rio and Rio State. Houses from the slums ["favelas"] were sliding down the hills and even apartment buildings at the base of the hills were crumbling in all the South Zone. Tropical rain storms!

8

It was in those days that I initiated research at the famous "House of Rui Barbosa" in Botafogo, a long but important story. Rui Barbosa was probably the most famous orator and statesman in Brazilian history – ambassador, candidate for President and important in the founding of the League of Nations in The Hague at the beginning of the 20th century. He was a legendary, almost folkloric figure in Brazilian history – an intellectual, lawyer of great causes and to boot a polyglot! The word was he taught the fundamentals of English to the Queen of England herself! Upon his death, they converted his home and acreage into a park, museum, library and research center, the library begun with his own vast collection of books. Of note is that the Rui Barbosa Estate was on Embassy Row in Botafogo, not a bad location.

The fact that the "Casa" possessed the best archive of "literatura de cordel" was an accident in Brazilian intellectual life. Because old Rui was so well known as a polyglot, they founded a section in Philology in the Research Center. Within this understandably rather serious section someone suggested they should also have an interest in the spoken and "popular" speech of Brazil. From there it was only one step for interest in "popular literature in verse" (a more accurate term for what would become known as the "literatura de cordel"), said literature serving as an archive of the Portuguese of the "masses of the Northeast." Due to the weight of intellectuals such as Manuel Cavalcanti Proença (my original mentor in "cordel,") Manuel Diégues Júnior (filmmaker Cacá Diégues' father) one of the best known cultural anthropologists in the country, the writer Orígenes Lessa and others just a little less important, the CRB came up with the funds for Proença to go to the Northeast and "rescue" what remained of the old "cordel" with the purpose of creating the definitive collection of popular verse in Brazil. So, they did it. In the end, the CRB collection at that time also comprised the personal collections of Proença, Orígenes Lessa and Diégues Júnior. All was done with the idea of preserving the "folhetos" and "romances" in verse and studying the Portuguese in them.

So it was that the "Casa" became my principal research home in Rio. It was at the "Casa" where I would meet Sebastião Nunes Batista from the most prominent of Brazil's folk poetry families of the Northeast. Son of Francisco das Chagas Batista, colleague of Leandro Gomes de Barros, the most famous poet of "cordel," brother of Pedro Batista, Sebastião would become one of my best friends in Brazil and my guide not only for the "cordel" but for other aspects of Brazilian life and culture, not the least the Afro-Brazilian religious rite in Rio, the "Umbanda." I would sit across the table from him in the old tiny library for "cordel' research, taking hand-written notes of the story-poems (before Xerox machines) and absorb his tales like a sponge.

All this was good stuff for the LETTER and innocent stuff for the DOPS, or so I thought. Sebastião was far from the only Brazilian in the 1940s who flirted with the idea of popular, Marxist leaders and a solution to the problems of the poor.

9

"Cordel" poets hung out wherever they could (meaning avoiding arrest by the police for selling their booklets of verse without a peddler's license to the many northeastern migrants living in greater Rio, living in the "subúrbios" but daring to declaim verse in plazas in the South Zone). One such place was the Largo do Machado in the old Flamengo District. At the end of December, I went to the Largo, going on a tip from Sebastião at the CRB, to see for the first time the folk dance-popular theater of "Bumba Meu Boi," one of the less famous but not less important aspects of Brazilian folklore. It really is a sort of folk dance – popular theater and would be performed by northeastern migrants living in greater Rio. At that time the "Largo" was known as one of the many places where Northeasterners could get together to socialize in Rio, all of them migrants. There were "romances" and "folhetos" of "literatura de cordel" for sale as well. The moment was a bit ironic in that I had naturally wanted to see "Bumba Meu Boi" in the Northeast (or in the North, famous as well in Maranhão State but also with a well-known variant in the Amazon Region), closer to the area of its origin.

The "Largo" or "Plaza" was filled "hillbillies," one of them dancing to the music of a "rabeca" a Northeastern folk violin, backlander style. It was then I met a renowned figure of northeastern culture in Rio – João José dos Santos or "Azulão – famous in Rio as an oral poet - singer ["cantador"] as well as for "literatura de cordel" in the South-Center of Brazil. Azulão rested from time to time from his role in the folk dance to drink beer in a local street bar ["pé sujo"] to the side of the plaza, and it was there we conversed. In the bar Azulão sang songs from the backlands and another poet from Ceará State improvised verse.

The play was described in my notes as follows, I a novice seeing it for the first time with no other knowledge of it: the cast of characters was Matthew ["Matéu"], a black woman (the part was done by a man in blackface,) and young men ["galans"] with hats with ribbons, mirrors and small toy swords adorning them, and the bull ["o boi"] itself, white with red spots. The bull was large, almost round, the bull's head with horns, a white sheet on top with those red spots, but all covering what must have been a wooden frame with a man "playing" the bull. The dancing and music were pretty, considering I did not understand one word of the Portuguese, but when I left at mid-night the play was not over yet. The "bull" had died, had been resuscitated, and was being followed by "friend bear" ["amigo urso"].

The presentation was sponsored by the Mayor's Office in Rio, without such funding it could not have taken place. To me the folk dance – play was colorful, interesting and fun, to a degree, but it was meeting the amazing Azulão and hearing him declaim and sing his verse and songs that was the highlight.

As I was leaving the dark plaza whose streetlights only did a partial job of lighting the area, I was suddenly scared out of my wits. I'm no fighter and of course as an American did not dare carry a weapon (am I kidding, especially after the gun incident in Recife), and North Americans were known by the muggers in Rio as "filet mignon" at the time. You had to watch your back. A man suddenly came up to me out of the shadows at the first street corner, flashed a smile, and said,

"Gaherty, surely you remember me? I met you outside that leftist Colonel Proença's house a few weeks ago. I just wanted you to know we have not forgotten about you. Seems you are on the straight and narrow these days at the Rui Barbosa Research Center, and although we have been keeping track of your friend Sebastião Batista for years (he impersonated a bona fide medical doctor a few years ago up in the backlands of Bahia State and made a modest living at it even without an official degree), he has caused no serious trouble since. He hangs out at the São Cristóvão Market on Sunday mornings and is the "letter guy" typing letters on his old typewriter for all the illiterate hillbillies homesick for their sweethearts and families in the Northeast. No harm in that I guess, unless the letters are political."

"I guess you are doing the "folklore" thing again tonight huh? That hillbilly shit is contaminating the South Zone, but what can you do? They outnumber all of us real "cariocas." The only good thing is all the easy "ass" you can get when the chicks get off the north zone buses and land on Ipanema Beach on a Sunday morning. If I were you however, I'd be careful talking to that poet you met tonight. He's known for some political stories and making some snide remarks about the current regime, none so far to put him in jail, but you can tell what side he's on."

"So Senhor Gaherty, it's good to see you again, work hard and have fun in Rio."

The reader is correct if he or she is beginning to sense *my* sense of paranoia in the hot summer of 1966-1967 in the "marvelous city" of Rio. At least I didn't get mugged.

10

And a good place to get mugged was during the wild New Year's Eve celebration in Rio that came up in the next few days. The celebration goes by the French name "Reveillon" and is without compare in Brazil and perhaps in the world. I arrived at Copacabana Beach at about ten p.m. There were thousands and thousands of people in the streets of the "bairro" itself and on the beach, many carrying white candles and vases or bunches of white flowers, a homage to Iemanjá, the goddess of the sea in the Afro-Brazilian Spiritist cults. The homage can be seen in many parts of Brazil wherever there is Afro-Brazilian religion. It is famous in Bahia but on another date, February 2, with a huge popular festival. Bahia's iconic singer, Dorival Cayimi wrote the song "Dia 2 de Fevereiro" commemorating the festival as it is in Salvador da Bahia.

The entire length of the great beach of Copacabana, a crescent like a half-moon, was jammed with people, many of them participants in the cults paying homage to the goddess, also representing the Virgin Mary in Brazil's religious syncretism. They were dressed in the traditional clothing of "candomblé:" the women in blue or white skirts and adorned with necklaces and bracelets ["pulseiras"] of gold or silver color, and the men, the "oguns" or male participants, were dressed all in white. Some people would go to the edge of the sea and place one or two candles in the sand, light them and offer prayers. There were many groups of perhaps one hundred persons, in circles with hundreds of lit candles. Iemanjá is also a principal deity of "Umbanda," the amorphous Spiritist rite prevalent in Rio, and who knows how many of the thousands were from that cult. Most of the people were black, but white women and men were among them. There are specific chants and dances associated with each cult and with the homage to Iemanjá, and it is not easy to describe the immense scene, so impressive for both its size and for the "movement" of the dancers.

At the touch of mid-night, all manner of fireworks and rockets were set off all along the six kilometers of the beach and the air (there happened to be no wind; all was calm) was totally filled with the smoke from the fireworks. The official offering to Iemanjá was done by the "Mothers" or "Fathers" of the saint [Mãe ou Pai de Santo], or the "Sons or Daughters of the saint," [Filho ou Filha de Santo], all in the clothing described. Some offerings were done by persons who entered the water, wading in the waves and tossing or pushing baskets with the offerings - flowers, food, whatever. The folk belief is as follows: if the offering is pulled into the sea by the waves, it is a sign that Iemanjá accepts it. If it returns to the beach, one must toss or push it out again. There were many small boats full of people in the middle of the bay, also tossing out their offerings. I saw baskets of white lilies (the favorite flower of Iemanjá) and bottles of sugar cane rum [cachaça], and wine and beer among the offerings. Some people entered the water in swim suits, but most were in the Afro-Brazilian attire. Iemanjá's colors vary from region to region, blue in Bahia, white in Rio. There were groups of "Spiritists" from one end of the huge beach to the other. Each group "constructed" or built a small barrier of sand to separate it from another group, and within the area they prepared a sort of "altar" of candles and flowers in the form of a circle. The "Oguns" and "Mães de santo" led the chants and dances. Groups varied, some much quieter than others, and there were many variations.

There was one group, I imagine of "Umbanda," where the women were smoking large cigars, and the leaders wore a sort of "headdress," Indiginous Style with feathers of tropical birds. I believe they were of what is called the "Caboclo" variant of "Umbanda." Specific drum beats accompanied the dances and chants performed alongside the altars with the bottles of rum, flowers and images of the "saints." One group caught my attention for the fact it was all male, nude to the waist and singing Indigenous chants. Yet another was of "Daughters" of the saint dancing around the altar. I saw several women in a state of trance or "possession by the saints," or in their parlance "cavalgadas" or "ridden" by the saints. As they say, "The saint had fallen," ["o santo caiu"] and the women had a "fixed" glare on their faces, balancing in the dance.

The beach was also full of tourists, mostly Brazilians, but also many foreigners. There were many couples, lovers tightly embraced in the Carioca night, and even a few "marginais" or vagrants in ragged clothing. The waves were strong and beautiful, reflecting the brilliant light that came from behind - light that came from thousands of open windows and terraces of the tall apartment buildings facing Copacabana beach. It seemed that each window had people viewing the spectacle, and this together with the reflection from literally thousands of candles along the beach plus the brilliance of the fireworks made for an unforgettable scene.

For the young "folklorist" Gaherty it was an incredible experience without equal in that Brazil of 1966-1967. Copacabana was impressive on any night of the year with its "movement," ["movimento"] but on New Years' Eve I believe there were few scenes to match it anywhere.

Apart from the "folkloric" scenario, there were thousands of revelers simply celebrating the coming in of the New Year. These were mainly from the middle and upper classes, many dressed in formal clothing - tuxedo and gown - mixed together on the great sidewalk of Copacabana and in the many beaches and nightclubs on its edge. The contrast of this latter group to the huge mass of the religious cults, the "other" Brazil with its deafening drum beat, chants and dances, was truly memorable, a true contrast of the cultures of the "Two Brazils."

The scene continued into the wee hours of the morning, the restaurants overflowing and there were traffic jams on Avenida Atlântica in front of the beach. In 1966 it was still the "small" avenue of only two lanes! I lasted until 3:00 a.m. before retiring to my modest boarding house on Posto 6 (another story to tell).

11

It was about this time, shortly after the New Year that I moved to "Dona Júlia's" boarding house [pensão]. She was originally from Ceará state and lived with her nervous daughter Dona Janaína on a semi-quiet street a few blocks back from the beach in Posto 6 of Copacabana, the place "researched and approved" by Dona Glória Forti, Caetano's mother. I learned only later that we were very near the home of no less than Carlos Drummond de Andrade, "Prince of Brazilian poetry" of the period, a famous poet of the Modernist Movement, and not far from the residence of João Guimarães Rosa who was for me the most artistic Brazilian novelist of the 20th Century.

I'm not sure where the boarding house should enter this LETTER, but here it is. It was yet another aspect of Brazilian life that you didn't read about in the papers but is part of what made Brazil so interesting. Life in that boarding house was "something else!" Dona Júlia cussed everyone and everything - politicians, crooks, capitalists, and ner' do wells - in her fierce and personal battle to survive as a widow in the Brazil of those years. It was a common phenomenon in the Brazil of that time: a rented room in an apartment owned by a widow trying to maintain her family in the battle to survive in a country with insane inflation, a life each day more difficult in that Brazil of the so-called "economic miracle" of the military regime and of Delfim Neto, the obese Minister of Finance. Perhaps more important, something I would accidentally discover days or weeks later, was that Dona Júlia's "pensão" was exactly in front of the building and apartment of the Ferreira Lima family and my future good friend Cristina Maria.

Dona Júlia was the epitome of the cliché in Brazil of that time of the "masculine woman" ["mulher macha"] of the Northeast. I never heard anyone swear with such vigor at the politicians, petty thieves in the local food markets and inflation, and even her clients who rented a room in the boarding apartment. I can only imagine what she said of me in my absence!

At that time of year, it was incredibly hot. I divided my time between research at the Casa de Rui Barbosa, visits to the Northeastern Fair in Rio's North zone, reading at home, cinema and the Carioca Carnival to be described in a moment. There was also time to do a lot of tourism (mandatory in Rio) with Don, the Peace Corps friend I had met in Bahia; we went to the great tourist sites. We enjoyed the beaches of Copacabana, Ipanema and Leblon, the Botanical Gardens, the Tijuca Area, Sugar Loaf, the North Zone of Rio and the São Cristóvão Fair and Market, and a bus trip to Petropolis to see the great Museum of Pedro II, the Bragança Emperor of Brazil after independence from Portugal. One might recall the "Brazilian" take on Independence when his father Pedro I, after Portugal and the royal family were liberated from Napoleon, chose to stay in Brazil rather than head home with his famous line "I'm staying," ["Eu fico."] All was done in the intense heat and high humidity of the Carioca summer.

A memorable night with Don my Peace Corps friend was our trip to the restaurant "Lisbon at Night" ["Lisboa à Noite"] in Copacabana where I dined on "Beef Portuguese Style," Roberto tried "lulas" ["squid in its own ink"] and most important, we listened to "Fado." We understood the owner also owned "O Galo" and "Maxims" in Lisbon and was a friend of Amália Rodrigues, the "diva" of Fado music from that era who had recently performed in Lisbon at Night in Rio. The "fado" made a strong impression on me - the woman dressed in black with black shawl, the man who at times "dueled" with her in song, and the musical accompaniment of the "guitarradas" or guitar style from Portugal. It was all just a small continental interlude from the main attraction – Brazil and Rio.

12

It was about that time that I met (where else but on Ipanema Beach) the young Cristina Maria who would become a good friend and "a sort of" girlfriend (more felt by me than she) and would share experiences which also marked my life as a young American bachelor in Rio. It all happened in that cliché of a moment when a young American takes a deep breath and stammers an "Oi, como vai?" to the good-looking chick at the beach on one of the hot, sunny mornings in Rio. Cristina was happy enough to meet a "gringo" who knew some Portuguese and seemed innocent enough. I remember she was with her little sister as well. I would see her again a few times before we would get to know each other well enough to discover we were "neighbors" in Rio. It was good fortune to live in the tall apartment building opposite that of the Ferreira Lima family (and Cristina Maria) which gave me the opportunity to spend time with her and her very hospitable family during those next few months.

It is a chapter a bit personal, and a type of "ingenuous love" still on my part, but despite everything, our time together would mark my life in that magical year in Brazil. As I said there was a serious girlfriend in Recife, and of course I spent all that time with the Chácara buddies in the Red-Light Zone of Boa Viagem Beach, but this was different. It was great to meet and "date" a classy, good looking young lady in Rio de Janeiro! I could afford to take Cristina Maria to the Castelinho Bar on Ipanema Beach where over time we got to know each other very well in one of the dark, corner booths. I think maybe I was falling in love with this very young but immensely well-built and intelligent Brazilian chick. The hormones were raging for both of us (the reader can use his or her own imagination). Still though, there were limitations in a nightclub crowded with "Cariocas" out on the town. One thing not so different from Nebraska though was the night everyone in the bar was "mooned" when a yellow VW Bug ["Fusca"] rolled by with two white buns staring us all in the face!

Among other things, it was Cristina Maria who introduced me to the music of Chico Buarque de Holanda, singer, composer and my favorite musician in Brazil. There were many occasions when we would watch the weekly, national televised show of MPB ["Brazilian Popular Music"] when figures like Chico Buarque, Nara Leão, Gerardo Vandré, Jair Rodrigues, and other greats of the times would compete for the "song of the year" or "musician" of the year. I think fans of Brazilian music who read this LETTER will get excited hearing of the wave of music following the Bossa Nova of the late 1950s and early 1960s. It was that year that Chico's "A Banda" won the prize and Gerardo Vandré's "Disparada" may have as well.

13

The São Cristóvão Fair in the north zone of Rio would become an important base for research on "cordel" in that hot summer of 1966-1967; it all began with the first visit to the fair in January of 1967. In the 1950s and still in the 1960s the Fair was an important gathering place for northeastern migrants now living in Greater Rio to meet and "cure homesickness" ["matar saudades"] of the old life in the Northeast. In 1967 the fair was huge with all the attributes of the weekly fairs in the Northeast - food, drink, hand woven hammocks, roll tobacco, clothing, tools and all the rest. More important, the fair served as a place to socialize and to hear the music of the old Northeast in the form of the trios playing music called "Forró." The trio consisted in a triangle, a drum and a small accordion or "sound box." The musicians were dressed in the leather cowboy hats of the Northeast, not the stylized version made famous by Luis Gonzaga of recording fame, but the small, short brimmed version seen throughout the Northeast.

On this, the first of many visits, I met an old black gentleman originally from Manaus who sold the story-poems of "Editora Prelúdio" of Sao Paulo and tourist trinkets ["bugigangas"] to make a meager living in the fair. He considered himself a "pious" man with the gift of preaching the word of God. I also bought "folhetos" from one of the veteran poets of the fair, Antônio Oliveira, whose stock was mainly from Ceará. He would receive the story-poems through the mail and sold me many "at discount."

On this visit, I also reencountered the poet Azulão who sold aside from his many own romances and "folhetos" the Prelúdio poems with their colored, comic-book style covers. Short, 38 years old, he used a small, primitive sound system, a sort of small amplifier - speaker, and a microphone to "sing" and sell his stock of poems. Extremely personable, with a real talent of showmanship, he mixed declamation and singing of the poem with many jokes and asides to the customers, who happened to be mainly men. At the same time, he kept a constant eye on his stock (there were small time thieves about) and sold story-poems to an avid public.

14

In this part of the LETTER to the "Times," there were many events or happenings in Rio that were unconnected, so I sent them with the title "Potpourri, Rio de Janeiro, January 1967 1."

1. I went to mass at the Fort in Copacabana near the far end of the beach next to Ipanema on that same Sunday afternoon after the São Cristóvão Fair, listening to "modern" sacred music. I must admit it was more than a desire to fulfill the Sunday obligation of a Catholic. A handout was given at the entrance advising the women at mass to not come with low-cut dress or blouse, a fact reiterated by the priest from the altar. Not all got the message.

2. I was with Sebastião Nunes Batista at the Casa de Ruy talking "business" about "cordel." Sebastião spoke of Rodolfo Coelho Cavalcante in Bahia and his extreme moralist vision in his poetry. Sebastião believed that it was all due to Rodolfo's conversion to Protestantism in his youth. There is no doubt his conservatism and moral stance did come from that important part of life. The poet told of a time when he was teaching in a primary school in Piauí State, and one of his young students asked for a kiss. He told her, "If you are going to be my disciple, no kissing allowed."

3. There was an unforgettable visit to the Benedictine Monastery in the old center of Rio, all arranged by Dona Júlia in the boarding house. It was the first time that I had seen the famous monastery, guided by Fathers Jerônimo and Tito. We had lunch in the large refectory with all the monks, and there was complete silence as we listened to a reading of sacred scriptures. Later they gave me a tour of the monastery which dated from the 16th and 17th centuries in Rio: altars "bathed" in gold and stained glass in the windows and ceiling.

4. End of January 1967. There were never ceasing heavy rains, floods and deaths in the entire greater Rio area. Water, electricity and gas at various times were lacking in the city, not to mention the "favelas" or slums. When I left the boarding apartment I always carried a small candle and matches, this to descend and climb the stairs of the apartment building where we lived on the seventh floor. It was on one of such days that the electrically powered cable car going to Sugar Loaf would stop intermittently in the middle of its

climb first to Urca Hill and then to the Sugar Loaf itself. The car swayed in the air; I speak from personal experience since it stopped once when I was in it. Imagine suddenly, complete silence, the passengers with baited breath, only the sound of the breeze outside and the car swaying back and forth in the wind.

15

Carnival in Rio de Janeiro. A premise: I, a bachelor and dreamer, came to Brazil in part to see this spectacle, based largely on an idealized notion of Carnival from the film "Black Orpheus" ["Orfeu Negro"] seen in my school days at Georgetown. I "did" Carnival ["Brinquei carnaval"] in 1967 with a truly international group, the main persons being Americans living in Rio and working at diverse places - USIS, Peace Corps, and the American Consulate. There were many students in the group as well - from Japan, Italy, Brazil and the U.S. One of the customs of Carnival in 1967 was for friends in neighborhoods to form a "block" and celebrate together, one big party. You all had to have a "block" costume, so it was decided to be "Hawaiians," buy a yard of flowery cloth, wrap it around your waist and/ or boobs and away you go. So it was. Through the Americans I gained access to parties associated with the American Consulate in beautiful parts of the city, i.e. Urca. It was during these days I met a pretty, young American girl from Chicago, a nurse and Peace Corps Volunteer living in Flamengo. We romanced some in those days, unforgettable days for the young gringo. The readers may wonder when I worked and what happened to the research. It was put on hold.

Hansen told me in a letter during that time that he was not expecting anything earth shattering from me for Carnival, after all thousands of tourists came to Rio each year to celebrate, but he encouraged me to just tell it like it happened. So be it. Allow me to tell of the episodes of Carnival.

February 1st. I met the people from the consulate and joined their group: Gloria, Paula, Wanda, Janie, Gino (an Italian from Trieste), and Mario from Florence.

On February 3rd, there was a party at Gloria's house to "plan" Carnival: dancing, drinking, carnival music, and guitar playing, a bit by me.

February 4th. We went to a big carnival party at the home of the Director of USAID in Urca. The dancing was outside on the patio and there was tremendous rain, heat, humidity, and all of us were completely soaked by the rain, but no one stopped "pulando" [dancing] happily to the sound of a true carnival band. We were also soaking wet from the sweat from the samba through the hours. The band was made up of Cariocas supposedly with a link to the great Samba Schools - there were trumpets, clarinet, trombone, and drums and the band played until the wee hours of the morning. And it was a night of much drinking by all. I weaved home through the streets of Copacabana to the boarding apartment.

February 5th. In the morning, everyone went to the beach to "sweat out" the hangover of the previous night. That night we all went as a group to Copacabana Avenue in front of the entrance of the Copacabana Hotel to see the arrival of the famous costume ball people who would attend the big dance in the hotel. A ticket to get in was extremely expensive and hard to come by, so we saw it all from outside. I forget the names of the famous participants, but they were well known in the press and were famous for entering the contests each year, doing the circuit of all the big balls, including ones later in Sao Paulo, Recife and Bahia, supposedly with a different extravagant costume for each ball. They appeared in the photos of the national weeklies "Manchete" or "Fatos e Fotos" in the coverage on Carnival. There is a whole minor chapter of "Brazilian folklore" regarding these folks, the story of the extravagant costumes and costume balls. I might add, another feature of Carnival was the annual international "diva" jazzing up the locals' interest and the press as well; in 1967 it was Gina Lollobrigida, and she was accompanied by that famous Rio playboy, Jorginho Guinle, "theoretical Marxist" and one of the wealthiest persons in Brazil.

February 6th. We went to the beach at Ipanema in the morning and then to another party at Gloria's house in the afternoon; that was followed by a surreal evening and night. It began with a wild ride in an old Buick convertible to the downtown. The car broke down on one of the main downtown streets and we were all pushing it to what destination I do not know when the police arrived. "Get that damned thing out of here! You are blocking traffic." I caught a glimpse of friend Heitor from the DOPS but for whatever reason he didn't approach me, perhaps because I was in the middle of the group. The secret police had enough to worry about with all the rest of drunken, partying foreigners in town. We were in the middle of what they called "street carnival" ["carnaval de rua"] - this was an important part of Carnival when the "blocks," some famous, others just neighborhood groups, would all fill the streets of Rio with dancing, bands, improvised costumes, lots of music and drinking. Somehow or other the car got started and we ended in a party at a distant "bairro" or district of Rio, a party in Jacarepaguá. This club was modest, the people equally modest from the humbler social class but with great samba music. Each district of Rio, rich or poor, has its version of a "country club," no matter how modest; there is a big carnival dance in each. Later in the wee hours of the morning we returned to President Vargas Avenue to dance ["pular"] and just watch the "movimento."

February 7th. We went to the downtown once again, this time in the middle of the day to Presidente Vargas Avenue to see the "movimento" or "action." There were tens of thousands of people dancing in the streets in "blocks" or "ranchos" parading on the main avenue which later would be the scene of the famous Samba Schools. Such groups were called "Sujos" or "Dirty Ones," or "Índios" with the dancers dressed as Indians. It seemed to be almost an atmosphere of hysteria by the masses in the streets. Incredible. That night we went to another dance at the Paissandú Club, "sambando" until 4 a.m.

February 8th. This was the "maxium night" ["noite máxima"] of Carnival. This time our entire group went first to Rio Branco Avenue and then to Presidente Vargas where we entered the wooden grandstands to see and experience the famous Samba School Parade. Gino, the Italian, had wangled tickets, I don't know how, and there was a big hassle to get in; with Gino's Italian "jeito," we joined thousands of others in the main grandstands on both sides of President Vargas, ready to party. We were almost in front of the main stand with the TV cameras showing the parade to all of Brazil in color via the new satellite system done by the military regime.

This was the "famous" carnival, the great night of the parade of the Samba Schools on President Vargas Avenue in the center of Rio. On the long night and next day, the gamut of Rio revelers would pass in parade. I add that even with the brilliance and spectacle of the show in 1966, it was still "pure" as the folklorists would say. The first to parade were the "Societies" ["Sociedades"], the big carnival floats with allegorical themes; I recall costumes of the bull of "Bumba Meu Boi," of northeastern cowboys, huge bumblebees, and then the Model-T cars (a carryover of the first carnival parades of "calhambeques" or "Model – T's," of upper class Cariocas at the beginning of the 20th century.). The floats, all interesting, had a moral and political aside: the beautiful "mulatas" riding on the floats and dancing samba were not topless! The Military Protectors of the Nation and its morality would of course not permit such a thing in 1967.

Then came the "cream," the famous Samba Schools (one always remembers the Samba School of "Black Orpheus"), by far the most impressive part of all Carnival for me. There were literally thousands of participants in each Samba School, each group from one of the poor "favelas" of Rio, mainly black and mulato participants, but with a smattering of white dancers ("wannabes" from TV or the movies or even upper-class Rio), each School with a theme and a theme song memorized and sung by all as they danced down the avenue in front of the spectators and the reviewing stand. The schools were highly organized with a fixed structure (one can perhaps include the entire phenomenon as a part of Brazilian Folklore; this was how it seemed to me). First came the "Comissão de Frente" [the "Board" at it were]. I remember one case when all, perhaps eight or nine men, were jet black and dressed in brilliantly white linen suits with a red carnation in the lapel - "this" was the "classic" clothing worn by the stereotyped Carioca "malandro" [slick rogue], an icon of old Rio.

Then came the "Passistas," the "star" dancers of each school, men and women, followed by a beautiful girl carrying the banner of the school, the "Porta-Estandarte." These dancers were the best! Then came the "wings" or divisions of the large total group ["as azas"], each with variations on the costumes and representing an aspect of the overall theme, comprising perhaps a thousand dancers. Then came the "bateria," the percussion section, also perhaps totaling hundreds of all manner of drums and percussion instruments. It was this group, all in unison, that maintained the "rhythm" and "beat" of the name "Samba School."

I recall the Salgueiro Samba School with its theme of "freedom," the red and white colors, a sub - theme of Tiradentes, a Brazilan martyr for Independence from Portugal, the abolition of slavery, all in incredibly rich costumes. Then came a traditional part of all the schools - the "Bahian Lady" wing - black ladies of all shapes and sizes, but most "big sized" with the huge skirts reminiscent of the Bahian "candomblé" costumes. There was also the school of Vila Isabel: costumes, dancers, percussion, and then Mangueira, perhaps the most famous school of all in its colors of pink and green! The night was long, and for me tiring; each school took from one to two hours to pass the reviewing stand, and there were many schools, a true Brazilian spectacle! We were standing the entire time, the wooden bleachers vibrating up and down with the flow of the "samba dancing."

The parade would go into the wee hours and then into daylight of the next day. Still awake, we experienced the dawn of that Carnival morning, a long, colorful and romantic time bringing back memories of "Black Orpheus" when Orpheus walked in the wet streets of dawn on Ash Wednesday, carrying his deceased lover Eurídice to the top of the hill opposite Urca and the denouement of the film. Due to a small but good camera, but now without a flash or batteries after six months in Brazil, I took few slides of Carnival, but did get one memorable one that morning along Getúlio Vargas Avenue - the lady was one of the "Passistas" of Salgueiro and appeared on the cover of one of the national magazines' coverage of Carnival that week.

That next day was Ash Wednesday, but the Cariocas were not finished. They organized yet one more parade on Avenida Atlântica in Copacabana with the prize-winning Samba School, the famous Mangueira. It was Carnival all over again, thousands of people dancing in the streets and "watching the band pass by." These were the words expressing the theme of one of Chico Buarque's great pop songs of the times, "A Banda," which captured the moment, the age and perhaps the spirit of carnival for all ages. That morning the noise, the heat and the humidity were almost unbearable.

In sum, it was a great spectacle, a great party and my dream come true of spending Carnival in Rio. It is difficult to explain; I am not normally one attracted to noise, to costume parties or balls, but being a bachelor and not wanting to be a "square," I did the whole thing. As the Brazilians would ask and answer at the time, "Did you dance?" "Yes, I danced." ["Pulou?" "Sim, pulei.]

It all was another part of my "research" as a folklorist studying the "cordel" since Carnival was one of its themes. Maybe that's a stretch. As the "Chácara" guys in Recife had said months earlier, "Folklore is a pretty lousy front for what you are really doing." Heitor Dias, my "friend" from the DOPS in Rio never showed up to spoil the fun, and it was a great part of the LETTER from Rio.

16

Pot-pourri of Rio Part II

Classical Guitar in Rio

It was in those days that I, an amateur classical guitarist, had an encounter with a guitarist living in Rio, Mr. Araújo. He told me of his youth in Rio and a friendship with Laurindo Almeida in their younger days. Both were learning to play classical guitar, and Laurindo made the decision to leave Brazil, believing that in his homeland there was no future for the instrument and style of play, and immigrated to the United States. The story did not end there - Laurindo evolved to become one of the world's famous guitarists, doing LP recordings, sound tracks for Hollywood movies, and no less important, he came to the top of the class of both jazz and "Bossa Nova" musicians. His friend Araújo stayed in Rio, played samba music on the radio, and obviously regretted that he did not follow the same path as Laurindo. Moral of the story: classical music in Brazil was a challenge in 1967, certainly for classic guitar. I met one of Brazil's best known classical guitarists in the airport in Rio, a Mr. Barbosa, leaving for a tour. And I knew a person or two in the Rio de Janeiro Symphony, but such people lived for the joy and challenge of the music and not the monetary rewards.

A climatic note

From time to time due to conditions of weather, climate, moon, I don't know what, the entire beach of Copacabana was exposed to what they called the "ressaca" or high tide and rough seas and gigantic waves which crashed across the two-lane Avenida Atlântica and up against the apartment buildings. As a student of Brazilian Portuguese, I thought it was interesting that "ressaca" also means "hangover" in Brazil.

"Payer of Promises" ["Pagador de Promessas"]

I saw for the first time the film "Payer of Promises," ["Pagador de Promessas"] so important for my research in Brazil on the "cordel." This play by Dias Gomes was made into an important "art" film which dealt with the theme of religious syncretism in Brazil, specifically, Bahia, and the intolerance of the Catholic Church to Afro-Brazilian practices. An important, albeit minor character in the play and movie was "Dedé Cospe Rima" ["Dede the Rhyme Spitter"] based closely on the real life cordelian poet Cuica de Santo Amaro. Cuica was famous, or perhaps infamous in Bahia, the "Hell's Mouth" of "cordel" at the time.

"Zumbi dos Palmares" – Grupo Arena

I also saw the play "Zumbi dos Palmares" from the "Arena" Theatrical Group, a group both praised and condemned in the era, depending on your politics, who daringly produced plays based on the national social consciousness, cleverly masked to be sure because of the brutal military censorship in vogue during the times. Zumbi was a runaway slave who established what was a revolutionary, independent colony of runaways in the interior of the Northeast. The military certainly did not need such models for the rebellious youth of the 1960s. The play was really in praise of liberty and an indirect slap in the face of the military dictatorship. The music was by a terrific young composer Edu Lobo who would suffer himself at the hands of the dictatorship.

Walking home alone from the theater that night, I was slapped on the shoulder from behind, scaring the crap out of me. It should not have been a surprise by now. Heitor of the DOPS roughly grabbed my arm and not mincing words said, "Gaherty, is your head coming out of your asshole? I warned you about getting out of line from that phony bullshit research you are being allowed to do. We know the "cordel" and some of those commie professors writing about it deal with the "pau de arara" shitheads who have invaded Rio, and Zumbi was an uppity slave of a couple of hundred years ago, but these young so-called "intellectual artists" who write these phony plays and music are all Marxists and headed for a bad end these days. You'd be smart to stay away from this shit. I'm keeping track, just be warned." His tone was different this time, so I just said, "Yes sir, I just heard the music was good and wanted to know more about Brazilian colonial history. That's all." He let go of my arm and I high tailed it back to the apartment.

Paquetá Island in Guanabara Bay

I did my first outing to Paquetá Island in the Bay of Guanabara. The boat was jam packed (me thinking of the ferry boats sinking in Asia at the time), Ai! My Peace Corps companion Ellen and I had to stand the entire time. We saw dolphins in the Bay of Guanabara, famous for its pollution. Gulp. Then we rented bicycles to go around the island, not daring to swim in the Bay's waters which were not a beautiful crystalline blue or green. An article in the national news magazine "Veja" ["See"] later confirmed our suspicions. The people on the ferry appeared the same as that on the streets during Carnival, but most of the tourists to the island seemed to be "povão" or the masses of Rio. The outing was well worth the time for its spectacular views of the bay, of the Brazilian navy ships, the international cargo ships, and the beautiful views of the buildings and beaches of Niteroi and then Rio on the return.

Hills and Slums ["Morros e Favelas"] of Rio

I climbed one of the hills a little way (alone), this one beginning on top of the tunnel at the end of Copacabana near Barata Ribeiro Street. The only way up was by a dirt path surrounded by vegetation; the path was quite steep and in slippery condition due to the recent heavy rains. There were rivulets caused by the rains and several places with wooden boards used as "bridges" over them. The houses, or better, the shacks above were of wood with metal roofs, all seemingly placed in mass confusion without order. There was no water source, but I saw women and children with buckets in hand descending and climbing the hill the entire time. There was one water spigot at the base of the hill where they filled the buckets (for the romantic, imbued with idealism from the movie "Black Orpheus," this was a scene recalling the first scene in the movie; it all seemed familiar). And many people were taking "sponge" baths from the buckets filled at the spigot.

At the base of the hill in the back of Ipanema, there were nice, even beautiful apartment buildings and still the occasional large home with a green yard surrounding it, this in contrast to the shacks up above. One only saw black persons. I walked a bit, now in the back part of Ipanema, and there the hill had come down. The only thing to be seen was the red soil of the caved in hill, a result of the heavy recent rains, and several shacks that had fallen down the hill. Way up on top you could hear the noise of machinery, one assumes from the city, working to try to stabilize the hill. At the time, there were articles in the newspaper speaking of the government's plan to evacuate the "favelas" in all of Rio, requiring the residents to move to the far-off district of the Baixada Fluminense, famous for its poverty and crime, where there would be new "proletarian" housing projects built especially for the poor. I was told that this same situation was repeated each year during the rainy season - the government threatening to tear down the slums in Rio. The problem for people living in the slums was that for many of the "favelados" on the hills above Copacabana, Leme, Ipanema or Leblon work in the South Zone was as maids, door men, night watchmen, or washerwomen for the middle or upper-class South Zone residents. "Cordel" had a great story-poem about the situation: Azulao's, "The Central Station Train," ["O Trem da Central"] to see the plight of such poor people. The government says the "favelados" do not maintain their modest houses and area because they do not own the property, all a vicious circle. But the rent, paid to whoever it is, is insanely high. The idea that living in a favela is cheap is a lie!

The Tea at the American Ladies Club

As mentioned, I was learning to be a good researcher and "folklorist." Witness the fact that I was invited one fine afternoon to give a talk to the respectable ladies of the "American Colony" in Rio. I went; I do not remember the exact address, but I think in Laranjeiras, and spoke of Northeastern Folklore, "cordel" and the rest. I believe I even donned a white shirt and tie for the occasion. My reward was a fine bronze "jangada" which I would tote back to the USA. The "Times," the INR and the DOPS should all have been proud of this patriotic moment.

Meeting Orígenes Lessa

This would be an important day - I finally succeeded in meeting and conversing at length with the writer Orígenes Lessa in his apartment on Avenida Atlântica in Rio. He was in the process of either a legal separation ["desquite"] or divorce so was in the process of moving apartments. But it was a great talk: he gave me "hints" about "cordel" that he knew like no one else in those years in Brazil, speaking of José Bernardo da Silva, Rodolfo Coelho Cavalcante, Cuíca de Santo Amaro and Manoel Camilo dos Santos, to mention the principal figures of "cordel" of that time.

General Costa e Silva "Crowned"

March 15, 1967. General Costa e Silva was "crowned," i.e. inaugurated, today as the new president of Brazil, succeeding his colleague General Castelo Branco. It was on this day that the "Tribuna da Imprensa" a major daily in Rio would mark the age by doing a historic edition on Castelo Branco. The final day of the Tribune's "countdown" to zero, that is, the final day of the Castelo Branco regime, had arrived. On that final day the entire front page was taken up by a huge, red number 1. The back page was replete with the homeliest photographs of the General. The publisher of the paper, Hélio Fernandes, received as his award the official notice of losing his political rights ["cassado" like the leftist politicians] and the paper was closed by the government. This was proof of the censorship and repression of the times, but was nothing in comparison with what would come later that year.

At Last, Pelé and Santos in the Maracanã

March 19th. We went to the Maracanã to see the game between Flamengo and Santos with King Pelé the Santos Star. The final score was Santos 1, Flamengo 0. It was a day of torrential rain, the playing field a field of mud. I saw little of the style of the "great one" because we were seated far from the field. Once again, the "molecagem" or shenanigans of those in standing room in the "moat" around the field was evident. In the interim between the periods one of them jumped the fence between the moat and the playing field and led the security police, the "macacos" or monkeys as they were lovingly called, in a mad chase around the field. The fans in the stadium applauded his every move, while booing and making fun of the police, a sort of Keystone Cops brigade. At one point the entire public was standing on their feet applauding the target. A curious aside, for the gringo, was seeing poor fans in the stadium with a soccer ball, cut in half, as a cap. But in the end, I succeeded in seeing in the distance the figure of number 10 in the white shirt, not a small thing!

"Plantation Boy" ["Menino de Engenho"]

I saw for the first time the movie "Plantation Boy" ["Menino de Engenho"], extremely well done with scenes from the old slave quarters of Itapuá sugar cane plantation as well as the Oiteiro plantation, both of which I had visited in Paraiba. It would have been very difficult to follow the plot of the movie if one had not read the book, one of José Lins do Rego's most famous in his Sugar Cane Cycle, a mainstay of the "Novel of the Northeast." A few days later I would meet, through friend Sebastião Nunes Batista, the director of the film, Nelson Pereira dos Santos, known for his role in the "New Cinema" of the 1950s and 1960s in Brazil. We all had a draft beer [choppe] in one of the café-bars facing Cinelândia in downtown Rio. This is one more case of the amazing ease of meeting important Brazilian artists in Brazil in the 1960s.

How to Get into a Hospital

An elderly lady in Dona Júlia's apartment boarding house suffered a heart attack; it took three days to get her into a hospital, apparently for a lack of beds. And the fete only took place through the "pull" ["pistolão] of Dom João, the Benedictine of the Monastery already described and friend of the family. This is one more lesson in Brazilian life: the "jeito" or "arrangement" as the only way to get things done—it's who you know!

Sensationalist News from the Northeast

News from the Northeast in the papers of Rio is, to say the least, sensationalistic, and really "yellow" journalism: the assassination of an ex-deputy by hired gunmen in Alagoas, the crisis in the sugar industry and the strike of plantation workers in Cabo and Palmeira in Pernambuco, the latter understandably unhappy due to not receiving their pay since last August and eating rats to not die of hunger; stories of floods and hunger in the entire area of five northeastern states.

Bus and truck traffic in Rio

You had to experience it. It raised the hair on the back of your neck. The streets were in horrible condition, potholes everywhere. There was a common comment by the Cariocas: "It seems like each intersection is "work in progress" by the Power Company, and little men come, dig a large hole and vanish. The hole stays for some months, and eventually more little men come, fill it in and disappear once again. The fleet of buses and trucks, thousands of them, seemingly all without mufflers and belching black smoke, dodge barricades by the Power and Light Company."

Outing to Petrópolis

The outing was again in the company of Peace Corps Volunteer and friend from Bahia, Don. The city was much larger than I had expected or imagined with a very large, bustling downtown business section. The road from Rio after leaving the dirty and run-down North Zone became a two-lane paved highway with many curves, always climbing (see the film "That Man in Rio" with Jean Paul Belmondo, now a cinema "classic.") The climate changed gradually as we went higher, and it was much cooler in Petrópolis where the streets were filled with flowers. Our goal was to see the Palace - Museum of Dom Pedro II, in effect, his "summer house." One could still rent horse-drawn carriages to roll through the city. In front of the palace itself was a large green area with many trees and needed shade including the ubiquitous palm trees. There were some which are particularly tall and in fact were called "The Emperor's Palms," planted supposedly during his times in the 19th century.

The first thing the tourist noticed was the floor of the museum - polished black and white marble at the entrance and the rest with a wide variety of colored polished wood which they said were variants of Brazilian rosewood ["jacarandá"]. All tourists were required to take off their shoes and put on the fuzzy slippers ["chinelas"], no exceptions! The idea was to not scratch or harm the beautiful wood. The ceiling in the different salons was plain and simple except for two large rooms with a finer decoration. The latter, perhaps strangely enough did not match either the décor of the Casa de Rui in Botafogo in Rio.

We saw the Emperor's medals, presents given to him or the royal family, coins of the Empire, and objects of silver and porcelain. In the Reception room, the carpet was from the age of Louis XIV of France, and we saw Dom Pedro's inauguration robe, velvet with touches of gold and Toucan feathers as decoration. Then we saw the Emperor's crown of gold studded with diamonds. There was a conference room, supposedly used after Independence, portraits of the royal family, and the nobility (the Viscount of Taunay among them, from the Romantic period of Brazilian literature), and paintings of nature and scenes of the sea and Rio. Really, it was a rather simple palace in comparison to those of Europe; it was of Neo-Classic architecture, like one of the mansions one might see in Recife from the sugar cane age: that is with columns and a triangular façade. The return to Rio greeted us with more rain, fog and pollution and horrible traffic. Due to a traffic jam, it took two hours to go from the bus station to Copacabana.

17

An unexpected eye-opening moment of Brazilian politics and the Revolution happened with Cristina Maria's Family. Her father, Jaime Ferreira Lima, was a federal deputy in the national congress from the State of Amazonas before the 1964 military revolution. He considered a leftist and had his political rights taken away ["cassados"]; he was on the "list" of the military like many others, some who fled the country or entered "voluntary" exile. I learned all this on a social occasion when I was visiting Cristina Maria and heard a conversation one pleasant evening in that summer of 1967 in Rio.

I was invited into Jaime's spacious library-office and met Orestes Spínola, a "cassado" deputy from Recife, facing the same political fate as Jaime, and there was a very interesting conversation between them. Orestes spoke of the old MEB, "Educational Base Movement," [Movimento Educacional de Base] of the 1960s in the Northeast before the revolution. He spoke of the MEB's efforts to better the Northeast and Brazil (incidentally and important for me, the MEB used the format of the story-poems of "cordel" to reach and teach and inform its public). He spoke at length of the problems of Brazil now in 1967: the corruption of the current military government; the exploitation of Brazil by foreign capital (with many examples and statistics thrown in by Jaime) and the sub-soil minerals being sold to foreigners and to their firms. Spínola explained that the new government closed the MEB for "reasons of subversion" because it was teaching the poor masses about the true reality of Brazil, this through the radio and even the story-poems of "cordel." The military government in effect condemned totally the politics and government in Brazil prior to 1964.

All this was new to me. The conversation opened my eyes to the opinion and status of the "opposition" of 1967, an educated and informed opposition. The two ex-politicians revealed that there was a tremendous problem of disinformation in Brazil at that timel. There was a battle to know the truth of the situation in Brazil taking into consideration the propaganda of the military government and the SNI, the "National Information Service" (the DOPS worked hand in hand with it). It was impossible to know the truth without having inside sources. I think the two politicians felt safe including me in their conversation in the privacy of Jaime's home, after all I was just a friend of the Ferreira Lima daughter and a young North-American researcher naïve to most of what was going on in Brazil.

I thanked the family, made my way to the apartment elevator, went to the ground floor and started across the street for the short walk back to the boarding apartment when suddenly a black car pulled up, old "friend" Heitor opened the door, and said, "Get in. We're going for a ride." I was shoved in between him and a burly fellow dressed in a black suit, white shirt and tie and told to keep my mouth shut until they ordered me to talk. The car drove out of Copacabana, entered the "aterro" or freeway to downtown, went into the Glória District where we turned off on a dark street, drove a few blocks and pulled up in front of a nondescript four-story office building. Heitor opened the car door, ordered me to get out, and follow him inside to an elevator which took us to the third floor and a dimly lit corridor and a just as dimly lit office with glazed windows and office door.

The furniture was sparse - a desk, typewriters, a desk telephone and two or three straight back wooden chairs along the wall. "Sit down, make yourself at home. We're going to have a conversation."

"Okay Mr. Gaherty. We know you've been spending time with that pretty piece of ass Cristina Maria at Ipanema and the Castelinho and that's cool, but you my friend were at the wrong place tonight. We have constant vigilance on Orestes Spínola and his friends, and that includes Ferreira Lima. They are both *persona non-grata* with the government and my superiors at the DOPS, for obvious reasons. The revolution has many enemies and it is our job to keep track of them. You probably know by now they are both "cassados," political jobs and rights taken away and told to keep their noses clean. As far as we know that's the case, but once again when you as a guest in our country, supposedly doing that phony folklore research (we're still okay with that since your guy Iverson is in touch with us and has informed us you are a bona fide researcher, but **that's as far as he knows),** who knows what can happen. It's easy to be snowed by the lies and clever shit such people may tell you. So, we're here to listen to you and find out exactly what you heard and what was talked about. No bullshit please. We can rough you up a little on the way to the airport and your expulsion from Brazil after you spend a night upstairs in a place you won't like. Talk."

This was getting to be just a little too "real" and I was shaking in my boots. Trying to get my thoughts in order was not an easy task, so I stammered all I could think of:

"Look, Mr. Dias, I was a guest at Cristina Maria's home, had dinner and was listening to some Chico Buarque MPB music. Mr. Spínola was at the table and I could see he was a friend of Jaime's and of the family. I considered it a privilege as an American to have this opportunity to get to know Brazilians and Brazil a bit better. Jaime and Orestes both freely told me of their political fate, being "cassados" since they were on the Left prior to the Revolution. They of course were critical of the turn of events in the last years since in effect their side is now out of favor. Orestes spoke most of the MEB mainly because he learned I had spent a lot of time in Recife, and was studying the "cordel," and thought it would be of interest to know its minor role in the ABC teaching of literacy of the MEB. And of course, they were critical of the U.S. and its efforts to aid the current regime, but, hey this was no more than I had heard in the bullshit sessions in the student bars in Recife. The family has been nice to me and I like Cristina Maria a lot."

I didn't go on to mention the topic of "disinformation" and the SNI. I said I thought it was important to consider that as an American scholarship holder and researcher in the 1960s, I was keeping my nose clean and knew it was good to not know too much, and in fact "folklore" was not considered a dangerous topic. The jokes of my friends in the Northeast about me and the CIA and what I was doing in Brazil did not fall out of the air. I told Heitor and his friend,

"The truth is that I keep my distance from all this, in part because principally I'm ingenuous and very naïve. Hey, I just gave a talk to the ladies from the U.S. colony on northeastern folklore. I'm not looking for any trouble and am just trying to be a good American in Brazil."

There was a long silence. I noticed that both Heitor and his friend had taken off their suit jackets revealing shoulder holsters and a weapon, maybe to cool off in the sweltering room or maybe to make me realize the "gravity" of the situation. They were both smoking and that didn't help much.

"Okay Mr. Innocent American, once again you haven't exactly thrown a bomb or robbed a bank, but you do not have seemed to have listened when I told you last time to stay out of the wrong places and see the wrong people. We'll telephone Mr. Iverson, inform him of your latest carrying on and see what he says. I'll call a taxi for you and you get your American ass back home to the boarding house. I suggest you cool it with the Ferreira chick, or at least find out who's visiting before you go for dinner. I think you know by now to stick to the folklore."

The taxi showed up, I was marched to the door and Heitor speaking very rapidly (I could not catch all the Portuguese, but heard the word "safado" ["son of a bitch"] repeated a couple of times) gave instructions for the ride home. No words were exchanged with the driver, he knew my apartment building number and dropped me off with a shit-eating grin and said, "I hope we don't meet again."

In the coming months, on a quick trip to the Amazon area, I would chance upon a person in Belém do Pará who gave hell to Ferreira Lima, calling him a communist, subversive and a thief. I know that Jaime had serious dealings and business affairs with his export-import company, I imagine in the North, and had done export deals with Hungary and other Eastern Bloc countries, in those days motive enough for suspicion by the right. The acquaintance from Belém seemed to share the opinion.

What I can say, and it was apparent then, was that the family treated me exceedingly well. I suspect they all talked about the "naïve gringo." I was Catholic, studious and was far from ever tempted to stick my nose where it did not belong (just as I was far from realizing the true situation in Vietnam in those years). There was one goal: do the research, defend the thesis and become a professor of language and culture in the U.S. Enough said.

Now at the end of March and April of 1967 the moment arrived to end the research in Rio and once again begin the short trips to other regions of Brazil, a return to the bus rides far from the coast and the Atlantic. So, I bundled off this the longest LETTER to Hansen and "The Times" and went in search of more adventure. Because I was on the road I did not get his answer until later, but in effect he said, "Keep up the excellent work. We've got you covered with the DOPS. What is most important is to provide a view of Brazil we can't get elsewhere, and you are doing that in fine fashion. Check in via the next LETTER with the travels. I would not worry about police harassment in Rio; that's old news in today's Brazil. Just be sure and keep Iverson's phone number just in case."

LETTER V

TO THE INTERIOR FROM RIO DE JANEIRO

1

Belo Horizonte, Ouro Preto and Congonhas do Campo

I traveled with Steve Baldini, also a Fulbrighter (B.A. level), recently graduated from Harvard with interests in politics, economics and economic development (more specifically he would reveal to me later). We left Rio at 7 a.m. on the bus and with beautiful weather. After the suburbs, one begins to climb immediately, but gradually, until you arrive in Petrópolis, a trip of one and one-half hours from Rio. To the side of the road there is dense forest, beautiful Ipé trees with blooms - purple and yellow flowers in the branches. At one point, there was an entire valley full of the same trees and beautiful flowers in the fields, houses, etc. Then we began to see the famous "Pine Tree of Paraná," with branches spread like an Elm tree in the U.S.; the tree had pine needles instead of leaves. We passed Tres Rios [Three Rivers] on the divide between the state of Rio de Janeiro and the state of Minas Gerais; the border had the Paraná and Paraíba rivers with dirty, yellow water, and strong current. Then came Juiz de Fora in Minas Gerais state. Already the architecture in Minas was different than in Rio; the roofs were not flat or with façades as in the Northeast, but in the form of a trapezoid. We began a gradual climb through undulating hills, but still with palm trees, much pasture land and many herds of cattle. The soil seemed little cultivated save for fields of corn planted by hand. It was curious to see rustic soccer fields "cut out" of the green carpet of grass in the pastures. It was the most comfortable and least surprising of my trips thus far in Brazil.

Belo Horizonte. We arrived on Good Friday and went to mass in the cathedral which was packed with people. Then we went to an Italian restaurant (chosen by Baldini of course) and the next day visited the Federal University of Minas Gerais, this because of Steve's interest and contacts. Steve separated himself for a few minutes from me at the university, saying, "This is just Harvard, economics stuff. Just sit down and read the paper; I'll be back soon." I recall little but that we did pass through the famous district of Pampulha in Belo made famous by the church with architecture by Oscar Niemeyer and could see in the distance the brand new huge soccer stadium, the Mineirão. To tell the truth, I was not "into" this part of Brazil and had little curiosity about it. What did interest me was the Mulatto Sculptor Aleijadinho and the famous colonial city of Ouro Preto with its fame of riches from gold and diamonds and precious stones as well as the place of the "Inconfidência Mineira," [The Minas' Effort at Independence late in the 18th century]. That's where we headed after the short stay in Belo Horizonte.

Ouro Preto

Ouro Preto (old Vila Rica) was the jewel of mining towns from colonial Brazil, the highlight of the area of the gold and diamond "rush" of the 18th and early 19th centuries. This area formed yet another in the "cycles" of economic development of the colony and the country. The riches of Minas Gerais would be transported to the principal port of Rio de Janeiro for export to Portugal. It is a fascinating chapter in Brazilian history.

We woke up at 5:30 a.m. for the bus trip from Belo Horizonte to Ouro Preto.

This was a land of small mountains, always green with pastures, and in one place with low clouds and fog in the valley after rains. The entrance to Ouro Preto, from a view a little above, seeing the valley and the main road passing through the city, was very impressive. In the town itself we wandered about, seeing among other things many churches - Our Lady of Mercy, the Church of St. Paul, St. Francis de Paula with its images, Our Lady of the Rosary, Our Lady of the Pillar and St. Francis of Assisi.

We also saw the University of Ouro Preto specializing in geology and minerals and the famous "Museum of the 'Inconfidence" ["Museu da Inconfidência"] – its main historic figure in 1798 - the patriot Tiradentes ["Tooth Puller"] - and other comrades were drawn and quartered for treason against the Crown, that is, the Brazilian-Portuguese Government, to foment independence from Portugal.

In the museum, of note, was a crucifix from the age of João V of Portugal, and I never saw anything else like it in Brazil: the agony of Christ with blood pouring from his wounds. It was terrible, in the literal sense, capable of striking terror into the viewer. There also was another cross, but of Italian Renaissance Style, of gold, but simple as the paintings and other objects from the beginning of that period in Italy.

In Ouro Preto, in general, I remember a delightful climate, the old streets of cobblestones ["paralepipedos"], the small corner bars and clubs, and the processions of Holy Week. But the main thing was the churches.

The Church of Our Lady of the Rosary of the Poor ["Igreja de Nossa Senhora do Rosário dos Pobres"]. The Church of Our Lady of the Rosary was built by slaves for slaves with its paintings of death, the last judgment, and hell and heaven; all were placed in the side chapels. The altars were painted and not "bathed" or gilded in gold. This was unlike other important churches in Vila Rica (the original name of Ouro Preto), one surmises because of its status as a slaves' church. It was built by one of the brotherhoods of Rio de Janeiro in the 17th century.

The Church of the Pillar [A Igreja do Pilar]. There was fine and detailed work by Aleijadinho, altars "bathed in gold," Baroque angels and much decoration, the richest church in Ouro Preto.

The Church of St. Francis of Assisi [A Igreja de Sao Francisco de Assis). This church also had much work of Aleijadinho, the high altar was truly fantastic "bathed in gold" and in brilliant color.

Congonhas do Campo, Easter Sunday, 1967

We left Ouro Preto for the next destination. The bus passed by green, undulating hills and arrived at a crossroads where we changed buses for the small carrier to Congonhas do Campo. On the road one saw beautiful "Lenten" ["Quaresma"] Trees; I wondered are these the same as the "Ipé"? The Vila of Congonhas was much smaller than Ouro Preto, situated in a valley between low mountains, the church of Bom Jesus dos Matoszinhos to one side, on top of a small hill, and the "Igreja da Matriz," [the main church] to the other. We attended Easter Sunday Mass and all the festivities, including the filming of it all by a TV station from Belo Horizonte, including a young lady carrying the head of St. John the Baptist on a tray!

The famous Church of Good Jesus of the Wilderness ["Bom Jesus dos Matosinhos"] was beautiful: in its interior, I recall images of dragons, two angels, and animals at the foot of the columns. The church was constructed on top of a hill with a road of cobblestones [paralelepipedos"] at its base in the plaza.

Most famous, despite the work of the Sculptor Aleijadinho inside the church, is what is outside: the soapstone sculptures of the Prophets of the Old Testament. "Aleijadinho" or "The Little Cripple" was mulatto, crippled and yet one of Brazil's greatest sculptors. Aside from his soapstone prophets and many of the images of the interiors of churches in Ouro Preto and Congonhas, the "Way of the Cross" in Congonhas may be no less important. In its fourteen stations of the cross, each represented in a small chapel, are multiple figures in wood of the personages of the Passion of Christ, all painted in brilliant colors. It is a true masterpiece.

As mentioned, on Easter morning there was fog and clouds; in the afternoon, all cleared and a beautiful day with fresh and super clear air was before us. It was all in an atmosphere of a small country town with music emanating from the speaker system in the central plaza, music in Brazil certainly "for movement." Many persons were in the plaza, most dressed simply, not like the "beautiful people of Rio." There were men in coats without ties, young ladies in groups walking around the plaza, arms linked and in modest fashion; other groups of men drinking beer in the bars to the side of the plaza and listening to music on transistor radios. Still others were listening to the Sunday soccer game - the Cruzeiro team from Belo Horizonte. There were small boys offering shoe shines near the bus station. And not lacking were young boys, a bit dirty or disheveled, offering "tours" in the churches for a few cruzeiros. There were wooden benches to the side of the plazas, just to sit and pass the time. And there were several fountains, all very simple, different from the "grandeur" of Ouro Preto. Boys played kick ball in the streets; one boy was playing with a toy wooden wagon. There were burros on the streets and many beggars as well. What I did not know at the time was that Congonhas was the home of the most famous Spiritist Medium of all Brazil at the time - Arigó.

The return to Belo Horizonte was on the "local," ["o ônibus pinga-pinga"] packed to the gills, people standing in the aisle and lots of baggage.

2

Brasília, March, 1967

Once again, I went with Fulbright Colleague Steve Baldini, he as "guide" and the one with all the contacts. The political capital of Brazil would be of much less "professional" interest for a folklorist, that is, with one exception: the "Satellite City" of Brasília Teimosa where the "candangos," the builders of Brasília, or their descendants lived. These were the construction workers, most from the Northeast, who built Brasília from 1955 to 1960. I was hoping to discover "cordel" literature among the migrants. It turned out that there were two or three well-known poets, among them Paulo Batista, one of the sons of the famous Chagas Batista of Paraiba, and brother of friend Sebastião Batista, and another poet, Leobo, of some weight. I failed in meeting any of them on this limited trip. And there was very little more "cordel" visible during my stay.

It is important to emphasize that the Brasília I knew in 1967 was still the "young" Brasília, still under construction as I shall note. One must see the French film "That Man in Rio" with Jean Paul Belmondo, filmed in part on the construction site of the original Brasília, to appreciate the frontier spirit of the place.

The trip to Brasília by bus from Belo Horizonte was eleven hours. I only recall much empty space between the two places. We went by a huge lake formed by the "Represa de Tres Rios" [The Three Rivers Dam], originally the largest in Brazil, this before the construction of Itaipú in the south. The mistaken conception of those outside of Brazil is that Brasília was built in the middle of the forest, as though it were another Amazon. This is far from the truth: the city was built on the "Planalto" ["the high plains"], a land of undulating hills, with savannah forest to be sure, but not like the Amazonian rain forest. And another thing - the soil was deep red, much like you might see in Oklahoma or Texas in the U.S. (but not in Nebraska where we take great pride in the rich black soil known for our corn crops).

After traveling the entire night, we arrived a little after dawn at the famous bus station that sits in the middle of Brasília on the crossroads. As the Brazilians from those years know, the city was built in the form of an airplane: the pilot's cabin at the front houses the principal buildings of the senate, the chamber of deputies, and their respective offices in a tall building in the form of an "H." Moving from the "cabin" of the airplane, now into the fuselage, on both sides of the street are the ministries, small sky-scrapers of glass of some six to ten floors, and between them is a large green area. In 1967 the road was one-way with two lanes on each side in front of the ministries. From there one arrives at the "center" of the plane at the crossroads where the bus station is located. On one side of the Center is the commercial zone of banks and commerce. This part of Brasília seemed like any other city in Brazil with traffic lights, but the original idea was to make a city totally free of traffic lights by using cloverleaves and the like on the main avenues. It was just a bit that way in 1967.

On the two sides facing the crossroads, still under construction, were the north and south "wings" of the city. In 1967 there was little to be seen in the north wing, just the construction of some residences and a lot of vacant land. To the south there was a commercial zone already mentioned, the "Superblocks" and elegant residences and the embassies in the distance. One could see the large lake with its beach, an effort by the new dwellers of the Planalto to cure their nostalgia ["matar saudades"] for the beaches along Brazil's coast. The residential area designed by Oscar Niemeyer, "The King of Pre-Fab Concrete," and Lúcio Costa, his colleague in city planning, featured the famous "Super Blocks." These were complexes of apartment buildings, each perhaps twenty stories high, and each block with six buildings. The idea was that they should be if not totally, then almost self-sufficient, each with food markets, post office, schools and the like.

In 1967 the greater part of the commerce took place along W-3 Street. What a romantic name! This contrasted with the poetic names of streets in Recife recalled in the famous poems of Manuel Bandeira, or of Salvador, and really of most other cities in Brazil. It reminded me of the suburbs in the U.S. - shopping malls and a street that extended for kilometers in the distance. The effect on this tourist was a bit chilling; it was so different from that of other cities in Brazil.

At the "tail" of the airplane was a large park which seemed, in my opinion, as though it came from the moon and was just as cold in its tone. It was designed by Brazil's most famous landscape architect, Roberto Burle Marx, a colleague and buddy of Niemeyer and Lúcio Costa. The most important part of the park was the television tower which one could ascend part way in an elevator and achieve a fine view of the center of the city. I took slides of everything.

To one side of Brasília was "the lake" - an elegant part of town for government employees, the upper crust of the capital, and of the foreign diplomats from the embassies. It was indeed an artificial lake, totally man-made by bringing tons of sand from outside the city for its "beach," once again to cure the homesickness of the residents for their real homes in Rio. We visited the American Embassy; I recall little; it all seemed so cold and artificial. Dan left me drinking a cocktail at the reception while he conferred with "friends" from Harvard. Or so I thought.

A short distance from the government center was the Casa da Alvorada, residence of the president of Brazil, constructed in the same architectural style as the glass and concrete ministries, very modern in appearance. We could only observe it from the avenue in front, but I noted the guards, soldiers with machine guns at the entrance to the palace. It was very modern, very clean and very cold.

As I said, surrounding the center of Brasília itself was the "satellite city" with its proletarian housing; there lived the "candongos" or construction workers and laborers who had built the city, most of them from Brazil's northeast. They arrived for the construction in 1955 during the regime of famous President Juscelino Kubitschek, and with the inauguration of the new city in 1960, most stayed. The memory of all this appears in one of the story-poems of the "cordelista" Apolônio Alves dos Santos when he writes of the "good 'ole days" of his youth, selling "cordel" in the streets in those days. All this would end, and he would move on to a modest dwelling in the north zone of Rio de Janeiro. It is interesting to see the film "Bye-Bye Brazil" with its young protagonist, a sound box northeastern musician like Luís Gonzaga, who ends up playing the northeastern clubs in Brasília doing "shows" in the style and get-up of the famous singer.

In 1967 this part of town was very poor, without good city streets, with the appearance of a "favela" isolated in the middle of the capital. The largest city was Taquaritinga, but there also was Núcleo Bandeirante, a euphemistic name recalling the pioneers and searchers for gold and Indian slaves from São Paulo who were the first to arrive in the region in search of riches. It was easy to catch a bus in the central station, go out to these places and return. Curiously enough in 1967 to go from one part of the city, be it north, west, east or south, one always had to return to the central bus station and then head out in a new direction. Núcleo Bandeirante seemed to me to be like one more "favela" - poor shacks, unpaved streets, and the people of poor appearance, many in rags. I made a rapid visit to the local market where I did find just a few story-poems of "cordel" by local authors; most of the poems were of the new style and format of the big publisher in São Paulo, Prelúdio Publisher, with its comic book style covers.

Steve and I returned to the center of the city and went to the large Plaza of the Three Powers [Praça dos Tres Poderes] where we saw the "infrastructure" of the Cathedral of Brasília. It was still in the beginning of construction with twenty "needles" ["agulhas"] representing the twenty states of the nation. The project was abandoned during our visit in 1967, or so I understood, because of a lack of funding and problems regarding the engineering and architectural plans. We passed by and saw other ministries - all very similar in style - of pre-fab concrete, lots of glass, generally rectangular and about twenty-five stories high, some occupied others empty. What one could see, in general, was the very modern art of statues and sculptures in front of the buildings, notably, the Aeronautical Ministry.

"Folklore" and reality of the times: shortly before our arrival, the building of the Ministry of Agriculture caught fire, a large fire that practically destroyed the edifice. Gossip had it that the bureaucrats employed in the ministry, coming from the "good life" in Rio de Janeiro with beaches, night clubs, etc. did not want to move to "the end of the world" in Brasília, thus, the mysterious fire. A short while after this blaze, the Brazilian government required that all countries move their embassies to Brasília. It took a while and there was a lot of foot dragging, but eventually all complied. Folklore or reality: Brasília created its own folklore. It was said that it was constructed due to the contracts of huge concrete firms, by chance, the owners being relatives or friends of President Kubitschek's family. Another tall story was: to force the senators and representatives of the national congress in Rio to go to Brasília, the government provided free passage by air each weekend to return "home" to the beaches of Rio! I understand that this was indeed the real situation in Brasília for some years.

It was at this point when we visited a session of congress where we listened to a few speeches and some debates, but with few congressmen present (Brazil was quickly becoming a dictatorship, so congress really was a "charade") that I learned a bit more about my traveling companion. As we lunched on the 14th floor of the congressional office building, the one in the form of an H, we encountered Samuel Jonas the friend from the Portuguese boarding house days in Salvador who at that time was on "business" from the mayor's office in Brasília. He greeted both of us, recalling for me that wild night in the whorehouse in Salvador when all the action was stopped by the police at midnight because of the upcoming election day. His big embrace of Steve however was greeted with, "I hear you have been doing excellent work for our friends in Washington, ferreting out information on the military's economic plans for the "March West" through the Amazon! Congratulations my CIA friend!" Steve grimaced, got slightly red in the face, and said, "Mike, you can keep a secret, can't you? Didn't you suspect something in Recife when I talked of the program at Harvard, my studies in economic development and the "grant" to Brazil? The "Agency" connection is not much different than your LETTERS to the "Times" except I'm getting two monthly checks instead of one, the first from Fulbright, and second was the "Agency" in D.C. My "research" is not a whole lot different than your Ph.D. folklore research - on-site and just a different topic. Better however to keep it under your hat." Jonas chimed in, "Sorry. I thought you two were on the same page on all this, but I'm cool with it." He proceeded to show us around the complex of offices of the mayoralty and ended with a warm "goodbye" in front of the congressional office building.

It was just as well neither of them knew of Iverson and the INR connection and my off and on encounters with the police or DOPS people in Recife, Salvador or Rio. As we say in Nebraska, "No sweat." At that point Steve and I returned to Rio on the bus, a long ride but with indelible memories which I share in this LETTER. I surmised the city would certainly grow and prosper in the coming years, like the rest of Brazil, and would change in character from the pioneering days I knew. I believe that I saw the city at a special time, yet in its infancy. Once again, one must see the French film "That Man in Rio," with Jean Paul Belmondo to see some spectacular scenes during the actual construction of Brasília in its infancy by the "candongos." I would see Steve again just one or twice in the coming months in Brazil but did later read in the "Diário de Pernambuco" in Recife in a small article on the international page news that an American research scholar had been asked to leave Brazil for revealing government insider information on land speculation in the Amazon to U.S. government sources. "Nossa!" as they say in Brazil; Heitor had warned me to not get into the wrong crowd, but in this case I guess he would have said "the right crowd," and I guess in this case Baldini was it!

3

The Stern Wheeler on the São Francisco River, April of 1967

This trip would be one of the most unforgettable for the gringo researcher in Brazil. The purpose was to see if any "cordel" was present along the important interior commercial waterway of the São Francisco River passing through Minas Gerais and Bahia and emptying into the Atlantic in Sergipe. It all began in a very calm way, the trip by bus from Rio to Belo Horizonte. The only thing upsetting the calm was a horrible accident - another bus turned over in the middle of the road. In Belo Horizonte I had dinner at the Italian Restaurant on Alfonso Pena Avenue (the same I had shared with Steve Baldini, my guide on the trip to Brasília), and I noted the traffic jams due to the soccer game between Cruzeiro and Santos in the "Mineirão" stadium.

What followed was the bus trip to Pirapora, Minas Gerais. We traveled at night and on bad roads, and a rare thing in central Brazil, it was quite cold on the bus, this despite wearing a long-sleeve shirt and a sweater. The other passengers kept their windows open to the cold, night air. The road was clay and gravel with many detours and the bus lacked in basic comfort.

The Arrival in Pirapora. I was lodged at the "Hotel" (modest, with only the basics of a single bed, a small desk, a lamp, but a clean bathroom with cold running water) of The Navigation Company of the São Francisco River - a small, simple but clean accommodation. The company was what they called a "mixed" company in Brazil in those days; the stock was divided between government ownership and private holdings. The day-to-day operation of the Company gave me the impression that it was just one more of the bureaucracies I had known in Brazil, that is, the government civil service offices ["repartições públicas"].

Pirapora was quite small, the main street paved with traditional cobblestones, the "paralelepípedos," and the others of clay. There were many poor shacks with naked children running in front, and there was no lack of pigs ruminating in the garbage to the side of the streets. In contrast, "O Velho Chico" or the São Francisco River itself was a magnificent sight below the rapids below the long bridge crossing it at Pirapora. There were many "gaiolas" or stern wheelers of the Company tied in to the main dock and other points along the river; there was also a variety of small motor launches and simple canoes. In the cataracts below the bridge there were several men fishing at dawn on the river. The locals told me there was no danger of "piranhas" in answer to the question from all the foreigners due to the stereotyped notion that all the rivers in Brazil held this small "denizen." I was told that if there was current in the river, there would be no "piranhas." Despite these words of wisdom, I would see "piranhas" in markets along the river all along the trip. These fishermen at Pirapora fished for "surubim" and "dourados." They used nets they would cast into the current, pull back toward themselves and after the cast, hope for good results.

You could see the ubiquitous "garbage men of the back lands" wherever you looked - flocks of vultures circling in the sky and picking up garbage on the ground. The next morning, I went to the main dock to see my steamboat for the trip - the São Salvador (the boat used in the filming of "Seara Vermelha" ["Red Harvest"] by the novelist Jorge Amado). At the boat, I had a conversation with a member of the crew; he had lived in Pirapora for 26 years and worked on the river the entire time. He recalled that in the "old" days it took from 50 to 60 days for the round trip from Pirapora to Joaseiro da Bahia, but with the construction of the Três Marias Dam up stream, and now with the current controlled, the river was much easier to navigate.

Later that first day I walked all along the docks; there were a total of eight stern wheelers of the Company docked at the side of the river. There were also many small dugouts and boats of fishermen and local cargo boats. The stern wheelers, called "gaiolas," dated from the nineteenth century on the river. Some were made in Brazil; three came from the Mississippi River in the U.S. (so they told me) and one from the Rheine River in Germany. They were all wood burners with steam engines powering the stern wheel.

I walked along the side of the river to the large bridge that crossed the São Francisco River. The bridge held a train trestle as well, the train's destination being Belo Horizonte first and then Rio de Janeiro. This was the same train of folkloric fame which carried the poor migrant-refugees from the dry Northeast to the "prosperous South," an important theme in Jorge Amado's "Red Harvest." The refugees had walked as far as Pirapora where they caught the train, or had arrived in the same place after boarding the stern wheelers in the trip upstream from Joaseiro da Bahia on the border with Pernambuco state.

There were many ladies washing clothes at the side of the river, most of them black; they were working in the tiny streams or rivulets that emptied into the great river, extending the clothes on the ground to dry. And near them were a plenitude of young boys fishing with wooden poles and using worms as bait to catch small fish that they later would sell to the men to use as bait in fishing the river. The men I saw fishing in the rapids below the bridge were dressed in shorts and wore large straw hats; they fished with round nets they would cast into the current and draw back to them. They told me the best fishing was for "surubim," a fish with rainbow colors that they would sell for 2,200 cruzeiros per kilo in the market.

That afternoon and evening was spent in the small restaurant of the Company at river side. There was pleasant conversation with a young man from Belo Horizonte who worked in the program of pest eradication in the region (an anti-malaria campaign); the goal was to kill mosquitoes that carried the disease. Spraying was the only known remedy for the problem. At dusk, I witnessed a soccer game of young boys on a small field at the side of the river, seen in that special light before sundown, the brilliant last light of day, incredibly beautiful. I thought: this is a photo of Brazil. One sees soccer the national game in the most unlikely places! The day had been quite warm, but with dusk and night coming on, the air cooled rapidly with a very pleasant breeze coming off the river. It turns out that the greater part of the residents of Pirapora work for the Company or fish in the river to make a living. There was little commerce in the town which could brag of only one market day for the week on Saturday.

The next morning, I walked "downtown" where I found only one, solitary vendor of "literatura de cordel," an old black man named Vicente. He sold only the story-poems with colored - comic book style covers of the Prelúdio Publishing House of São Paulo because "they were pretty with the colored covers." Two years before he had bought some poems of the northeastern style from a seller from Juazeiro do Norte, Ceará, and he was still trying to sell them. When I commented that we in the United States had no such tradition, he commented that the booklets of "cordel" had a "pretty rhythm" and added that "Brazil has a lot of foolish things, but some good things as well." He was happy that I took his picture, and he bragged, telling customers of the "Americano" who had interviewed him for a "great study."

I spent the second night once again at the restaurant of the Company, the "Bambuzeiro" at the side of the river, dining on fresh "Surubim" with a spicy side sauce. After the dinner hour, the place was converted into a Brazilian "nightclub" ["boite"], albeit in modest, country style. It was indeed the center of night life in Pirapora including the new "yeah-yeah-yeah" music and many young ladies who appeared like magic with the pleasant evening breeze on the river. After a few of those tall icy "Brahama Choppe" beers I couldn't resist dancing with one of the cuter chicks. Rosário, a bit of an ironic moniker considering the ebb and flow of the evening, was about five feet six, dark-eyed, long shiny black hair, sensuous lips and no less sensuous body sheathed in a skin-tight blue dress and with ample firm flesh all in the right places (it took little time to discover this in one of those Brazilian "slow" dances emanating from the tiny trio of piano, guitar and drums in the corner of the dining room now cleared for dancing). I guess I should have figured that where there are sailors, in this case, the crews of the many stern-wheelers, there would be ladies interested in keeping them happy … for a price. Rosário complimented my Portuguese, laughed at my efforts to dance to Brazilian music, wondered why I was in the place - I was the first "gringo" she had ever seen in those parts - but was not opposed to continuing the evening in my modest room in the "hotelzinho." It had been what seemed a very long time from the comforting touch of Cristina Maria in the dark Castelinho in Rio or some steamy time in Peace Corps Volunteer Ellen's apartment in Botafogo, but Rosário had her own "fieldwork and advanced degree" in sex in that far-off, isolated corner of Brazil! "Play it again Sam" quickly got us through that unforgettable night alongside one of Brazil's most famous rivers. We parted early the next morning with my wallet a little lighter and me with a whopping headache from the "Brahma" beer.

The First Day, the Departure and the Unexpected

Later that morning, due to my luggage, I caught the local taxi from the hotel to the dock and the São Salvador. There was a big crowd arriving at the same time to wave goodbye to the boat, passengers and crew, waiting patiently while the hold of the boat was being packed with no end of "stuff." There was time and the opportunity for the curious, passengers or not, to climb aboard the boat, look around and share comments and opinions with their neighbors. We left the dock with a long whistle from the stern wheeler that caused the ears to hurt, the first time I a landlubber from Nebraska would hear such a piercing, unique sound. I was impressed with the cleanliness of the boat, the crew all in their "uniforms" of white and blue (white t-shirt, blue denims), white traditional sailor hats, the same as those on the high seas, all apparently in order.

Scarcely having left the dock, entering the middle of the river and heading north toward our destination of Joaseiro da Bahia, the boat suddenly stopped in the middle of the river and then turned to shore and a rustic "dock" made of boards at the side of the river. There was a slow and arduous process of extending boards from the stern wheeler to the new "dock," thus creating a sort of ramp from the shore to the small barge attached to the side of the steam boat. The idea was to bring cows, steers, bulls and horses to the barge which would be sold in other small towns upstream. The "roundup" began. The cattle descending the chute from the land to the barge spooked, turned around and headed back up the chute to the land on the river bank. Then some cowboys responsible for this new "herd" of livestock plus all the crew of the river boat took off up the hill, out of sight, and about two hours later returned with the missing cattle still thirsting for their freedom. The cowboys returned literally dragging two big steers which they pushed aboard the barge.

After this first unexpected delay in the trip, that first night I was introduced to "on board service." In first class where I was lodged they set up several small round tables on the front deck for dinner; the passengers seated themselves with no particular seating order, but according to personal choice. The same tables after the supper and during the next day were used for breakfast and lunch and then for card tables and a place for conversation. Conversation was always very lively - the men debated the merits of the small towns along this "River of National Unity." It is important to note that there was a large refrigerator on the main deck jammed full of soft drinks and bottles of beer, the large bottles of Antártica or Brahma of the times, this to "irrigate the conversation" as they say in the vernacular. I spent many hours "drinking in" this source of gossip and folkloric tales of the São Francisco River.

Throughout the entire trip the steam boat stopped two or three times each day to load wood, cut logs provided by poor folks along the river. The "sailors" of the crew lugged the same on board on their shoulders protected by a sort of burlap bag on the shoulder and stacked the wood next to the big boiler in the front of the boat.

There was a beautiful sunset that first night, and the air cooled rapidly, folks on board needing a light jacket for the cold. At dusk we stopped in a small clearing to deliver the mail, a tiny settlement with poor shacks without electricity, but with roses in front, something I would note throughout the trip. All along the trip along the banks of the river one could see small "gardens" ["roças"] dedicated to growing garden vegetables. And to the side of these gardens one could see poor houses, shacks really, the ubiquitous stick shacks with mud wattle walls and thatched roof, and many times with banana trees alongside.

There was traffic along the river but boats were small in number. There were canoes crammed with foodstuffs moved by the rower ["barqueiro"] propelling the boat with a long pole. The gringo student of Brazilian Literature had to think of stories by the great João Guimarães Rosa of the small boats on the "Grande Chico."

I slept well that first night, considering that I was not yet accustomed to the accommodations - the small cabin with bunk beds. My roommate was a gentleman in his 60s or 70s, a retired pilot on the river. This gentleman diverted me with stories of his days on the river, myself not being able to distinguish between fact and fiction, but enthusiastically accepting all as a great adventure on this river of "national unity." And, little by little, I was accustoming myself to the constant sound of the steam engine, the "chug, chug, chug" of the stern wheel, turning, turning and never stopping. It ended being a very calming sound helping me to fall into a deep sleep.

The Second Day, Life on Board, Routine on the River and the Cast of Characters

I woke up to a dawn with a chilly wind from the river and to a breakfast of "mingau," hot bread and delicious coffee. Then there was another unexpected stop - the crew was making their way along the banks of the river cutting grass for forage for the cattle and horses on the barge. Some hours passed until we arrived at the town of São Francisco, Minas Gerais, seeing from afar the church tower of the small town, its only high point. The dock was constructed of stone, a project well done, and there were vendors waiting for our arrival with salty snacks, chickens for sale, and cheese (of course, the famous "Cheese of Minas Gerais"). There was a lot of movement among the crew, and soon I discovered why - they had left the boat and were now returning lugging huge bottles of the local sugar cane rum ["cachaça"], famous in the entire region. It was at this point that I discovered that the hold below the third-class river level deck of our steam boat was full of empty jugs, brought from the South, and they would be exchanged for new full jugs of the "good white stuff" ["branquinha boa"] for the return to Pirapora and points south to Belo Horizonte. There also was a warehouse of SUDENE [Superintendency of Development of the Northeast] to the side of the river, but the town seemed calm with a scenario that was now becoming familiar: wood stick houses alongside the river with canoes and small boats, one or two larger boats with sails and women washing clothes at the side of the river.

A little while later there was another stop, this time to cut grass or fodder plus load wood, and the accompanying scene of poor women washing clothes at the side of the river, pounding the clothes against rocks to wring out the water. At yet another stop in a small town where there was an American Mission (Protestant to be sure) dozens of school children came out to meet the boat - very clean children in their school uniforms, a huge contrast to the poor, naked children normally seen along the banks of the river during the trip.

A beautiful moment—we found ourselves passing another stern wheeler from the Company, this one heading up stream, the bow low in the water, loaded down with freight and with less space for passengers. One could see huge bales of cotton stacked on the lower deck. And again, there were many fishing boats on the river, an occasional motor boat, but my general impression was that the region was little habitated, and little developed economically. The passage of time was scarcely noted, giving the impression things were as they had been for many years.

At this point the river was very wide with several islands, the latter unpopulated. The water was muddy, and the current was strong. At the side of the river was thick vegetation with a small vegetable garden seen occasionally, with manioc plants, banana trees, corn and vegetables.

The days got a little long, but I managed to climb the ladder and steps up to the top deck of Steerage. There I met and had long talks with the pilot ["prático"]; he told me of the Company which now was federal, and that salaries were much less than they were for private concerns. He believed that all that was done well before was now just part of the governmental bureaucracy. The crew consists in about fifteen "sailors" who tie the lines at the docks, clean the boat, prepare and serve the meals, scrub the decks, bring the wood aboard and cut the forage for the cattle and horses on the barge. There are five or six officers in light brown uniform and officers' hats with epaulets on their shoulders, including the pilots who know how to navigate the river, and the commander. I had a slight problem with this latter gentleman today when he scolded me for climbing a ladder from first class up to the pilot's cabin, finding a chair and sitting in the same in a swim suit while taking the sun and reading a novel! In my defense, I truly did not know the rules on board. After the captain left, muttering to himself, "Those damned passengers!" So it was. It's his ship!

My notes reveal my impressions of the passengers in first class: there were a few young ladies. Their general appearance was that of country girls from the interior, poor, simple, dark skinned, and among them two or three who were cute. One I talked to a bit was Margarida who worked in Três Marias and was returning for a "short" visit of three months to her sister's plantation in São Romão. There were also older folks, but also of very simple dress. One man sporting the broad brimmed straw hat of a "Colonel," drank beer all day long and told of being a pilot "on the other river," the Paraná in Southern Brazil; he said he was comparing the two rivers and their system of navigation. In third class, on the lower deck just inches above the water line, there were several men in cowboy outfits including the traditional leather cowboy hat, and one "vagrant," with long, dirty and messed up hair. These people would get hot coals from the ship's boiler, put them in small cookers and cook their meals on the coals. They slept in hammocks strung on the lower deck, on the same level as the livestock in the barge. I discovered that the cost of passage was the same, corresponding to class of course, whether you were going up or down river, the down trip taking seven days, up-river fourteen days. That was indeed a very Brazilian thing in those days, not distinguishing between the costs of a passage for seven or fourteen days.

The stern wheelers also served as mail boats; they stopped in what seemed the end of the world, in clearings along the river, and delivered letters or perhaps one package. The river was at its best at dusk when the water reflected a sky of soft and large clouds. It was at that moment of the day when the colors are their most brilliant, a little before sunset, a wonderful scene. During the day it was much warmer (thus explaining my request to the Captain to put a chair outside the control cabin which happened to provide some shade); the mornings were fresh and cool, and dawn was even a bit cold.

That night we arrived in Januária, the most famous city of Minas Gerais for sugar cane rum ["cachaça"]. Later we docked in Manga, the largest town before we would leave Minas Gerais and enter the state of Bahia. They all commented that Bahia was the more developed state economically along the river.

I had another conversation with one of the functionaries of the Company who was on board. He told me of the reorganization of the Company into what was known now as a "mixed company." "Seventy-five per cent of the stock is in the hands of the federal government which chooses and names the President; the rest of the stock is in private hands, including those of employees of the Company. Navigation of the river is controlled by the Brazilian Navy and Brazilian Merchant Marine. There is a special course for piloting and navigation and the candidate must pass an exam to be a pilot on the São Francisco. Most interesting is that once one passes the exam, he has the right to be a pilot on ships of the high seas as well as on the river boats. The course of study is in the same school of navigation." The employee of the Company spoke of the diverse stern wheelers - the "Venceslaus" from the United States, and this same "São Salvador" from the filming of the movie "Red Harvest."

An aside: - a moment that really made the gringo enthusiastic: very early this morning we passed by a tiny villa named Maria da Cruz, and at the exact moment of passing a group of about ten cowboys came storming down the main street toward the dock on their horses trying to "down" a bull. They caught the bull using the northeastern "method" - grabbing the tail and pulling on it hard - thereby rolling the animal to the ground, and then tying it up and dragging it to the dock. This was a scene directly from the famous stories of northeastern folklore and the "literatura de cordel" like "The Mysterious Bull" and a plethora of story-poems about cowboys and valiant back landers. These "Knights of the Backlands" were dressed from head to foot in leather - the broad brimmed leather cowboy hat of the backlands, vest of leather, as well as leggings or chaps. It was easily the most picturesque moment of the trip up to that point! Such moments reinforced the concept of the real existence of a folkloric Brazil!

Maria da Cruz was to be noted: it was very small but pretty with a blue church on top of a hill in the center of town facing the banks of the "Rio Chico." A huge barge from Tres Marias dam, a barge used in transporting automobiles, was moored unexpectedly in this tiny town. It turns out it had broken its moorings at a dock above Pirapora and then passed through the rapids below the bridge, and had only come to a stop here.

We stopped for almost an hour in Januária where we unloaded large sacks of empty jugs of sugar cane rum [cachaça], all coming from the center-south of Brazil. On the docks one could see huge bales of cotton, but none came on board the São Salvador for our trip down river. Dozens of kids, almost all black, in bare rags, played alongside the boat, swimming in the shallows. The ubiquitous washer ladies were also in evidence, washing and wringing out the clothes along the river bank. At this point several new first-class passengers came aboard, and several more with cowboy hats "camped" in third class on the lower deck. Now in first class there were more passengers than available private bunked cabins ["camarotes"]; the newly arrived passengers slept on cots on the first-class deck during the night, but the cots disappeared first thing in the morning. I went below to visit the "general quarters" of the crew; I saw sleeping cots below deck with the "floor" above made of steel as above second and first-class decks. One could imagine the intense heat they all experienced at least until a cooler dawn.

My pilot "friend" from Paraná is a big beer drinker and he likes to talk. He told me of his birthplace in Joaseiro da Bahia, the residence he left there thirty years earlier, saying he had left at least "a million and a half" [cruzeiros] there. He now lives on and works on the river boats on the Paraná River navigated in southern and southwestern Brazil in the States of São Paulo, Paraná and Matto Grosso. His Portuguese was not easy to understand, like that of many other "back landers" aboard; the Portuguese of one of the pilots of the São Salvador who has become a friend was much easier to comprehend.

I spent the next day, first with "mingau," "café com leite" and bread, speaking with a student from the town of Manga and watching the movement of the crew on the stops for wood and forage for the livestock on the barge. And once again I went down to the lower deck, this time near the boiler, and saw more cots used by the crew and the hammocks strung by the poor, third class passengers, and then an entire beef hung up and being cut into pieces by the cook-butcher. I also chatted with the "maquinistas" or engine crew; the machinery seemed in impeccable condition, all highly polished and oiled. I noted the poor, lower deck passengers eating manioc flour mixed with dried beef or jerky, all as was the custom, using their hands and no utensils.

The Rock of Lapa and Good Jesus of Lapa
["A Pedra da Lapa e Bom Jesus de Lapa"]

The next day dawned with heavy fog on the river, and far in the distance one could begin to make out the principal destination of my trip - the Rock of Good Jesus of Lapa. A larger town along the river, perhaps of some six thousand inhabitants or more, it had a dock busy with small motor craft, many with canvas roofs, and the same with hammocks "armed" or strung across the boat, one with the placard "I go and come with God on board" ["Com Deus Vou e Volto"]. These small motor boats were crammed with cargo; I saw sand, huge piles of rope, fruit, fish, etc. The usual washerwomen were along the banks of the river near the dock and dozens of black boys were swimming in the river. And there were many canoes as well.

The dock itself, better made than many smaller ones we had seen along the course of the river, was of concrete and stone, and in front of it there were many large carts drawn by oxen being prepared to haul the freight from the river boats up into the town, bulls of the Brahma or Zebú Stock familiar in the Northeast. One could also see carts drawn by horses. Suddenly there was noise and mass confusion - one of the bulls, it seemed the largest to me, had gotten loose and was playing havoc with the entire scene; men were shouting, some trying to catch the bull, others running away as fast as their legs would carry them. I recalled scenes of Bull Riding at the Central Nebraska Free Rodeo near Lincoln, my home town.

From the docks to the town there was a road of sorts, or at least it looked like a road, totally filled with mud from the recent rains. To the side I saw the poorest houses I had seen up to that point in Brazil, the usual shacks made of sticks, and these not even covered with mud wattle or adobe bricks, and with roofs of broken tile. Many seemed to serve as food and drink stands for the pilgrims arriving in Lapa. The effect was that of a miserable slum without any sign of vegetation or anything green, created by and for the poor pilgrims. The same streets were filled with goats and pigs running loose, one imagines, looking for the day's sustenance.

I do not know if I am mistaken, and it could well be the case, but at that moment in 1967 it seemed to be an edge of town totally without planning, that is, an organized layout of the streets. It all just seemed to have evolved from the existence of the Rio Chico and its importance as a prominent place of pilgrimage, but perhaps I am wrong. Up the way to the shrine, in the town itself, the streets were not the accustomed cobblestones [paralelepípedos] of the Northeast, but were of rock itself, and they were relatively clean.

I don't believe I have yet come to speak of the "reason for being" for the city. Good Jesus of Lapa grew in fame as a great stopping place for religious pilgrims searching for the help of the famous saint Jesus Christ himself. The place became known when a monk, Francisco da Soledade, made the Rock famous by his life of faith and charity. As it had to happen, there were miracles attributed to him and his fame grew, as monk and saint. A similar thing would happen in Juazeiro do Norte, but here it was the fame of Jesus himself, the patron saint of Lapa, rather than that of the "Taumaturgo of the Backlands," Father Cícero Romão Batista. With the passing of time, the pilgrimages grew until recent days when thousands of pilgrims arrive in Bom Jesus for the festival of the patron saint. The visitors include poets of the "literatura de cordel," famous among them the "Apostle Poet" Minelvino Francisco da Silva of Itabuna in Bahia. The effect, really, is that of a town which came from nothing and was created mainly for religious pilgrims, migrants and tourists.

The high point, literally and figuratively was the Rock itself, described better as a gigantic rock with many caves inside. It was visible from way down the river, long before we arrived at the town itself, in part because the land surrounding it is entirely flat. The rock rose up massively and perhaps in a bit of a frightening way (depending upon romantic readings of the visitor). The hill or rock practically surrounded the town on one side; it was from 70 to 100 meters high with pointed rocks on all sides, making me think of the famous "Pedra Bonita" in Pernambuco State, also a frightening place with its own story of religious "fanaticism" in Brazil. It was at Pedra Bonita where another cult arose - that of a self-proclaimed messianic figure who urged the religious sacrifice of animals, dogs and even babies in the year of 1825. See José Lins do Rego's famous fictional account of the place, people and event in his novel of the same name "Pedra Bonita."

There were at least some fifteen caves within the rock or hill, one with the renowned chapel, yet another replete with statues and images of saints, and the "miracle room." The latter was jammed with photos on its walls and especially human body parts made of plaster of paris; these were the "ex-votos" or objects left by religious pilgrims faithfully "paying their promises." Many "ex-votos" extended from the floor to the ceiling of the cave. There were also wooden models of stern wheelers, a testimony of shipwrecks on the river and crew and passengers saved by the saint. The miracle room was indeed like the same phenomenon already described in Juazeiro do Norte, that of Father Cícero Romão Batista.

In front of the entrance to the chapel there were the customary "holy women" [beatas], old women, many dressed in rags, but always in black, and beggars, almost all requesting alms and offering to tell the "Story of Good Jesus" to the tourist. To the left of the entrance was a large tower, tall and made of stone, an edifice that reminded me of the medieval towers of European castles and of fairy tales, perhaps those made famous by the brothers Grimm. I also thought of the prison-tower of the famous play of the Spaniard Calderón de la Barca, "Life Is a Dream," ["La Vida Es Sueño"] and its prince-protagonist Segismundo. For someone of another culture, the tower even resembled the minarets of Muslim Mosques. Upon entering the large cave itself, I recognized an elderly lady passenger from the São Salvador making the final part of her journey on her knees, thus showing respect and I suspect, paying her promise to the Saint.

The day we arrived was the day of the weekly fair-market, a sight very familiar to the gringo researcher in wanderings in the Northeast; there were stands with raw meat covered with flies, "rapadura" or hard sugar cane sweet, and skinny, hungry dogs everywhere. Unhappily I saw and purchased very few cordelian poems and these in the style of the colored, comic-book style covers from Prelúdio Publisher in São Paulo. So it was that the "marketing" of São Paulo's "cordel" reached far with its big city tentacles, a fact lamented repeatedly in those months by the poets and publishers in the old Northeast. And it turns out the poets of "cordel" arrive in town only during the feast days of Good Bom Jesus, from June to October, clearly because customers abound in those days. We were unfortunately in the month of April.

The Trip Continues, the Brave Rancher and the Prospector

My friend from São Paulo and the Paraná River continued to drink his beer, beginning at 8:00 a.m. and conhaque the rest of the day. Two good looking young ladies came on board at Carinhana; dress them in the ultimate styles of Copacabana and you will see what a backlands beauty truly is! Last night I watched the same two young ladies ironing clothes using a table as an ironing board, but most interesting was that that were using an old fashioned heavy metal iron filled with hot coals to do the ironing.

We passed by a villa called Sítio dos Matos and the entire crew (except the officers and pilots) jumped overboard for a refreshing swim in the river. At yet another stop, this in the middle of the night, it was a strange sensation to dock in total darkness from the river and be confronted with a dock with bright electric light, really a very advanced dock of concrete and rock, and behind it loomed large warehouses with white columns. With a little imagination one could imagine oneself in front of a Roman temple with its columns but in the middle of the Brazilian outback.

Then I noted the presence of one more person in the cast of characters on the São Salvador. He was a rancher from the region who talked with me of his past military service in Salvador da Bahia and of his fun life with the ladies of the night and the nightclubs in the same city. Sporting a revolver at his waist, on another occasion he bragged of his extraordinary talent as a marksman, and for some strange reason, I believed it all. And he went on about his swimming abilities, saying to me, "I can swim from one side of this river to the other (and the river was very wide) and with you on my back!" I wholeheartedly agreed, not asking for proof. He spoke of his father's ranches, the vast numbers of cattle in their herds, of the pickup trucks, the jeeps, and the Rural (a popular Brazilian station wagon-jeep of those days), and how he liked to have comfort when he traveled. He told me of his school days and studies, up to the third year of the "Science" curriculum, and commented on the ignorance of the back landers who populated the region. He was headed for the city of Iboitirama where he was planning on buying one hundred head of cattle. And as it had to be, the conversation came around to women: he said he was not a whoremonger, but if a woman came around with "easy" talk he would not turn down the opportunity. A man always had to be ready, and a real man had to have a mustache, "It attracts the women!" The reader may recall that I experimented with growing a beard and mustache in Recife earlier in the year, a custom I abandoned due to itching in the heat and humidity and being called a "Fidelista" and Communist.

A scene right out of a Hollywood film occurred a little later that day. Arriving at I don't recall what stop along the river bank, all of us passengers were on deck, leaning on the rail, watching the customary business of docking, the local villagers arriving to celebrate the sight of the stern wheeler, and all the vendors with their wares. Leaning on a railing on the first-class deck, I heard a "pst . . . pst." This was the usual custom in the backlands to get someone's attention; a custom I had adopted, that is, until someone told me it was not a sign of "good upbringing." Be that as it may, it was used all the time in the backlands and by all kinds of people, so I kept using it. Thinking the "pst" was directed to someone else, I paid no attention, but the "pst . . . pst" came again. It was then I spotted an elderly man staring right at me. The old fellow had a head of grey hair, a white beard not very well kempt, and was dressed in simple but not poor clothing. What he really wanted was to talk to me, now waving with that Brazilian motion of open hand down turned telling me to come closer. He turned out to be Mr. Francisco and he told me of a recently discovered mine he was working, just a short distance from the town where we were docked. It was a mine of semi-precious stones - amethyst, tourmaline, aquamarines, topaz and others. He pulled a rather dirty piece of cloth out of his pocket and inside was a pile of all kinds of semi-precious stones. He thought, as might be expected, that I a North American would know of someone who might want to buy the mine or maybe buy it myself. Being the innocent American I was, I told him I was merely a student doing research and that I had absolutely no contacts with foreign capitalists, and beyond that, just had the budget of a struggling student. He, sad and disappointed, left me at that point, perhaps not totally convinced of my story. But, my o my, the scene could only remind me of a vague memory of Humphrey Bogart. The famous film "The Treasure of the Sierra Madre" was a classic film of a search for riches by a cast of characters that rivaled that of the valiant back landers and bandits of "cordel" of the Northeast (I mean "Valiant Vilela" and Lampão and António Silvino). But even if I had had the dough, I would not have had the courage to get off the stern wheeler and follow the old prospector. Once again - "Living is

Very Dangerous" (in this Brazil) said João Guimarães Rosa in this novel "The Devil to Pay in the Backlands."

The final part of the voyage ended the next day with our arrival in Xique-Xique, a medium size burg still in Bahia. The dock was quite busy with small fishing boats and some cargo boats including some with sails. It was in the local fair that I saw and found a "clay bull" the most beautiful that I had seen in all the Northeast, and lots of ceramics, and a very large fish market. A young fellow showed me a "dourado" of ten kilos, and showed another he said was a "piranha." Could it be? It was big.

I had arrived at Xique-Xique with a new plan, and in the end, a rather quixotic plan. The fact was the trip on the sternwheeler was getting to be a bit tiring and I was ready for a change of scene. At the designated end of the riverboat trip in Joaseiro da Bahia, down the river yet a couple of days from Xique-Xique, I had planned to catch a bus to Salvador da Bahia to meet a girlfriend from the days in Rio. Recalling a concept from the basic notions of mathematics which seemed correct to me - the shortest distance between two points is a straight line - and having sought some advice while on the river boat (bad advice in the end), I decided to get off the boat in Xique-Xique and catch some transport directly to Salvador, thus economizing two days of travel yet on the river boat. They told me the transportation from Xique-Xique would be easy - perhaps a third-class plane (DC -3), or if not, certainly, a bus "direct" to the coast. As they say in Spanish, I left "Guatemala para entrar en Guatepeor," from the frying pan into the fire! I should confess that I learned later that if I had continued on the boat to Joaseiro, there I would have found a well paved direct highway back to Salvador.

So I got off the stern wheeler, but not without saying goodbye to my friend the "prático," some crew members, but not the Captain, and with my bag in hand, went in search of the marvelous transportation spoken of aboard ship, already thinking of the encounter with the young lady in Salvador.

4

To not mince words, in Xique-Xique there was no airplane (it was to arrive sometime the following week), no bus, nothing! So I "contracted," a fine word, a local guy, a sort of taxi driver of the backlands, to take me on what would surely be the worst road in all of Brazil, to the next town, Irecê, where "certainly" I could catch a bus to the desired destination of the capital of the state. So I arrived exhausted, filthy dirty and in bad humor in the town of Irecê. There was bad luck again - the bandied about and promised bus had already left for the east. Therein began a small adventure that would add to the "folkloric" adventure just finished. The "deal" turned out to be to stick out the proverbial thumb and hitchhike in a Rural Station Wagon with two employees of the São Francisco Navigation Company (the same one that ran the river boats), ostensibly heading for Salvador. What they were doing in Irecê I never discovered, but the departure was set for the next morning. The "hotelzinho" [small hotel] where I stayed that night anxiously waiting to get "the hell out of Dodge" was the poorest and dirtiest I had seen thus far in Brazil. They told me (and pardon me, oh citizens of Irecê), that the town had 5000 inhabitants and was the best region for growing beans and rice in all Brazil. I never experienced that "grandeur" and only saw the principal street which was in the process of being paved, and beyond that, the northeastern cactus.

So, "we took off." The first two hours I traveled in the back end of the Rural, with no seats. It was dirty and hot; the rear of the "Rural" Jeep filling rapidly with the thick dust stirred up by the crazy, bone rattling and insane pace the Company driver insisted on keeping. The road was of clay and full of pot holes, an impossible road that would cover me with a coat of mud and dirt - just like Sonia Braga – Gabriela - in the "slave market" where Nacib would find her in "Gabriela Clove and Cinnamon." I was used to the way many Brazilians drove, including the taxi drivers of the "School" of Emerson Fittipaldi or Aryton Senna (once again, the Brazilian joke - the Indianapolis drivers supposedly got their training as taxi drivers in Rio or São Paulo), and the many bus drivers trying to break the speed record on the freeway in Rio de Janeiro. This driver topped them all.

It turns out I had a traveling companion, a surprise to me, in the back end of the Rural - a genuine "country girl" from Iboitirama. She was a girl or perhaps a grown lady; I could not tell from the dust and dirt covering her as well. At the first opportunity she fled the Rural, frightened I believe and scared within an inch of her life! I never found out for sure, but the Company guys told me that this was all a "test" to see if the gringo was a weakling or not, for later they allowed me up front in the cab, now considered "real people." We ended the trip as good friends, and I think respecting each other. The trip that followed was a constant whirlwind of partying - beer, conhaque and women! They knew every small-town bar and whorehouse from the São Francisco River to the Atlantic Ocean and Salvador! Well, not quite (I had adopted cordelian hyperbole along the way). We stopped in Miguel Calmon. The truth - I would have never survived the trip if it were not for the alcohol to "desensitize" the discomfort of it all!

But now, just a traveling "buddy," I could appreciate the classic countryside of the Bahia Interior - first the deep backlands with cacti, goats, Brahma cattle and many people walking along the road, others on bicycles, and yet others on burros. We saw and passed by large trucks with people jammed like sardines in the back end and even sitting on top of the cab. Once we stopped to give a ride to a young girl, she could not have been more than fifteen years old, with two tiny children at her waist, all in rags. I will never ever forget the face of that child-mother: black eyes like pieces of coal, thin, the image of misery. I failed in exchanging one single word with her, either because of her backland's speech or by the simple fact I was a gringo. For me, knowledgeable of the great "cycle" of "cordel" of the droughts and the refugees of the same, she was the spitting image of this sad reality of Brazil.

Upon arriving at the city of Miguel Calmon, my "guides" told me the mountain range nearby produced the best drinking water in all Brazil - a water that appeared to me to be brownish colored, and I thought, tasting the same. If these were to be my last words, this was just one more "trick" pulled on the gringo. But, Miguel Calmon was a pretty place, the image of prosperity in comparison to what I had seen in Xique-Xique. It was green with many small plazas and houses with flower gardens.

Then we passed through the "diamond zone" of Bahia, rich in minerals, but according to my friends, "exploited" principally by foreign firms. Here also there was the constant conversation, now nothing new, of an incredibly rich Brazil, of great hydro-electric potency but with the lack of resources to develop it, of the poverty of the same rich Brazil, and the love of the Brazilians for my now deceased hero, President John f. Kennedy. After leaving Miguel Calmon at eleven a.m. (departure had been set for 8 a.m.), we passed by Jacobina, the center of gold mining in Bahia. There the old reliable Rural (a well-known and beloved vehicle in the interior of Brazil) broke down and after a long wait, we were pulled by a large truck for a six-hour ride into Feira de Santana. I, like the many peasants I had seen on the ubiquitous trucks hauling freight in the interior, rode seated on top of the cargo in the back of the big truck. I felt like Don Quixote, all beat up from my adventures, being taken back home on the broken-down burro of a neighbor. There in Feira I got the "milk route" [pinga-pinga] bus to finally arrive in Salvador.

The city seemed like paradise to me in comparison to what I had seen the past few days; it would bring the reencounter with Ellen, the girl friend from Rio, and lots of tourism: all the coast with its beautiful beaches, the sea so beautiful as previously seen in the earlier phase in Bahia, the beach and lighthouse of Barra, the lower city and the Mercado Modelo, a show of "maculelê", dancing and carrying on in the Boite Anjo Azul, dinner in the Restaurante Paris and the restaurant in the old Teatro Vila Velha, the Club Cloc, the Pelourinho, and days later, the departure.

There was one unpleasant reminder of my tap dance with the DOPS, this time from Sérgio the same agent who had cornered me two months earlier when I had the encounter and interview with, in his words "the "commie" Brazilian Literature professor at the University of Bahia." Ellen and I were having a pleasant lunch in the restaurant in the Modelo Market when the DOPS agent in the usual white linen suit, narrow black tie and straw hat suddenly appeared at the table and with no invitation from us sat down, took off his hat, lit a cigarette and said,

"Gaherty, you have been a busy guy since we last talked. My colleague Heitor Dias in Rio has kept me (and all of us following you about in Brazil) apprised of your scrapes in Rio and for that matter your travels to Minas, to Brasília and your latest jaunt on the riverboat. That's where I come in. You and I already had a talk about Jorge Amado, that commie turncoat from here in Bahia and all the crap he pulled as the representative of the Party in the Brazilian congress in the 1940s, his being kicked out of Brazil by the Vargas Regime, the voluntary work for the Communist International in Hungary and of course the Marxist tripe he sells all the naïve Brazilians who read his lousy books for the sex and the rest. We know all about his novel "Red Harvest" ["Seara Vermelha"] and his view that banditry, religious fanaticism and political bossism in the Northeast can all be alleviated with a Marxist Revolution. How he got the cinema Reds to do that film on the riverboat is a mystery to me. The question is: were you really doing "folklore" and "cordel" research or are you once again sympathizing with Amado's crap and the Fidel and Ché Guevara land reform crowd? If you didn't have those INR connections in D.C. and Brasília you would be somewhere below the lion pen in the São Paulo zoo. Don't forget that." He put on his hat, left the cigarette smoldering in an ashtray on the table and walked out of the restaurant.

Ellen was shaking and asked me to order a strong "caipirinha" which she slammed while she interrogated me, saying, "What in the hell is going on here? You never told me in Rio you were involved with any funny stuff. This is creepy." I said, "Don't worry. I do have some U.S. government connections and I am writing the LETTERS for the "Times" but the research is real and let's have a good time tonight." So it went until a teary goodbye at the Salvador airport with promises for a final reunion in Rio when we both wered to be headed home in a month.

Epilogue to the São Francisco

Thinking back, on the way back to Recife, I mused that the river boat trip was the most picturesque and most interesting of all my travels in Brazil, at least up to that point. The countryside was relatively pretty but with nothing spectacular apart from the beauty of the river with its dawns and sunsets on the water (the views of the bay of Salvador and of course Rio de Janeiro surpassed by far that scene). But the experience on the stern wheeler [o "gaiola"] on this river so historic for all Brazil, together with the Brazilian cast of characters, a unique group at that, was wonderful. Really, I had the feeling of being in the "birthplace" of the land of "The Devil to Pay in the Backlands" ["Grande Sertão: Veredas"] of the master João Guimarães Rosa. And of course, to experience ten days on the same stern wheeler as in the movie "Red Harvest" ["Seara Vermelha"] of the great hero Jorge Amado was an education. I always thought that it would have been much like this to travel in the middle of the Mississippi River in the nineteenth century remembering the stories of Mark Twain, i.e. "Life on the Mississippi." In sum, it was a unique, memorable experience, I felt like I had lived a small part of the history of Brazil.

LETTER VI

THE AMAZON AND THEN
LAST DAYS IN RECIFE

1

Adventures in the Air to Belém and Manaus

After the beautiful days of rest and tourism, reliving days of nostalgia in Salvador da Bahia, I had said goodbye to my friend, she returning to the life of Peace Corps Volunteer in greater Rio, and me to my final stay in the Northeast. Upon arriving one more time in "the land of 'cordel'," I came to realize that I was lacking a visit to one last possible area of collection, the Amazon Basin where there had existed an important variant of "cordel" in the 1930s in Belém do Pará and then possible poets and vendors in the state of Amazonas itself with its capital city Manaus. I asked the Fulbright Commission for additional funding, and a modest amount was granted, so I programed the trip.

Adventures in the Air

Although this trip did not turn out to be anything especially significant for cordelian research, it was one more picturesque adventure in the great Brazil. We left Guararapes Airport in Recife on a Curtis 46 airplane, the military version of the DC - 3; the fare was "Tarifa 3," the only fare available to me considering the modest financial resources remaining to me. The airline was the old standby Varig. The first stop was in Fortaleza where the plane was temporarily grounded, but after a certain amount of time we took off again, heading for São Luís, the capital of Maranhão State. There the old wreck stayed on the ground. We had tried to take off from São Luís, warming up the engines at the end of the runway, but then received the order to taxi back to the hangar.

So we changed planes once again, now to a DC -3 of Paraense Airlines, a small regional carrier in the North and the Amazon. With no more problems, we arrived in Belém do Pará late in the afternoon. On that trip viewing the ground from the air it was all new to me, and I was very impressed by the dense tropical forest which could be seen immediately after takeoff from São Luís. THIS was the famous Amazon forest so dreamed about and imagined from readings in graduate school. We flew at a very low altitude, the only way the old DC - 3 could travel, so the result was a marvelous view of the land. There seemed to be no cleared areas - all was forest! At first view Belém seemed pretty with wide tree-lined avenues in the city center, but with extreme humidity and heat.

Steve Baldini was with me again; I began at this point to wonder if part of his job was to keep an eye on me! There began a series of interesting events; I do not remember the exact sequence, so I tell it in a rather "impressionistic" manner as it comes to my mind now. Through Steve's auspices we went to visit Mr. Buck Highlander, Director of CARITAS and its distribution of food in the region through this international Catholic Charity organization. The conversation was both interesting and revealing as to the problems that CARITAS faced in the region, and more importantly, the total situation in the region. The principal function of CARITAS at the time was the distribution of "Food for Peace," the distribution of seeds, and giving instructions for health and hygiene, principally in Amapá Territory (the huge island off the coast of Pará). Buck spoke of problems with Protestant Missionaries along the route of the new Brasília-Belém Highway and their accusation that the Capuchin Priests were selling the food of "Food for Peace." He spoke of protests by students on the left, the burning of a USA flag, of rocks thrown at the USIS (United States Information Service) building and his impression that the predominate sentiment in the area was almost totally anti-U.S. Mr. Highlander was very preoccupied with this situation because he saw the good that foreign firms were doing in Brazil at that time, "firms of conscience," "good firms." According to him the propaganda from the left had destroyed much of the good will of such firms. He spoke, in an aside, of the Tapajós Indians and the Mundurucus spread throughout the Amazon forest, now decimated by poverty and sickness.

At that point, despite profiting from the conversation, I left in a bit of a hurry, needing to go back to the airline office to confirm my passage to Manaus for the next day. I left Buck's house, hurrying to catch the only taxi I saw in the streets and not realizing that the streets of Belém were only paved up to perhaps a half-meter from the sidewalk. Therefore, stepping quickly into the street, and seeing a little old lady on the other side of the street, certainly with her eye on that single taxi, the one I wanted, I tripped and fell in a hole, seriously twisting my ankle. Seated there on the pavement, I thought to myself I had surely broken the ankle if the pain I felt had anything to do with it. A Good Samaritan came by, helped me up and pointed the way to a "Pronto Socorro" [first aid station] in the neighborhood. The doctor there examined the ankle, wrapped it, and recommended that I be careful not to put too much weight upon it. The result was my "forced" vacation in Belém.

2

Trying to make the best of the situation, the next day I limped down to the docks of Belém to see the famous "Ver-o-Peso" [Check the Weight] market. I was thinking that this part of Brazil would be especially interesting to Hansen's readers of the "Times" since it's the Amazon that intrigues most North Americans. Despite the ankle, I ended up experiencing the most fascinating market that I had seen up to that point in Brazil, and one needs to remember that I had already seen the most famous markets and fairs of the Northeast and the Northeastern fair in Rio and the markets along the São Francisco River in Minas Gerais and Bahia. I saw the docks of Belém with huge freighters of the high seas; these navigated the Guarujá Bay outside of Belém and then the Amazon itself. The docks were a whirl of activity. There was a plethora of fishing and cargo boats and an "anthill" of human activity loading and unloading the same. I saw huge blocks of ice that bare footed men with no protection on their feet dragged from the dock to the boats.

At the Ver-O-Peso there was a tremendous variety of fish, mountains of crabs in baskets, along with ceramics and tiles. The vendors were "armed' with large machetes cutting up the fish for sale. Outside the market there was much activity: there were stands of all types full of vegetables - herbs, greens, manioc flour, and beans. And snake skins. One thing got my attention: almost all the outside market seemed to be controlled by Japanese - Brazilians. I learned later through the "cordelian" verses that there was a large Japanese colony in Belém, and in fact, prejudice against them by the Brazilians during World War II had been fierce. But now there seemed to be scarcely a "Brazilian" in the vegetable stands. Looking more closely I saw that indeed the market reflected the greater Brazilian "mosaic" or "melting pot;" there were Portuguese, foreigners, mestiços of all colors, Indians, Blacks and the Japanese in the market. This indeed was the "Brazilian Mosaic" so bandied about in the documentary films about Brazil.

I have not said yet that the Ver-o-Peso had a tremendous quantity of canaries, parrots, macaws, monkeys and even capibaras (that pig-like rodent in the Amazon) as well as many tanks of colored, tropical fish. The tourist shops in Belém and Manaus to come were very different from the ones in the Northeast due to the abundance, naturally, of articles made of alligator skin, snake skin, and for the butterflies (including the Blue Morpho), all native to the forest. They even sold key chains made of piranha heads and other local "gadgets."

Inside the market I met and conversed with two sellers of "literatura de cordel" from the region. The first was Raimundo Oliveira, active in the Belém market for years, a seller of the story-poems of the São Francisco Printing Shop of Juazeiro do Norte of José Bernardo da Silva; Oliveira, a man with just one arm, was a very pleasant person. He spoke of Editora Prelúdio in São Paulo and its "infiltration" of the market for "cordel," even with vendors in faraway Manaus. He refused to be photographed and did not want to sign any of the story-poems of his own authorship that I purchased. One of them was indeed a "classic" of the entire story of the Rubber Boom in the Amazon and the inscripted laborers from the Northeast. In the plaza outside the Ver-o-Peso there was another cordel vendor but with poems of "local" authors, that is of the region, of Cunha Neto and S. Simião, the latter a native of São Luís do Maranhão, but now a resident in Belém. Simião was not present but was on a boat trip to Santarém to sell his "folhetos." In this visit in 1967 I was not too familiar with the local "cordel" and did not know much about the Guarjarina Press, one of the most important in Brazil in the 1930s and 1940s. Be that as it may, by 1967 the originals of the Guarjarina Press were not being sold on the streets but were in private collections because the press itself had not operated for twenty years.

The docks of Belém were literally jammed with large ships, cargo ships and smaller traffic, among them small boats with sails in a style like the famous "saveiros" of Salvador da Bahia and the Recôncavo Bahiano. And there were many diesel boats. The Guarujá Bay in Belém was extremely wide and there were many islands in the distance. One sees them much better from the air: what appeared to be a huge lake was the Guarujá River with a large island to the north, and in the distance on the other side of the island was the Amazon River itself.

The next morning I met Richard and Susan, Peace Corps Volunteers from the U.S. from the State of São Paulo on an R and R tourism trip to know the North. They learned of a small tourist boat which offered for a reasonable price to take us to see the rivers of the region. I happily joined them for the jaunt. To arrive to the dock of the tour boat we caught a local bus passing through a riverside part of town the likes of which I had only seen in films - all the houses were on stilts above the water, and all seemed extremely poor. There were boys on the bus with "hats" made from cut-in-half soccer balls, a reminiscence of the national mania. We arrived at the "Amazon Queen" run by a certain Mr. Standish, the boat, clearly resembling the "African Queen" of the Bogart and Hepburn film. Leaving the dock, we passed all manner of small boats, with sails and with motors, some serving as houses for their owners. Then we entered the Rio Pará passing by the Rio Gumá and tributaries of the Rio Cumdú. According to our guide and host and pilot, Mister Standish, the totality of all these waters together was equal to the volume of the Amazon. According to him no less then fifteen small rivers converge at this point and come together near the Island of Marajó some fifty kilometers distant. It indeed was a watery world.

There were many fishing boats of all kinds, but when we entered the Rio Guamá the banks of the river closed in beside us, the river now being a straight "ribbon" of water. Forgive the gringo but it did not seem dissimilar to me from the narrow water of the Jungle Cruise in Disneyland, not such a stupid idea when you think about it - Disney did a lot of research before he built his park. Then the forest closed even more; it was now much denser with all kinds of trees and vegetation - from the ubiquitous coconut palms to the gigantic "umbrella trees" so famous in the region, trees that stand like towers above the rest of the forest. The undergrowth along the banks was also dense with vines, grasses; it was a true "wall" of vegetation. There were abundant clearings with shacks supported on sticks or poles, "pirogas" or canoes, and small row boats, these rowed using a long pole. Many children were in the clearings, all waving to us as the boat went by, dressed poorly or with no clothes at all. I saw women within the shacks spying at us through holes which served as windows, apparently trying to hide from us. There were many native dugout canoes and fishing nets strung from the coconut trees. Many trees extended their branches out over the water, and the small kids climbed up them to jump or dive into the muddy water. We saw the "four-eyed fish" swimming on the surface, black and yellow Orioles ["Rouxinóis do Rio Negro"] and the famous Blue Morpho butterflies of the region.

At one point we entered a sort of narrow canal, almost without sunlight and totally wet soil; the pilot said the tide climbs to this point. There were other huge trees, large flies, cacau trees (imported to this region), and rubber trees. In sum, I felt for the first time that I had begun to see a bit of the real Amazon. (It was something you would never see from the big ships which plied the middle of the Amazon as though as on a huge lake, not reaching its small tributaries.)

On the return we passed by a mattress factory that used palm fronds as its prime material, and then at the entrance to Belém, the Yacht Club, and all along rows of houses on stilts. Trying to link my previous experience in Rio de Janeiro to the region, I asked Mr. Standish about Ex-Federal Deputy Ferreira Lima (the reader may recall my short infatuation with his daughter and my time with the family in Rio). "Well," said Standish, "he's a damned communist, a lawyer who earned his money in real estate, who was elected by his friends, and had no real solution for the problems of Brazil. If he is rich, it is because he robbed folks." Shocked and repentant of having asked the question, I believe I had just learned a lesson in the politics of the "Two Brazils," my own experience in Rio and the opinion of the "masses" in Belém. Whether what the pilot of the boat said was true or gossip, I rooted for and believed in the concepts expressed by the daughter and the father. One only had to hear their side of the story matched by no end of facts and logic in the telling. The story goes a long way to explain the politics of the Military Regime, now dictatorship in 1967, and the paranoia of the Left. The dictatorship would go on in late 1967 with a proven record of oppression and even torture.

A footnote on the boat trip: I was stopped outside my hotel after the boat ride, this time by a local DOPS agent who said they knew I was on the boat and had talked to Standish about Ferreira Lima. The only way I figure they could have known was that Standish was charged with telling the locals about any foreign passengers and conversations. The government indeed had big ears and long tentacles, in this case hardly worth their time. I told him all I did was ask the Captain his opinion on the matter, my curiosity just being what citizens up North thought. He said, "That pretty much corroborates what we already knew. No harm done." Damn! This was getting old.

That night we had dinner at the "Club Militar" on the banks of the Guarujá Bay, a beautiful scene and a restaurant famous for the local dish "pato no tucupi," [Tucupi Duck]. The next morning, I went to visit the well-known Goeldi Museum with its gardens, forest and zoo to the side, the latter with all manner of tropical birds and some not tropical - vultures, owls, raptors, parrots, herons and the obligatory animals: alligators and very large snakes. The museum was important for its interest in the Indigenous culture in the region. It had showcases with ceramics from the Marajó Tribe, believed to be the tribe "of most advanced culture" in Brazil (these are the words from the signs of the Museum itself). They were possible "migrants" from the Rio Solimões in Ecuador. I do not opine on this issue. The gardens and forest surrounding the museum were beautiful, and in them I experienced the first cool breeze I had felt in Belém which no longer seemed like a furnace. The truth is that the heat of Belém does not reach the extremes of the sandy deserts of Africa. I had expected "a heat of a thousand devils" ["mil diabos"] by being so close to the equator. If you mix in some sunshine, you quickly feel exhausted. That alone must explain why life truly goes at a slower pace and there is an obligatory nap in the heat of the afternoon.

An aside: I went one more time to the river where there was a swimming contest in progress - swimming from one side of the Guarujá Bay to the other and returning! A young Japanese man won, an incredible distance.

Now with the ankle feeling a bit better and not anxious to spend more time n Belém, I wanted to continue the journey. In these paragraphs of tourism I have not narrated the anxious telephone calls to the airline office trying to continue the journey. The fact was I was quite angry with them and of traveling in third class. But there was no other way. It may be of interest to see a summary of the travel details of those days. A small odyssey by the gringo tourist in the North of Brazil in 1967 follows: *

1. The beginning of the trip started in Recife on the Atlantic Coast where we passengers embarqued and disembarqued last Friday in Fortaleza, the first stop on the planned trip, leaving Recife on the C-46 of Varig Airlines.
2. The C-46 broke down in São Luís de Maranhão; we waited one hour and Paraense Airlines came to the rescue taking us late that afternoon to Belém do Pará. Of note: in those days the prop flights flew only during daylight.
3. The accident with the badly, twisted ankle caused me to miss the Varig flight on last Saturday to Manaus.
4. I tried to change plans and catch a Vaspe flight on Sunday, at eleven a.m. to Manaus.
5. The eleven o'clock flight was first announced as delayed, programmed for departure at two p.m.
6. The same flight was announced as "delayed" until three p.m. The same flight was announced as delayed until seven p 7. p.m. Then it was cancelled.
7. On Monday, the happy gringo with ticket in hand climbed aboard a Paraense flight to Manaus: a DC - 4 on the tarmac, motors warming up, and suddenly called back to the gate. A long wait. Finally, we took off for the dreamed of, fabulous Manaus.

The asterisk * only represents the "outgoing" journey; there were other events on the "return" to be told in a bit.

3

IT WAS WORTH THE WAIT! A large benefit of flying third class in those days was the necessity to fly at a relatively low altitude. Below the DC - 4 with four prop engines one could see the great Amazon region - river after river, our trajectory following loosely that of the Amazon River. One could see all manner of tributaries to the larger Amazon, flooded land along the river, all seeming like a huge swamp. The forest was dense with just a few clearings spotted from the air with signs of human activity, probably small farms. It was the rainy season of the "tall waters" and great thunderheads in the distance; the plane swerved to the left, then the right, leaving the flight plan I am sure to avoid the tropical storms, the passengers with seatbelts fastened, white knuckles and trying not to become air sick.

There was one stop in Santarém along the Tapajós River, not too small a river itself but with very dark waters, these not mixing with the "coffee and milk" ["café com leite"] waters of the great Amazon itself.

An aside: On board the DC - 4 to Manaus were some North American scientists carrying plastic sacks filled with water and small fish, species they had caught near Belém and were taking for analysis by the instruments on board their research ship docked in Manaus. One of the scientists sat beside me on the trip and showed me the fish. The ship was well known in the region for diverse reasons. I found out the locals labeled it a "spy ship" of the gringos.

At one point now near Manaus we saw from the air the confluence of the Rio Solimões with the Rio Negro which came in from the North. This was the famous "Encounter of the Waters" in Brazilian tourist jargon; one saw the water that looked much like Coca-Cola of the Rio Negro in contrast to the muddy, almost yellow water of the Solimões; the two joined to form the great running of the Amazon east to the sea almost one thousand miles distant.

Wanderings in Manaus

We landed in Manaus and I caught a Kombi (the Volkswagen Van of the times) to the city center. At the international airport of Manaus to the side of our jalopy-like DC - 4 were the most modern of huge international planes, first class air travel! A good thing still in the 1960s was the free transport by the airline of its passengers to the hotel, even for third-class passengers!

I was lodged in the "Pensão Garrido" where I later met a Bolivian (one thinks of the well-known Brazilian novel "Emperor of Acre" by Márcio Souza) who admitted to making a living from international contraband. We had dinner in a small café near the docks which made me think of the scene from "That Man in Rio" with Jean Paul Belmondo, a café that would have fit just as well in a Bogart film. The Bolivian spoke of the latest news - Manaus would soon be a "free port" city which would certainly bring population growth as well as monetary growth to Brazil.

The next day I made my first visit to the very large market at the dock in Manaus, an experience! Very picturesque with regional flavor, the exterior market was the most interesting - these are like the "leftovers" from the principal market, a beautiful wrought iron edifice inspired by the steel construction seen in the Eiffel Tower in Paris and the Santa Isabel Elevator in Lisbon. The outside market was built on large, long wooden planks extended into the Rio Negro water. Small boats were docked and were being unloaded of their cargo of vegetables, fruit, chickens, jute and such; the larger part of the launches were motor launches. The customers would walk very carefully on the boards and make their purchases, stepping from one boat to the next, from land to water and back. There were huge piles of bananas and pineapples. It makes the fan of "cordel" think of Manoel Camilo dos Santos' famous "Trip to São Saruê" - a poetic land of great abundance. Rumor had it that there were tarantulas in the bananas so "look out!" They told me all these products came from farms and even truck gardens at the side of the great river. It is difficult to describe the atmosphere of the place, but it was exactly as I had imagined - a civilization and economy constructed on and based solely on the river.

The river traffic was heavy, much more than on the Pará at Belém, and a world apart from what now seemed to me to be the miniscule traffic just seen on the São Francisco River. There was incredible heat in this open-air market, especially when the sun was overhead, and it was all quite dirty, but no one seemed in any hurry to escape the sun. Another part of the dock was different: the commercial traffic of "classic" transport boats on the Amazon. These boats, generally diesel with two decks, were the "maritime taxis" of the Rio Negro and the Solimões (which becomes the Amazon downstream from the Encounter of the Waters). They were similar to the "Gaiolas" of the São Francisco, with cabins on the upper deck, hammocks strung, and space for freight below, but were different because of the diesel engines instead of the steam driven stern wheelers. Crammed with passengers, there was much activity, many people selling and buying at the market and on the dock. Along the dock I noticed many beggars, many crippled in one form or another, and many people selling limes or bananas in small quantities trying to earn a few pennies. I had never encountered to this point in Brazil so many and such a variety of insects - ants, flies and an almost invisible "no see'um" which had a terrible bite.

The area was impressive by the size of it all and all its activity - long lines of passenger boats docked in rows, cargo boats getting ready for departure with people on board who had spent the market day in Manaus, others heading long distances to a series of towns up and down river from Manaus. I had never been to the Orient with its great floating cities, but Manaus seemed to me to be a culture based on water and the rivers, and at that time, a principal source of transportation in the region, at least for the humble masses.

On the mainland, near the docks and facing the river, I found what I had been hoping for - a vendor of the romances and story-poems of "cordel," all his wares extended on a wooden table. His stock was from Juazeiro do Norte from the printing shop of José Bernardo da Silva (the astute reader might recall I had seen and interviewed the famous fellow in Juazeiro), the classic romances of the Northeast. It turns out he had bought his stock from a vendor who lived in Fortaleza most of the year and came only occasionally to Manaus. He also had story-poems from Prelúdio Publishing House in São Paulo. But I met no poets or any sign of local printing shops.

Then I walked to downtown Manaus, full of the movement of customers. There were many shops with appliances and electronic devices, all very modern and colorful, much like the commerce in the center of Recife but with an "Amazon" flavor. In the middle of the 1960s Manaus had 200,000 inhabitants. The city was being converted into among other things a major manufacturing area for computers! The "free port" law fixed for a period of twenty years hopefully would completely change the old riverside city with its colorful period of the rubber boom (and the semi-slavery that that entailed) into a regional commercial center in that great region of the Amazon in Brazil. I noted the basic infrastructure of asphalted streets first seen in Belém and then Manaus that were still lacking in the interior of the Northeast. This was the impression of someone studying folklore and not economic or political development.

One saw all the shops open to the air, shopkeepers flirting with the girls that walked by, the home appliance stores with refrigerators, stoves, stereos, and tape players. There were watches for sale everywhere, and all manner of electronic gadgets. How about a Rolex for $5? Above all one noticed the usual very Brazilian "movimento" with blaring music and noise from loud speakers bellowing the latest music hits, especially the "iê-iê-iê" of early Brazilian rock n' roll.

It was time to visit the most famous monument of the region, the great Opera House or "Teatro Amazonas" in Manaus; it was of national and international fame dating from the epoch of grandeur and riches of the Rubber Barons. The interior's phenomenal decoration was that of Italian, English and French furnishings - wall coverings, furniture, murals, a floor of imported marble from Portugal, when not the floor of various colors of Brazilian rosewood. They say that in that golden age of the Rubber Barons it cost from twelve to fourteen "contos de reis," a figure translated in 1967 to several million "cruzeiros" in the inflated money of Brazil in the 1960s. Local folklore had it that the Rubber Barons sent their laundry to be done in Europe! And that the big names of European Opera would come to Manaus for a one-night stand! Perhaps. The exterior was equally impressive: it was white and rose colored with a gigantic domed roof of mosaic, a beautiful and impressive plaza in front, and sidewalks made like others in Bahia, Recife or Rio, of the famous white and black mosaic stones. I noted that the chairs on the main floor of the opera house were colonial in style, all caned like the furniture in the colonial mansions of the sugar cane barons of the Northeast. Several of the latter came to mind: the colonial house of Portuguese blue and white tiles of friend and author Ariano Suassuna in Casa Forte in Recife, or the "Casa Grande" now headquarters of the Joaquim Nabuco Research Institute of Gilberto Freyre in Recife and yet the "big house" of the José Lins do Rego sugar cane plantation in Paraíba.

Another outing was to the City Park of the 10th of November (I do not recall the importance of that date). The Manaus zoo was disappointing. It was a place for picnics and swimming in the clear black water the color of Coca Cola coming from the Rio Negro and what seemed like very thin animals dying from lack of care. The high point of the outing to the zoo took place on one of the most picturesque buses I had seen in Belém and now Manaus - the entire exterior of the bus was made of wood, except of course those parts like axle, motor, wheels, etc. The sides, the floor and the roof of the bus were of wood, as they told me, to avoid the rust of the fluvial climate of Manaus. Seated, awaiting departure on that steamy, hot afternoon, just "hanging out" as it were, suddenly I saw a man come aboard with a strange animal hanging from a stick he carried. It was a sloth, exempt I surmise, from paying for a ticket.

Atmosphere of Smugglers and More

That afternoon, I had time on my hands and ended up seeing, smelling and "incorporating" myself (as the Spiritists of Brazil say) in the atmosphere of the market and the docks, especially enjoying the traffic on the water. One boat brought only crocodile skins. There was a kind of floating city, recalling the famous floating city victim of a huge fire, some say set on purpose by the city government to do in the "mess over there." Notorious for its filth, prostitution and drugs (recall the film "That Man in Rio" with Jean Paul Belmondo, a film that today is a great "accidental" documentary of Brazil of those times with its scenes of Manaus' "floating city" and of its scenes from Brasília in its infancy.) The inhabitants of the "floating city" accustomed to the periodic fires, move to the interior or other houses built by the city of Manaus as a "solution" to the problem, a policy like that in Rio de Janeiro in the same period with the accidental" burning of "favelas" and the moving of the "victims" to the Baixada Fluminense, a proletarian area outside of greater Rio.

Down the way from the market was the official wharf or dock of Manaus; this was where the ocean-going ships were docked. The dock was a phenomenon in itself; it floated on very large pontoons, a necessary construction in order to withstand the rise and fall of the river during the rainy and dry seasons, a matter of 70 feet according to one source. This floating dock had to be able to accommodate the said ocean-going cargo ships as well as local river traffic. I saw large trucks unloading raw cashews directly in the holds of the ships; one of the ships I was told was heading for Germany. It was impressive to realize we were almost one thousand miles from the point where the Amazon empties into the Atlantic, and that these huge ships are here in the middle of the forest. The day ended with a gorgeous sunset on the water and the easing of the heat and afternoon on the river and its multitude of boats. Many of the same, now with lights or lanterns lit, made for an unforgettable scene for the gringo researcher. It seemed mysterious, exotic and romantic recalling to mind the romantic description Jorge Amado painted in words so many times of the "mysterious" city of Salvador da Bahia. I thought, "Gaherty, you're not in Nebraska anymore."

That night I ate dinner one more time in the same restaurant near the dock, a place of adventurers, smugglers, political refugees, and with some young ladies of dubious character. A man near my table had a long scar along his cheek and should have had stories to tell. I was drinking beer with my Bolivian acquaintance who plied me with interesting stories of the time - of the free trip sponsored by the Bolivian Communist Party to the Soviet Union, air fare and three months of board and room. It was an excellent opportunity for poor Bolivians to see a bit of the world, an opportunity that existed nowhere else. My Bolivian friend swore that he "had no politics" and that it would be a clever idea to send all the Communists in Bolivia to Russia for six months, to get to know the country and its Socialist system, and then decide if that is what they wanted for Bolivia! The night wore on, the conversation waned, and I returned perhaps miraculously, to my humble boarding house without being mugged.

Officially that is, there was another encounter with an undercover detective (from DOPS I guess) who cornered me on the dark street, scaring the crap out of me before he showed me a badge and said, "I've got to admit this is interesting duty they laid on me since you arrived in Manaus. You know, you might as well get used to it buddy, you are on our shit list. It's not every day I get to hang out in such a colorful place. You're lucky "Scarface" there in that dive of a place did not corner you on the way to that shitty men's room and put a shiv in your side just for pocket change. (The agent had been sitting at a nearby table taking it all in.)"

"What interests us is your Bolivian friend. He's got a dossier a foot long, you name it: smuggling, Communist connections, just one of dozens hanging around Manaus today. Gaherty, you seem to have a penchant for picking new friends! I could hear bits and pieces of the conversation, but now is your chance to fill me in on the details. I'm in no hurry; let's get a "cafezinho" like civilized folks and you can tell me all about it."

"It's getting to be old hat," I thought to myself, "just get on with it and get out of here."

"Okay, it's pretty simple. I'm traveling alone, and he came up to my table and started the conversation. I liked the chance to speak some Spanish here in Manaus and he didn't seem threatening." I retold the entire conversation: the Bolivian's "work" in Manaus and the tales of the Bolivian government's trade and friendly terms with Moscow and the free trips to recruit young desperate people to the "cause." (This was the time of Ché Guevara's misadventures in South America trying to spread the Fidelista doctrine.)

"Yeah, we know, we're all too familiar with all that. Why do you suppose we were worried by Francisco Julião and the Peasant Leagues in the Northeast, the whole bunch Fidel sympathizers, and incidentally, you've been nosing around asking questions about Julião a while now."

I didn't have much more to say, adding, "The guy told me the Russian benevolence didn't work, at least on him, and that they should send all the Bolivians there to find out what Bolshevism is really like."

Mr. agent seemed satisfied and noted that for the most part I seemed to be just doing the standard tourism; he paid for the coffee and had one last word of advice: "It's good to be curious, and I can appreciate you want to see different angles of all that's going on around here, but that place is one of the most notorious hangouts for people who end up dead, and you're damned lucky I escorted you home. What else are you planning, hopefully not going back there?"

I said, "I've got a tourist trip on the milk boat tomorrow and then I'm getting the hell out of here. Does that suit you?"

"Glad to have your company. Just the same we'll be watching."

In fact the next day would bring the last adventure in Manaus, and not the least interesting, in this odyssey to Brazil.

The Milk Boat

Waking at 4 a.m., I went to the dock to be a passenger on the Milk Boat, an excellent way, and not the slightest touristy, to see the agricultural and riverine economy near Manaus. Remembering my farm background once again in Nebraska, it seemed like a great idea. I would get to experience not only the Rio Negro, but also the Solimões (the name of the Amazon River in the western Amazon region, but down river from Manaus when it joins the Rio Negro it becomes the Amazon proper), and the Paraná and Carreira rivers.

The boat was equipped with a hold full of ice to be prepared for the large milk cans to be picked up on the route of the ranches in the region with dairy cattle. The main deck was for passengers, mainly humble folks after a day of "doing the market" ["fazendo feira"] and other shopping in Manaus, returning to their modest homes along the river. And the boat was propelled by a large diesel motor. It looked like the "Amazon Queen" of Belém but was larger.

Immediately after departure we were all served "café com leite" and bread, both excellent, particularly keeping in mind that early hour. The boat's captain was a Cearense from Crato (the "progressive" city in the Valley of Cariri in Ceará, a rival of the city of Juazeiro of Padre Cícero Romão). After the departure from Manaus I entered in conversation with a rancher returning home to his place (being a farm kid these encounters were always particularly interesting to me); he was the owner of 800 hectares (about 1500 acres), one part of his property near Manaus but another farther into the interior. I recall from my notes on the trip, "He only raises cattle because he does not have the necessary capital or the hand labor to cultivate his lands. He spends the winter (the season of heavy tropical rains, from January to May) in Manaus and goes out to the ranch only in the "summer"." He opined that the new Free Trade Zone would harm traditional ranchers because their crops and products would now enter competition with the new ones from outside, these free of import duties, but he was enthusiastic about the new possibilities for local industry and for agricultural equipment."

We entered first the Rio Negro and then proceeded to the gigantic Solimões. At this point the river was extremely wide with a strong current, and now particularly dangerous for navigation due to the considerable number of large tree trunks floating in the current, coming from upstream in this season of "high water" (April to May). Then we entered the Carreira River, a much smaller steam with many large cattle ranches alongside. The terrain was extremely flat, already cleared (the trees and vegetation were leveled) for some kilometers from the river which was constantly rising.

In the summer season this tributary, now so strong, dries up completely. The channel was very narrow and on both sides, at water level, the forage grew wildly. And there was an abundance of water birds in the area. I saw yellow and white birds, dozens of white herons with long, fine "stilt" legs and large and fine beaks. The birds hunt insects and small fish and are seen all along the river. Stock still, they seemed like marble statues, their whiteness in contrast to the brilliant green of the surrounding vegetation. There was no end to the variety of small birds as well.

At one stop the crew hauled aboard a gigantic fish; I think it was the legendary "Pirarucu" weighing almost fifty kilograms. They dumped it into the hold. This "fish storage" seemed to contrast with the "mission" of the milk boat, picking up full cans of milk, exchanging these for the empties from Manaus it would hand back at the small, country docks. It was a flexible mission indeed open to receiving and trading many products of the region. I was disappointed to not see crocodiles; they tell me these inhabit the swamps, still waters and smaller streams in the interior (the famous "igarapés"). Along the river there was an abundance of houses, structures of all sorts spotted on both the outgoing and return trip to Manaus. And along with the large cattle ranches there was also subsistence agriculture in the region - small plots of whatever could be cultivated in garden size plots, like manioc and other vegetables.

The houses were all of wood, some a bit finer than others, but most generally small and simple, many of just one floor. The better ones were painted, at least in the front, and generally in vibrant colors. The roofs were of thatch, but a few houses had tiled roofs. The typical house was linked to the river by a "sidewalk" of planks, and the house to other out buildings with the same planks. The "dock" of each small house was very rustic, the floor of wooden planks with a small "house" setting on the planks (the latter looking like the old out houses on the farms of 19th century Nebraska), the whole thing built up on stilts.

Transportation and communication among the houses on the river was always by dugout canoe or a very small motor boat, the larger of these with the capability of transporting people or perhaps a few head of cattle. All the houses were built on stilts and sat about two meters above the water; the reason was that all this land floods during high water season. Some of the ranches had "corrals" as well built on stilts where they kept cattle safe from the water, fed on the cut forage already mentioned. I saw many such "corrals" along the river. My rancher friend on the milk boat informed me that literally thousands of head of cattle in the region are lost either from drowning or from a type of pneumonia contracted from standing in water.

The people I saw at river side were visibly poor and dressed accordingly: the men wore shorts and a straw hat; the women in simple cotton "chita" dresses; the children were nude. It seemed that at each house where the boat stopped there were a dozen small children spying behind the open windows, just watching us go by.

As I already mentioned, the amount of river traffic in the region was impressive, much more than on the São Francisco River in the backlands of Minas Gerais and Bahia, and one could constantly hear the "chug, chug" of diesel motors of the boats that went by. The boats seemed to follow a certain style: round in front and back, one deck, just like the milk boat.

Returning to the purpose of our boat, the milk boat, there were stops at dozens of plantations or ranches where we swapped empty milk cans for full ones, sometimes not even bringing the milk boat to a stop. There was a quick exchange and I might add a dexterous one by the boat's crew, sometimes emptying the full milk can into large ones on the boat and returning the empty. The larger cans on the boat were of course cooled by the ice in the hold below deck. I did not see any effort at cleanliness but suppose that was taken care of later in Manaus.

Another impression: the cattle seemed much fatter and healthier than the Brahma stock you see in the Northeastern interior. There was Brahma stock in this region but lots of other breeds that seemed to me to be the Ayrshire or Guernsey familiar in Nebraska. And there was a lot of Holstein stock for milking. What impressed most however was the land itself, flat, open pastures, all cleared, all green and fertile, not the dense vegetation we saw on the "Amazon Queen" in the tributaries around Belém. Evidently this land had been cleared and was under production for a long time.

The return trip was uneventful. We passed by the "new" floating city on the outskirts of Manaus with row upon row of houses on stilts. I forgot to mention that there were many jute plantations, with the jute drying on wooden stands. Upon arriving once more at the confluence of the Solimões and then the Rio Negro, I noted the "floating gas stations," the many buoys and markers and finally the wide view of Manaus itself.

So, the excursion was excellent, not for any great cultural or historic importance, but a beautiful "photo" of Manaus and surroundings in the 1960s. And like I said, interesting to the farm boy.

4

The Return to Recife and More Surprises of Brazilian Aviation

Everything was going too well! What was going on? The Paraense DC -3 was programmed to leave for Belém do Pará at 6 a.m. We left only one hour later, that is, at 7:00 a.m. That's the good news. Right after departure, on route to Belém, I noticed smoke and flames coming out of the right-hand engine. It did seem to diminish a bit as the landing gear went up. Happily, the pilot noticed too. We landed in Santarém and an interesting scene followed: they ordered all the passengers to get off by going down the normal small ladder (it was a small airplane). Later, all of us were wandering about on the tarmac; I happened across the pilot and asked out of simple curiosity, what was the problem? These were his words, not distorted I think by translation (but paraphrased): "Hey dude, I don't know, I'm just the pilot. I just drive this thing. The mechanic will look into it." What bothered me a bit was his appearance: he sported no uniform or any other sign of a pilot of an on-going airline, but was dressed in "civilian" clothes. He did not fill me with confidence.

A bit later we took off in the same airplane and returned to my by now "beloved" Belém. There, drinking beer in a bar, I ran into two Germans and an Australian, all just "hanging out" in Belém, trying to get the hell out of town. They were from the crew of a freighter and were let go once it arrived in port with no guarantee for further job or passage. I took advantage of the short stop to go see the Theater of Belém, very pretty, nice looking but nothing frankly in comparison to the Teatro de Amazonas in Manaus. I read in a local journal that many towns and cities in Amazonas State were now flooded and asking for federal support, and that the same thing is happening, of all places, in Ceará (land of great droughts) with almost 4000 families out of their homes. At least there seems to be a bit of variety in the calamities that strike that poor State and its history.

So once again, we lifted our wings for a flight to Fortaleza, and on the final point of takeoff at the end of the runway, we all heard a "tunk, tunk, tunk" and were called again to return to the terminal where there was a delay of one hour and once again we took to the air. This time successfully.

On the Way to the Northeast Once Again

May 20th. Now in Fortaleza, strange as it may seem, it was my first time in that city. I went to the central market where I talked with old Benedito, an agent for "cordel" for many years. He had an excellent stock from the entire Northeast, principally from the printing shop of João José da Silva in Recife and José Bernardo da Silva in Juazeiro and Joaquim Batista de Sena in Fortaleza itself. At this point, there were few cordelian titles I did not recognize, but it was good to pick up a few new ones. Unhappily I did not get to meet Joaquim Batista de Sena, an important figure of "cordel" in Fortaleza at the time.

I did the "obligatory" tourist thing in Fortaleza, buying a beautiful "marriage hammock" ["rede de casal"], one of the more important artisan products still excellent in Ceará at the times. It was a present for the Peace Corps girlfriend in Rio. I asked myself later: with whom could she have slept in it later? Oh, "saudades." The price was 30.000 cruzeiros, not a small amount of money at that time. For myself and more important, I bought a nice wooden carving of Father Cícero Romão Batista, some nice wooden "jangadas" and a few examples of the traditional weaving of Ceará.

Then on a short outing, not on the tourist map for Americans in Fortaleza at that time, I did a zig-zag walk along the beach until arriving at an incredibly poor fishing village, a sort of "sea side" fisherman's "favela." It was made up of wood stick shacks, deplorably dirty, something sad for me, but very "folkloric," There was a picturesque scene with the arrival of several fishing "jangadas," (not those of tourist films), coming into the beach. All the fishermen and their families were extremely poor, in rags, and with a truly modest catch for the day – fish about six inches in length. The sails on the 'jangadas' were all patched. But there was one truly beautiful moment - I observed for a very long time an old man, really a master at his craft, tossing a large round net into the waves at the sea side, time after time in search of a catch, and he caught little.

A visit to the José de Alencar Theater (Alencar was one of Brazil's greatest writers during the Romantic Period of the 19th Century, author of plays and novels) was of use not only for my research on Brazilian Literature but to complete as so far as possible my "mission" of seeing and knowing more of Brazil. Now it was back "home" to Recife and the coast.

5

In those final days in Recife, there would be student protests and the strife to come. In truth, the large part of research on "cordel" and Brazilian literature for the Fulbright was done. And I was very satisfied with my LETTERS to Hanson; these last days would just tie up loose ends.

I was mentally and physically ready to leave Brazil. I passed those final days of May and the beginning of June reading, going to U.S. films (satisfying my nostalgia for home) and wandering about the city, seeing places so far unseen. And now, with another perspective, the city seemed smaller to me and "provincial" in the Brazilian sense, different from those months before when I had arrived, a newcomer to the Northeast from Rio de Janeiro.

This time I was lodging in a different boarding house, not the old Chácara das Rosas. The new one was on the Riachuelo Street with its owner, Dona Carméia, a very pleasant lady. Gossip had it that the old Chácara, sitting on very valuable real estate, was in the process of being torn down and in its place would surge a high rise apartment building, sign of the times in Recife. The new boarding house was just down the street from the old Chácara and near the Law School and its park.

Social life was good - reunions with old friends from the Chácara and others. There was a "serenata" on the beach in Olinda and clubbing at the "Toca do Pajé." And there were nights spent with students from the universities, another night in the Club Calhambeque and a dinner at a Brazilian barbecue restaurant [churrascaria"].

There would be one more "photo" of folklore. My friend Pedro from Campina Grande learned of a Xangô initiation to take place in a distant district of west Recife, something I did not expect from him (recall he was studying pre-med and his father was a Spiritist medium in Paraíba). The event would be an initiation rite of a "daughter of the saint" on the site of the Mãe de Santo Maria da Aparecida, all in homage to St. George. We arrived at the site which was on top of a hill and the path leading to it through the trees. Then we saw the initiation: the main room with symbols of Xangô - arrows, bows and the like. First came the customary chants including the appeal to Exú to not interfere with the ceremony and accept a sacrifice to him. Then the daughter of the saint appeared, dressed totally in white, seating herself, legs crossed in front of her, in the middle of the main room, and her head was shaved. Chickens were sacrificed and provided the blood that was allowed to drip down the front of her head and then on her entire body. The chicken's feathers were then dropped on her and stuck wherever there was fresh blood. Later the feathers were removed and were burned, the smoke expected to purify the initiate. She remained seated in that position for several hours, sitting in the middle of offerings that included various kinds of fruit, soft drinks and "cachaça." Later that night the main "batuque" or cult ceremony would take place. It turns out that "Maria" was a man, one of those personages not so rare in Xangô, although not the rule. She/he had very long nails, a lisping speech, and wore a white embroidered blouse. She showed us the room where the "saints" were venerated, with all the images of the "Orixás" or saints, which of course corresponded to many Catholic saints. It was in this room that the sacrifice itself would take place, first offered to Exú (a devilish, mischievous personage and at times dangerous) and then to St. George. I remember the altars dedicated to Exú (his symbol the trident), to Iansã (St. Barbara), and to Oxum (St. George with his lance) and Xangô (St. John the Baptist and his sword) and to Iemanjá (the Virgin Mary). So "Maria" reigned in her blue blouse and white slacks and turban. The daughter of the saint was also in white, and others were in street clothes. Many firecrackers and rockets were shot off during the ceremony, and as mentioned, that night there would be the main cult gathering with chants, dances and an offering of food. It was interesting enough; at that point in my academic and research career I had not really studied the "notions" of the Afro-Brazilian religion. Later that same day, looking back and reflecting, I found it very interesting that I was taken there by a northeastern friend, a student of science and soon to enter medical school. The friend early in our friendship and my research in the Northeast had seemed "closed" to such things of his land, but now he seemed to have his mind "opened" to Brazilian reality. I would like to think that perhaps my own curiosity and influence might have played a part in that. I am certain that I opened the minds of many northeastern colleagues in the Northeast to the "literatura de cordel."

6

There were now signs of unrest on the horizon: in the newspaper, there were items of news in Brasília - two federal deputies pulled revolvers on each other in a session of congress, and there were problems in Pará State between Indigenous tribes and the military.

Then one night just two days before my scheduled departure on Varig to Rio and Pan Am to Miami the protests in the streets continued; they were student manifestations and many of these repressed by the military. On one occasion, the protesters tried to take refuge in one of the principal churches of the city, São Pedro dos Clérigos if I'm not mistaken. There was an unspoken law that the churches were "out of bounds" but that apparently was just a law. The soldiers entered the church and many protesters were beaten, a clear violation of said law. That next night before my departure my buddies from the boarding house, many good friends from the Chácara days, were drinking beer at the old "Bar Acadêmico," and it got a little beery, loud and boisterous with many shouts in favor of the protestors and students. The street protests were planned to continue that night. Someone said, "Let's join them." I said, "No way, this is nothing to mess around with."

At that moment, the shouting got louder outside, and there were hundreds of people running through the street along the Law School Park, some carrying sticks and beer bottles and stones they were launching at the heavily armed military police in hot pursuit. Suddenly there was tear gas everywhere and a couple of live canisters spewing the foul stuff right in front of the bar. "Merda! Let's get the hell out of here." We all bolted for the exit off Riachuelo and suddenly at least a dozen cops ("os macacos") were right in front of us, forming a phalanx of belly clubs and armed in army helmets with bullet proof vests.

"Stop right there you sons of bitches." My buddies Pedro and Zé took off and were run down and were being beaten with the night sticks right in front of us. Pistols and rifles soon appeared. The rest of us, maybe a half dozen or so were backed up against the wall of the bar, afraid to even move. An officer came forward, said, "You're all under arrest. Don't move or you'll be mincemeat." I heard the sirens, then two paddy wagons appeared from nowhere. We were ordered to get in, pronto. I yelled, "I'm an American citizen and don't have anything to do with this. Let me go." The answer was a soldier grabbed me by the arm, and said, "Tough shit, you commie sympathizer. Get in the wagon." I thought I had broken a knee as he pushed me into the wagon and I was slammed to the steel floor in the bedlam that followed.

The truck's engine roared, we took off and were soon zooming through the tear gassed filled streets. It was dark now and pure bedlam outside. After what seemed just minutes, the truck screeched to a stop, the door was opened and someone said, "Get the fuck out of there. March!" My knee was throbbing and I could scarcely climb out of the wagon, but managed to limp across a sidewalk, up some stairs into a long concrete hall and then a room with brick walls, no windows and a cold concrete floor. I couldn't catch most of the Portuguese, but fellow prisoners were yelling obscenities at the soldiers before a steel door was slammed on us in the room and another squirt of tear gas followed. Coughing, unable to breathe, I was lying on the floor with my arms over my face and mouth and nose, just trying to lie still. I remember trying to say one of those Catholic prayers from church days at home when I must have blacked out.

When I came to a few minutes later, it was deathly quiet. We were all huddled on the floor and I was cold and my body hurt all over. You could hear sirens outside, yelling, horns honking and occasional gunshots. I guess a couple of hours passed when a soldier in an army helmet yelled through the grates in the steel door, "Keep your goddamed mouths shut and don't move or make any trouble. You've had your chances you motherfuckers. We'll deal with you with this is all over." I smelled urine and discovered I had pissed my pants at some point, and the smell of shit and vomit permeated the cell. That's all I remember in that long night, huddled together with people I had never seen before, save for one or two familiar faces in the room, guys from the boarding house, all of us frightened and dumbstruck.

There was no food or water offered that night or the next morning, but at some time, a soldier came up to the cell door window and yelled out, "We want the American. Curran (unfortunately my last name sounded like a swear word when you tried to pronounce it in Portuguese, something like "scoundrel"). Get your ass over to the door." I managed to get up, thread my way through the bodies around me and limp to the door, and shouted back, "Here I am." A couple of voices behind me said, "Don't tell the bastards anything companheiro." Another said, "The gringo sonofabitch and CIA snitch is getting out of here. Stop him." But the door opened, two more soldiers grabbed me by both arms and half dragged me down a hallway to another room, and in the blur of it all a flashback came to me, "This is like that damned holding room from the airport six months back." They shoved me into a wooden straight back chair, handcuffed me, threw a can of water on my face and said, "We're going to have a talk and it better be good."

There were three soldiers in the room, but soon a couple of civilians in the now familiar cheap, dark suits with white shirts and narrow ties appeared, one of them the same guy from the airport months earlier. He looked at me, pulled up another chair right in front of me, slapped me hard on the face, and said, "Curran, it looks like the jig's up and the shit's hit the fan for you my friend. No more feeble excuses. We want straight talk and an explanation: How in the hell are you here and what in the shit did you do to get into this mess? If we find out you were involved in the protest I'm afraid it won't go easy for you. There are lots of "fidelistas" wandering the streets here in Brazil and some of them are American."

I said, "Okay, where do I start?" He said, "From the beginning, but you better make it quick. I've got a whole roomful of sorry bastards to rough up after we finish with you."

What could I say, truth was the only option. "Officers, you obviously know who I am and I've been stopped and questioned by you guys or your cohorts in the DOPS five or six times and all without doing anything wrong. It's always just been a case of talking to some Brazilians you find suspicious, but people just talking and explaining what's going on in Brazil to me. I'm a graduate student, I've got a study grant to study your folklore and literature, and that's all I've done. And I'm just one day from finishing the grant and heading home to write the damned dissertation."

"Make that in the preterite, gringo. You WERE heading home. We'll see."

"I was in the 'Bar Acadêmico' where all of us used to hang out and drink beer and eat in those days last June and July when I was doing serious research at the Law Library and the Joaquim Nabuco Institute. They were good buddies, we drank a lot of beer and I learned a lot of Portuguese. We even went whoring in Boa Viagem so does that sound like I was into subversion or revolution against the Regime? Shit. They were good days. Tonight was just another beery night. True, we probably swilled too much Brahma, and a couple of people got boisterous and shouted "Viva Fidel" or some such shit, but we weren't involved in the protest. Then all hell broke loose outside, someone said, "Make a run for it" and you know the rest. I AM an American citizen and you know; I've got that INR connection in Brasília, so will you let me at least call him again?"

Geroaldo (that was the agent's name) put out his cigarette inches from my manacled hand, smirked, stood up, walked around the room a couple of times, and said, "If we weren't getting some help from your Army and aid agencies, I wouldn't consider it but there might be ramifications if your dead body ends up in the surf beyond the reef. You got anything else to say?"

"Yeah, but I'd like to say it in front of you and the INR man Iverson." In all the melee they had not confiscated anything in my pockets, so I pulled out the old billfold with Iverson's number, gave it to him and waited. "Look Geroaldo, just for your information. I think we're on the same side. My whole family served in the military, my Dad in the Merchant Marine, my oldest brother in the Army Air Corps at the end of WWI and in Korea, my other brother a Naval officer in the Pacific. I may not have been in the service but am not a fucking draft dodger either like some of the Peace Corps people here. The NDEA scholarship and the Fulbright are just as important as carrying a rifle. We're going to eventually teach in the universities and prepare dozens if not hundreds of students to know about your country, learn your language and prepare them to defend the interests of the United States wherever it's needed. I just needed to say this, no matter what."

The officer said, "I appreciate that but you aren't the first person with a good story. Sit tight and we'll see what happens. We've got Iverson's number from last time so I'll see if we can get him on the line." Two black telephones appeared, on one he was on talking in a very rapid Portuguese, something about "Tell them it's urgent. We've got their stooge here in jail in Recife and need to decide what to do with him."

They came up with a bottle of that mineral water the Brazilians drink to not get some vile disease and a couple of stale sweet rolls, uncuffed me and allowed me to finish them while we waited for the phone call. Maybe a half hour passed, the phone rang, he muttered some words under his breath and handed me the phone.

"Hello Mr. Gaherty. This is Stanley Iverson. DOPS tells me you got caught in a jam of some kind and are in a tight spot up there. To tell you the truth we're not surprised; you've been skirting trouble for awhile. But we're on the same page and your reports via the LETTERS are on spot. Tell me your side of the story."

I blurted out all I could remember and tried not to forget anything. Iverson listened and said he would call me back in a few minutes. The longest minutes of my short life! When he came back on the line, he was all business:

"You do nothing but listen and follow my instructions. We've got a relationship going with these folks, but we can't push it. They are in charge. But the wheels are turning and here's the deal: you get to spend the rest of today and tonight as their "guest". I myself am catching a flight to Recife tomorrow a.m. and you will be released from custody. The exit permit from the police saying you don't owe any taxes after a year's stay in Brazil and an official statement you haven't committed any crimes will be in my pocket. You'll be allowed to gather your stuff and there will be a short, escorted ride to the Guararapes Airport where we'll get you on the direct flight to Rio and a ticket on the midnight Pan Am flight to New York. I'll have more to say when I get there. Be careful of your mouth and don't get these guys worked up any more than they already are, okay?"

"Yes sir. Thanks. I hope you know I've been on the up and up about all this."

"Yes, indeed, Mike, you have gone far and beyond what we anticipated. See you tomorrow."

Geroaldo hung up the phone and personally escorted me to a tiny cell on the second floor, a bunk bed with a single sheet, no pillow, an iron stool in the corner and just a small window high up on the cell door. They brought me the usual "guest" meal, a plate of rice and beans and another bottle of water. He said, "We'll see you in the morning. Be a good boy."

I found out the next morning that prayers can be answered and there is such a thing as a guardian angel, in this instance, a tall, bespectacled, suave American with a smart sport coat, white shirt, tie and a formal, leather briefcase to his side who entered the cell. He stretched out his hand, smiled, and said, "I'm Stanley Iverson. Mike, we finally meet. Sorry about the circumstances but mister it could have been a lot worse. The guard will take you to a john down the hall, go wash your face (he tossed me one of those travel kit toothbrushes and tiny tube of paste from the airplane). When you finish, a guard will bring you to the main office downstairs. I'll be there."

I followed orders, and still felt like crap, limping on the bad leg, and met him in what was a more "civilized" office with a desk, roll chair and a divan in front of it. Geroaldo and another fellow, apparently his superior, a big shot in the DOPS, and Iverson waited. The boss man smiled, addressed me and Iverson and made what sounded like a short speech,

"As a representative of the government and the Military Revolution of 1964, it is a pleasure to have an opportunity to help our friends of the alliance between Brazil and its neighbor fighting Communism and subversion in the hemisphere. Mr. Iverson and his friends in Brasília have interceded on more than one occasion when difficulties arise when a United States citizen meets misfortune. So, Mr. Gaherty we are happy to tell you that your stay in Brazil is shortly coming to a close, we wish you a safe trip home, and incidentally we congratulate you on the research you did. Mr. Hansen has made us aware of the important contribution you have made in your

LETTERS to the "Times" explaining much of Brazil to a foreign audience." He handed Iverson a packet of very formal looking papers, shook his hand and then mine, a bit reluctantly, and said, "Your taxi is waiting."

Once outside, Iversen said he would not be letting me out of his sight and offered to help me in those final hours. We returned to the boarding house where my buddies stood quietly, obviously impressed with my "associate;" I explained that indeed I was finalizing the stay, thanked them all, packed my stuff (one huge suitcase full of "cordel' poems), and we got in the taxi. (I could only imagine the scene with my buddies: laughing and saying, "Hey we knew that folklore shit was a lousy cover.") The trip to the airport was quick, Iverson saying little, but when we got on the airplane to Rio, he had a lot to say.

"Mike, I hope you appreciate all this. I know it's part of the job, but those DOPS guys give me the shivers every time something like this happens. Hinges get greased when they need it, and this was one rusty hinge. They will have someone on this flight and for sure at the airport for the Pan Am flight in Rio, just to make sure all goes as planned. I'm not wired and don't think anyone around us is, so we can talk. I just want you to know that Hansen is apprised and is very much relieved I've got you on the plane. He has raved about the LETTERS and said the minute you land at JFK he'll be at the airport, buy you a good pastrami on rye and a cold beer and have a long talk. I don't think personally you were ever out of line, but shall we say, you were in the wrong spot at the wrong time and with some shady folks. I suggest you give it all a rest, get all this amazing material together and write a cracker-jack dissertation. I'll be one of the first to read it."

I didn't leave Brazil quite the way I planned and missed a few goodbyes, but there was an immense sigh of relief settling into the comfy wide seat in tourism in Pan Am. I think the stewardesses in those snappy uniforms saw that sigh, and plied me with more than one scotch and a hot meal until the plane banked through the clouds and mist in New York.

EPILOGUE

Hansen was there at JFK, looking like a newspaper man in the tweed jacket, with ruffled hair and a pipe in his hand. He said the <u>Times</u> had arranged a one-day layover before a non-stop flight to Omaha and then on to Lincoln. Would I mind if we spent a couple of hours over that New York deli dinner and get caught up on things? Who was I to refuse? The taxi took us to a busy deli somewhere in Manhattan (I was in a daze and surely didn't know where in the hell I was, and besides was physically and mentally exhausted from the last few days). We sat down in a quiet booth in back and after the first of several beers, he urged me to tell him all about it in my own words.

"Where do I start? You really have the basics in the LETTERS and will get the rest in the last I'll write at home in Lincoln and get to you as soon as possible. Brazil was all I dreamed it would be, I really was treated terrific with all the research, the incidental friendships and those amorous moments to boot. I think I grew up a little bit. I don't know where Brazil is headed, but I'm worried. In those final days in Recife, the new General President Costa e Silva came into power and inaugurated that AI – 5 (Institutional Act n. 5) which in effect seals the arrival of the dictatorship, total censure of the press and what I think will be a total lack of freedom. I just hope my friends make it okay."

Hansen listened, puffing slowing on that pipe, letting me quaff the last beer, and finally said,

"Mike, you know this was actually the first time the <u>Times</u> entertained such an arrangement, I mean my original letter to you, our agreement, and your subsequent LETTERS. I want you to know it has turned out splendidly; readers of the International Section took interest in what you wrote and I daresay were soon "hooked" and waiting for the next installment. You indeed do write well and have proved it. I know you will have to write an academic piece on the "cordel" in that dissertation, but I would like you to know that once it is finished and you are "doctorized" we plan to publish the LETTERS through some good friends at a good New York publisher and I think you will be well on your way to getting a fine post at a good university. I can say personally that you made Brazil and its people come alive to me. I'm sorry for any inconveniences caused, but it turned out well."

I stammered a thank you but then remembered, "There is one big favor you can do for me. That Di Giorgio classic guitar is still at my friends the Forti's house in Rio. Can you get it shipped home to me in Lincoln? I left some unfinished loves in Brazil, but that's my true love." He chuckled, said he would arrange it and was about to walk me to a taxi taking me to the hotel.

"Oh," I said, "I've got that ole Irish Catholic guilt thing going here. There was one small item in the final days in Recife I did not or have not put in the LETTER. It's a little personal, but I think you'll understand. I went one final time to the Zone out in Boa Viagem with the boarding house buddies, for old times you know, spent some time with a peroxide Brazilian blonde, and a few days later experienced a good deal of discomfort in the old tool. The buddies said, "No problem, it happens all the time, we know a guy who can fix that." I told the doctor, "We got to do this quick." He gave me a whopping dose of tetracycline that took care of it. Like I said, it all started with Sputnik and ended with the clap."

Hansen roared with laughter and almost choked on his pipe. After a few minutes he said, "When we get the LETTER I'll think about it. I'm not sure if your prose and scholarly efforts should end with a thud or is it a loud clapping noise?"

ABOUT THE AUTHOR

Mark Curran is a retired professor from Arizona State University where he worked from 1968 to 2011. He taught Spanish and Brazilian Portuguese languages and their respective cultures. His research specialty was Brazil's folk-popular literature or as it is known in Brazil, the "literatura de cordel," and he has published many research articles and fourteen books on the subject in Brazil, the United States and Spain. Subsequent books are mainly autobiographical and/ or reflect civilization classes taught at ASU in the series "Stories I Told My Students."

Published Books
A Literatura de Cordel. Brasil. 1973.
Jorge Amado e a Literatura de Cordel. Brasil. 1981
A Presença de Rodolfo Coelho Cavalcante na Moderna Literatura de Cordel. Brasil. 1987
La Literatura de Cordel – Antología Bilingüe – Español y Portugués. España. 1990
Cuíca de Santo Amaro Poeta-Repórter da Bahia. Brasil. 1991.
História do Brasil em Cordel. Brasil. 1998
Cuíca de Santo Amaro – Controvérsia no Cordel. Brasil. 2000
Brazil's Folk-Popular Poetry – "a Literatura de Cordel" – a Bilingual Anthology in English and Portuguese. USA. 2010
The Farm – Growing Up in Abilene, Kansas, in the 1940s and the 1950s. USA. 2010
Retrato do Brasil em Cordel. Brasil. 2011
Coming of Age with the Jesuits. USA. 2012
Peripécias de um Pesquisador "Gringo" no Brasil nos Anos 1960, ou, À Cata de Cordel. USA. 2012
Adventures of a 'Gringo' Researcher in Brazil in the 1960s. USA, 2012
A Trip to Colombia – Highlights of Its Spanish Colonial Heritage. USA, 2013
Travel, Research and Teaching in Guatemala and Mexico – In Quest of the Pre-Columbian Heritage, Volume I – Guatemala, Volume II – Mexico. USA, 2013
A Portrait of Brazil in the Twentieth Century – The Universe of the "Literatura de Cordel." USA, 2013
Fifty Years of Research on Brazil – A Photographic Journey. USA, 2013
Relembrando – A Velha Literatura de Cordel e a Voz dos Poetas. USA. 2014
Aconteceu no Brasil – Crônicas de um Pesquisador Norte-Americano no Brasil II, USA. 2015
It Happened in Brazil – Chronicle of a North American Researcher in Brazil II, USA. 2015

Diário de um Pesquisador Norte-Americano no Brasil III, USA, 2016
Diary of a North American Researcher in Brazil III, USA, 2016
LETTERS FROM BRAZIL. A Cultural-Historical Narrative Made Fiction, USA, 2017

Professor Curran lives in Mesa, Arizona, and spends part of the year in Colorado. He is married to Keah Runshang Curran and they have a daughter Kathleen who lives in Albuquerque, New Mexico. Her documentary film Greening the Revolution was shown most recently at the Sonoma Film Festival. Katie was named "Best Female Director" at the Film Festival in Oaxaca, Mexico.

The author's e-mail address: profmark@asu.edu

His website: http://www.currancordelconnection.com

Printed in the United States
By Bookmasters